PENGUIN BOOKS

WIDESPREAD PANIC

'Extraordinary ... Ellroy's legion of fans will love it'
The Times

'Purgatory is rarely this much fun'
Financial Times

'His most compelling novel in ages'
Daily Telegraph

'A characteristically vigorous tour of his established
territory ... Like drinking a pint of espresso'
Times Literary Supplement

'Great fun'
iPaper

'Unfolds in shimmering Ellroyvision'
Wall Street Journal

'Wildly entertaining and memorable ... a spiritual
companion to *L.A. Confidential*'
NPR

'Devious and delicious ... Ellroy's total command of the
jazzy, alliterate argot of the era never fails to astonish.
This is a must for L.A. noir fans'
Publishers Weekly

'The dean of Los Angeles crime novelists'

D1328644

'If you love Ellroy, you'll love this wild ride'
Washington Post

'Fascinating, gripping, dubious but unique'
Crime Time

'Brilliant'
Belfast Telegraph

'Graphic, stunning'
BookReporter

ABOUT THE AUTHOR

James Ellroy was born in Los Angeles in 1948. He is the author of the acclaimed 'L.A. Quartet': *The Black Dahlia, The Big Nowhere, L.A. Confidential* and *White Jazz*. His novel *Blood's A Rover* completes the magisterial 'Underworld USA Trilogy' – the first two volumes of which (*American Tabloid* and *The Cold Six Thousand*) were both *Sunday Times* bestsellers. His previous novel, *This Storm*, is the second instalment in Ellroy's 'Second L.A. Quartet'.

Widespread Panic

JAMES ELLROY

PENGUIN BOOKS

PENGUIN BOOKS

UK | USA | Canada | Ireland | Australia
India | New Zealand | South Africa

Penguin Books is part of the Penguin Random House group of companies
whose addresses can be found at global.penguinrandomhouse.com

Part I originally published (in slightly different form) in e-book format
as *Shakedown* by Byliner Fiction in 2012

First published in the US by Alfred A. Knopf, a division of
Penguin Random House LLC in 2021
First published in the UK by William Heinemann in 2021
Published in Penguin Books 2022
003

Typeset in 10.74/13.1 pt AlbertinaMTPro
by Integra Software Services Pvt. Ltd, Pondicherry

Printed and bound in Great Britain by Clays Ltd, Elcograf S.p.A.

The authorised representative in the EEA is Penguin Random House Ireland,
Morrison Chambers, 32 Nassau Street, Dublin D02 YH68

A CIP catalogue record for this book is available from the British Library

ISBN: 978–1–529–15758–1

www.greenpenguin.co.uk

To
Glynn Martin

and to
Lois Nettleton, 1927-2008

SHAKEDOWN

Freddy Otash Confesses, Part I

SHAKEDOWN

(Teddy Diaz Conjugues, Part)

CELL 2607

Penance Penitentiary
Reckless-Wrecker-of-Lives Block
Pervert Purgatory
7/16/2020

I've spent twenty-eight years in this fucking hellhole. Now, they tell me I can memoir-map my misadventures and write my way out.

All that religious shit I disdained and disobeyed has played out true. There's Heaven for the good folks, Hell for the beastfully *baaaaaad*. There's Purgatory for guys like me—caustic cads that capitalized on a sicko system and caused catastrophe. I've sizzled in my sins for two decades plus. I've relived my earthly life in dystopian detail. My cunning keepers are currently dangling a deal:

Record your jaundiced journey. Trumpet the truth, triumphant. Hop to Heaven, and hit that high note.

Baby, it's time to *CONFESS*.

Purgatory is shitsville. You're stuck with the body you had on Earth when you died. You eat nothing but coach-class airplane food. There's no booze, no jazzy intrigue, no wilt-your-will women. Violated victims bop by my cell. They remind me of my many misdeeds and jab me with red-hot pokers. Gay gauchos hurtle down from Heaven and scold me for outing them back in the homo-hate '50s. It was my *job*. I entrapped soiled celebrities and putzo politicos, and cornholed them in *Confidential*. I sold my soul to that maladroit magazine. Now, I'm sordidly SORRY.

So *what?*

Sorry's for limp-dick losers. Confession salves the savage self and rips it to righteous redemption. Hear my plaintive plea, O watchful world:

Get me the fuck out of here!!!!!

My keepers have poised me with pen and paper. They've compiled a complete run of *Confidential*. My synapses soar with a million malignant memories. Freddy Otash, 1922–1992. I'm a rogue cop, a private eye, a shifty shakedown artist. I'm the demonic deus ex machina of my tattered time and place. I'm the hellhound who held Hollywood captive. I'm the man with the sex-scorched secrets you irksome earthlings want to hear.

Confidential presaged the infantile Internet. *Our* gobs of gossip were repugnantly *real*. Today's blowhard bloggers and *their* tattle texts? Pussyfooting punks *all*. We stung the studios. We popped the pooh-bahs. We hurled the hurt, wholesale. We voyeur-vamped America and got her hooked on the shivering shit. WE CREATED TODAY'S TELL-ALL MEDIA CULTURE. We crazily crafted a lurid language and made it our own.

It's the lexicon of the lowdown. It's the dialogue of the dish. It's the slithering slur and the thrill of the threat. I think and write in algorithmic alliteration. Language must lambaste and lay on the lash. Language liberates as it offends. *Confidential* taught me that. My confession will make this dizzy dialect divide you in two. There's Sin and Atonement, fuckers—there's nothing else.

Purgatory's a punitive proposition. Montgomery Clift pitchforked me yesterday. *Confidential* labeled him "the Lavender Lilliputian" and "Princess Tiny Meat." JFK followed Monty. I dumped the dish on his dope habit and call-girl cavalcade. Marilyn Monroe penance-poked me next. Marilyn was a snout trout. She dispensed head to rogue pharmacists, *XXX*-exclusive. They dispensed noxious Nembutal back. Maybe I shouldn't have tattled the tale—but I was within my First Amendment rights!!!!!

I'm consumed with candor and wracked with recollection. I'm revitalized and resurgent. My *meshugenah* march down memory lane begins NOW.

I was working Hollywood Vice in '51. We got word on a fuck pad, operating out of a crib at the Villa Elaine. I hotfooted it over there."

We're bopped back in my booth. There's my audience: four showbiz *machers* in worse shape than me. Walkers, canes, and oxygen tanks clog the aisles to the kitchen. Fractious Freddy O.'s holding court.

It's late summer, '92. I'm seventy and in *baaaaad* fucking shape. I've consumed scads of scotch and sucked three packs a day since I shot out the chute. I've got emphysema and a bum pump. I'm aching to make eighty. It's a lunar-looped long shot.

Sol Sidell said, "Get to it, Freddy. You roll to the pad, and then what?"

Sinful Sol. A jailbaiter from jump. He produced beach-blanket flicks in the sick '60s. I pulled him out of the shit, circa '66. He was reefer-ripped and poking two underage twists.

I said, "Okay, I roll to the crib and peep a side window. Shit—there's Sam Spiegel, the cat that produced *Lawrence of Arabia* and *The Bridge on the River Kwai*. He's muff-diving a three-hundred-pound chick. That was a boss beef, back in '51. I told Sambo it's dues time. It's a morals bust, or a monthly donation to the Fred Otash Retirement Fund."

My pals yukked. I wrapped into my Reuben sandwich and felt a twisted twinge in my chest. I downed digitalis. I saw Jules Slotnick suck on his oxygen mask and light a Camel Light. Julie produced turgid turkeys about farmworker strife. Call him Mr. Guilt for Gelt. He made all his live-in maids blow him. He held their green cards as a hedge against their refusal to bestow daily head.

Sid Resnick said, "Give us another one, Freddy."

The Sidster was Mr. Holocaust Heartache. He produced *schlock-umentaries* for Islamic TV. He was the King of the Chubby Chasers. He longed for it *laaarrrge.*

I cruised my cranium cracks for a story. Two elderly gay cats sashayed by the booth. That fed me my cue.

I pointed to them. "I got tipped to an all-male pajama party, back in '56. I paid some LAPD hard boys a yard apiece to bust it, and brought my camera along. Those cats were piled up in a five-way with Rock Hudson, Sal Mineo, and a dude with giant acne cysts. *Confidential* wrote it up. Universal paid me ten g's to keep the Rockster's name out of the story."

The booth roared and *re*-roared. Julie Slotnick gasped for breath. Al Wexler yukked out a bagel chunk. It flew and flopped to the floor.

Alky Al owned six porno bookstores and nine nose-job clinics. He plowed a truck full of migrant Mexicans and left six dead. I got it mashed down to a Mickey Mouse misdemeanor. Al *owed* me, *laaaaarge.*

I killed my sandwich. Alky Al blew a faux fanfare. I laid out my lifelong credo: "I'll do anything short of murder. I'll work for anyone but the Reds."

My boys clapped and guffawed. A bad twinge hit my heart. I downed digitalis and deep dips of scotch.

Corned beef and sauerkraut socked my system. I got floaty and deep dyspeptic. I brought up a bread crust. It popped on my plate.

The booth tumbled. My pals vaporized. My vision blurred black. Calendar sheets shot backward. Decades disappeared and devolved. Maybe I'm dead. *Maybe I'm just dreaming this shit—*

There I am. I'm fetching fine in '49. I'm beefcake, boss, and bangin' them bonaroo bitches, three at a pop.

I'm handsome and heavy-hung. I'm a lustful Lebanese. Call me a camel cad from the get-go. I'm an ex-Marine. I trained troops at Parris Island and sent them off to Saipan, savvy. I joined the LAPD in late '45. I went on the grift *faaaaaast*.

I formed a 459 ring. They worked my downtown foot beat. They popped pawnshops and dumped dope-pushing pharmacies. I fingered the jobs. My gang cadged cash and dope. They were 2:00 a.m. creepers. I was their Rogue Cop Rajah.

I'm corrosively corruptible and tempted by the take. I live for the scurrilous score. It's my existential fate. I had a squaresville home life in bumfuck Massachusetts. My mom and dad loved me. Nobody butt-fucked me in my bassinet. I live by a cool-cat code. There's shit I won't do. My code got catastrophized on 2/4/49.

I hogged a hall mirror. I combed my hair and noosed my necktie. Sy Devore tailored my formfit uniform. The squadroom buzzed *baaaad* all around me. It's a Code 3 squawk—shoot-out at 9th and Figueroa.

Two men down. One traffic cop/one heist geek. The cop's nudging near death. The geek suffered superficial wounds. Both men—ensconced at Georgia Street Receiving, *right now*.

The squadroom bebop buzzed. The squadroom phones rang incessant. The buzz bombarded me. I heard murderous murmurs laced with a lynch-mob gestalt.

I heard heavy footfalls. Booze breath bristled me.

"If you're through admiring yourself, I've got something."

I turned around. It's a Robbery bull named Harry Fremont. Harry has a rancid rep. He stomped two pachucos dead during the zoot suit riots. He pimped transvestite whores out of a he-she bar. He was shit-faced drunk at noon.

"Yeah, Harry?"

Harry said, "Be useful, kid. There's a cop killer at Georgia Street. Chief Horrall thinks you should take care of it. This is an opportunity you don't want to pass up."

I said, "Take care of *what*? The cop he shot isn't dead."

Harry rolled his eyes. He passed me a key fob. He said, "4-A-32. It's in the watch commander's space. Look under the backseat."

I *got* it. Harry locked on my look. He went *Nooowww, he gets it*. He winked and waltzed away from me.

I steadied myself and stood still. I loaded up on that lynch-mob gestalt. I lurched through the squadroom and zombie-walked downstairs. I hit the garage.

I found the watch commander's space. There's 4-A-32. The key fits the ignition. The garage was dark. Ceiling pipes leaked. Water drops turned wiggy colors and morphed into wild shapes.

I gunned the gas and pulled out onto Spring Street. I drove *slooooow*. The heist geek was jacked in the jail ward. It was a lockup-transfer ruse. It was forty-three years ago. It's *still* etched in *Sin*-emascope and surround sound. I can *still* see the passersby on the street.

There it is. There's Georgia Street Receiving.

The jail ward sat on the north side. The squarejohn ward sat to the south. A narrow pathway bisected the buildings. It hit me then: *They know you'll do it. They know you're that kind of guy.*

I reached under the backseat. I pulled out transfer papers for Ralph Mitchell Horvath. I grabbed a .32 snubnose revolver.

I put the gun in my front pocket and grabbed the papers. I slid out of the sled. I popped down the pathway and went through the jail-ward door.

The deskman was PD. He pointed to a punk cuffed to a drainpipe. The punk wore a loafer jacket and slit-bottomed khakis. He sported a left-arm splint. He was acne-addled and chancre-sored. He vibed hophead. He looked smack-back insolent.

The deskman did the knife-across-throat thing. I handed him the papers and uncuffed and recuffed the punk. The deskman said, "Bon voyage, sweetheart."

I shoved the punk outside and pointed him up the pathway. He walked ahead of me. I couldn't feel my feet. I couldn't feel my legs. My heart hammered on overdrive. I lost my limbs somewhere.

There's no telltale windows. There's no pedestrians on Georgia Street. There's no witnesses.

I pulled the gun from my pocket and fired over my own head. The gun kicked and lashed life back in my limbs. My pulse topped 200 rpms.

The punk wheeled around. He moved his lips. A word came out as a squeak. I pulled my service revolver and shot him in the mouth. His teeth exploded. He dropped. I placed the throwdown piece in his right hand.

He tried to say "Please." This dream's a routine reenactment. The details veer and vary. The "Please" always sticks. I'm alive. He's not. That's the baleful bottom line.

The cop lived. He sustained a through-and-through wound. He was back on duty inside a week.

Vicious vengeance. Wrathfully wrong in retrospect. A crack in the crypt of my soul. Harry Fremont passed the word. Freddy O. is kosher. Chief C. B. Horrall sent me a jug of Old Crow. The grand jury sacked him two months later. He got caught up in a call-girl racket. An interim chief was brought in.

Ralph Mitchell Horvath. 1918–1949. Car thief/stickup man/weenie wagger. Hooked on yellow jackets and muscatel.

Ralphie left a widow and two kids. I got the gust-wind guilts and shot them penance payoffs. Money orders. Once a month. Fake signatures. All anonymous. Dig—Ralphie's dead, and I'm not.

Memory Lane. I'm fetching fine in '49. I'm full-fuck filleted in '92.

I holed up at my pad. I lingered through Labor Day. I looped the lane and took last looks at my loved ones, lewd ones, and lost ones.

I scoured scrapbooks. The old photos got my gears going. I'm there with Frank, Dino, and Sammy. I broke legs for them. They cringe and crawl away. There's boocoo pix of my bed at my old pad. I called it "the Landing Strip." I was Mr. Three-Way then. I swung with stewardesses, starlets, and stars. Liz Taylor and I swung with a stew named "Barb" on many groin-grabbing occasions. There's pix of my lost love, Joi Lansing. There's pix of my *true* love, Lois Nettleton. I was young and hung then. *Aaaahhhh*—sweet motherfucking mystery of life!!!!!

There's my dictionary and thesaurus. They were teaching tools for the wrathful writers at *Confidential*. Utilize alliteration and instill intensive slurs. Homosexuals are "licentious lispers." Lesbians are "beefcake butches." Drunks are "bibulous bottle hounds" and "dyspeptic dipsos." Vulgarize and vitalize. Create a *craaazy* populist parlance. Make it sinfully *siiiiing*.

My pals popped over on Labor Day. We built burgers and boozed big. They left at 2:00 a.m. A male nurse corps shagged them and shot them down to their limos. Walkers wobbled, oxygen tanks toppled and rolled. It rubbed me raw, Daddy-O.

I settled in and watched a *Dragnet* rerun. I bought the juicehead judge in four of Jack Webb's drunk-driving beefs. I shtupped Jack's wife, soaring songstress Julie London. She said I was the biggest and the best.

I noshed a dozen Famous Amos cookies. I'd seen the episode before. Sergeant Joe Friday busts some hirsute hippie punks. I missed Jack. We shared some yuks. He kicked off back in—

A hydrogen bomb hit my heart. Mushroom clouds claimed me. Monsters morphed out of them. Johnnie Ray. Monty Clift. Politi-

cians pounded and movie stars mauled. It's a calamitous kaleido-
scope of condemnation.

They jumped me. They went *J'accuse, j'accuse, j'accuse!!!!!* I gasped.
My left arm exploded. I hit the medical-emergency button on my
phone.

Then some pixilated pops. They're the *Herald*'s horror headlines.
TATTLE TYRANT, MR. FEAR, SHAMAN OF SHAME. Then a crunching
crash. My door's down. There's a mask on my mouth.

I'm dead. Thence comes Purgatory and this confession.

MY FUCKED-UP FOOT BEAT

Downtown L.A.

10/4/52

Central Division. The doofus day watch. Freewheeling Freddy's at loose ends.

I disbanded my 459 gang. My main men got hooked on Big "H." They were decidedly desperate and snitch-prone. I'd gambled away my gelt. I was living on a schmuck cop's pay and was suffused with the blues. William H. Parker became Chief in '50. He instituted righteous reforms and riddled the ranks with a phalanx of finks to sniff out miscreants and misconduct. I drove a Packard pimpmobile. I won it in a darktown dice game. Parker's punks tattled to the hellhound *Jefe*. I got called in and grindingly grilled. Parker warned me not to be a Bolshevik. He said, "I've got my four eyes on you."

It rained that day. It was some mad monsoon. Wild winds whipped me along on my foot beat. I stopped at a lockbox phone and called the station. The deskman told me to hotfoot it to 668 South Olive. They were shooting a *Racket Squad* episode in the lobby. They needed a hard boy to shoo off autograph hounds.

I headed over there. I caught a taut tailwind and slalomed in the slush. It was a medical building. The lobby was all lit up. I caught a frazzled fracas, right off.

Lights, cameras, boom mikes. Here's the *action*, straight up.

A jug-eared cat was hassling a boss blonde. He wore pegged chinos and a gone jacket. She was built, va-va-voom.

The cast and crew orbed the scene. Jug Ears grabbed the blonde's arm and applied abrasions. It gored my gonads and hit my heartstrings. I walked up behind him. He saw my shadow and swift swiveled. I notched his nose with a palm shot. I looped a left to his larynx. I kneed his nuts as he dropped.

The blonde genuflected. I tipped my hat. Jug Ears cradled his busted beak and moaned for his mama. The cast and crew clapped.

The blonde said, "He's my ex-husband. He stiffed me for three months' alimony."

I kicked him in the head and lifted his wallet. Jug Ears mama-moaned anew. The cast and crew whistled and stomped.

The wallet weighed in heavy. I fanned the cash compartment and counted a sea of C-notes. I handed them to the blonde. She dropped them in her purse and dropped a dollar on her ex-hubby. She said, "For old times. He was good in the sack."

I laffed. I reached in my pocket and handed her a card. Understated class *shows*. There's my name, phone number, and "Mr. Nine Inches."

She dropped the card in with her cash stash. A guy yelled, "You're up, Joi. Scene 16-B."

She winked and walked away from me. I cuffed Jug Ears behind his back and pay-phone-called the station. Holly*weird*: they filmed the scene with the ex coma-conked and cuffed on the floor.

I walked outside and smoked a cigarette. A black-and-white cruised by and hauled the ex to Georgia Street. I thought of Ralph Mitchell Horvath. A kid returned my calling card. She wrote on the back: "Joi Lansing. 39-25-38. Googie's, tonight at 8:30."

I've got a boss bachelor pad, straight up from the Strip. It's jammed with Jap flags and shadow-boxed Lugers. There's a periscope perched on my porch. I peep neighbor women and gas their gestalts.

I'm a voyeur. It's vampiric. I study people. I rage to know their secret shit.

My bedroom features a *biiiiiiig* walk-in closet. I've got sixty Sy

Devore suits. My dresser drawers drip with lacy lingerie. My lynx-like lovers leave me *mucho* mementos.

I've got a file on Ralph Mitchell Horvath. I culled it from PDs and penitentiaries statewide. I know *all* Ralphie's secrets.

He poked a Mexican sissy in reform school. He fathered two half-wit kids. He pimped his wife to cover his poker debts. He scored prescription goofballs from a Chink pharmacist.

I dug up that dirt. It bought me distance on Ralphie. It held off his hold on me. Know your foe. I've known that godless gospel since my crib.

I dressed sharp for Joi Lansing. I wore my crocodile loafers and hid my heater in a shoulder rig. A spritz of Lucky Tiger—and a short stroll to the meet.

Googie's was a coffee cave on Sunset and Crescent Heights. The space-age aesthetic rubbed me raw. Fluorescent lights/Naugahyde/chrome. A hip hive for showbiz shitheels headed for Hell.

I walked in. Joi Lansing table-hopped. She wore a too-tight gown and a meager mink stole with a pawnshop tag attached. The joint buzzed per a sneak peek in Glendale. A Googie's regular played a love scene with Bob Mitchum. Bad Boy Bob slipped her tongue. They toked a reefer in the RKO backlot. She blew him in his '51 Ford.

A hubbub juked the joint. I knew I radiated *FUZZ*. I crashed into a booth and unbuttoned my jacket. A flit flamed by and ogled my piece. He hopped to a hen party, one booth over. Dig *this* dirt: the barman at the Cockpit Lounge ran an all-boy slave auction. Adlai Stevenson got embroiled and embarrassed. The hens hooted—*ha, ha, ha!!!*

Joi sat down. I pointed to the pawnshop tag. She pulled it off and dropped it in the ashtray.

I said, "Thanks for the invitation."

Joi said, "Thanks for the revenge. That guy fractured my left wrist on Saint Patrick's Day, '49."

"You're too young to have an ex-husband."

"Yeah, and I'm estranged from number two. I'd head to Reno

for a quickie, but it might not work. We got hitched in T.J., so the paperwork could get dicey."

"Is there anything I can do?"

"Well, you're a policeman."

I lit a cigarette and held the pack out. Joi shook her head.

"He's on parole, and he's a grasshopper. You could call Narco. That might do me some good."

I shook my head. "Give me his address. I'll think of something."

"He'll be *here* at nine-thirty. He's been living at the Y since I kicked him out, and the fry cook here takes his phone calls. He's a nonunion grip. I stiffed him a fake message after I met you. You're a producer at Fox, with a job for him. You're meeting him in the parking lot."

I laffed. "You just assumed that I'd do it?"

Joi laffed. "Come on, Freddy. That stunt you pulled downtown, and 'Mr. Nine Inches'? What won't you do for money or gash?"

A Mex busboy sidled by. I grabbed a belt loop and stopped him. He saw my roscoe and got the shiver-shakes.

I socked him a sawbuck. "Go to the kitchen and get me a bag of weed. You'll be on the night train to Culiacán if you don't deliver."

Manuel went *Sí, sí* and moved out. Joi laffed and bummed a cigarette. I blew a high smoke ring. She blew a higher one. They hit the ceiling and mushroomed, Hiroshima-esque.

Manuel meandered back with the *mota*. I told him to scram. The hen party parsed a new nugget. Ava Gardner sacked Sinatra. She's shacked with a heavy-hung extra at Monogram.

I said, "What's your real name?"

Joi said, "Joyce Wassmansdorff."

"Give me the fill-in."

"I'm from Salt Lake City. I'm twenty-four. I went to the MGM school, and went nowhere."

"But now you're up-and-coming?"

Joi stubbed out her cigarette. "I'm uncredited in six pictures, and credited in four. I've got *Racket Squad*, *Gangbusters*, and a comedy with Jane Russell in the can."

"Give me some dirt on Russell."

"What's to give? She's a Goody Two-shoes married to that quarterback for the Rams."

I eyeballed the room. Paranoia pounds me, periodic. The two crew cuts by the take-out stand? They're Bill Parker's boys. I'd seen them at Central. They were purse-lipped puritans out to bag bent cops.

Joi said, "You'll need money to enjoy my company."

I *re*-eyeballed the room. I exercised my X-ray vision. A punk I popped for flimflam made me and beat feet.

Joi said, "It's nine-thirty. Look for a little guy with a big pompadour."

I bopped back to the parking lot. Pompadour lounged upside a '51 Merc. I closed in close. He orbed my shoulder rig and went *Oh shit*. He wore light-colored slacks. Piss coursed and covered his cuffs. I dug in, diplomatic.

"Don't contest the divorce. I'll negotiate your alimony payments. Send the check directly to me. I'll take my cut and deliver the rest to Miss Lansing."

Pompadour held up his hands. It was *Don't hit me, hoss*. I pulled out the bag of weed and caught his left mitt in one motion. I pressed hard and finagled a full fingerprint spread.

A drizzle drifted down. I gestured toward the street. Ex-hubby #2 took off running.

"Hollywood could use a guy like you."

I turned around. There's Jolting Joi. She knows from opportunity.

"You mean I could use Hollywood."

She kissed me. I kissed her back. That's how it all started.

I know from opportunity. It costs money, honey. I heisted a bookie room two days later.

A Hitler mask hid my face. I entered with an empty grocery sack and exited with four g's. I blew half the swag on Joi. I bankrolled my biz with the remainder. A Beverly Hills pharmacist fed me piles of pills to push. Harry Fremont sold me eight ice-cold roscoes. Joi scared up a scrape doctor. I told him I'd be out seeking nice-girls-in-a-jam. Guns/dope/a felonious physician. My girlfriend as conduit to a coruscatingly corrupt culture.

Joi hit Hollywood in '42. She was fourteen. She matriculated at MGM and met Everybody. She was luridly low-rent *and* confoundingly connected. She knew Everything. She was a one-babe Baedeker. She knew bartenders, bellhops, busboys, call girls, casting directors, and cads. She knew pornographers, pushers, and pimps. She knew troves of tramps in trouble. She was out to crown me King Shakedown. Joi greased Holly*weird* with my handouts. Scores of scurrilous scamsters licked up my largesse. We were buying bleak and blowsy blackmail dirt.

I worked LAPD. I scored an off-duty gig. I was now the security boss at the Hollywood Ranch Market. It was licentiously legendary and open-all-nite. I bagged shoplifters and check kiters. I lived within my means and never gave Bill Parker's goons a hook to entrap me. I took Joi to Ciro's and the Mocambo. I saw Intelligence Squad cops cataloguing the scene. I braced them as a brother. I ballyhooed my big nights, financed by big days at the track.

I sold guns. I sold pills. I brokered abortions. I hawked a filthy film called *Mae West's Menagerie*. Shack jobs were verboten for LAPD men. Joi and I trysted at her mom's pad in Redondo. She said the word was moving out and metastasizing: Freddy O.'s The Man to See.

Gigs rolled in. I pounded a perv who'd whipped out his whang on Duke Wayne's wife. Duke paid me five yards and gave me the skinny on Red Hollywood. Dino Martin called me. He knocked up his maid with soon-to-hatch triplets. I bribed a Customs cop and got Dolorous Dolores deported. Dino paid me two g's and dished the dirt on a stunning string of starlets. They bounced on my bed and dug up dirt on my regular retainer. Want C-notes and riotous ruts in the hay? Call Mr. Nine Inches.

I got Lana Turner a scrape. She banged an alto sax named Art Pepper in a bout of bebop abandon. Putzy Pepper wanted her to keep the kid and threatened exposure. I planted two reefers in his sax case and buzzed the fuzz. He got nine months at Wayside Honor Rancho.

Joi knew a classy clique of Hancock Park housewives. They were unbearably unbodied and entrenched in ennui. They needed furtive fucking. She saw money in it. Put "pimp" on my résumé. I'm on Stud Patrol as of now.

Opportunity is love. That cold concept socked my sick soul.

Joi said Liberace had a job for me. We were in the sack at her mom's place. Her eyes twinkled and twirled me some all-new way. She drew dollar signs in the air.

The moment vibrates in VistaVision and swervy Swish-O-Scope. A piano noodles a nocturne and pounds a polonaise.

A fey factotum met me. The yard was tropically tricked out and football-field size.

Flamingos flitted. Toucans tooled and bit bugs. A path cut through ten-foot-high fronds and floral explosions. Everything was green, purple, and pink.

We hit a clearing. It was paved with stones embossed with musical clefs. The pool was shaped like a piano. Liberace sat in a deck chair. A leopard with a mink collar snoozed at his feet.

The factotum sashayed off. I pulled up a deck chair. The leopard stirred and snarled at me. I scratched his neck and kissed his snout. He went back to sleep.

Liberace said, "You're fearless. You're the kind of man I need."

"I'm here to help you out, sir. Joi said you've got a guy bugging you."

The factotum sashayed back with cocktails. Two highball glasses glowed pink. The guy served us and skedaddled. My drink tasted like radioactive bubble gum.

Liberace said, "Bottoms up."

I yukked. "A kid's putting the boots to you, right? Pay up, or he'll rat you to the Legion of Decency. All those dago mob guys that book your act in Vegas will hightail it. Your TV show will be canceled if word gets out you go Greek."

Liberace sighed. "Inimitably candid, and so, so true. He's a dishwasher at Perino's. What was I thinking?"

I sipped my pink drink. "Pictures?"

"Of course, dear heart. He lured me to a motel with a wall peek."

A hi-fi speaker sparked and kicked on. Judy Garland belted, "Someday he'll come along / The man I love." The leopard lolled and licked his balls. Liberace goo-goo-talked him.

"Five thou, sir. You get the pictures and the negatives, along with my assurance that it won't happen again."

Liberace pouted. His chest heaved. Sequins popped off his toga. The leopard loped to the pool and arced his ass over the edge. A giant shit ensued.

The factotum ran up. He wielded a turd-scoop contraption. Liberace reached under his chair and snagged a scrapbook.

"Ex-convicts are a weakness of mine, I'm chagrined to say. I've got mug shots of him, and quite a few other rough-trade conquests. It's my new hobby. I paste pictures, when I'm not wowing my fans or practicing Chopin."

I grabbed the book and leafed through it. It was the fucking lavender lodestone. I counted twenty-six K-Y cowboys wearing neck boards. Names/dates/penal-code numbers. A smutty smorgasbord of malignant maleness. Parole holds and prosty beefs galore.

Liberace jabbed a pic of one Manolo Sanchez. The guy vibed baleful bantamweight.

"He broke my heart, while his evil lezzie sister took snapshots. Feel free to get tough."

I nodded and flipped ahead. Three glum glamour boys popped off the page. Ward Wardell, Race Rockwell, Donkey Don Eversall. All booked for possession of pornography.

I pointed to the pics. "Blue-movie actors, right? They peddle it on the side. You see the movies, you get a yen, you make a phone call."

"That's correct. I went to a screening at Michael Wilding and Liz Taylor's house. Michael screened *Locker Room Lust* and *Jailhouse Heat*, and supplied the referral."

"Referral" ripped me. "Could these guys get it up for women?"

Liberace whooped. "Could, can, and *do*, sweetheart. And Donkey Don is the eighth wonder of the world, if you follow my drift."

I tingled. I thought *Parlay*. I saw dollar signs and movie-star movement on my Landing Strip.

"So, Michael Wilding's a gay caballero?"

"In spades, love. His house is known as the 'Fruit Stand,' which perturbs lovely Liz no end."

I yukked. "And Liz wants a divorce, so she can move on to her next husband and break the all-time world record?"

Liberace slapped his knees. "Yes, and she's pulling ahead of your girlfriend in that department."

I cracked my knuckles. Liberace swooned. The cat almost creamed in his jeans.

"Tell Liz to meet me at the Beverly Hills Hotel, tomorrow night. Fill her in on my résumé."

Liberace *re*-swooned. The leopard snarled and shooed a toucan up a tree.

Perino's was high swank and old money. It catered to sterile stiffs and dotty dowagers. I drove over at close-up time and parked by the back kitchen door. It was whipped wide open. Sassy Sanchez was scour-scrubbing pots.

I slid out of my sled and hunkered low on my haunches. I ran reconnaissance. I noted a line of lockers by a walk-in freezer. I had Salacious Sanchez alone.

He mambo-minced to his locker and primped. A mirror magnified his mug and tossed it back at me. I squinted and claimed a close-up. *Aaaaaaaah*—the top locker shelf. There's a stack of photo sheaths.

He picked his teeth. He squeezed blackheads. He dewaxed his ears. I walked in and crept up behind him. I pulled my beavertail sap. His neck hairs bristled. He wheeled and pulled a shiv.

Flick—the blade sliced my Sy Devore blazer. He shrieked shit *en español*. It ran the your-mama gamut.

He pirouetted and parried. We were in knife-fight tight. I risked a ripe stab wound and roundhoused him to the head. My sap socked him, full force.

The seams ripped his face. The business end tore an eyebrow loose and gnashed in his nose. He dropped the knife. I kicked it away. I grabbed his neck and squelched a scream. The deep-fry dipper was four feet away. It was spitting hot grease off spuds lyonnaise.

I dragged him over. I stuck his knife hand in the grease and frog-fried it. He screamed. I held his hand in the grease and burned it to the bone. Spatters spotted up my London Shop shirt.

I dropped his hand. I walked to the locker and grabbed the photo sheaths. I flipped through them.

Ooohhh, Daddy. It's Liberace Goes Greek—Kodacolor prints and negatives.

Sanchez screamed and careened through the kitchen. He dumped a dish rack and spasm-smacked the walls. His hand was charbroiled and crackle crisp. Flayed flesh flew off.

The night was young. I was up five thou and blasphemously blasted on blood and aggression. Revelation ripped me. I knew I could mix my own fruit shakes. I pocketed two Liberace negatives.

I called R&I. They delivered the dish on the smut-film troika. The boys shared a pad in Silver Lake. Plus a bent for the sex-soiled and seditious. *Semper fi*—they met in the Marine Corps and ran rackets out of a bondage bar down in Dago. They sold forged green cards. They peddled Spanish fly. They led Rotary groups to T.J. for the mule act. They sold dildo dupes of Donkey Don's sixteen-inch whanger.

They fell in the shit in '50. They sold Spanish fly to a nervous nympho and pledged a date with Donkey Don. The Donkster reneged. The nympho impaled herself on the gearshift of a '46 Buick. San Diego PD filed Felonious Assault. The judge tossed the case. Here's a ripe rumor: he was Race Rockwell's regular trick.

I popped out to their pad. It was a wizened wood-frame job,

buried in bougainvillea. I rang the bell at 11:00 p.m. and got no answer. I picked the door lock and let myself in. I crept flashlight-first and inventoried their shit.

The boys possessed Nazi armbands/Mickey Spillane novels/combat-pinned Marine blues. Plus *mucho* moviemaking equipment. Plus cheesecake mags going back to '36. Plus souvenir snapshots from the Klub Satan, Tijuana, New Year's '48. El Burro sports spiffy red devil ears.

I walked out to the porch. I chain-smoked and sucked on my flask. I recognized the ribbons on their uniforms. The boys savaged Saipan and stormed Guadalcanal.

I sipped bonded bourbon. I got a light load on. A jalopy jammed up at 1:00 a.m. The boys bounced out and made for the door.

I whipped out my badge and flashlight-lit it. It was deep dark out. I couldn't catch their capitulation. Call it a cool coup d'état. The dominant dog now rules their pack.

"My name's Otash. You're going into business with me."

Extortionist. Entrepreneur. Enterprising Enforcer. I ran that roundelay as I licked my lips for Liz.

I got half looped with the lads and laid down the law. I'm taking 20 percent of your smut biz. You get police protection. You're now the naughty nucleus of Freddy O.'s stud farm. Get ready to bring the brisket to some housewives in heat.

Donkey Don laid a ladle of bennies on me. I buzzed through my day-watch duty downtown. I broke up a fistfight at the Jesus Saves Mission. I chased a raft of Red agitators out of Pershing Square. I popped a whipout man at the Mayan Theater. I busted a psycho kid blowtorching two lovebirds in a '49 Ford.

My tour of duty tapped down. I went by the Criminal Courts Building and read up on divorce law. I reserved a bungalow at the Beverly Hills Hotel and scrounged refreshments off local merchants. Lou's Liquor Locker supplied champagne. Hank's Hofbrau coughed up cold cuts. Fast delivery was assured.

I swooped by my pad. I traded my cop suit for a choice chalk-stripe ensemble. Oh *yeah*—it's your ardent arriviste poised to pounce!!!!

The bungalow was big, boss, flouncy, and flamboyant. The bellman harrumphed at my ham and cheese hors d'oeuvres. He rolled his eyes and split. I paced and smoked myself hoarse. The bell rang at 8:00 p.m. sharp.

There she is—Elizabeth Taylor at twenty-one.

She stood in the doorway. I fumbled for chitchat. She wore a tight white dress. It caressed her curves and clambered up to her cleavage. She said, "If I move too fast, I'll split a seam. Help me over to that couch."

I grabbed an elbow and steered her. My hand trembled, my heart trilled. I sat her down and poured two jolts of '53 domestic. We perched on the couch and offered up toasts.

Liz raised her arm. A dress seam split down to her hemline. She said, "Shit. I didn't *have* to wear this. You're just the bird dog for my divorce."

I yukked. Liz said, "Don't marry me, okay? I can't keep doing this for the rest of my life."

"Have I got a chance?"

"More than you think. Hotel heirs and queer actors haven't worked out, so who's to say a cop wouldn't?"

I smiled. I sipped champagne. Liz snagged a slice of ham and snarfed it. Her wicked white dress constricted her. She looked plaintive, plain, and pure.

I unzipped the back. I slid in some slack and brought breathing room. Liz sighed—*Aaaaah*, that's good.

The shoulder straps slid slack and fell down her arms. Liz deadpanned it. Our knees brushed. Liz retained the contact.

"How do I cut loose of Michael? I can't cite mental cruelty, because he's a sweetheart, and I don't want to hurt him. I know you have to show just cause in order to sue."

I refilled her glass. "I'll bug your house. You get Wilding looped and get him to admit he digs boys. I levy the threat in a civilized manner, and he consents to an uncontested divorce."

Liz beamed. "It's that *easy?*"

"We're all civilized folks. You probably earn more money than him, but he's older, and has substantial holdings. You broker the property split and the alimony along those lines."

"And how are you compensated?"

"I get ten percent of your alimony payments, in perpetuity. You keep me in mind and refer me to people who might require my services."

Liz lounged on the couch cushions. Her dress collapsed past her brassiere. Our eyes found a fit. The rest of the room vaporized.

"And how will I keep you in mind? There's lots of people vying for my attention."

"I'll do my best to make this a memorable evening."

It started out clumsy and sweet. My punch line cued the first kiss. Liz was victimized and vanquished by too-tight attire. She shrugged her dress off. It wiggled down to her waist.

I carried her into the bedroom. The hoist popped buttons off my shirt. They shot across the room. We laffed. I heard the radio a bungalow over. Rosemary Clooney sang, "Hey, there—you with the stars in your eyes."

We got naked. We were built boss, stratosphere stacked, and hung home wrecker heavy. We were the boffo best of L.A. '53.

We made love all night. We drank champagne with Drambuie chasers. We smoked cigarettes and spritzed gossip. We put on robes and climbed to the roof of the bungalow at dawn.

An A-bomb test was scheduled in nowheresville Nevada. The newspapers predicted priceless fireworks. Other bungalow dwellers were up on their roofs. There's Bob Mitchum and a young quail with the quivers. There's Marilyn Monroe and Lee Strasberg. There's Ingrid Bergman and Roberto Rossellini. Everybody looks fuck-struck and *happy*. They've all got jugs for the toast.

Everybody laffed and waved hello. Mitchum brought a portable radio and tuned in the countdown. I heard static and ". . . eight, seven, six, five, four, three, two, one."

The world went *WHOOSH*. The ground shook. The sky lit up mauve and pink. We raised our booze bottles and applauded. The colors bristled into bright white light.

I had my arm around Elizabeth Taylor. I looked Ingrid Bergman straight in the eyes.

L.A. '53 was my ground zero. That blast still shoots shock waves through me.

There was smog in the air then. People coughed and gasped. *I* never noticed it. That bomb-blast moment *made* me. My L.A. was always mauve and pink.

I worked LAPD. I walked a downtown foot beat. I rousted Reds during the "Free the Rosenbergs!" fracas. I pinched pervs, purse snatchers, and pickpockets in Pershing Square. My smut-film biz laid in loot. Donkey Don Eversall plied his python all over Hancock Park. Joi was Donkey Don's dispatcher. She koffee-klatched with horny housewives and set up the dates. Liberace gave me girl-talk gossip. Liz Taylor and Michael Wilding went to Splitsville. I got 10 percent of Liz's alimony bite. Joi, Liz, and I threeskied on my Landing Strip. Liz knew a Pan Am stew named Barb Bonvillain. She flew the L.A.–Mexico City route and had half of Hollywood hooked on Dilaudid and morphine suppositories. Bad Barb was six-three, 180, 40-24-36. She scored high in the women's decathlon, Helsinki '52. All four of us locked loins. The Landing Strip lurched. We murdered the mattress and banged the box springs down to the floor.

L.A. '53—*ring-a-ding-ding!!!!*

Joi and I crashed the Crescendo and the Largo most nights. Cocktail waitresses fed me slander slurs. I tipped them, titanic. It brought back my kid-voyeur days, rabidly redux.

A fragmenting frustration set in. I *had* the dirt. It would take an armada of shakedown shills and photo fiends to deploy it. I racked my brain. I knocked my noggin against the bruising brick wall of unknowing. Extortion as existential dilemma. A confounding conundrum worthy of those French philosopher cats.

My cop life could not compete with the lush life. I was a double agent akin to that Commie cad Alger Hiss. Liz Taylor drove me to Central Station and signed autographs for the blues. I knew that word would leak to Chief William H. Parker. I was full of a finger-stabbing *FUCK YOU*.

Ralph Mitchell Horvath haunted me. Nightmares nabbed me as I slid into sleep. Joi and Liz nursed me with yellow jackets and booze. My bedtime mantra was *He Deserved to Die*. It was beastly bullshit. I couldn't convince myself that it was true.

I spent nuke-bomb nights at the Hollywood Ranch Market. My office was two-way-mirrored and overlooked the aisles. I scanned for boosters and looked down at the legions of the lost.

Their pathos pounded me. Bit actors buying stale bread and short dogs of muscatel. Six-foot-two drag queens shopping for extra-long nylons. Cough-syrup hopheads reading labels for the codeine content. Teenage boys sneaking girlie mags to the can to jerk off.

I watched. I peeped. I lost myself in the losers. A goofy ghost came and went with them.

He was about twenty-three. He slouched in windbreakers and wore cigarettes as props. He breezed through the aisles at 3:00 a.m. He always looked ecstatic. He talked to people. He cultivated people. He studied people the way I peeped windows as a kid. I saw him out on the sidewalk once. He played the bongos for a clique of fruit hustlers and junkies. A girl called him "Jimmy."

The fucker appeared intermittent. I made him for an actor living off chump change and aging queens. I saw him kiss a girl by the bread bin. I saw him kiss a boy in the soup aisle. He moved with a weirdo grace. He wasn't froufrou *or* masculine. He was in on some exalted joke.

I saw him boost a carton of Pall Malls. I cornered him, cuffed him, and hauled him upstairs. His name was James Dean. He was from bumfuck Indiana. He was an actor and a bohemian you-name-it. He said that Pall Mall cigarettes were queer code. The *In hoc signo vinces* on the pack meant "In this sign you shall conquer." Queens flashed their Pall Malls and ID'd each other. It was all-new shit to me.

I cut Jimmy loose. We started hanging out in the office. We belted booze, looked down on the floor, and gassed on the humanoids. Jimmy habituated the leather bars in East Hollywood. He ratted off pushers and celebrity quiffs and filled a whole side of my dirt bin. I told him about my smut-film and male-prosty gigs. I promised him a date with Donkey Don Eversall in exchange for hot dirt.

We'd hit silent stretches. I'd scan the floor. Jimmy would read scandal rags.

They were just popping up. *Peep, Transom, Whisper, Tattle, Lowdown.* Titillation texts. Lurid language marred by mitigation. Insipid innuendo that left you craving *more.*

Politicos got slurred as Red—but never nailed past implication. Jimmy loved the rags but cruelly critiqued them. He said they weren't sufficiently sordid or precise in their prose. He called them "timid tipster texts." He said, "You've got better skank than this, Freddy. I could give you three issues' worth from one night at the Cockpit Lounge."

A bell bonged. It was faint and far off. Memory is revised retrospection. Oh *yeah*—fate fungooed me that night.

A newsboy pulled a red wagon into the market. It was stacked with magazines. He started filling up racks.

A cover caught my eye. Priapic primary colors and hard-hearted headlines screamed.

You get the picture. The magazine was called *Confidential.*

THE BEVERLY HILLS HOTEL

8/14/53

Joi woke me up. I was nudging off a nightmare. It was a dark double dip. Ralph Mitchell Horvath, shot in the mouth/Manolo Sanchez with skeleton claws.

I looked across the bed. *Shit*—Liz was gone.

Joi read my mind. "She had an early call. She said to remind you that Arthur Crowley wants that phone date."

I lit a cigarette. I chased bennies with Old Crow. *Aaaaaaah,* breakfast of champions!!!!

"Remind me again. Who's Arthur Crowley?"

"He's that divorce lawyer who needs your help."

I said, "I'll call him when I go off-duty."

Joi stepped into a skirt and pulled her shoes on. She dressed as fast as most men.

"No more girls for a while, okay, Freddy? Liz is great, but Barb is like Helga, She-Wolf of the SS. Really, that stunt with the armband and the garters? That, and she hogs the whole bed."

I laffed loud and lewd. My wake-up whipped through me. It canceled out all dreary dreams and coarse cobwebs. Late summer in L.A.—*ring-a-ding-ding!!!!*

Joi kissed me and bopped out of the bungalow. I shit, showered, shaved, and put on my uniform.

The phone rang. I snagged it. A man said, "Mr. Otash, this is Arthur Crowley."

I buffed my badge with my necktie. A mirror magnetized me. *Man-O-Manischewitz*, I look good!!!!

"Mr. Crowley, it's a pleasure."

Crowley said, "Sir, I'll be blunt. I'm swamped with pissed-off husbands and wives, looking to take each other to the cleaners. Legal statutes are in flux, and divorce-court judges are demanding greater proof of adultery. Liz Taylor told me you might have some ideas."

I lit a cigarette. Benzedrine arced through my arteries and piqued my pizzazz.

"I *do* have ideas. If you have flexible scruples, I think we can do biz."

Crowley laffed. "I'm listening."

I said, "I know some Marines stationed down at Camp Pendleton. I was their DI in '43 and '44, and now they're back from Korea and looking for kicks. It's a parlay. Hot rods, good-looking shills, walkie-talkies, phone drops, and Speed Graphic cameras."

Crowley hooted. "*Semper fi*, sir. You're a white man in my book."

"*Semper fi*, boss. We'll work out the details at your convenience, and I'll round up my boys."

"And, in the meantime? Is there anything *you* need?"

Benzedrine was a groin groper. One thing *did* come to mind.

"My Landing Strip's got two empty runways tonight. Liz told me you're conversant with the concept."

Voices vibrated outside the bungalow. They were *mucho* male and brazenly brusque. I heard foot scrapes and coughs.

Crowley said, "Liz explained the concept, so I called you prepared. I'll send two stenos over."

"Mr. Crowley, you're a pisser."

"It takes one to know one, sir."

We hung up. The voices vibrated. I caught key-in-lock sounds. I walked into the living room. The door whipped wide.

It's William H. Parker.

With two plainclothes bulls. Both six-four. They live to hurl hurt. They're mastiffs on a mission to maul for their master.

"Send not to know for whom the bell tolls—"

I unpinned my badge and tossed it at Parker. It hit his chest and dropped on the floor. The mastiffs moved. Parker went *Get back*. The mastiffs pawed the carpet and growled *loooowwww*.

I unhooked my gun belt and dropped it on a chair. I called up some cool. Freon Freddy, the Shaman of Shakedown.

"Hit me, Bill. Shack jobs, living above my means, bending the rules here and there. My head's on the chopping block, baby. Guillotine me."

The mastiffs smirked smug. Pious Parker parsed out a grin.

"You are currently engaged in an intimate relationship with a Pan American stewardess named Barbara Jane Bonvillain, now in Federal custody for possession of narcotics procured in Mexico. I must inform you that the outsized Miss Bonvillain is a Communist agent and a personal emissary of Marshal Tito, the Red boss of Yugoslavia. As if that weren't enough, Miss Bonvillain is really a man. She underwent a sex-change operation in Malmö, Sweden, in late 1951, before her stellar efforts impersonating a woman at the '52 Olympics. You fucked a man, Freddy. You're a homo. Get the hell off my police force."

You're a homo."

"You're a homo."

"You fucked a man."

"You fucked a man."

"You're a homo, you're a homo, you're a homo."

I drank myself into a stunned stupor. I passed out on the floor. I got intimate with insects inhabiting the rug. They were dung desperadoes. They were my filthy fellow travelers, lower than lice.

"You're a homo, you're a homo, you're a homo."

I drank, I passed out, I woke up. I went eye-to-eye with a big beetle. We discussed the man-bug metaphysic. It was infused with frissons from that freaky frog Camus.

The beetle said that life was horrifically happpenstance and that we were all fucked by fate. Bugs were biologically bid to live off larvae and leaves. Men were massacred by lascivious lust and bumbled into bed with he-shes. *You didn't know that she was a he. Hit your bennie stash and find your way out of this funk.*

I obeyed the beetle. The Benzedrine outrevved the booze. I talked shit with the beetle for hours. We went feeler-to-feeler on the floor.

I called Abe Adelman at the State License Bureau. I promised him two g's for PI's ducat, quicksville. I bid the beetle adieu and climbed back into my civvies. I drove straight to the Hollywood Ranch Market.

L.A. looked like Pompeii, postearthquake. The summer sun skimmed the sky and scattered death rays. Hes were shes and shes were hes and the most gorgeous girls were gargoyles. I got to the market and ran up to my office. Jimmy was scanning the August *Lowdown.*

He said, "You're wigged out, Freddy."

I said, "I've been talking to a bug."

"What did he tell you?"

"Some shit you wouldn't believe."

"I would believe it. It's the basis of our friendship. We tell each other shit the world wouldn't believe."

I smiled. "Tell me something typical. I've had a jolt. I need to get my feet back under me."

Jimmy said, "The barman at the Manhole is pushing horse."

I said, "I'll file it away, in case I need him."

Jimmy said, "I've got a picture of Marlon Brando with a dick in his mouth."

"I'll give you a C-note."

Jimmy passed the Old Crow. I took a pull and felt the floor meet my feet.

"How was your date with Donkey Don?"

Jimmy held his hands two feet apart. Jimmy said, "Ouch."

I roared. We passed and repassed the jug. Jimmy lit a Pall Mall.

"I'm up for a role on *GE Theater,* but this Paul Newman punk will probably get it."

"I'll plant a bag of weed on him, and lay on the fear. You'll get the gig."

"Thanks, Freddy."

I thought about the talking bug. I looked down at the aisles. I felt fate beaming back at me.

"I've got all this good dirt and no place to put it. It's driving me fucking crazy."

*S*emper fi.

I assembled my ex-Marine cadre. My porno-prosty boys proceeded priapically apace. My Camp Pendleton pals came up to L.A. and joined Operation Divorce. The two crews crossed over. I had six certified psychos, culled for my command. My Pendleton pit dogs were blood-blitzed from killing Commies in Korea. They were out for chaotic kicks and required tight tugs on their chains. Our marks were adulterous wives and husbands. Donkey Don lured ladies to hot-sheet hotels and instigated insertion. Flashbulbs flared as I kicked in doors, camera cocked. My Pendleton pits were adroit and adept at rolling surveillance. They tailed wayward wives and whorehound hubbies to hotels and walkie-talkied me. Joi was the mouthwatering man bait. She worked off Arthur Crowley's *craaazy* crib sheets on the hubbies' habits. Joi was sinful seductress *and* cold cocktease. I kicked the doors in just as Joi's zipper dropped.

Operation Divorce was a Marine Corps maneuver and a mad moneymaker. Operation Otash was the ultimate umbrella command. I had an army of snarky snitches on my payroll. My PI's license arrived and served to cinch my sinful sanction. I did not much mourn my severed service with the LAPD. I paid vulture Vice cops for tips on quivering queers, jittery junkies, dipsos deep in the DT's. I built fat files on celebrity secrets and hoarded the horrors hard in my heart. Knowledge is power—the Beverly Hills Hotel bug told me that. The one puzzle piece still missing: how to *systematically* carve cash from all of it.

Jimmy joined in. I kicked putzy Paul Newman's ass and held a bag of maryjane primed with his prints. Jimmy got the *GE Theater* role and groveled with gratitude. I hired him to hump the husband of a divorce-seeking dowager sick of hubby's hijinks. Jimmy was a swift switcherooer—if it mamboed, he'd move on it. He boffed five babes in one week—topping Donkey Don's extant record. I camera-caught the wives as Jimmy shot them the *schvantz*.

L.A. '53—radioactive ring-a-ding-ding!!!! That mauve-and-pink sky, ever mine.

Then, at long last—the confounding convergence.

I was on the Landing Strip. I was lolling with Liz and a winsome waitress from Biff's Charbroil. My mail slot creaked. An envelope hit the floor.

It was a Western Union telegram. I opened it and read:

> *Dear Mr. Otash,*
>
> *We here at* Confidential *are looking for a man conversant in the celebrity secrets of present-day Los Angeles, preferably a man with prior police experience. Would you be willing to meet me in a week's time, to discuss a possible collaboration?*
>
> *Sincerely,*
> *Robert Harrison,*
> *Publisher and Editor In Chief*

Ava Gardner's Dusky Dee-lite."

"Johnnie Ray's Men's Room Misadventure."

"Bad Boy Bob Mitchum: Back in Reeferland AGAIN?"

Oh *yeah*—*Confidential* contaminated. *Confidential* kicked up chaos. *Confidential* came to *work*.

I wired Harrison and confirmed the meet. I booked a boss bungalow at the Beverly Hills Hotel. I borrowed textbooks from Arthur Crowley's library and studied libel, slander, and defamation of character. I learned to think and talk like a language-lucid lawyer.

Jimmy bagged back issues of *Peep, Lowdown, Whisper, Tattle,* and *Confidential* itself. I studied linguistic loopholes and cultivated codes of mitigation, equivocation, ambiguity. There's innuendo, inference, implication. There's many wicked ways to scandal-skin a cat.

I alter-egoed myself in a week's time. I discovered *sinuendo* and scandal language. I moved into the bungalow a day early. That talking bug and I conferenced and concurred:

Confidential was the grooved-out grail of this shook-up generation. Disillusionment is enlightenment. *Confidential* trafficked truth and harpooned hypocrisy. It was a devoutly decorous document. It was the *meshugenah* Magna Carta of our hopped-up and fucked-up age.

It's now 9/21/53. It's now precisely 10:00 a.m. The doorbell rings.

Caviar, canapés—check. Martinis mixed *magnifico*—check. My dossier on Bondage Bob—malignantly memorized.

I opened the door. There's the Sultan of *Sin*uendo. He's a nervous nebbish in a dreary drip-dry suit.

He said, "Mr. Otash."

I said, "Mr. Harrison."

He walked in and went *Oooh-la-la.* I poured two mighty martinis and pointed to the couch. We raised our glasses. I said, "To freedom of speech."

He said, "The First Amendment. What it hath wrought."

We clicked glasses. He made the you-and-me sign. He said, "Strange bedfellows."

You're *stranger*, dipshit. *You* wear women's lingerie and love the lash. *You* published "Honeys in Heels," pre-*Confidential.*

"Get my attention, Mr. Otash. Open strong, baby. I need dirt, and a man to excavate it. Hit me, sweetheart. Show me why the cognoscenti says, 'Fred Otash is the man to see.'"

I flashed my Marlon Brando snapshot. Bondage Bob perused it. He spazzed and spritzed me with a mouthful of martini.

It drip-dried on the sofa and my silk suit coat. Bondage Bob coughed and called up composure. He said, "Holy fucking shit."

"May I give you a candid assessment of your situation, and explain how I might best serve you?"

"Hit me, doll. I didn't fly three thousand miles for some namby-pamby chitchat."

I shot my cuffs and showed off my Rolex. Twenty-four-karat gold/diamonds/rubies. I buzz-bombed Bondage Bob with my bold opening thrust.

"You publish what is rapidly becoming the premier scandal magazine in a very crowded field. You compete with *Whisper, Tattle, Peep, On the Q.T., Lowdown,* and others. Your competitors rely largely on true-crime exposés, reports of miracle cures for various diseases, and rehashes of your own articles on celebrity misbehavior. The specific strengths of your magazine are its staunch anti-Communist stance and *sex*. Frankly, I find your articles that play on the *greed* of your readers are both unbelievable and devoid of the heat that people turn to *Confidential* for. There are no emerald mines in Colorado, and no Uruguayan herbs that triple the size of the male member in two weeks' time. You're *lying*, sir. You're hoping that bilking your readers with stories like that will both boost your sales and help defray the costs of the libel suits that are being filed against you with greater and greater frequency in circuit courts all over America. My good friend, the esteemed jurist Arthur Crowley, has informed me that magazines that publish filler pieces chock-full of boldfaced lies create what he calls a 'gap in credibility and verisimilitude.' This calls into question the veracity of all the articles published in said magazines over time, leaving said magazines vulnerable to both individual lawsuits and the looming specter of what Mr. Crowley calls the 'lynch-mob-like and Communistic specter of the emerging class action suit,' wherein aggrieved parties band together under the aegis of left-wing lawyers in order to posit a common beef and destroy the First Amendment right of free speech that we hold so sacred here in America. The mitigating, equivocating, and temporizing language that runs through your groundbreaking articles on celebrity misconduct will not save you. You may use *alleged, purported,* and *rumored* as much as you like, but they will not legally extricate you in the end. My first two salient points are these: you must dramatically boost your sexual content, and everything you publish in *Confidential* must be entirely true and verifiable."

Wooooooooo!!!! Bravura breath control and artful articulation!!!! Bondage Bob's flabbergasted and flushed.

He fidgeted. He licked his lips. He crossed his legs and went submissive sissy. I saw restraint-rope scars on his wrists.

"Nuisance suits are costing us twenty-five thou a month. Those Commie lawyers are coming out of the sewers like rats."

I socked him my Second Soliloquy:

"Informants must be both credible and coercible, as well as vulnerable to exposure of their own misdeeds. I served as an officer of the Los Angeles Police Department for close to a decade. I have access to every crooked cop in this town, and they will rat out any celebrity, socialite, Communist, miscegenist, or alluring lowlife that they know of for a simple retainer. The scum that they rat out will rat out six others to stay out of your magazine, and the mathematical equation that I am positing will extend indefinitely. I can tell that you're thinking, *Informants alone will not suffice,* and that assumption is correct. You may know that we are entering a bold new era of electronic surveillance. I propose that we install standing, full-time bugs in every high-class hotel in Los Angeles. I will bribe the managers and desk clerks of said hotels to steer celebrity adulterers and queers to specific rooms, where their sexual activities and conversation will be captured on tape. The best bug man on earth is a hebe named Bernie Spindel. I will meet with him soon. Mr. Spindel would love to enter your employ, and has a gift for you. He bugged a bungalow at the Miramar Hotel in Santa Monica last week. The manager of the hotel is a masochistic child molester with a quite understandable urge to be punished for his aberrant behavior. I will physically chastise him on a monthly basis, which will deter him from hurting children, as well as keep him under my thumb. He will have strict orders to place all celebs in bungalow number nine. Bernie's gift is a tape of Senator John F. Kennedy fucking Ingrid Bergman, and detailing his preposterous plans to run for president of the United States to her, while she yawns and prattles on about her kids. Be forewarned: the fucking is short-lived. I'll be frank: Senator Kennedy is a two-minute man."

Bondage Bob. He's gaga, goo-goo-eyed, *gone*.

"So, we—"

I cut him off. "*So*, we also bug all the gay bathhouses. *So*, I have extortion wedges on the informants who supply the dirt for our most explosive pieces. *So*, I polygraph-test them to assure their veracity. *So*, I create a climate of fear in Hollywood, which is the most gorgeously perverted and cosmetically moralistic place on God's green fucking Earth. *Because*, I have an unerring nose for human weakness and have sensed for some time that we have entered an era where the gilded and famous all secretly harbor a desire to be exposed. *Because*, I am willing to burglarize any psychiatrist's office in order to get the dirt on their celebrity patients. *Because*, I am willing to quash lawsuits through the threat and application of physical force."

Bondage Bob *guuuuuuuulped*. "What *won't* you do?"

I saw Ralph Mitchell Horvath. I said, "Commit murder or work for the Reds."

A pin-drop silence sizzled. I let it linger *loooooong*.

"Would you consent to an audition? To test your inside knowledge?"

I nodded. Harrison hit me. I bopped to his beat, beatific.

"Senator Estes Kefauver?"

"Whorehound. Shacks with Filipina prosties at the downtown Statler."

"Sinatra. Give me the latest."

"Caught his new girlfriend muff-diving Lana Turner, went on a six-day bender with Jackie Gleason, and wound up with the DT's at Queen of Angels."

"Otto Preminger?"

"Mud shark. Currently enthralled with a sepia seductress named Dorothy Dandridge."

"Lawrence Tierney?"

"Brawling, psychopathic brother of noted grasshopper Scott

Brady. Digs the boys at the Cockpit Lounge, and the occasional girl who looks like a boy."

"John Wayne?"

"Quasi–drag queen. Fucks women and looks stunning in a size fifty-two-long muumuu."

"Johnny Weissmuller?"

"King Schlong. Well known to have fathered nine kids out of wedlock, with nine different women. Current holder of the White Man's World Record."

"Duke Ellington?"

"Current holder of the Black World Record."

"Van Johnson?"

"The Semen Demon. Sucks dick at the glory hole at the Wilshire May Company men's room."

"Burt Lancaster?"

"Sadist. Has a well-appointed torture den in West Hollywood. Pays call girls top dollar to inflict pain on them."

"Fritz Lang?"

"Known to film Burt's torture sessions, and screen them for a select clientele."

"The Misty June Christy?"

"Nympho size queen. My shakedown bait Donkey Don Eversall gives her the big one on a regular basis. Donkey Don's got a wall peek at his crib. My pal Jimmy Dean made an avant-garde film of their last assignation. It's called *The Stacked and the Hung.* The premiere is Friday night, in my living room. You're cordially invited."

"Alfred Hitchcock?"

"Peeper."

"Natalie Wood?"

"Child actress in transition. Rumored to be ensconced at a dyke slave den near Hollywood High."

"Alan Ladd?"

"Dramatically underhung snatch hound. A man on the horns of a brutal existential dilemma."

Bondage Bob. The big magazine mogul. He's gaga, goo-goo, pulled into putty. He's martini-mangled and *mine.*

"Mr. Otash, the job is yours."

I said, "The bite is fifty grand a year, and expenses. My operating costs will go at least double that."

Now, he's green at the gills. *Now*, he knows there's No Exit. It's a fabulous fait accompli.

"Yes, Mr. Otash. We have a deal."

We shook hands. We jacked gin and vermouth. Bondage Bob said, "Jean-Paul Sartre's a pal of mine. He'll love *The Stacked and the Hung*."

That talking bug rocked across the rug and waved at me. I swear this is true.

Jimmy timed the fuck. It ran 1:46. Jack Kennedy and Ingrid Bergman banged the beast with two backs.

Pillow patter tapped the tape. Jack said, "*Aaaaah*, that was good." Ingrid said, "Vell, for vun of us, perhaps."

I roared. Jimmy howled. The market was 3:00 a.m. dead. We gargled Old Crow.

Jimmy said, "We wrapped *GE Theater*. I invited Ronnie Reagan to the premiere."

I said, "He hates the Reds. I'll hit him up for some snitch-outs."

The tape groaned and ground down to squelch. Jimmy turned it off. I looked down at the floor. A dippy denizen bought this month's *Confidential*.

Jimmy said, "When I'm famous, keep me out of the magazine."

I said, "When you're *in* it, you'll know you've arrived."

My first ops check arrived. I retained Bernie "the Bug King" Spindel. We spent a week whipping wires to wainscoting and laying mike mounts into mattresses. I bribed hotel honchos up the yammering ying-yang. We drilled, bored, spackled, threaded, planted, and wired all the high-end hotels. Regular retainers would result in records of sicko celebs sacking up in those rooms. Bondage Bob had bountiful bucks. We wire-whipped full-time listening posts at the Beverly Hills Hotel, the Hotel Bel-Air, the Beverly Wilshire, the Miramar, the Biltmore, the downtown Statler. A Biltmore bellboy tipped us, right off. Gary Cooper and a jailbait jill jumped into that bugged bedroom. *BAM!!!*—our system socks in sync. Bedsprings bounce, voices vibrate, mikes pick up tattle text and lay it to the listening post. *BAM!!!*—my Marine Corps mastiff retrieves the tape. *BAM!!!*—the babe is sixteen and a Belmont High coed. Coop says, "You're built, honey. Tell me your name again." The girl gasps, "I've always loved your pictures, Mr. Cooper. And, wow, you're really *big*."

The dirt. The dish. The scandal skank. The lewd libels revealed as *real*. It all came to me and to *Confidential*. Freddy O.'s in unstoppable ascent.

Jimmy cut his movie and dubbed in a sizzling sound track. The proud premiere was *the* L.A. Moment of Fall '53. I served pizza, booze, and pills from a felonious pharmacy. My pad was packed with movie *machers* and Marines, stupid starlets, stars, and studs. Dig: Liz, Joi, Ward Wardell, Race Rockwell, Donkey Don Eversall. Ronnie Reagan, Harry Fremont, Arthur Crowley, Bondage Bob, and Jean-Paul Sartre—existentially seeking the scene. A six-foot-six drag queen, Rock Hudson, ex–U.S. Congresswoman Helen Gahagan Douglas. Charlie "Yardbird" Parker, nodding on Big "H."

It's the egalitarian epicenter of postwar America. It's a colossal convergence of the gilded and gorgeous, the defiled and demented, the lurid and the low-down. This seedy summit set the tone for the frazzled and fractured frisson that is our nation today.

I dimmed the lights. Race Rockwell ran the projector. The sound track hit: Bartók, Beethoven, bebop by way of Bird. There's the opening titles: *The Stacked and the Hung*, starring Donkey Don Eversall and June Christy. Photographed, edited, produced, and directed by James Dean.

The applause ran apoplectic. There's the first shot. It's a Hollyweird motel room. It's a through-a-wall-peek peep at you know what.

June Christy enters the room and drops her purse on the bed. She looks apprehensive. She lights a cigarette, she checks her watch, she taps her toes and paces. It's soundless cinema. The camera stays static—the lens is lashed to that peek.

June hears something. She smiles, she walks offscreen, she walks back on with Donkey Don. Donkey Don winks at the wall peek. He's in on it. June sits on the bed. Donkey Don whips it out and wags it. My pad shakes and shimmies. There's gasps, wolf whistles, shrill shrieks.

I looked around for Jimmy. June devoured Donkey Don, tonsil-deep. Where's Jimmy? Fuck—he's jacking off by the pizza buffet!!!

'53 to '54. My mauve-and-pink skies. Sales-graph lines in escalation. *Confidential* hits a million a month. *Confidential* makes two million in rabid record time.

It's all ME. I'm awash in the sicko secrets I've cruelly craved my whole life. I've got L.A. hot-wired. My city teems with tattle tipsters on my payroll. Hotel rooms are hot-sheet hives hooked up to my headset. I know everything sinful, sex-soiled, deeply dirty, and religiously wrong. It's wrong, it's real, and it's MINE.

My Marines lived in listening posts. They caught Corrine Calvet cavorting with a car-park cat at the Crescendo. They caught Paul Robeson, ripped to the gills at a Red rally. They caught Jumping Johnnie Ray again. I verified all of it and fed it to *Confidential*. Gary Cooper and Miss Belmont High? Quashed for ten grand.

'53 to '54. A-bomb parties on Liz Taylor's rooftop. Cavalcades of color against the dim dawn. The camaraderie and opportunity. The sense that this march of magnificent moments would never stop.

Sales graphs. *Confidential* covers. Dipsos, nymphos, junkies, and Commies, exposed. That cover I regret, that ball I dropped, that *malignant* moment. That page in Purgatory as I pause my pen.

It's January 16, 1954. I'm at my pad. I'm booking a threeski for the Landing Strip. I quashed a story on Marilyn Monroe's Mexican marriage. Marilyn grovels, grateful. She knows a sapphic sister with a sometimes yen for men.

The phone rang. I picked up. Arthur Crowley said, "There's trouble, Freddy."

I said, "Hit me."

"I got a tip. Johnnie Ray's been to a libel lawyer, and he's suing the magazine. I know that you verified the story, but he's going forward anyway. I strongly suggest that you nip this in the bud."

"Men's Room *Mishegas:* Jittery Johnnie Strikes Again." I verified the story. *Confidential* ran it. This was untold grief.

"My Marines are on maneuvers, Art. There's no one to handle it."

"*You* handle it, Freddy. Take care of it, before that tip gets back to Bob Harrison."

I hung up. My nerves were nuked. I took three quick pops of Old Crow. Joi was tight with Johnnie. They girl-talked regular. I liked Johnnie. Jimmy screened *The Stacked and the Hung* for him, personally.

I dropped three yellow jackets and obliterated the day. I woke up at midnight. Johnnie always hit Googie's after his closing set. He always parked in the same spot.

I walked over. I recall spring heat and a brisk breeze. I lounged on Johnnie's Packard Caribbean. Johnnie bopped out at 1:15.

He saw me. He got the gestalt. He said, "Hi, Freddy."

I said, "Don't make me, kid. I'll keep you out from now on, but you've got to stop it here."

Johnnie said, "You're a parasite, Freddy. You feed off the weak. I'm not backing off. I don't see any of your goons around, so you'll have to do it yourself."

I said, "Let it go, Johnnie. You can't win this one."

"*You're* the weak one, Freddy. Joi told me you cry out for your mother in your sleep."

I trembled. "One more time, Johnnie. No lawsuit. Do this for me, and the magazine will never come near you again."

Johnnie spit on my shoes. "You're a mama's boy, Freddy. Joi told me you fucked a tranny, which makes you more queer than me."

I saw red and black-red. I hit him. My signet ring slashed his cheek. He went down on his knees. I picked him up and hurled him against his car. I heard bones crack and teeth shear. The bumper ledge gouged his head. I kicked him and tore a chunk of his scalp free.

He said, "Okay, okay, okay."

I said, "I'm sorry, kid."

Johnnie spit blood. Johnnie spit teeth and gum flaps. He shot a big fuck-you finger my way.

The market was 2:00 a.m. deadsville. Jimmy and I quaffed Old Crow. We stood by the mirror and gassed at the ghoul show. I was spritzed with Johnnie Ray's blood.

Jimmy said, "I'm up for the lead in *East of Eden*. Elia Kazan's waffling. It could go either way."

I said, "I'll lean on Kazan. He's susceptible. There's some pinkos he didn't rat to HUAC."

Jimmy gazed down at the aisles. My hands hurt. I cracked my signet ring. My shirt cuffs were soaked red.

The Legions of the Lost. They're down there. They're damning me. They're hexing me to Hell. They're my comrades in chaos. They're saying You're One of Us.

"Jimmy, do you know why you're a freak?"

"I don't know, Freddy. Do you know why *you* are?"

I said, "I don't know, but sometimes it all gets to me."

PERVDOG

Freddy Otash Confesses, Part II

CELL 2607

I'm balefully *back*. It's time for my next contaminated confession. I'm *still* stagnantly stuck in the Hell Adjacent Hilton and yammeringly yearn for a heavenly reprieve. I'm *still* stuck with the fucked-up and failing body I had when I crapped out, back in '92. It's *still* confession/repentence/atonement. It *still* comes down to *that*. Here's the draconian drill:

I'll repugnantly reprise some shit I pulled in phantasmagoric '54. I'll be freewheeling Fred Otash at thirty-two. '54 was a ring-a-ding-ding year. I'm going to *diiiiiiig* going back.

So, succumb to the seditious soul of a scandal-rag scoundrel—because wicked words on paper are pop-pop-popping your way.

Freaky Freddy O. rides again.

ATOP MATTRESS JACK KENNEDY'S BOSS BUNGALOW AT THE BEVERLY HILLS HOTEL

2/14/54

It's a wind-whipped winter nite. It's cloudless clear all the way to noxious Nevada. Uncle Sambo is detonating a payload-packed A-bomb in some deserted desert burg. We're here to grok, groove, flip, flash, and gas on the show.

We've got a ripe rooftop perch. I'm here at Bondage Bob Harrison's behest. *Confidential*'s running a *farkakte* feature on radioactive waste as a dick-enlargement bonanza. Bob's got a mad chemist brother. He's calling his priapic product "Megaton Man."

We're here. That means me and my Marine Corps mastiffs: Race Rockwell and Ward Wardell. Mattress Jack has slipped his gilded guests binoculars and Hyannis Port toggle coats. My cool contingent carries burglars' tools and comes with B and E know-how. The plan: burglarize Senator Jack's bungalow in the wiggy wake of the blast.

Dig the guest list. There's Jack the K. and insolent Ingrid Bergman. There's Bob Mitchum and Juicy Jane Russell. There's Tarzantoned Lex Barker and liquor-looped Lana Turner. Jimmy Dean's on *my* guest card. He's *still* peddling snapshots of Marlon Brando with a dick in his mouth. Jimmy's got director Gadge Kazan in tow. He's *this close* to snagging the top role in *East of Eden*. Gadge is a maladroit midget. His flicks send me somnambulistic. He ratted some

Comintern cads to HUAC and earned *Confidential's* fevered fealty. He snitches recidivistic Reds to Bondage Bob, subversively sub rosa.

Senator Jack served rum drinks topped with floating hashish cubes. I opted for the Benzedrine-spiked reefers. Jack Baby loves my larcenous Lebanese ass. I flew a bitching bevy of call girls down to Acapulco last year. They trashed Jack's paparazzi-pounced honeymoon and made Jackie jump into my bed. Jack's a *c'est la vie*, Daddy-O, noblesse oblige sort of guy. Jackie was grovelingly grateful.

A portable radio announced the countdown. Waiters stood by with postblast drinks and hors d'oeuvres. A doomsday disc jockey intoned: "ten, nine, eight, seven, six, five, four, three, two, one—zero."

Bombs Away, Motherfuckers!!!!!

A magnificent mushroom cloud morphed into mauve and pink. Man, what a suck-your-soul sight!!! My balls contracted. My boys and I hopped off the roof, down to ground level. Ground zero popped pink particles high in the sky. The gilded gang applauded and roared.

We deviously ditched the party. None of the bomb babies saw us. Jack's bungalow was right there, off the roof. I demobilized the door lock with a celluloid strip. We locked the door behind us and worked with pocket penlights. Chop, chop—fuckers. I'm giving us eight minutes, tops.

Our top target was address books. They were stashed in handbags and overcoats discarded for Jack's toggle togs. It's a scandalrag caper. I'm out to notch names/numbers/addresses. The lurid love shacks of the heavy-hung and hard up. Nubile names and fuck-struck fone numbers. Noxious names and homo-hideout addresses. Non sequitur names that might mandate bracing breakins themselves.

It was all for *Confidential*. Knowledge is power. You naïve *nudniks* know that. *My* misanthropic motive? A demonic desire to know the world's secret shit and hoard said shit for my personal titillation and shakedown potential.

The clock's ticking. We crisscrossed the crib. Ward and Race went for all the boss booty. *Ooooohhh*—overcoats draped on hotel-suite chairs, high-line handbags galore. My job was forensic frame-up. I secretly secured three fingerprint cards from Beverly Hills PD Burglary.

Dig: three hot-prowl/rape-o/459 men. Bad lads, already ID'd. At large for six Beverly Hills jobs. Forced oral cop/straight rape/thirty-four thou in stolen furs and jewels.

It gets wicked worse. There's a Little Lindbergh Law kidnap. She's a Beverly High cheerleader. There's multiple motel-room rapes before she's cut loose. The BHPD wanted these fucked-up fiends, *baaaaaaaaad*. Heh, heh—I made Scotch-taped transparencies of the three print cards. George Collier Akin, Durwood N. M. I. Brown, Richard "Rattlesnake" Dulange. Fred O. judge-and-juries a frame job on YOU.

I got out my print cards. I laid the treated transparency tape across three thumb and full-fingerprint spreads. I pulled off my single-digit tapes. I laid prints on chair backs, waist-high wainscoting, touch-and-grab bedroom planes.

J'accuse—Akin, Brown, and Dulange—you were here. You robbed Senator Jack Kennedy's hotel suite. You done been FRAMED.

Ward and Race dumped furs and address books. They stacked them in Senator Jack's ostrich-skin suitcase. We were six minutes in. I saved the best booty for last.

Mattress Jack was a hellacious hophead. He had legal scripts from half the pharmacists in L.A. I made for the bathroom and Jack's mad medicine chest. Oh yeah—Dilaudid, Dexedrine, Dolophine sulfate. *Ooooohhh*—the nifty new Nembutal suppositories!!!

Jack collected lissome locks of women's pubic hair. He traveled with them and kept them in unscented sachets. I found his stash in an attaché case under the bed. They were lewdly labeled. I've always gassed on La Bergman and Anna Magnani. I left the attaché behind. I took two love-lashed sniffs on my way out the door.

—⁓—

Ward and Race left me the address books. Bomb blasts and burglary—the total take vibed ten g's. Don Wexler knew a fence. We'd lay off the furs soonsville. We split the wallet cash three ways.

I popped two of Jack's delectable dexies and leveled the load with a one-grain Dilaudid. I drove to Googie's to log tattle tips from the late-nite legions who lingered there.

Tipsters crept up and crowded my table. Here's baritone sax Gerry Mulligan. He lays out alto sax Art Pepper's yen for lush high school chicks. Pepper pounded his pud at the sight of pom-pom-girl garb. He haunted Hollywood High and Hami High and left drool stains on the football field bleachers.

Comme ci, comme ça. I laid twenty clams on Gerry. He amscrayed to score some Big "H."

Billy Eckstine dropped by to schmooze. The mellifluous Mr. B. was mad for miscegenation. He played all the colored clubs on 46th and Central. He loved *Confidential* and lauded its sheer linguistic flair. He called it the "scatterbrained scat of white men working hard to be hip." Billy was right. I told him I'd insert the quote in the next issue. Billy went on to *coon*fide his own recent affairs. And, Freddy, dig—all these bints *want* to see themselves linked to me in *Confidential*.

"All these bints." As in Ava Gardner, Bette Davis, ex–U.S. Congresswoman Helen Gahagan Douglas. Lezbo basketball player Joan "Stretch" Perkins—hiding her secret yen for men from her sapphic sisters on the USC team. Plus the Misty June Christie, Anita O'Day, four boss bitches on work furlough from Tehachapi, and smack-back Chet Baker's willowy white wife.

I laid two yards on Billy. He showed me a pic of Stretch Perkins. She's sinking a *looooooong* hook shot against UCLA. I emitted low growls. Stretch ran six-six and 190. Billy grokked my Landing Strip antics. He affirmed that Stretch dug threeskies. He said he'd set Joi and me up with her.

Low growls and bilious boredom. Billy bopped off. Jilted lovers bopped up. They ratted out their cheating wives and hubbies as the Black Dahlia killer. The Dahlia was stale bread. I fobbed them off with a five-spot apiece.

It was 2:00 a.m. My dope cocktail coursed through me. My thoughts tumbled and tossed. That A-bomb blast blazed behind my eyelids. I saw three big squarejohns in gray suits by the bar. They vilely vibed fuzz. I thought of William H. Parker, still running spot tails on me. I blinked, the squarejohns squiggled, they might have been A-bomb/dope fantasia.

I thought about the magazine. Sales were up 16 percent for January '54. Shame shot through me. I thought about my thump job on Johnnie Ray. Johnnie was tight with Joi. They koffee-klatched and gal-talked. Johnnie threatened to sue *Confidential*. He refused to desist. I had one rancid recourse. Johnnie gave Joi the blow-by-blow. Joi was righteously repelled. She resisted my rigorous romancing and refuseniked threeskies with Liz Taylor. Maybe Stretch Perkins would loosen her libido and liberate her heart.

Another jacked-up Joan jumped me. Joan Hubbard Horvath. Ralphie's widow. I had two grand in my pocket and no place to go at 3:00 fucking a.m.

So, I cadged an envelope from my waiter.

So, I went by the penance pad.

Lower Hollyweird. Camerford between Vine and El Centro. A smudgy small wood-frame job, just short of a shack.

I parked across the street and bopped over. I popped the envelope in the mailbox and bopped back to my sled. A light popped on. The Horvath hut glowed internal and infernal.

I'm a devious dipshit. I made too much noise on purpose. Hey, lady—I killed your husband. It's been five years and eleven days now. I've never seen your face.

Just newspaper pix. Pixilated pokes at you in wilted widow's weeds. The *Herald* ran headlines. WOUNDED COP SURVIVES SHOOT-OUT. GUNMAN SLAIN IN ESCAPE ATTEMPT.

There's a *biiiiiiig* pic of Fractious Freddy. There's zero per throw-down guns and Ralphie's unarmed status.

I lit a cigarette and sat there. I played "Willow Weep for Me" in my head. Time tipped by. Joan Hubbard Horvath walked out on the porch. The front-room lights boffo backlit her.

She wore a dark wool dress and brown loafers. She sported a short shag hairdo and wire-rimmed specs.

She looked *toward* me. I looked *at* her. I'm a good whistler. I whistled "Willow Weep for Me" all the way through. I made the crescendo a cri de coeur and a long-suppressed sob.

Joan Horvath looked in her mailbox. The song went *soooooooooo* soft—

THE SECURITY OFFICE AT THE SLEAZOID HOLLYWOOD RANCH MARKET

2/15/54

Jimmy Dean and I lolled by the two-way mirror. We looked down at the dregs and the dreck and the dreamy drag queens dragging themselves through the aisles. Shifty shoplifters shot their gaze to our opaque eye in the sky.

Jimmy said, "Aisle six. That fat guy slid a Swanson's TV dinner down the back of his pants."

I lit a cigarette. "The checkstand guy will spot the bulge and nail him."

"You're abstracted today, Freddy."

"I had a late night, and I don't feel like messing with chumps."

Jimmy pulled a chair up. I collapsed on my couch. Jimmy tossed a magazine on my lap.

"I talked to Billy Eckstine after you left Googie's. He told me you're entranced with a certain lezzie athlete. I heard she frequents Linda's Little Log Cabin, and I thought you might appreciate page twenty-six."

The *Trojanette Sporting News.* Glittery glossy and a boss booster rag. Page twenty-six: a fulsome foldout of Joan "Stretch" Perkins.

Woo-woo!!! She's a Viking Valkyrie. She's a blitzkrieg blonde with bleached-blue eyes. She's bigger than Barb Bonvillain—richly revealed to be a man some quack diced and dehomoized.

There's Strapping Stretch. She's Stunning Stretch in USC

crimson-and-gold silks. She wears no makeup. She looks heavenly wholesome. She's smiling because she's bigger than everyone— men insistently included. And I know and dig that that means *ME*—you towering temptress.

I tossed the magazine back to Jimmy. He said, "Something's eating you."

"Joi moved out last night, while I was at Googie's. She left me a note: 'Fuck you and go to hell. You're a storm trooper, and the world is wise to your shit.'"

Jimmy yukked. "Joi's vivid, but I found you a new roommate—at least for a while."

"Stretch Perkins?"

"No such luck. Liberace called me. He wants you to look after his leopard while he goes on tour. You're the only man for the job. The fucking leopard would kill anyone else."

I yukked. "I'll consider it. Tell me some other shit I don't know, and make it entertaining."

Jimmy lit a cigarette and blew concentric smoke rings. Gadge Kazan told me the trick got him *East of Eden*.

"I did two days on *Ride Clear of Diablo*, at Universal. Lew Wasserman knows we're pals, and he chatted me up on the set. He said Rock Hudson's going batshit with boys of all races, colors, and creeds, and Morty Bendish at the *Mirror's* getting ready to blind-item it, and he's passing the specific dirt and some motel-room infrareds on to some guys at *Transom* and *Whisper*. He wants you to put the squelch on it and find Rock a wife, so maybe the appearance of being married will put the skids to all those persistent and wholly accurate rumors."

I roared righteous and laffed lewd. I folded my fitful funk and tossed Jilting Joi and Jittery Johnnie Ray aside. I popped two of Jack Kennedy's Dexedrine and went rippled and revitalized.

"Call Lew, and put him on your side in all matters pertaining to your career. Tell him we're in. I'll lean on Bendish and the *Transom* and *Whisper* guys. We'll negotiate the wife search when I glom the infrareds, and we'll split Lew's paycheck fifty-fifty. Hit the studio casting pools and hustle up some good-looking skirts who know an opportunity when they see one, and who know how to keep their mouths shut. No semipros, nothing garish. Withhold the 'He's a fruit' punch line until we've narrowed down our list of candidates. Call Rock now and tell him to be discreet and order in his woof-woof, for the time being. Tell Lew that *he's* the one to break the news to Rock—and to tell him the good news that as far as women are concerned, nothing lasts forever."

Rippled, revitalized, ready to roll. *Bam!!!!!*—scratch a righteous and reptilian American, and the lines between OPPORTUNITY and LOVE blur.

Jimmy split to find Rock Hudson a wife he'd never pour the pork to. I checked the a.m. papers and ran the radio. As expected—the 459 at Jack Kennedy's suite went unreported. As expected—a BHPD Burglary dick called me. As expected—he called everybody on Senator Jack's A-bomb-bash guest list. As expected—he mentioned the burdensome B and E in *sooooo*-discreet terms. *But*—he laid the vivid verismo on ex-cop Otash, X-clusive.

"We know who did it, Freddy. It's those rape-o shitheads who kidnapped that cheerleader chick. They left prints up the wazoo. Those humps are bought and paid for."

Don Wexler called half an hour later. Dig: we got 11.6 thou for the furs and jewels in Jack the K.'s hotel suite.

I went through the five address books we stole. *Confidential* thrived on insider tattle. I had pink and red leather books for Ingrid Bergman, Lana Turner, and some society sob sister named Connie Woodard. She scribed for the Hearst rags and wrote up the pampered party lives of the L.A. elite. I had black books for *Baaaaaad* Bob Mitchum and Senator Jack his own self.

I tapped La Grande Bergman first. The names and numbers were prissy predictable. Fat voyeur Alfred Hitchcock. Yawn-meister Gregory Peck. Dago directors Roberto Rossellini, Vittorio De Sica, Michelangelo Antonioni. So far, so *what*? Ingrid swung with Rossellini, circa '50. She popped his out-of-wedlock whelp and caused a stir. So *what*? *Confidential* ran that stale story already. The rest of the numbers? Studio stiffs, fag hags, anonymous suck-ups to the stars. Plus—Jack the K., *biiiiiiiig* surprise: Ingrid was a WOMAN—if it mamboed, he'd move on it. Plus *this*: all the dizzy data was in *Confidential's* master file already.

I tapped Bob Mitchum's black book. It was all call girls/all day and all nite. Note the boffo bust measurements next to the numbers. Half these babes peddled their poon out of Googie's. *Yawn*. They were all in *Confidential's* comprehensive call-girl file. Note to Bondage Bob Harrison: run an All Call Girl Issue soon!!!!

Next up: Hearst hack Connie Woodard. *Aha*—here my hackles hopped.

Call girls to Commies. *That's* a puzzling parlay. Note these noxious names. We've got Joe Losey and John Howard Lawson. We've got Comintern cultural commissar V. J. Jerome. There's dyspeptic Dalton Trumbo. Don't stop now. There's blustery blowhards blasted and blacklisted, Moscow's minions all, plus all the mock martyrs known as the Hollywood Ten.

We had all the names and numbers in our "Known Commo" file. *So what?* It's the confounding connection to the Woodard cooze that made it all pop!!!

And—*here's* a hot one. Gnaw on *this* non sequitur. He ain't no apoplectic apparatchik. He ain't no rank Red, no way.

Steve Cochran.

Steve the Stud. Mr. Twelve Inches. B-movie thug and cad supreme. Star of dreary drive-in drivel like *Highway 301*, *White Heat*, and *The Damned Don't Cry*. Steve the Stud's ruff and tuff, on- and offscreen. He's a brawler and a sicko psychopath. Men fear him, women crave him. He's the hungest among us. He treats women ruff and tuff—like they licentiously like it. He beat two pachucos who tried to mug him half dead. A fruit honked him at Grauman's Chinese. He bit the guy's nose off and spit it back in his face.

Woooo-woooo!!!!

A hunch hit me, hard. Call it the Cochran Confluence. I had two address books left. Lana Turner's and Jack K's. Said books would yield boring bupkes. Except for this: said books would unify the Cochran Confluence.

I cracked the books and riffled pages. Steve the Stud's right there, alphabetical.

Bingo. Both books. Add on Commophile Connie Woodard. Here's my hunch: it all meant Something Big.

I drove back to my pad. I brooded and worked the phone until 10:00 p.m. sharp. Then I dressed sharp and drove out to the Valley.

Something Big.

My phone work confirmed it. I tapped my contact at PC Bell. I gave him four names and pledged him a thou to run phone bills. Dig this, demonic:

Jack Kennedy called Steve Cochran nineteen times the past two months. He called from his Senate office and his Hyannis Port home. Steve the Stud called Jack fourteen times. He called from his well-known fuck pad in West Hollyweird.

Connie Woodard called Steve Cochran twenty-four times the past two months. She called from her crib in high-rent Hancock Park. Steve the Stud called Connie twenty-one times.

Lana Turner called Steve Cochran thirty-four times the past two months. She called from her Holmby Hills manse. Steve the Stud called Lana twenty-six times.

I logged the insidious info and let it pulse and percolate. Dumb domestic shit ditzed me. Joi left a note, taped to the bathroom mirror. She called me a "Merchant of Hate and Violence" and preeningly prophesied my short and loveless life. I checked my answering-service messages. Liberace begged me to babysit Lance the Leopard. I left a message with his service: "Okay, I'll do it."

I popped two dexies and leveled the load with four belts of Old Crow. I put on my choice chalk-stripe suit and spritzed on Lucky Tiger. I pondered the Cochran Confluence and Joan "Stretch" Perkins, nonstop. I called Bernie Spindel on my way out the door.

I said, "We're working tomorrow. It's a bug-and-tap on Steve Cochran's place."

Bernie said, "*Oy,*" and hung up.

Linda's Little Log Cabin: a lezbo lair and rustic rendezvous raft. A shadowed shack. Shellacked wood beams and show tunes tuned low. A make-out mood. Wraparound booths wrapped in cigarette smoke. Butch bunkers and fetching femme nests.

I walked in. I knew the drill. Central Vice validated the dive and took 5 percent. Linda Lindholm owed me. She liked lewd Latin stuff. She went through wetback wenches, *mucho mas*. Linda laid *las chiquitas* low. Linda went from burning love to boredom in six seconds flat. Frame-up Freddy stepped in then. I reefer-rousted the girls and bounced them back over the border.

Linda saw me. She stood at the bar and made that *gimme* sign. I dipped a double sawbuck her way. She pointed to a back booth.

I walked over. I smelled Jungle Jaguar perfume—straight up/ no chaser. She stepped out of the booth and stood up to meet me. Gilded goddess, I'm yours.

She towered tall. She backlit and bashed my base desires and made me simmer *soooooooft* in her glow. She wore a sleeveless madras shirtdress and saddle shoes sans socks. She emitted Valkyric vibrations. She looked like Kirsten Flagstad sang *Tristan und Isolde*. She said, "Hello, Mr. Otash," and held out her hand.

I took it and bowed. She had a husky kid voice. It was cool contralto cut with prep school—straight up/no chaser.

We slid into the booth. We sat across from each other. A table lamp lit Stretch, A-bomb mauve and pink. Her bare arms were my size. She raised a hand and tossed her hair. Her underarm hair showed. Her *craaaaazy* credentials crackled by torchlight. Kirsten Flagstad to Anna Magnani. She took on an Italian Neorealist glow.

She said, "Billy told me that you wanted to meet me. I like meeting new and interesting people, so I said okay."

I said, "I saw your picture. That's why I'm here, and I know you can guess why. But my intentions went out the window the second I saw *you*."

Stretch smiled. "Billy said you're the man to see in L.A. He considers me trouble-prone, because I sort of like girls. I'm training for the '56 Olympics, and I don't want to bollix that up."

Drinks appeared. On the house. Linda brought them herself. A Manhattan for Stretch. Old Crow for me.

We tipped glasses. "You're nineteen. Everyone's a new and interesting person to you. That leaves you vulnerable. Lezzie girls, and colored guys like Billy, and guys like me are trouble, so if you're trouble-prone, you should consider who you let into your life."

Stretch sipped her drink. I held my hands back and tried not to touch her.

"If the stern-big-brother routine is a ploy, it's a new one. People usually don't meet me and start warning me away in the same breath."

"I like the idea of you being reckless, and me getting you out of jams. Here's my first bit of advice. Billy told me you want to be linked to him in *Confidential*. That's a dumb move. It'll mess you up with the USC regents and the Olympic people."

Stretch shrugged. "I'm nineteen. I'm restless. I'm as notable as an intramural athlete who happens to be a girl can be. I'm big, and I'm rather awkward, and a certain type of man and woman go for me, and want to meet me and test themselves with me, and I'm very curious as to who those people are."

I folded my hands on the table. Stretch folded her hands over them. Her hands were bigger than mine.

"So, I go for you. I wanted to meet you, and I've met you. I've explained my intentions, so here's something you might find interesting. I'm looking after a real-live leopard for the next three weeks. You can visit my pad and meet him, and I won't let him maul you or kill you."

Stretch laffed. She temptress-tossed her hair. It was straight and dirty blond and center-parted. She had big buck teeth.

I locked up our fingers. It went to a cute tug-of-war. Her hands were stronger than mine.

"Are you in a jam right now?"

"No."

"Can you sniff out bad intentions and walk away, fast?"

"Yes."

"Will you call me if you're unsure about somebody?"

"Yes."

"Have you got enough money to live on?"

"Yes, and I'd never let man, woman, or beast set me up in a place and expect favors."

I yukked. "It's a code you've got, right? It's like me. I'll do anything short of murder, and I'll work for anybody but Communists."

Stretch yukked and unlaced our hands. The booth was warm. We popped sweat. Stretch wiped her brow and her underarms. She tied her hair back with a rubber band and gave me This Look.

"I'm glad you like me there. It means that you're discerning, and that you dig the offbeat."

My nerves were shot to shit. Stretch scared me and scattered me and lust-lashed me some new way. Stretch read me her restricting riot act.

"I like to make out and take naps with men. I'm putting the rest of it off until I sort some things out."

I lit a cigarette. Stretch lit up out of my pack. She blew four concentric smoke rings to my three. I felt dope-ditzed and sex-socked—and lost-lifed some new way. I laid my head on the table. Stretch ran her hands through my hair.

"You're okay, Uncle Freddy. I know you killed a man when you were a policeman, and Billy said maybe you shouldn't have. I'm forgiving with people, if they don't mess with me directly."

I raised my head and pulled her hands down and kissed them. I caught her scent and my scent, all merged up.

"What else did Billy tell you about me?"

"He said we were both curious and lonely, in the exact same way."

Jungle Jaguar. The widow's withered scent. The Joan-to-Joan parlay at 1:00 a.m. A penance payment in my pocket and a picture in my head.

Liz Taylor in *A Place in the Sun*. The final shot. Monty Clift walks the last mile. The mad mise-en-scène goes silky subjective. There's a climactic close-up. Liz looms, *laaaaarge.*

She parts her lips. Transposition/transfiguration. I kiss the merged Joan Perkins and Joan Horvath for the fade-out.

Camerford and El Centro. There's the house. There's late living room lights.

I parked and walked over. I mimicked Monty's last mile and made the mailbox drop *laaaast.* I looped back to my sled and waited. I whistled "My Funny Valentine" at dirge speed.

Joan Horvath walked out. She wore the same stay-at-home ensemble. She held a cigarette and a highball glass. She tossed her dumb wool skirt and sat down on the porch.

She caught me mid-chorus. I hit a high note and made the secondary theme soar. I looked *at* her. She looked *toward* me. The moon moved out of a cloud bank. I saw gray flecks in her shag cut.

Those steel-rimmed glasses gave her 3-D vision. She saw through me like some creature in a monster matinee. I shut my eyes to shut her gaze out and deploy the big close-up. A black curtain closed off her kiss.

BERNIE SPINDEL'S BUG VAN

Outside Steve Cochran's Apartment Complex
West Holly*weird*
2/16/54

Bernie said, "I'm wary of this job. This psycho cocksucker scares me."

Studly Steve lived on Havenhurst between Fountain and the Strip. Three sparkle-Spanish buildings/one cool courtyard. Six pads per building. Call girls and minor movie minions ensconced within.

It's 9:14 a.m. now. Steve's home. His coon maroon Merc's parked out back.

I lit a cigarette and gargled Old Crow. I had a case of the yammering yips and the mean megrims. I kept seeing things. Strongarm cops in surging surveillance. Women I wanted wicked *baaaaaaaad* and weren't there. Waiting wilted me. I wanted WORK. I popped two Dexedrine to goose things along.

Bernie said, "He's got four rooms, plus bathroom. I checked with the County Planning Office. The walls are soft stucco, and all rough-finished. They'll be easy to drill and respackle. I broke in last night and carved some paint chips. It's a new paint job, so it should be easy to match."

We wore TV repairman jumpsuits. Master keys would get us in. Steve the Stud was filming some crime lox called *Private Hell 36*. Bernie spot-tailed him yesterday. He said Steve got his all-day calls at 9:30 a.m.

I said, "We'll piggyback the listening post on Sweetzer. Burt Lancaster's got his torture den in the same building. My Marines will monitor both locations. We'll have a man hot-wired in at all times."

Bernie went *Oy*. "Burt swings both ways. Ward Wardell told me. He buys his boys from a swish named Dwight Gilette."

I said, "To each his own. You're a big cheese at your synagogue, and you've got eight *schvartze* girlfriends."

Bernie went *Oy*. I pointed across the street. Studly Steve's rolling. His cherry Merc's wheeling southbound.

We loaded up. Drills, spackle paste, paint and brushes—*check*. Wire rolls, condenser mikes, friction tape—*check*. Wire clamps, spatulas, industrial vacuum—*check*. Toolbox packed with close-work tools—*check*.

We packed two big metal cases. They were marked "Acme TV Repair." We vacated the van and coursed through the courtyard. We hit Steve's door at a sprint. Bernie jabbed keys at the door lock. Key #3 got us in.

I popped through the pad. It was cool, cozy, and tidy tight. Living room/ bedroom/kitchen/bathroom/washroom. One connecting hallway. One demented decorating motif:

World War II. Ripe real regalia. Booty from Berchtesgaden and Jap flags salvaged from Saipan. Swastika wall banners. German helmets as cereal serving bowls, sunk in the sink. SS-motif ashtrays. Rising-sun rugs. Showy shadow-boxed Lugers. Beaver pix of Eva Braun—*der Führer's* freaky *Frau*. Choice tchotchkes on chairs/ tables/wall racks. Dig *this*, deranged: Jap shrunken heads, beady-eyed beasts, all wearing fit-to-size Brooklyn Dodger hats.

Bernie slavered, slack-jawed. I got out my Minox spy camera and shot it all. I smelled Smear Job. Let's foto-fuck this creep.

Steve Cochran, the Big Dick *Bürgermeister* of the L.A. Reich. Nazi nests at Warner's, Metro, and Fox. We'll loose-link it to last year's Nazi/flying saucer piece. Bondage Bob Harrison partied with Paraguayan parasite Alfredo Stroessner and wicked Juan Perón. They hid hordes of Hitlerites, circa '46. Commie columnists called *Confidential* "fascistic," "nativistic," "hucksteristic," and "the voice of vile volition in the vox populi." The coruscating Cochran exposé would lash those leftist lies!!!!!

Bernie jerked at my jumpsuit and jacked me half off my feet. "Freddy, let's *go*. Quit gawking. We've got work to do."

So, yeah—we *worked*. We whipped wires to wainscoting and wiggled them under rugs. We drilled white walls and wedged in bug mounts. We rigorously respackled and repainted. We vacuumed up Spackle dust. We planted microphones in cracks, crevices, crawl spaces. We ripped the receivers off the two telephones and planted condenser mikes. We studied standing lamps and stuck bug mounts under the shades. We bugged the bedroom and looped the living room. We supersocked in the *sound*.

Tick, tick, tick. Four-plus hours' work. I was sweat-swacked and dexie-ditzed and stomp-the-stars elated. We repacked our gear. Bernie sighed and went *Oy. Opportunity is love*. That maladroit maxim moved through me.

The Sweetzer listening post. A two-bedroom flop in a Deco dive off Willoughby. We recorded Burt Lancaster's torture tilts with stacked starlets there. Plus three call-girl cribs. Plus an opium den in the back of the Hunan Hut—"Home of the Shanghai Shipwreck Cocktail."

The pad was wire-whipped, floor to rafters. Cable cords and outlet plugs jammed up the joint. We manned tape rigs round the clock. Bernie set up a transceiver in Steve Cochran's living room. It went optimum operational at 6:00 p.m. 6:00 sharp came and went. I slipped on headphones and listened to dead air.

Jimmy Dean dropped by. He brought nudie pix and brief bios for Rock Hudson's wife candidates. Dig: six backlot babes who cadged coffee for cast and crew and blew select directors. I told Jimmy they looked *goooooood*. Jimmy donned earmuffs and manned the Hunan Hut rig. He passed on choice *sinuendo*. The delivery dinks pushed pills packed in with their pupu platters and pork fried rice. Bela Lugosi and Peter Lorre toked "O" in the den. They schmoozed their guest shots on Vampira's late-nite TV show. Vampira went lez in the Los Amigas home for girls. She was running a lez string out of Googie's, as we speak.

More dead air. I got bored and called my answering service. *Oooooh*—Miss Joan "Stretch" Perkins called. She wanted to know if she could pick up Lance the Leopard and install him at my crib. I called Stretch back and set it up. I urged caution. Stretch blew me a fone kiss and said she'd make out with me soon.

Joi called. Johnnie Ray called. The answering-service girl said they got catty. "Tell Mr. Otash he's hung like a cashew—and who knows better than me?" "Tell Mr. Otash he's an evil storm trooper—and soon the whole world will know."

Fuck that shit—I went back to line hiss and dead air.

Time ticked. I chain-smoked and scratched my balls. The Hunan Hut delivered dinner. I noshed Noodles à la Chang and China Joe's Chop Suey. Steve Cochran's phone rang at 8:29.

Steve picked up. The voice activator vibrated. "It's Lew's War Surplus. We've got a clearance sale on Schmeisser machine pistols, Nazi daggers, and Jap shrunken heads—flamethrower-fried on Iwo Jima." Steve bought three daggers and three heads. The guy said he'd fix them up with Dodger baseball caps.

More dead air. I doodled on scratch paper. I wrote "Freddy & Stretch" and drew a heart around it. Time ticked. Steve's phone rang at 10:52.

I picked up. Static and line fuzz futzed with the call. I got a woman's voice. I got Steve's voice. I got static, fuzz, garbles, line lint, lewd laffs, and static stew.

I cuffed the console. I hit the squelch switch. I ditzed dials and got this:

The woman said, "Well . . . I don't know . . . are you . . . can sign up the talent?"

Steve said, "Are you kid . . . concept . . . time has come. . . . Celebrity smut. You want to talk—"

The call static-stuck, fuzzed and futzed, and diminuendoed to dead air.

Googie's hop-hop-hopped. The Iris Theatre ran a sneak peek of some 3-D dog. The Googie geeks retained their 3-D glasses and goofed themselves out of their gourds.

Jejune jerkoffs. Their revelry ran rampant and rubbed me raw. Tattle tipsters took note of me. I got stuck with stacks of stale bread.

Yawn. Orson Welles sliced the Black Dahlia. Check *The Lady from Shanghai.* Grok the symbiology. *Yawn.* Bill Holden's in the DT ward at Queen of Angels. He's banging night nurses two at a pop. *Yawn.* I've got morgue pix. The Carole Landis suicide, back in '48. All-nude. Full bush. Kodachrome color—if I'm lyin', I'm flyin'!!

Snore. There's a plot to throw the '54 World Series. The Jewnited Nations is pulling the strings. *Snore.* Grace Kelly's a nympho. She turned Johnnie Ray straight in a mop closet at the Crescendo. *Snore.* I know you won't believe this—but Pat Nixon hatched Count Basie's mulatto love child!!!!!

I believed all of it and none of it. I was back at the listening post. Unknown woman: "Can sign up the talent?" Steve Cochran: "Concept . . . time has come. . . . Celebrity smut."

Quivering question marks broiled my brain and skimmed under my skin. I couldn't stop the scurrilous scroll.

Then:

The Googie's geeks froze. I froze. Four fuzz walked in and waltzed the floor. Not just any cops. The LAPD Hat Squad. Sergeant Max Herman. Sergeant Red Stromwall. Sergeant Harry Crowder. Officer Eddie Benson.

LAPD Robbery. Hunter-slayers of heist men. All six-four and 220. All in pearl gray suits and white panama hats. The PD's hardest hard boys. Chief William H. Parker's personal pit dogs. Mastiffs on a mission to maul for their master.

I stood up. They whipped up and braced me. Red Stromwall said, "Hi, Freddy."

Max Herman said, "The Chief wants to see you, Freddy."

Harry Crowder said, "I like your suit, Freddy. Where'd you steal it?"

Eddie Benson said, "You were always a dipshit, Freddy."

Max Herman tugged a belt loop and made me his bitch. Red

Stromwall poked me with a beavertail sap. Harry Crowder and Eddie Benson flanked me and dwarfed me and made me mince minuscule.

We marched out to the parking lot. A PD plainclothes car rumbled, off by itself. Bill Parker sat in the backseat. I looked in. He looked out. I said, "How's tricks, Bill? Your wife still doing her act with the mule?"

Harry Crowder kidney-punched me. Red Stromwall sapped me. Max Herman said, "Don't screech, Freddy. You'll sound effeminate." Eddie Benson tossed me in the backseat.

I caught my breath and caressed my kidneys. Parker wore civvies. Parker spoke in his foghorn South Dakota drawl.

"Joan Hubbard Horvath, the widow of the man you killed in the line of duty, was murdered in her home last night. Her kids were off on a school trip. It appears to be a hot-prowl sex snuff. The house was ransacked, and the woman was strangled and stabbed. We found a total of fourteen envelopes bearing your fingerprints. Two of them were stuffed with twenty- and fifty-dollar bills."

Parker paused. He evil-eyed me. He made with the *malocchio.*

"The victim fought. We found beard and skin fragments under her nails, and I can see that you're unmarked. Her assailant had AB-negative blood. Your PD file reveals that you have O positive. This exonerates you as the actual killer, but not as an accomplice or a material witness. I would advise you to provide me with a plausible explanation for your prints on those envelopes."

I evil-eyed Parker. I made my *malocchio* more hopped-up and hateful than his.

"I killed Ralph Mitchell Horvath under the PD's implied dictum that cop killers must die. He was unarmed. I planted a throwdown gun on him and shot him in the back. Then the cop he shot recovered, which rubbed me the wrong way. I've been laying penance payments on Joan Horvath, going back five years. I've never spoken to her. You're a good Catholic boy, Bill. You get the guilts sometimes, so you know how it is."

Parker lit a cigarette and blew smoke in my face. I coughed the smoke back in his face.

"There's more to this, and most of it makes you look bad. First off, we've seen you talking to the Beverly Hills PD, and we make you and your boys for the 459 on Senator Kennedy's hotel suite. You screwed up the print transparencies, though. You laid down prints for *all three* of those shitheels who've been terrorizing Beverly Hills. That was a big mistake. George Collier Akin left the gang two weeks ago. We have very sound intelligence on this. He insisted on killing the girl they kidnapped, but Brown and Dulange held him back, and the girl was released. George Collier Akin is alleged to be casing solo hot-prowl jobs in my jurisdiction, and I've told Max and the boys to find him and kill him. They may seek to consult you in the course of their investigation, and I would advise you to cooperate. It might prevent the Beverly Hills PD from filing charges on you."

Parker paused. Parker went *Shoo, you cockroach*. I stepped out of the car. The Hats surrounded me, hail-fellows all.

Max Herman shook my hand. "Here's to you, Freddy."

Red Stromwall shook my hand. "Be good, kid."

Harry Crowder shook my hand. "We miss you, Freddy. Keep your chin up."

Eddie Benson shook my hand. "Stay clean, dipshit."

I cut free and stumbled back into Googie's. I beelined for the front door and plowed busboys and waiters, en masse. I knocked over drink trays. Customers went *eeeek* and crap-your-pants cringed. I grabbed a double scotch off Gene "the Mean Queen's" table and guzzled it, sans consent. I capsized a waitress and sent milk shakes and club sandwiches airborne. I crashed out the front door and snagged my Packard pimp sled at the curb.

The Strip was one block north. I blew a red light and whipped westbound. Ciro's was close. I floored the gas and flamed through late-nite traffic. I swung hard right and racked my undercarriage all up the porte cochere. I fender-bended Ferraris and Facel-Vegas and didn't give a fucking shit. Two car-park kids tried to corner me. I decked them and downed them and bashed them in the balls. They went ball-bashed falsetto and mewed for their mamas in Miami and Milwaukee.

I crashed into the club. The floor was packed tight-tight. Johnnie

Ray stomped the stage. He woman-wiggled and wanton-warbled his hit song, "Cry." He wiggled the mike and wailed like a jilted fishwife. He sobbed, he sighed, he tossed his spit curl and spun his hearing aid out into the crowd.

Joi and Liberace sat front-row center. I charged up. Patrons saw me. They stood up and went *Whoa* and *Halt now!!!!!* I dumped waiters and a fat broad at Bing Crosby's table. I made the front row. Joi and Lee looked up. Joi lip-synched, "You loser cocksucker."

I poured her Tom Collins down her dress and ice-cubed her chi-chis. Joi roundhoused me and fell flat on her ass. Patrons yowled. Johnnie blew his crescendo and cried for real. I dumped Joi's purse and found her Seconal stash. I guzzled out the contents. I chased five fat red devils with Lee's double martini. Lee *loooooved* it. He pinched my cheek and swooned. I lurched and lunged and levitated my way out of the club. I slid into my sled and sluiced eastbound on Sunset.

Some new solar system subsumed me. Streetlights went mauve and pink. A-bomb particles parsed and pierced my windshield. I eyeballed passersby. Every man's face went gargoyle, every wom-an's went succubus. Steve Cochran sang "Das Horst Wessel Lied." I ripped Nazi flags off his walls.

There's Vine Street. I cut south and cut east on Camerford.

The Horvath house was hot-lit, postmidnite. Nosy neighbors gawked. Outside arc lights glare-glowed the pad and strafed the sky. I parked behind a row of black-and-whites and K-cars. Plain-clothesmen and bluesuits pounded the porch. Kids' toys and fur-niture were loose on the lawn. The front door stood open. Print men dusted walls. Foto men snapped fotos. Lab men fiber-swept the floors.

Burglary dicks checked window openings and cluck-clucked. I saw Harry Fremont at work. The red devils ripped me and turned it all topsy-turvy. I went blank. Arc-light glare burned my eyes. Joan Horvath and Joan Perkins kissed me like Liz in that close-up. I went black-blank and blinked. I saw Bill Parker and Red Stromwall pass a flask on the porch. I slid my car seat back to deflect the arc light. I got snug and supine. I said, "Please, God—make me safe," and passed out.

I passed out cold and woke up windshield-warmed by the sun. My windows were up. A cop type stood in the street and eyeballed me. I didn't recognize him. He got into an unmarked unit parked in front of me. I grabbed a stray piece of paper and wrote down the rear plate number.

It all came back. I prayed my way out of the sunlight and blinked back to black. Rosie Clooney sang, "Hey there, you with the stars in your eyes."

I made the *Mirror*. NITEKLUB INFERNO: P.I. FRED O. IN FRANTIC FRACAS. I made the *Herald*: CONFIDENTIAL COP OTASH IN CIRO'S BROUHAHA. The hot headlines heartwarmed me. They instilled instant pride. Joan Horvath dead-deadened it. Freddy, what thou hath wrought.

Bondage Bob called and congratulated me. The insidious ink spiked *Confidential*'s early-morning sales. Ciro's was Sheriff's turf. Bob called Gene Biscailuz and pledged ten thou to his reelection campaign. It covered the cost of my ten-minute tantrum and frosted out possible beefs.

Joan Horvath got a bleary blip in the *Herald*'s local spread. WIDOW WOMAN SLAIN IN HOLLYWOOD HOME. BURGLARY-SEX MOTIVE CITED.

Bob and I biz-talked. I tossed him the tattle on the Rock Hudson wife hunt and laid out the lowdown on the would-be wives. Bob knew candidate Claire Klein. She played shakedown shill at *Whisper*, back in '51. Her part-time gig at Universal was a plain ploy to meet extortable men. I weighed in: We've got to scoop the fan mags on this one. Dole out the dish on Rump Ranger Rock's disingenuous dates with real women. Sock in the subtext. It's a shadow shuck. Hollywood will fuck you when no one else will.

Bob agreed. He added, And we'll double-cross Rock on his wedding nite and expose his boy bent. We yukked the irksome irony. I dumped the dirt on the Steve Cochran gig. Bob pooh-poohed the Nazi-Jap fetish trove and called Steve a history buff and no more. He himself paid five thou for a swastika-print bikini once worn by Leni Riefenstahl. His girlfriend turned heads at that big Polio Fund pool party.

"And, Freddy—I heard Cochran leans left, if anything."

I closed with the cloying clue of "Celebrity Smut." Bob told me to work the listening post my own self. "*And*—if it pans out, we'll send in a female ringer to entrap Steve—Claire Klein might be good."

Bob signed off with "Sayonara." I offered "auf Wiedersehen," boss. I shit, showered, shaved, and made myself march to the mirror. I saw myself and saw where all this was going. Freddy, what thou hath wrought. I called Harry Fremont and made a lunch date.

I drove home. A basketball hoop was nailed beside my front door. Stretch sank long hook shots. She wore her USC silks. Neighbor kids watched. Lance the Leopard lounged in my doorway. Kids patted him and fed him potato chips.

I snuck up behind Stretch. I said, "If you convince me you're really nineteen, I'll toss your hair and kiss your neck."

Stretch laughed. She dropped the ball and pulled her hair to one side. The kids scoped the exchange. What's this repob? *She's bigger than him.*

"I was born January 18, 1935, at Good Samaritan. That means you can go ahead."

I caressed her bare shoulders and kissed her neck. I stood tiptoed to do it. The kids clapped. Lance the Leopard looked over and growled.

Stretch sank three long ones and swiveled. She grabbed my belt and pulled me inside my own pad. Lance followed us in. He detoured to the front bathroom and guzzled toilet water. Stretch waved to the kids and kicked the door shut.

I crapped out on the couch. Stretch stretched out and laid her head on my lap.

"My mom showed me the *Mirror*. Did you have fun at Ciro's last night?"

"Do you live with your mom and dad?"

"I live with my mom. My dad was killed on Saipan, when I was eight. What did you do in the war?"

"I was a drill instructor at Parris Island. I trained Marines who got killed at Saipan, but I never went overseas myself."

"Why not?"

"Because I knew I'd get killed, and I didn't have the stones to take the risk."

"Why?"

"Because I'm fearful and selfish, and I have to get whatever it is that I want, and that's as far as I'm going with this line of questioning."

Stretch balled my hands into fists and kissed the knuckles. She kicked off her sneakers and dangled her feet off the couch. Lance hopped on my favorite chair and licked his balls.

"You're watchful, too. You forgot to mention that. And you're diffident and circumspect around me. And none of the girls at Linda's hates you, even though you broke half the liquor bottles during that Beverage Control raid in '48. And you're chagrined for digging on me, even though you spy on people and expose them in print, and beat the crap out of people who threaten to sue your low-life magazine."

I smiled. "I stole the bottles I didn't break, and Billy Eckstine bought them off me at half price."

"Billy likes you. I wouldn't be here if he didn't."

"Billy's Billy, and he's not all moonlight and roses. He tried to promote you to me and my recently ex girlfriend."

Stretch pried my fists loose and placed my hands on her breasts. Hey there, you with the stars—

"Billy overrates me, in lots of different ways."

"You're nineteen, and you're looking around. I get that you're bold—and you think the rules don't apply to you. That's as far as I'll take that line of chat, until I see you start making mistakes."

"You're saying the only thing that you can teach me right now is efficacy?"

"I'm saying that for some people, opportunity is love, and you might be one of them."

The dizzy duo at the listening post. Leashed Leopard and Large Lady. Race Rockwell and Ward Wardell *swoooooned.*

Stretch wore a tweed skirt, saddle shoes, and a pink oxford shirt. Lance wore a spiked collar that Bondage Bob bought him for Christmas. I brought three pizza pies and a cold case of Brew 102.

Stretch loomed and she-lorded it over three big men. Lance roamed the rooms and let people pat him. Race fed him anchovy pizza. Ward showed off our new corkboard. There's Operation Rock Wife bold-bannered—with nude pix and dippy dossiers tacked below.

We snarfed pizza pie and went to work. Race worked the Hunan Hut tap, I worked the Cochran line. Ward worked Call-Girl Line #1. Stretch got Call-Girl Line #2. Cool kicks motivated me. It was the lez line. Bernie Spindel and I hot-wired the crib—Flores south of Sunset. The *sin*sational sapphic scene sang dusk to dawn and entrapped occasional big-name babes and butches. Let's see how Stretch registers and reacts.

We pulled chairs up to the consoles. We plugged in. We donned headphones. Lance noshed pizza crusts and crapped out on the floor.

I sat close to Stretch. We played kneesies and lazy-linked hands. I got two hours of dead air. Some unknown male called Steve the Stud at 8:19 p.m. Steve called him "Cal." They schmoozed *Private Hell 36.* Steve dished Howard Duff and wife Ida Lupino. Duff was a souse. La Lupino was a snout trout. She blew him behind the food truck. Dorothy Malone sizzled. "I've got this celebrity smut angle I'm working on. She'd be a prime candidate."

Bingo!!!—Celeb Smut Lead #1/8:27 p.m.

The call capped at 8:33. Dead air dinged in its weary wake. I watched Stretch work the lez line. Her headset was clamped tight. She notched notes in her fone log. She evinced deep delight and entrenched ennui.

Boredom banged me. I snagged Claire Klein's buff shot and dossier off the corkboard and sat back down. Stretch snatched the buff shot and studied it. She winked and went *Oooh-la-la*. She said, "Rock should marry *her*."

I winked back. Claire was boss-built and credibly credentialed. Born: New York City, 8/11/21. World War II Wave lieutenant. Court-martialed and DD'd on a pandering beef. Emigrated to Palestine, '47. Seduced and tortured Arab spies for the Irgun and the Stern Gang. *Shit*—the A-rabs are my put-upon people!!!!!

Claire hits America. She moves to L.A. and gets a California teaching credential. She teaches algebra at Le Conte Junior High. She gets part-time studio work. Claire's a climber. She takes scalps and moves on. Bob Aldrich, Otto Preminger, Henry Hathaway, Willy Wyler. She visits Burt Lancaster's torture den. Burt wants to spin her on his wall-mounted dartboard and toss darts at her legs. Claire won't play. Burt comes on coercive. Claire shows him the shiv strapped to her left leg. Burt amps up the ante. Claire drops names.

Mickey Cohen, Lou Rothkopf, Sammy Dorfman, Baldy Stein. The kosher kowboys in the L.A. rackets. All zany Zionists. All demented and dyspeptic. Burt backs off—Claire's bad to the bone and calamitously connected.

Steve the Stud's phone rang. Log it—10:21 p.m.

Steve picked up. Unknown Male #2 jabbered. Steve called him "Fritz." They schmoozed the Jap sword and Jap-shrunken-head market. Fritz called it "a growth industry." Biz was up, up. Biz was bullish per Nazi-knife cutlery, all swastika-embossed. Plus Nazi helmets recut into chafing dishes and soup tureens.

Steve said, "I'm moving out of my kraut phase, Fritzie. Find me some Makarov pistols and some NKVD memorabilia. I wouldn't say no to daggers from some Ivan's Lubyanka stash."

The call droned on. I exhumed Bondage Bob's dish: "Cochran leans left, if anything."

The call capped out—10:42 p.m. Dead air doused me and slid me into sleep. I went someplace safe and soft. I snored in sync with Lance the Leopard, laid out at my feet.

Time ticked. Safe and soft became wet and warm. I swam in the River Styx. Joan Horvath rebaptized me. She wore a Nazi-print bikini and swim fins. Stretch jerked off my headset. Such innocence, such glee.

"Dig this, Uncle Freddy. The dots connect. Claire Klein's hooking, part-time. She tricked with that Communist Party cultural guy V. J. Jerome, who's supposedly infiltrating Hollywood, and the third spoke of the wheel was Babs Payton, who's been on the skids since she dumped Franchot Tone, according to the fan mags my mom reads. They went at it for two hours straight, and then they drank vodka and slurped borscht."

OLLIE HAMMOND'S ALL-NITE STEAKHOUSE

Wilshire and Serrano

2/18/54

We drank lunch. My appetite was up, up. I kicked assiduous ass all morning. Morty Bendish at the *Mirror*. The *Transom* and *Whisper* guys. I told them Rock Hudson was *my* gig, X-clusive. They kvetched, moped, and moaned. Blood bloomed on my beavertail sap. I sacked their civil contracts and ratched their rights of free speech.

Harry badged our waiter. He slipped us a jug at the PD's stock half price. Old Crow and Dexedrine—va-va-voom!!!!!

"Let's get to it. You want in on the Joan Horvath snuff. You've been waxing sentimental on that nutty broad for years. The price is five yards to buy in, and a yard a pop for special favors."

I flashed my flash roll and peeled off ten C-notes. Frazzled Freddy always comes flush. Harry cadged the cash and smiled smug.

"It looks like a hot-prowl 459, gone way bad. The guy came in a cracked window and left rubber-glove prints on the sill. He had Joanie's purse in his hands when she woke up and fought him. She scratched him, and we took AB-negative blood spill and dark and coarse beard fragments out from under her nails. That's good, so far. But there wasn't enough blood to run individual comparisons on. In this case, that means that blood type can exonerate, but it can't convict."

I gargled Old Crow. "Go on, and tell me why you called Joan a 'nutty broad.'"

Harry made the jack-off sign. "One, she married Ralphie Horvath, had two kids with him, and stuck with him. Two, she was overqualified for a low-life thief and punk like Ralphie. She had some big education, and was some kind of Russian-history scholar, but all she did was stay at home and tend to her snot-nosed kids."

I lit a cigarette. "Here's the big question. Did George Collier Akin do the job?"

Harry shook his head. "I'm not so sure. Bill Parker's convinced himself, he's convinced the Hats, and you know what that means. Parker saw the hospital pix of that girl that Akin, Brown, and Dulange abducted, and now he's running hot, with a thermometer so far up his ass that it hurts. He wants Akin dead, the Hats want to kill him, and it's true that Akin broke with Brown and Dulange when they wouldn't agree to snuff the girl. Okay, we can assume that Akin—who's a hot-prowl man from way back—is off working solo, and most likely in L.A. city. So far, so good—but I go back to '43 with this evil cocksucker—and the Horvath caper doesn't look like his kind of deal."

I stubbed out my cigarette. "How so?"

Harry said, "Okay. He's got dark and coarse facial hair, so that matches. I checked his Quentin file, and he's got AB-negative blood, so that matches, and it's pretty rare. But I popped Akin for eight hot prowls in '43, and he always wore a rubber red devil mask, cut down low on his neck, to protect him from scratching and gouging, and to further terrorize his victims—because he is *the* most sadistic son of a whore I've ever met—so if the Hats want to put him down, who am I to raise a stink?"

I gargled Old Crow. It rerouted my dexie surge, *molto bene.*

"He *wanted* to kill the cheerleader girl, but he's never killed *any* women, prior to that, that you know of."

Harry twirled his glass. "Never. He spent '43 to '51 in Quentin. He paroled out in November, hung up his parole, and went rogue. We've had six more hot-prowl/assaults possibly attributable to the

Red Devil Bandit since then—all with grievous bodily harm short of murder. Then this fuck hooks up with Brown and Dulange, and it's the BHPD's grief from that point on."

I said, "He split from Brown and Dulange two weeks ago. You 'assume' that he's working solo, but you're 'implying' that he's not strictly adhering to his Red Devil Bandit MO, and you've got no reported hot prowls that you're sure he's good for."

Harry sighed. "You nailed it. Never let it be known that the infamous Freddy O. drew a dumb breath."

I chained cigarettes. "What else? Describe the crime scene."

"The pad was ransacked. I think he was looking for something besides purse cash and whatever else he could carry away. There was over six grand of your penance money stashed in Joanie's clothes closet, and he didn't bother to find it or steal it. This whole deal reeks of personal animus. It's an I-hate-you-and-I'm-going-to-kill-you job, and that spells revenge."

I flashed my flash roll and rolled off five more C-notes. Harry snatched them up.

"You're a white man, Freddy. I'll have complete background paper on Joanie by tomorrow."

I got noxiously nostalgic. "Harry," "Ralphie," "Joanie." '49 to '54. A kid cop THEN. A Pervdog of the Nite NOW.

"I remember that day in the squadroom. You were younger and not quite so fat. 'Hey, kid, you look bored. Go shag this Ralphie guy and kill him.'"

Harry went *nix*. "Can it, Freddy. You can't pull the shit you pull in your everyday life and think that this jive crusade of yours will render you squeaky-clean."

Clean," *shit*. "Jive crusade"—malignantly more so. Harry Fremont was bent and bought and paid-for since the year one. He knew bewilderingly bupkes per Opportunity is Love.

I drove back to my pad. The door was whipped wide open. I heard screeches, yowls, growls, *eeeeks*, and roars. I ran inside and grokked on the grief.

Catfight. Lance the Leopard versus Joi Lansing—my exultant ex and extortion partner par excellence.

Joi was packing left-behind undies. Lance smelled thievery. He pinned Joi to the back wall and clawed her clothes to torn tatters. Her dress dripped off of her. He sharp-shredded her brassiere. His claws caught frayed fabric and rip-rip-ripped. I sensed sexual intent. Lance lashed at Joi. He orgiastically ordered up a cross-species striptease.

I laffed. Joi screeched, *"Freddy?"* I grabbed Lance's spiked collar and pull-pull-pulled. Lance went sulky submissive. He cursory-growled and slither-slunk to the bathroom. I heard him lap up a toilet-water aperitif.

I said, "What's shaking, baby?"

Joi said, "You loser shitheel."

I stepped toward her. She stepped toward me. She launched a left hook and landed it mid-face. She ripped a right. I let it land and pushed her down on the bed.

She said, "One for what you did to Johnnie, and one for that stunt you pulled at Ciro's. And tell Lee to get that rape-o cat declawed."

I pulled a chair up. Joi grabbed her purse and dug out her cigarettes. I lit her up.

"It's good to see you, kid."

"You insouciant shitheel. I'm never coming back to you, and I'm never working with you again—not in this lifetime."

I laffed. "How's this sound? Rock Hudson needs a wife. Lew Wasserman's protecting his reputation and Universal's investment. I could let you be the girl, for ten percent of the alimony deal when you dump him."

Joi kicked out at me. Her shoes flew wide and missed me. Her nylons were nicked and rife with runs. Lance clawed *cloooose*.

"I'm never coming back to you."

"I heard you the first time."

"No more shakedowns, no more bait jobs, no more three-ways."

"Come *on*. You're saying no more Liz Taylor in the sack?"

Joi blew smoke up at me. Her fierce façade cracked a tad. She'd landed two good ones. I wiped blood off my lips.

"The world's hip to you, Freddy. Your 'Tattle Tyrant holds Hollywood hostage' shtick is wearing people thin."

"Who's 'people,' babe? Come *on*. Name some names that mean something to me."

Joi rehooked her brassiere. "How's Steve Cochran sound? He said he's seen you and Bernie Spindel lurking around his place. He ran a bug check and came up empty, but he's got you pegged as Public Cockroach Number One, and he said you're heading for a good ass kicking."

Steve the Stud. There's a grabber. It's an irksome inkling of *Something*.

I lied loud. "His building's full of call-girl cribs. Bernie and I were planting some taps. 'Lurking,' shit. He's talking out of his ass, and the magazine's got no stake in him."

Joi flipped her burning butt at me. It singed my Sy Devore coat.

"You're jealous. Steve's got all the goods you're envious of. I know you, Freddy. You've got to know what's going on with him, and you'll pay me for the debrief."

My throat clamped and closed tight. My hands shimmy-shimmied. I whipped my wallet out and tossed bills on the bed.

Joi culled the cash and counted it. *Confidential* comes up flush. A grand for a five-minute snitch.

"I ran into Steve at Johnnie's. He told me he's making a 'message' smut movie, based on a hillbilly song by Bill Haley and His Comets, whoever the hell they are. He's trying to recruit some name actors and actresses, because the film will only be shown privately, so no one's career will get hurt. The song's called 'Thirteen Women and Only One Man in Town.' The atom bomb destroys the world, except for thirteen women and a man in this little desert burg, and the man has a giant dick, and he's on a crusade to repopulate the world. *Get it?* Steve's out of his gourd, and he's the director, the writer, and very obviously the star. He said he's got financial backing, but I don't believe him. *Get it?* He wants to lure thirteen women to the desert and get laid, and odds are, there's no film in the camera, and it's all some pipe dream."

"Celebrity smut." Steve Cochran's name in Jack Kennedy's

address book. The phone records. Steve calls Jack/Jack calls Steve/ Steve calls Jack.

I smelled *Something.*

"Five grand, love. I'll hot-wire you and send you in to bait him."

Joi smiled. "You're malleable, Freddy. You've always been easy to manipulate. It's the only thing that attracted me to you."

I rolled to the Ranch Market. A radio broadcast broiled, up in my office. Dig: sodden Senator Joe McCarthy rips Reds and socks out southland subpoenas. Dig, ditto: Jolting Joe and Bondage Bob are jungled up—larcenous land deals and sleazoid slum holdings. *Heh, heh*—Fractious Freddy knows all and holds all trump cards tight.

I turned off the radio and checked my in-box. Harry Fremont delivered, quicksville. *Bingo!*—a background brief on Joan Hubbard Horvath.

Joan, the big brain and undulating underachiever. She matriculates at UCLA, circa '39–'45. She logs advanced degrees in Eastern European languages. She speaks fluent Italian, Polish, and Russian. She works as an interpreter for the California State Senate, circa '46–'47. She marries riotous Ralphie Horvath, circa '48. She hatches his second-rate seed. She's got no visible means of support, then to now. *But*—this bodes *BIG*—Red Stromwall finds a Bank of America passbook tucked in Joan's undie drawer. *AND*—the current balance exceeds fourteen grand.

That's a brain broiler. *That's* prongingly provocative.

I recalled that cop car parked at the crime scene. I recalled that rear plate number I wrote down. I buzzed Central Burglary and braced Harry Fremont. Who's this cop cad working for? The plate number ain't LAPD. Harry said the suffix denoted a Fed sled. Maybe FBI or Treasury.

I downed two Dexedrine and gargled Old Crow. *Aaahhh*—my bloodstream blossomed and swelled. I called my answering service and checked my messages. *Aaahhh*—the wide world wants Freewheeling Freddy!!!

Joi called. Her koffee klatch with Steve the Stud was set for

7:00 p.m. Stretch called. She said she'd pop by my pad later. Bond-age Bob called. Update me, sweetheart—what's with heavy-hung Steve? Jimmy called. It's official—Claire Klein's in for the Marry Rock gig. Midnite at Googie's—be there for the meet and greet. I called Bernie Spindel. Six-fifteen at Havenhurst. Joi's jamming up Steve the C.

Wow—Frantic Freddy's in demonic demand!!! He's *THE* man to see!!!

Joi kvetched. She emphatically emasculated my last stirring state-ment. We wire-whipped her in the back of Bernie's bug van. Freddy, the mike-mount's too tight. Freddy, the lead wire's bunched up in my brassiere. Bernie, quit honking me—get your fat paws off my tits.

The wire job ate up fifteen minutes. We shooed Joi out and reparked on Steve Cochran's side of the street. Joi broadcast static and high heels hitting pavement. Our earmuffs caught every rustle and riff. Bernie worked the transceiver. The live feed fed furtively in. *Knock, knock*—Joi's at Studly Steve's door. *Creak/gnash*—door-lock noise—Studly Steve's letting her in.

Static/voice burble/sound overlap. Bernie ditzed dials and reca-librated the rustles and riffs. We got settle-in sounds. Glasses clink/ Steve serves drinks/cigarette lighters click.

Joi sighs. That's her "We're seated" signal. It's laying in, loud and clear. Incriminate yourself, shitbird. Smut's a felony bounce. *Confi-dential* gonna get yo ass. San Quentin's surging yo way.

Joi said, "Who decorated this place, Hermann Goering?"

Steve said, "It's set decoration for the movie. I'm deep into the immersion aspect of it all. There's this subplot I'm working on. The guy who's out to repopulate the world is a former Nazi sym-pathizer, and he renounces Nazism and moves into a one-world mind-set. Apostasy is a major theme of this movie. It's not all fun and games, and hide the salami."

Joi hooted. "Baby, you're avant-garde."

"I'm *beyond* it, you mean."

Joi: "*Yeah?* Well, who else thinks so? By that I mean, how many name people have you signed up, other than yourself as the star?"

Steve: "Anita O'Day and Barbara Payton have inked contracts, as they say in the trades. Lana Turner's on the ropes and considering it."

Joi: "That's week-old bread at half price, sweetie. Anita's a junkie, and Babs is turning cheapie tricks out of Stan's Drive-In. And, Lana—she's just jerking your chain."

Steve: "Hang on to your hat. I've inked Gene Tierney. You've *got* to gas on that one. She scored in *Laura* and *Leave Her to Heaven*, and she was Jack Kennedy's fiancée, back before he married that lockjawed stiff Jackie."

Ooooh—Jack the K. jumps in. *Ooooh*—his name in Studly Steve's address book.

Joi: "My ex, Freddy, sent some girls down to Acapulco, to spice up Jack's honeymoon. I know from Jack, believe me."

Steve: "And I know from Freddy O. My pals in politics have been passing along rumors. The studios are putting together a slush fund to put the skids to *Confidential*. Freddy and his storm troopers have been ratting out all these fags, dykes, and politically enlightened people. The boom's coming down on Freddy, mark my words."

Bernie made the jack-off sign and went *Oy*. The sweats swept over me. "Slush fund." "Politically enlightened people." That read *RED* in my book.

Joi: "Name names, lover. Your pals in politics. Who've I got looking over me, to make sure that the you know what don't hit the fan, if I appear in this movie of yours?"

Steve: "Jack Kennedy, for starters. Joe McCarthy, even though he's a fasco in the *Confidential* mode. Also, we've got Senator Bill Knowland, and Senator Hubert Humphrey. All these heavy guys are pals of mine, and these guys will put the squelch on any rumors that might seep out about the film, and you've got my word that it will only be screened for high-ticket people in politics and the industry—people who want to see—pardon my French—movie stars fucking and sucking and preaching the anti-A-bomb gospel as only I can write it. This is a high-ticket endeavor from jump street, lady—and you can get in on the ground floor."

Bernie went *He craaaazy*. Bernie grabbed his crotch and went *Oy*. Static broke through the broadcast. I doused dials and cleared the feed.

Joi: ". . . and it's not like I don't need the coin. But I'll tell you, though—the idea of screwing on film flips my switch. As long as the film doesn't make the rounds, like that photo of Marlon Brando with his mouth full."

Steve: "Marlon wants to appear in the film. I have this on good authority."

Joi hooted. "You're out of your gourd. As Bondage Bob Harrison says, 'I've got your good authority swinging.'"

Steve scoffed. "Mr. V. J. Jerome's my good authority. How's that for naming names? All the Group Theatre actors take their orders from him. And don't give me that fasco smear that he's in the employ of the Comintern. V.J. knows quality entertainment when he sees it."

Joi scoffed. "Okay, we're naming names. Okay, name me *one* name that can do me some good if and when my movie and TV career goes in the tank."

Steve: "Harry Cohn. How big is *that*? He runs Columbia, and he's bankrolling my film. He will personally see to it that nobody outside of a very elite circle of people see this movie. This is not a smut flick like you see at those Elks Club smokers."

The transceiver fritzed and glitched and broadcast stark static. It consumed the conversation. Bernie doused dials and replugged the console. I snared snippets of chat.

Steve: "Come on. It's not like you've never auditioned."

Joi: "Well . . . it's . . . not like I'm in any kind of ordained situation."

Line buzz/fuzz/stuck static. Wire warp and burned bulbs—the console's coughing smoke—

I dumped my headphones and hauled out of the van. I ran across the courtyard, *rapidamente*. I circled Steve the Stud's building and peeped ground-floor windows. I saw Steve's noxious Nazi regalia and Joi's skirt and shoes, shorn in a heap. I saw Jap flags and shadow-boxed shrunken heads, and heard gruff growls in bass-baritone. I tracked a trail of nylon stockings and men's Jockey briefs. I peeped one last *Walpurgisnacht* window—

And saw Joi gobble Steve the Stud, tonsil-deep.

Call me *Cornuto*. Call me shame-shattered and shit-shorn of power and agency. I made the midnite meet at Googie's. I surged with self-pity. Stretch called my answering service. She dumped our date and cited early practice. The Pervdog of the Nite knows better. Stretch now roils recumbent in savage sapphic embrace.

I sat alone. I nursed a numb-your-soul highball. Joi walked in the back door. She saw me and glimpsed my sick sorrow. I was l'*étranger* out of cool Camus—gallows-bound of my own device.

Joi went *oooh-la-la*. She rolled her eyes and held her hands two feet apart. She shot me the finger and walked back out the door.

I bebopped to a boo-hoo beat. Cuckold/*Cornuto*/jilted Johnny left in the lurch. Somebody save me. I'm sunk in this sink of self-hate.

Jimmy Dean and Claire Klein walked in the back door. La Klein wore blue jeans, Bass Weejuns, and a baleful Beethoven sweatshirt. She was rangy, busty, dark-haired, and unadorned. She had that proud/New York Jew/don't-fuck-with-me look.

I stood up. I primped. I blew off the blues and bloomed in the glow of new love.

They ambled over. This was biz on Bondage Bob's timecard. I snapped my fingers. My funk went *finito*.

A wetback waiter wafted into view. I ordered a pitcher of off-the-menu/high-test lemonade. 150-proof bourbon. Some ambiguous amphetamine. Pounded potions from Hop Ling's Hormone Hutch.

Jimmy played emcee. "Claire, this is Freddy. Freddy, this is Claire. I'm here as a full partner in this enterprise, and to ensure that Rock doesn't get hurt."

Claire said, "I'm here to marry him, not skin him alive."

The waiter bopped back. I played host and poured drinks. I said, "Don't smoke. This stuff tends to ignite."

We settled in. I studied Claire. I gassed on her crooked teeth and bold brown eyes. Here's my first fitful impression:

She's an agent provocateur. She lives to make shit shimmy to her own beat and bounce to her terms.

She said, "Jimmy's been briefing me. Steve Cochran, and all that."

She lived to pry. I caught that. I rerouted a reply.

"*All that*'s the Rock deal, for the moment. Now that I've seen you in person, Miss Klein, I've got some ideas."

Jimmy sipped laced lemonade. "We're listening, boss."

I sipped lemonade. Claire sipped lemonade. Her pupils popped, instantaneous. Her brows broiled with sweat.

"Here's the drift. Six dates, covered in *Confidential*. Atypically wholesome by *Confidential*'s standards, but we'll lay in some anti-Commie repob, to justify that. You play yourself. You're the bohemian algebra teacher at Le Conte Junior High. You meet Rock at Scrivner's Drive-In. You were sipping a pineapple malt, and some pachucos hassled you. This works an antipachuco message into the text. Rock walks into this fracas and beats up the pachucos. A flame sparks. He gives a pep talk to your algebra students. It's heartwarming. You have six dates. Your separate worlds collide and merge. Rock takes you to Ciro's and the Mocambo. You take him to culture caves and groove on le jazz hot. He proposes, you accept, the squarejohn press covers the wedding. You shack for the foreseeable future, and Jimmy watchdogs Rock and diverts him off boys. There's some bylaws I'll run by you when I know you better, and I'm not so afraid you'll scratch my eyes out."

Jimmy hoot-hooted. He eye-strafed the room and pupil-popped a built boy with bleached-blond hair. He ducked off to cull contact. I had Claire Klein to myself.

She said, "Let me guess the bylaws. Then I'll tell you what's acceptable, and what's not."

"Shoot, baby."

Claire said, "No side deals with Rock, his boyfriends, or any men I meet through him. No obvious extramarital liaisons with men I want to work on my own, or men I just plain like. Quit my job at Le Conte, or turn it into some jive fable of me helping underprivileged kids. Fink out all the skeevy goings-on I see in my swanky new Hollywood life."

I sipped laced lemonade. I made This Gesture. It meant bravo/stalemate/your move, mama-san.

Claire lit a cigarette. Bold girl. Brilliant girl. She understands chemical combustion. Her lemonade fails to ignite.

"No deals. Your bylaws stink. And, before you ask, yeah—I did pull a knife on Burt Lancaster. And, before it comes up, I was at Ciro's the other night, and caught your act with Joi Lansing, and if you think she'll ever play bait for you after the Cochran gig, think again. I'm better at this line of work than she is, and I'm not letting you lay down restrictions, even if it means blowing this 'Rock's wife' caper sky-high."

I took it in. I lit a cigarette. Freon Freddy. My lemonade fails to ignite.

"Okay. Do what you want. And, before you ask, yeah—I'll consider you for any bait gigs that might come up for the magazine."

Claire blew smoke rings. "It's not all a one-way street, baby. I've got quite a bit of inside dirt, and I've got no qualms about sharing it, especially as it pertains to the Reds and their sort of filth. I've finked to HUAC, and I'll fink to you—and at least you'll properly compensate me."

I made This Gesture #2. It meant capital C capitulation and wrung-out relinquishment.

Claire laughed. She flashed her crooked teeth. I went all woo-woo. Hey there, you with the stars in your eyes.

"Freddy O.'s a pushover. It's the last thing in the world I expected."

I said, "Let's go someplace and fall down. Let's crawl into a hole and not come out for a while."

Claire said, "Not tonight. I've got test papers to grade, and I can't let those disadvantaged kids down."

OUTSIDE THE HORVATH DEATH PAD

2/19/54

Late nites become me. They obfuscate and overtake me. They send me where I'm supposed to be.

I pulled up and parked on Camerford. LAPD yanked their crime-scene guard. The shit shack now stood dark. The clock marched toward midnite. I ran my radio and notched *Nachtmusik*.

Stan Kenton's "Machito." Jimmie Lunceford's "Uptown Blues." Gonesville, Daddy-O. Mad music to B and E by.

I ditzed the dial and extended the interlude. I got bop, by way of Bird and Deranged Dizzy. Bop bops me and sends me where I'm supposed to be.

I brought my evidence kit. I brought my burglar's tools. I was jazzed and jacked-up exhausted.

I'd worked Operation Rock Wife all day. Sexville, Daddy-O. Close contact with Claire Klein had me *goooooooone*.

Jimmy handled Rock and played director. *Confidential* supplied a foto man. I called Harry Fremont and brought him into the gig. Harry sprung three badass beaners from the Lincoln Heights drunk tank. They portrayed the pachucos who mob-menace Claire. We staged our stirring scene at Scrivner's Hollywood. Claire sips a pineapple malt in her '51 Ford. Rock lurks nearby. Swish carhops swarm him. He signs *mucho* autographs.

Jimmy feeds the cholos their motivation. He stamps them Stanislavskiites at the gate. Dig it: you want white pussy *baaaaaaad*.

They surround Claire's car. They coochie-coo her and weenie-wag her. Claire shrieks. Rock rocks to the rescue. He pounds the three pachuco punks to the pavement. LAPD rolls up and rousts the beaners. Harry Fremont cued them in advance.

It all worked, *perfecto*. Our fotog shot film and stills and got it all in four takes. Rock meets Claire. It's love at first sight. Jimmy counseled reluctant Rock. Brother, you *have* to. Lew Wasserman decrees that you take a wife.

I called Harry and pledged him five yards for his work. Harry shot me leads per the Horvath snuff.

Lead #1: he ran the plate number on that cop car I saw at the crime scene. *Bip*—it's a Fed sled/FBI/on loan to serpentine Senator Joe McCarthy and his L.A. Commie hunt. Lead #2: the Hats pulled in a shitbird pal of George Collier Akin's. He was a hump hot-prowl man himself. The Hats were hammering him *haaaaaaaard*.

Bird bopped me. Dizzy dinged me. I pulled on rubber gloves. I grabbed my evidence kit and *rolled*.

Shadows shrouded me. Streetlights were dim. I poured across the porch and braced the front door. I pulled a #4 pick and jammed the jamb upside the latch spring. The door popped open, *faaaaast*.

I pulled my penlight. I locked myself in. I laid my evidence kit on a chair. Harry got me the PD's print manifest. Joan's prints and her kids' prints were inked in.

Smudge-and-smear locations were noted. No other known or verified prints were found and logged in. Here's *my* job: roll overlooked touch-and-grab surfaces. Contrast and compare.

Chez Joan. It's all there for you to touch and taste. *She's* there for you as your own. Go forth, Pervdog—contrast and compare.

I roamed. I spread print powder on unlisted surfaces and pulled up dust and palm sweat. I worked back toward Joan's bedroom and saved it for last. I hit the kids' bedroom. It broke my hard heart. I pulled an unlogged little-kid print off a bed rail. I checked shelves and drawers for stashed booty and got zilch.

The kitchen reeked of overripe food and dumped trash. I rolled it, regardless. I dusted the breakfast-nook table and pulled up a full-digit print. I checked the print manifest and compared tents, arches, and whorls. *Eureka*—it's an unknown.

I inked it on a fresh print card. My pad prowl was now two hours and ten minutes in. My heart hurtled on overdrive. I stepped into Joan's bedroom and stood there.

Stale perfume stung me. It was Tweed or Jungle Gardenia. The Pervdog's a scent dog and knows whereof he speaks. I caught Joan's underscent. It jazzed me and fucked me up, in caustic concurrence. I penlight-flashed the walls and saw something.

A small borehole. Right there. The east-facing wall. Just above the floor. White Spackle paste caked at the edges. One frayed wire sticking out.

I knelt and flashed a close-up. I'm a bug-and-tap pro. I know bug-and-tap work when I see it. *This* was a bore-and-tap access point. The frayed wire was old. The bug-and-tap mounts had been removed. The Spackle paste was old and crumbled. The bug-and-tap removal man did a shit camouflage job.

Stale perfume. Tweed or Jungle Gardenia, mixed with her—

I went through the bedroom drawers. Joan's underthings were stacked neatly. The stale perfume scent became her scent, all by itself.

I racked out at the Ranch Market. Bondage Bob called early and drilled me out of a dream. Joi rolled her eyes and held her hands two feet apart. Joi flipped me off and walked out of my life.

Bondage Bob reprised my dreary dreamscape. He demanded dish on the Steve Cochran gig. I laid out the lowdown on Joi's bait job. Bondage Bob popped his perceived punch line:

Luscious Lana Turner On Skids—Soon To Sign Smut Contract!!!

We discussed Steve the Stud's phone bills. He called Jack Kennedy and society scribe Connie Woodard. We discussed my address-book thefts at Jack's hotel suite. Connie's a Hearst hack. *But*—she's got listings for the blustery blacklist boys of the Hollywood Ten. Plus V. J. Jerome and other Red rogues. Bob considered Commophile Connie the key to my perceived Something Big. Joi's bait-and-bug job confirmed it.

Steve the Stud blathers per his "political pals." The address book/ phone bill parlay. Connie Woodard calls Steve twenty-four times. Steve calls Connie twenty-one times. Jack Kennedy calls Steve nineteen times. Steve calls Jack fourteen times. Commophile Connie's once removed from Jack the K. Bondage Bob called it all a "pinko porridge"—now running into *Red*.

I told Bob I'd jump on Connie Woodard, and hung up. I omitted the time-consuming cost of my Horvath-snuff crusade. Time tumbled down on me. I reflex-popped two Dexedrine and turned time my way.

I had a pile of pilfered paper from the L.A. DA's Office. Writs and rejoinders, summonses and subpoenas—all signed, sealed, and loaded with legalese. I crafted a subpoena for Joan Horvath's college transcripts. I stamped it and forged it under the seal of DA Ernie Roll. I filled in the blur of blank paper and laid in the lawyeresque. I figured the UCLA admin hacks would kick loose within one week.

Rain and wild wind whipped me west on Wilshire. The run to Westwood Village took an hour and a half. My Packard pimpmobile carved a course westbound. Water-wilted pedestrians got out of my way.

I parked and ran into the main admin building. I flashed my Special DA's Investigator badge at a wowed desk lady. Ernie Roll shot me the shield. I'd pulled him out of the shit with two Jailbait Jills at a Jonathan Club soiree.

The desk lady pledged quick compliance. I winked to seal the deal. L.A. was winter storm–struck. The haul back to Holly*weird* would take two hours plus. I had time to kill. I schlepped over to the north campus library and ordered up microfiche.

The Hearst-hack *Herald*. Constance Woodard's column. Look for pro-Commie calumny cloaked in society slush. Look for Steve the Stud and Jack the K. puff pieces and mere mentions. See what jumps out.

The microfiche ran from December '53 back to August '51. Connie's column was called "Connie's Column." A small pic denoted all her one-page spreads. I recalled La Woodard from Jack K.'s A-bomb party. She was a knock-kneed redhead of the spinster-idealist ilk. She'd be richly ripe for Red recruitment.

I moved microfiche through a machine. I read Connie's columns. My hackles hopped at the start. Every Hancock Park hoedown, every debutante do and cutesy cotillion contained a rip on the Reds. It was *tooooooooo* much of a good thing. It was *waaaaay* out of print proportion. I scrolled back and hit May 16, '53. Jack K. attends a lawn bash. It fetes limp-wristed loser Adlai Stevenson. Connie properly prongs Adlai and calls him "pink in more ways than one." *Ooohhy*, Connie—you got *dat* right. *But*—she singles out Jack's kid brother, Bobby the K. She suck-up cites his tight ties to Joe McCarthy. And, *dig*: McCarthy has already disgraced himself. He's now anathema to astutely informed anti-Reds.

Tooooo much of a good thing. *Waaaaay* out of print proportion.

What's going on here? Connie's got Jack's name in her address book. It's right beside John Howard Lawson and V. J. Jerome. She calls Jack. She calls Steve Cochran. Steve's anti-A-bomb. That's suspect in itself. Steve's making "celebrity smut." He's "leaning left these days."

I scrolled back through Connie's columns. I skimmed for Jack and Steve worked into the word stew. '53, '52, '51. There—August 18.

Steve's captivating kids at a Shriners wingding. Connie's ever the muddled muckraker and gooey gadfly here.

"B-movie heartthrob Steve Cochran broke hearts at the Shriners last night, and not the hearts of the willing women so often attributed to him. No, readers—and he didn't brawl his way through the corridors of Children's Hospital, nor did he hit any doctors or slap any nurses who got in his way. He simply showered affection on those less fortunate than he, and in the process he claimed the hearts of many, including myself. Isn't it time the world looked at this very talented and humane young man as the gifted and sensitive artist that he is?"

I was floored, flabbergasted, and flipped into a rage. It's the Parthenon of Puff Pieces. It's the deus ex machina of disingenuousness. Connections, deflections, lies unworthy of *me*. I sensed it was *Something Big* at the start. Now I knew it was *Something Wrong*.

I levitated out of the library. Something Big/Something Wrong. I surfed the tsunami east on Sunset. It was some mad monsoon. A homing instinct homed me in on Havenhurst Avenue. I cut south and pulled up by Steve Cochran's courtyard.

Sit-still surveillance. Hard rain to hide me, couched curbside. Old Crow to kill the cold.

I dialed down the defroster and kept the windows clear. I strafed eyeball paths to the rear carport and Studly Steve's door. Time faltered and failed to trample my trance. Hours passed. Steve Cochran and Joi Lansing came out of the carport and headed for home.

His home. *Her* home now. They lugged *her* luggage. The matched set *I* bought her. Monogrammed at Mark Cross.

Some cute couple. A matched set. The Stacked and the Hung. Joi wobbled on too-high heels. A Band-Aid on Steve's right cheek set off his jawline and failed to mar his good looks.

Boo-hoo. Nobody knows de trouble ise seen, nobody knows my sorrow. Somebody, save me. Who said size doesn't count? I'm sunk in this sink of self-hate.

I bolted. I cut down to Fountain and came back up Crescent Heights. I parked in the rear lot and entered Googie's. I saw her, straight off. She wore her culture-cave ensemble. Blue jeans, Bass Weejuns, baleful Beethoven sweatshirt.

I primped. I popped two Sen-Sen for instant fresh breath. She was alone. She sat in a back booth. I feigned the nonchalance of the cool and the callous and walked straight up.

She twirled her ashtray. She sipped absinthe on the rocks and nibbled french fries.

"Joi's shacking with Steve Cochran. Jimmy called and told me. He said he helped Joi pack the rest of her stuff."

I said, "The Teletype travels fast. I just found out myself."

"I hope this consoles you. Jimmy said there was a very big girl asleep in your bed. She's about as tall as that colored guy from KU. Joi hexed her and poured liniment on her basketball shorts."

I laffed and took a jolt of Claire's absinthe. It stung my too-taxed liver and looped to my head. Claire tossed french fries on my place mat.

"Bondage Bob cut you a check for your wardrobe. He wants you dressed to the nines for your Mocambo date next week. You're doubling with Rock and Jimmy. Jimmy's bringing Liz Taylor. He's inked for some big oater set in Texas, soon. Rock and Liz top-bill him. Jimmy and Liz are strictly platonic. They'll make sure Rock doesn't light out after some hunky chorus quiff."

Claire lit a cigarette. "I'll sell Liz some Israel bonds. She's devoted to the cause now. She's sub rosa with this wheeler-dealer, Mike Todd. She never stays unmarried for long. Mike's a *landsman* of the old school. Liz is forbidden fruit to him."

I laffed. "Liz is low-hanging fruit of the new school. *Confidential* winks at divorces, and the magazine will always be kind to her."

Claire tossed a changeup. "I shivved that Mex who whipped his chorizo out on me. Jimmy got him lit up on the Method, but he whipped it too close to my face."

I tossed a changeup. "Harry Fremont saw a Fed intel file. He said you were in on the King David Hotel bombing, back in the British mandate."

"I planted the bomb. And then I played girl sabra and lovingly carried out dead Englishmen."

"The PD guys took the Mex to Georgia Street Receiving. You were kind. It was a superficial flesh wound. He got off easy."

Claire twirled her ashtray. "You've got a history with Georgia Street. Harry loves to dish. He said your guy didn't get off so easy."

"Let's not get into scalp counts. I couldn't possibly compete with you."

Claire smiled. "You've got lineage. The Lebanese come to fight. You're a Christian, so your people were surely considered elites."

I made the jack-off sign. "I fell off my camel and landed in L.A. My whole life's nothing but a prelude to you."

Claire yukked. "I'll never say yes, and I'll never say no. At some point we'll want to fall down together, and we'll both know the moment when it comes."

I got chills. I chugged Claire's absinthe. Wormwood whipped my wig and winged me back to Weimar Berlin. I joined a bevy of bohemians at the Hotel Adlon. We're there to cull the cusp of the abyss.

"What are you doing in L.A.? You didn't come here to teach school and see what happens next, and you're overqualified for studio gigs and bait jobs."

Claire said, "People here love to talk. Jimmy, Harry, Bob Harrison. I've come to understand that you're interested in Connie Woodard, and I'm interested in her, too."

I said, "Don't stop now."

Claire said, "I came to L.A. to kill a man. I don't know his name, but I think Connie Woodard might. It's all design and opportunity with me, as it is with you."

I drove home. I drove home jazzed and jacked to the gills and SCARED down to my shit-stained shorts.

The pad was queerly quiescent. Stretch dropped her USC silks on the living room floor. She left a note propped by the phone.

"Harry Fremont called. Meet him at the Central DB tomorrow. 10:00 a.m. Hat Squad. A 459 suspect. Mandatory."

I walked back to the bedroom. A bedside night-light was on. Stretch was crapped out on my bed. She was tucked in under the covers and dead asleep. Lance the Leopard was curled up on top of the duvet. Stretch was too tall for the bed. I covered her feet. Lance growled at me. Don't mess with my woman, you hump.

I know when I'm licked. I walked back to the living room and fell asleep on the couch with my clothes on.

The Hats had a hump in the hot seat. A claustrophobe closet/one table/six chairs. One fat phone book in vivid view.

He's Delbert Davis Haines/white male American/DOB 6-12-18. He's tight with George Collier Akin. They met and compared notes at Quentin. Haines did a doomsday dime for 459 plus rape-sodomy.

Harry Fremont dragged a dragnet and hauled him in. He was alibied up for the Joan Horvath homicide. He blew blues clarinet at a round-the-clock romp at the Riptide Room. Dexter Gordon, Chet Baker, and Art Pepper alibied him.

Harry said he'd made pay-phone contact with Akin. Haines said Akin was casing cooze for a Red Devil Bandit comeback. He's bidding Beverly Hills bye-bye. He's back on L.A. city turf.

The Hats hovered. They straddled chairs and loomed over Haines. I kicked my chair against a side wall and scoped it. Haines was a junkie. He skin-popped Big "H" and held off a habit. He was snaggletoothed and pustule-pocked. He wore a Sir Guy shirt and slit-bottom khakis. He was one mean motor scooter and bad actor.

Max Herman said, "You could waltz, Delbert. We've got nothing on the books we can hold you on."

Red Stromwall said, "Or we could concoct something and hold you indefinitely."

Harry Crowder said, "Or we could get ugly."

Eddie Benson said, "You know what we want and who we want, and the sooner you give it to us, the less likely it is that we'll lay on the grief."

Haines said, "Who's that guy kicking his chair back? I think I've seen him before."

Max Herman said, "That's Mr. Otash. He's a former Los Angeles policeman, currently employed as a private investigator."

Haines said, "He's a greaseball. I'm very much attuned to racial distinctions. I'm on the editorial board for the National States' Rights Party, and I write for *Thunderbolt Magazine*."

Red Stromwall said, "Let's stick to the topic at hand. George Collier Akin. You know what we want."

Haines picked his nose and ate the goober. He said, "I want your wife to suck my big dick."

Red phone-booked him. *Wham!*—a big roundhouse shot. His face hit the table. His nose cracked. Blood blew out.

He tried to wipe his face. Harry Crowder grabbed his hands and cuffed them to his chair slats. The ratchets racked deep and drew blood.

Haines giggled and licked blood off his lips. He wagged his well-hung tongue at the Hats.

"I'm the Lizard of Love. Check my rap sheet. I'm a go-down man from way back."

Harry Crowder said, "We like Akin for a burglary-homicide two nights ago. Lower Hollywood. Camerford off Vine. The victim's name was Joan Horvath. Does that ring a bell with you?"

Haines said, "Your wife rings my bell, eight nights a week. She's a go-down girl from way back."

Harry phone-booked him. He sidled a sidewinder shot. Haines' head whiplashed. Nose blood and mouth blood blew wide. Two teeth hit the far wall.

Eddie Benson said, "Joan Horvath. Camerford off Vine. The B and E snuff there. She wakes up and fights him. Does this sound like Akin? Has he mentioned the job to you?"

Haines licked his lips and torqued his tongue. He said, "Your wife mentioned that you're hung like an amoeba. That's why she brings me all the woof-woof."

Eddie phone-booked him. He ripped a reverse sidewinder. It tore one eyebrow loose. Blood spattered the opposite wall.

I said, "Joan Horvath was pushing forty. She had some gray hair, and she was on the stout side. I bet Akin likes it younger and firmer, and Harry Fremont told me the Red Devil Bandit doesn't range that far north and west."

Haines licked blood off his lips. "Hey, the greaseball speaks, and he don't speak with forked tongue."

Max Herman said, "Tell us what you mean by that."

Haines said, "I mean the greaseball speaks *la verdad*. The Red Devil Bandit likes young gash he can terrorize. He likes the pads off Washington and Jefferson, down near USC. I can get more specific if you give me that waltz and lay a big dinner-and-drinks chit for Kwan's Chinese Pagoda on me."

Max Herman said, "You're on."

Red Stromwall said, "We'll throw in a shower and a run by Georgia Street. We know all the doctors there. They'll fix you up."

Harry Crowder said, "Delbert's a white man."

Eddie Benson said, "Let's not go overboard."

Haines looked straight at me. "Severance Street, the first block south of Jefferson. The Bandit's casing a pad there. He might hit tonight. The chick's a predental student. She's got short dark hair in a pixie cut."

Max uncuffed Haines and handed him his handkerchief. Haines wrung his wrists and grabbed the chair back. He staggered and struggled to stand up.

I said, "You don't make him for Joanie? There's no way he'd go for that?"

Haines haw-hawed. " 'Joanie?' Do I detect something there?"

The Hats haw-hawed. They shared wicked winks. Max said, "We make him for Joanie, and that's all that counts."

—⁓—

Harry and Eddie took Haines to Georgia Street and ensconced him with the jail-ward doc. I went with them. Georgia Street, redux. I walked the wicked path I walked when I whacked Ralphie Horvath.

Eddie ribbed me. "Must bring back some memories. Eh, Freddy?"

Haines had no fixed address for George Collier Akin. The Hats preferred to hit hot-prowl men in the act. Max dug up a map of Severance south of Jefferson. Red stiffed cold calls to every house on the block. He pinned the pixie cut. She was one Louise Marie Vernell, age eighteen.

Red laid out the sick situation. Louise gave in to gasps. She rented a room in a coed boardinghouse. Max decreed evacuation. Red dispatched three patrol sleds. Patrol cops took the tittering tenants and their landlady to the downtown Statler. The PD picked up the tab. The girls gassed on the service and posed for pix with the cops.

We waited. The dead-of-winter day dipped to dusk. Max buzzed Bill Parker. I heard his side of the call. He said, "Yes, Chief" fourteen times and hung up.

I packed my .45 automatic. The Hats packed Python Magnums. Harry made the booze run. He brought back six short dogs of bonded bourbon and boocoo potato chips.

We rolled out in two K-cars. I rolled with Max and Red. Max laid in Ithaca pumps and a box of throwdown guns. We pulled ahead in the pole spot. Harry and Eddie bird-dogged behind. We hit South Severance at full dark.

Louise left her lights on, upstairs. They beamed I'm-home-alone/come-and-find-me rape rays. The pole car took the back-alley slot. The follow car took the Severance slot.

Max and Red played host. We shared short dogs and potato chips. The car was cold. The booze built its glimmering glow. Max and Red teased and taunted me.

You're okay, Freddy. We miss you, Freddy. *Confidential's* a shit rag, Freddy. How many felony extortions have you pulled this year, Freddy? The Chief's got his four eyes on you.

It sailed sadly by me. I was off with Stretch and Claire and the mystery man she vowed to kill. Plus Studly Steve and Commo Connie Woodard. Claire per Connie: "I'm interested in her, too."

Time ticked by. *Tick, tick, tick.* I entertain ripe revelations. Claire scares me more than Georgie Akin and the Hats. *Tick, tick, tick.* The hellhound Horvaths. They've haunted me and hurtled me *here*.

The teasing and taunting ebbed. Time ticked toward 10:00 p.m. Max and Red booze-dozed their way through ten-minute naps. I popped two Dexedrine and wound myself up.

I saw something. It was something evil and something wrong. The something walked northbound. In our direct direction. There's a red blur where its head should be and black below that. It's getting close. It's veering toward the boardinghouse back gate.

The boys woke up. The Something's *très* close. It's got its hand on the gate latch. Said latch is unlocked. Our K-car's shadow-shrouded. We see it. It can't see us.

The Red Devil Bandit. That red-rubber mask. The fangs and horns. He rapes and maims. He didn't maim and kill Joan Horvath. We're past all that now.

Max and Red pulled their belt guns. I pulled mine. The Red Devil Bandit opened the gate and closed it behind him. Max mouthed One, two, three, four, five. We got out and followed him.

We were silent. We went tiptoed. The Red Devil Bandit heard zilch. He stood in the walkway and eyed the upstairs light. Harry and Eddie stepped out of a shadow. The Red Beast saw them. They held pump shotguns.

The Red Beast turned to run. He saw three more men and three more guns out. He saw me.

Max said, "Kill him, Freddy."

I stepped up. I aimed. The Red Beast stood still. I fired at his face. It blew up, red-on-red. Red rubber and red blood exploded. The shot rang loud *loud*.

Harry and Eddie shotgunned him and tumbled him back off his feet. He's dead now. He's no danger. This is how this works. All five of us walked up and emptied our guns. We fired point-blank and shot him to bits.

INFERNAL INTERMEZZO:

My Furtively Fucked-up Life

2/22–3/18/54

Yeah, I did it. Yeah, it was wrong. Yeah, I enjoyed it. He got what he paid for. I knew I'd pay for what I did—somewhere down the line.

The Hearst rags loved it. HATS SLAY RED DEVIL BANDIT!!! CELEB P.I. ASSISTS!!! Dig the fetching fotos. I stand with Max, Red, Harry, and Eddie. They dwarf me. We point to something red and dead on the ground.

More headline hullabaloo. TIPSTER TATTLES RED DEVIL BANDIT!!! DARING BLASTOUT ENSUES!!! More fetching fotos. Georgie Akin's 1943 mug shots. A posed my-hero shot. Fractious Freddy with Max Herman and Red Stromwall. We strut. Louise Marie Vernell smarmy-smiles up at us.

BHPD blew a stakeout on Durward Brown and Richard Dulange. The Hats hunted them down and killed them four days later. The Hearst rags loved it. More headline hullabaloo. MOTEL MASSACRE!!! HATS GUN DOWN KIDNAP-RAPISTS!!! ALL GANG MEMBERS NOW DEAD!!!

Many more fetching fotos. The Hats with Chief Parker. Mastiffs maul for their master. Big backslaps and yuk-yuks. Many mentions of me. Max Herman sez, "We needed Freddy O. on this one. Freddy's our boy. He's the Man to See." Red Stromwall sez, "God bless Freddy O. What's a daring blastout without him?"

Yeah, I did it. Yeah, I knew it was wrong. Yeah, I loved the hack hullabaloo. Don't fuck with Freddy O. He's the Man to See. Too bad the world sees back. Too bad the world's inside him.

The Googie's gang saw me and tipstered me and fed me scandal skank. I scored scads of sinuendo for the magazine. Homos, lezbos, dipsos, hopheads. Underhung *Untermenschen* and big-dick barracudas. Heavy hermaphrodite action sunders the Sunset Strip!!!

Freddy O.'s the Shaman of Shame. He's got to *see* you. Meanwhile, *you* see *him*.

I saw Joan "Stretch" Perkins and Claire Klein. We talked about things and around things. I saw them, they saw me. They taunted, tickled, and teased me. Stretch wanted kid love, with all the va-va-voom verboten. We slept in my bed. Stretch wore basketball silks. I wore pajamas. We necked to a naughty nexus and stopped cold. Lance the Leopard got between us. It was nighty-night then.

Stretch taunts and teases me. She knows things about me. She knows I killed the Red Devil Bandit in cold blood. She knows it all pertains to the hellhound Horvaths—and that I'm not done with them yet. Claire Klein taunts and teases me. She won't fall down with me. We meet at Googie's most nights. We smile and drink. Our hands often brush. We discuss Operation Rock Wife. I'll be taking over Jimmy Dean's stewardship soon. He'll be off to shoot *East of Eden* with Gadge Kazan and that big Texas flick with Liz and Rock. Claire wants to kill a man. I *see* that. It consumes her. She *sees* that I'm going at the Cochran gig and the Commie Connie connection circumspectly. She's an I-want-to-*see*-it-and-know-it-all-now girl. And most assuredly a psychopath. She withholds from me. I withhold from her. Our boundaries wiggle, wilt, and hold firm. She scares me. I don't scare her. I'm not the Man to See. I'm the man to help her fulfill her murderous destiny.

Stretch provides innocence. Claire turns my lifelong voyeurism back in on me. I want to know her secret shit—but fear the price she'll make me pay. She knows that I killed the Red Devil Bandit to impress her. She intends to kill a man. I intend to kill the man who really killed Joan Horvath. The hellhound Horvaths. It all comes back to them. Claire *sees* that and knows that full well. I told her that I killed a man so she'll love me. She failed to reply. She won't love me until I find the man that *she* wants to kill. In the meantime, my will to work rages.

I work the Cochran gig. Bondage Bob wants a wild and sex-soiled serialization. I live at the listening post. The bugs and taps work *gooooood*. I listen to Studly Steve fuck my ex-woman Jøi Lansing. They deliriously defame me. They underestimate me. Joi tattles, taunts, and teases me. She knows there's bugs and taps in place. She hasn't told Steve. She knows I'm listening. She wants me to hear. That means she wants me to *see*.

Sound equals sight. My imagination seals the sensory gaps. Information insistently issues. Steve's recruited Lana Turner and hunk hubby Lex Barker. Lurid Lex *loooooves* underage stuff. The casting-call aspect of the celeb smut film proceeds. I'm on it. I'm on the Connie connection just as assiduously.

I haunt the UCLA library. I bug the admin folk: where's the Joan Horvath transcripts? The admin folk go *Soon, soon*. I read and reread Connie's columns. Connie's a codified Commie. She's Comintern. She's a Red Reptile couched in cold cover. She's seditiously subtle. Her words work on a mini-microdot level. She's linked to Steve Cochran. Steve rolls Red. I'm building a scandal-rag exposé and a damning derogatory profile. I'll leak it to Joe McCarthy or some more rigorously responsible cat. I'll get Claire the name of the man she wants to kill in the process. She'll love me then or she won't. I'll love her whatever the outcome.

Work. Operation Rock Wife. Rock and Claire like each other and look good together. Lew Wasserman's pleased. Rock orders in bunboys from a dial-a-dick service owned by Bondage Bob's wayward kid brother. He gets his regular woof-woof.

I fotograph Rock and Claire's at-the-doorway kisses. It's sterile stuff. Rock's a movie star and a very sweet man. He's engaged to wed a batshit bomb thrower and more. Only in America, only in L.A., only in Holly*weird*.

Work. Allies and adversaries. Old friends passing through.

The Hats hold their hands in. They swing by Googie's and

torque me as I tally tipster dish. How's the boy, Freddy? Do you miss us, Freddy? The Chief misses you, Freddy. You're always in his thoughts.

I looked for them when they weren't there. I listened for them at the listening post. They imparted the impudent theme of We See You. I saw them everywhere. I popped pills and saw them. I drank and saw them. I adamantly abstained and saw them most of all.

Work. I got my FBI kickback on that Horvath house print. Bad news: there's no file print extant. I *lived* at the listening post. I wore headphones and willed the next static-stung stammer that would tell me something big and something wrong. I waited for UCLA to call. Commie Connie confounded me. She never left her Hancock Park home. I needed to prowl the premises. I needed to booby-trap bugs and hot-wire the whole hut.

Connie hid from me and hindered me and immolated my imagination. I parked across the street and ran my radio. Joe McCarthy proclaimed his presence in L.A. Bondage Bob told me a Fed listening post had been set up someplace/somewhere. I saw my wires crossed with their wires, strung as strangling cords.

Work to constant communion. The Horvath house as soiled sacristy. I vowed vengeance. I exonerated the Red Devil Bandit and ran my rationale for his death. Joan heard me. I know that. Vigilance is love. I hold vigil most nights. I know that Joan hears me and sees me.

Connie's casa: a cool contemporary job at 1st and Beachwood. Two stories. All aluminum and glare-glinted glass, up and down. Some dippy Dane's idea of swank.

Sit-and-brood surveillance. A raging rainstorm brings a brainstorm. Hey, lady—we've got fone lines down. Let me in to check your fones, willya?

I perched in my Packard pimpmobile. Bernie was due. He had the pseudo repair tools and the know-how. He'd wing it, whambam. One fone/one condenser mike/one half-ass tap. No time to tackle bug mounts.

Raging rainstorms rip me, recollective. They wash my broiled brain and cleanse it clean. Last month. The Willoughby listening post. Stretch Perkins works Call-Girl Line #2. She hears Claire Klein and Barbara Payton trick with V. J. Jerome. The appalling apparatchik's in Connie's address book. That's Cold Connection #1. Here's Cold Connection #2:

Last month, ditto. Claire and I nosh the news and flare-flirt at Googie's. Claire lights me large with this line:

"I came to L.A. to kill a man. I don't know his name, but I think Connie Woodard might."

Hence, my bristling brainstorm. Hence, my ripe resolve. Work the Connie Connection *now*.

I yawned. My ass dragged. I was up late last nite. My landlord lashed my lease and tossed me out, temporary. Lance the Leopard laid waste to his rose gardens and crotch-sniffed his crotchety wife. I rented a boss bungalow at the Beverly Hills Hotel. Stretch helped me move. We hung up corkboards and tacked on *Confidential* sales graphs. Plus notes for my tricky troika: Operation Rock Wife/the Cochran Gig/my Horvath Crusade.

Lance *loooooooved* his new lair. Room service served his cheese-burgers and fries in a dog dish. Lance slept with Stretch. I slept on the couch.

I yawned. I dexie-dosed my case of the blahs. Bernie showed. He'd scrounged a PC Bell repair truck, for vivid verismo. He parked in Connie Woodard's driveway and drilled her doorbell.

She opened up. There she is. She's still rangy, nervous, and knock-kneed. She's the Specious Spinster and Miss Soviet Suck-Up of 1924.

Bernie schmoozed her. I rolled down my window and heard it. He went *Oy, lady*. She went *Oh dear—are you sure? Ooohhh*—she talked butch bass like Lauren Bacall.

She let Bernie in. He shut the door. I timed the house call.

Twenty-two and a half minutes. Bernie tips his cap and walks back out the door. Connie holds the door. Her russet hair's wrapped in a bun now. She waves *toodle-oo*.

Paydirt.

Bernie tapped the living room fone and shoved a short-range transceiver under the couch. We rented an upstairs office at a bank building off 1st and Larchmont. We laid in listening-post paraphernalia. Casa Connie to the post: two short-range blocks. We should get *gooooood* signal feeds.

Bernie donned earmuffs and manned the tap. I called Harry Fremont from a pay phone. I groused and proclaimed my predicament.

There's this woman. She's a shut-in. I've tapped her. I need to pad-prowl her. Rig me a ruse. I need four hours. She's a Commie.

Uncle Sambo needs you. Violate her sissified civil rights. I'll pay you five yards.

Harry said, "*Jawohl*, boss."

Babs Payton car-hopped and hooked out of Stan's Drive-In. It was hard by Hollywood High. She hit *her* Hollyweird high with *Kiss Tomorrow Goodbye*, circa '50. She was Mrs. Franchot Tone for six seconds. Tom Neal beat Timid Tone half dead and battered Babs with his lurid love. *Tattle* told the torchy tale, circa '51. Babs screeched into the skids. *Yeah*—she was ripe for Steve Cochran's *sexploitation*.

I pulled into Stan's. A comely carhop cadre caught sight of Big Freddy O. Babs and I go back. We badger-gamed businessmen in my cop days. Babs snared the schnooks at the Kibitz Room at Canter's Delicatessen. She lured them to the Lariat Motel on Lankershim. She socked the saps into the saddle and made with the moans. I kicked the door in and played irate husband. I glommed the gelt and kicked the cads back out the door.

Babs roller-skated over. She wore red-and-white jodhpurs and a too-tight jersey top. She said, "Here's trouble." She hooked a tray to my passenger-side door.

I dropped a C-note on the tray. Babs got the gestalt. She got in and sat beside me. The C-note went *poof!!!*

"Okay, I'll play."

"I thought you might want to."

Babs scooched down and swung her legs up. Her skate boots nudged her knees and fit fetishistic. She posed pouty and ran the rollers on my dashboard.

"I'm on my break for the next fifteen minutes. Before you start, let me state no more shakedowns. I'm not going back to the Kibitz Room or the Lariat Motel."

I laffed and lit a cigarette. Babs bummed a smoke and lit it off my lighter.

"*Freddy*, the point of all this is—"

"Steve Cochran. The smut film he's making, and don't ask me how I know about it."

Babs said, "Ha-ha. You're jealous, because Joi's in the flick, and she left you for Steve. I don't blame you, I'd be jealous, too. Ha-ha, and too bad for Joi, because as crummy men go, she's gone from the frying pan into the fire."

I rebuffed the rude remark. "Update me. The film, who Steve's conned into appearing, the start date, the whole schmear."

Babs shrugged. "Smut's smut, and I know from smut on an intimate level. Okay, Steve's wrapping *Private Hell 36* this week, so we'll start pretty soon. Probably within the next two weeks. Lana Turner, Lex Barker, and Gene Tierney have dropped out, which I know don't surprise you. Steve's stuck with me, Joi, and Anita O'Day, and he's recruiting an additional ten girls out of one of the call services some of us have been known to work for, which makes the full thirteen women that Steve and his big dick will repopulate the world with, after the A-bomb wipes everybody else on Earth out. Need I say that Steve's hipped on the A-bomb like nobody I've ever seen."

I went *Don't stop now.* Babs rolled her rollers on my red leather dashboard. It rubbed me wrong. I nudged her knees and kiboshed it.

Babs tapped ash out the window. "The premiere is sometime later this spring, in Harry Cohn's rec room. Smut's smut, and what's smut without some straitlaced boys to let their back hair down while they watch it. And since Harry's Harry, and a tyrant, a perv, and, most especially, a suck-up, these are some powerful boys, as in Senator Bill Knowland, Senator Joe McCarthy—if he don't trip on his dick between now and this so-called 'premiere'—and Senator Jack Kennedy, who I know you know from, but probably not on the intimate level that I do."

"Why would Jack's name be in Steve's address book? Why would Jack and Steve be calling each other, regularly?"

"Because Steve's Jack's pimp and dope supplier in L.A. Because Steve rolls left, and Jack's a barely suppressed bleeding heart, right below the surface."

I dipped through the dish. I strung it and strained it and micro-scoped it minutely. Nothing surprised me. Babs bops banal, so far.

"Claire Klein. I know you trick three-ways with her, and don't ask me how I know. If you start by saying she scares you, it wouldn't surprise me—because she scares me, too."

Babs made the hex sign. Babs waved faux wolfsbane. Babs made the sign of the cross.

"Claire don't scare me. Claire terrifies me. She likes to shave men's pubic hair with her switchblade, and half the tricks we go out on *love* it. She carries a Makarov pistol with a silencer in her purse, and we've been tricking with these Russian consulate guys, and they speak Russian with her, so I don't know what they're saying—"

I cut in. "*And* V. J. Jerome, that Commie culture-vulture guy—"

Babs cut back in. "Yeah, there's him, *and* Claire's cutting side deals, to swing with these Russian guys and shave their wives, and all the time she's pressing them, and she's digging for leads on some Commie scientist back in the '30s and '40s, who's got this weirdo 'Robin Redbreast' code name, and then she's pressing them on some society writer named Constance Woodard, and about this time I lose track of all Claire's crazy shit, and start praying to the Good Lord that I never have to work with her again."

I drove to Googie's. I perv-peeped Claire through a back window. I trembled. I smeared nose prints on the glass.

Claire sat in her back booth. She sipped absinthe and nibbled french fries. She wore tight blue jeans. Note the knife bulge on her left leg.

I walked in. The dinner din diminuendoed. There was just my heartbeat and hers. I trembled and tumbled toward her. She saw me. She read me right and tumbled telepathic. *She knew that I knew.*

I sat down. She read me. Here's fright-fraught Freddy. Freddy's got the frets.

"I saw the bug mounts when Babs and I tricked with V. J. Jerome. I thought it might get back to you. Babs even joked about it. 'Half these trick pads are hot-wired, and you never know who's listening. Most likely it's Freddy Otash."

I guzzled her absinthe. I grabbed the goblet too hard. The glass sheared and shattered. Sharp shards cut my hand.

Claire pressed her napkin into the palm and balled my fist around it. Claire unbuttoned my shirt cuffs and rolled up the sleeves in one go.

She ran her hands up my arms. She tugged at the hairs. She removed the napkin and blotted blood off my hand.

"You should assume that I want you to know everything that I do and say, and that it's all in our common interest. 'Opportunity is love,' as you've put it before. I'm sure you've spoken to Babs. And I'm sure she's told you a few things. You know why I'm here in L.A., and I know you're not here to deter me or prevent me from doing what I intend to do. From here on in, we should credit each other with the ability to learn and extrapolate. We'll have our moment together when we've accomplished what we need to, and it will be all that much sweeter then."

I said, "Robin Redbreast" and "Connie Woodard." My voice sheared. Claire pulled her shiv and picked glass shards out of my hand.

Stretch said, "You're scared. It's like you've seen the world's worst ghost."

My bungalow bid me to safety. Stretch was safe. Lance was safe. I *needed* that. I *wanted* to be someplace dark and depraved with Claire Klein.

I held my hand up. I heal fast. My cuts had crusted into crisp little crosses. I'd been stigmatized.

Claire was a Navy nurse, circa '43. Claire knew from knives. She cleansed my wound with high-test absinthe. She placed my hand on her breast and held it there. A part of me passed into her.

"Uncle Freddy, you're shaking. And what's with your hand? Don't tell me you've had some kind of religious visitation."

I walked up to my wall graph. *Confidential*'s daily sales had spiked spectacularly. I scanned my treacherous troika graph. I drew arrows between Operation Rock Wife and the Cochran Gig. I linked former to latter and wrote "Claire Klein & Babs Payton" below. I arrow-linked "V. J. Jerome" & "Connie Woodard." I wrote "Russian consulate guys" & "Robin Redbreast" below that.

Stretch walked over. Her eyes grazed the graph and ran right to "Robin Redbreast." She got goose bumps. They sprouted and spread up her arms.

I said, "The Sweetzer listening post. Monitor Lez Line #2, every chance you get. I'll pay you two yards a week."

She orbed my hopped-up hieroglyphics. She said, "As long as you tell me how all this plays out."

Transcripts. One fat file box. She was Joan Marcelline Hubbard then. She's Joan Horvath of My Heart now.

The admin folks delivered. They called me this a.m. They stridently stressed that rules and regulations apply. View the contents here. Return the box by 9:00 p.m. Don't snitch documents. Don't mooch monographs. The honor system applies.

I took a table all by myself. I tallied tabbed file folders and crafted a chronology. Joan Marcelline Hubbard. DOB 11-6-18. She hails from the hellish-hot San Joaquin Valley. She's farmworker stock. She graduated high school in '35. She picks fruit with a wetback work crew. She digs her way out of the Depression. She applies to UCLA.

She's accepted. She hits Westwood in the fall of '39.

It's all language labs and lit crit. She learns Russian/Polish/Italian. She flaunts her fluency in class and stages stirs. La Hubbard's a hambone. She's a distaff disc jockey on Bruin Radio. She shoves Shostakovich down the throats of the campus illiterati. She rewards them with reductive Rachmaninoff and cheesy Tchaikovsky. She riffs on Russki literature. She writes her own commercials for Russian restaurants. She's a regular at Karlov's Kasa Kiev. Karlov kicks back kash. She writes her own commercials for Polish Pete's Pirogi

Palace. Pete pays her in cold cash and kielbasa cutlets. She works her way through college in this mad manner. She's a noted campus cutup. She's a sinfully self-promoting cheerleader chick.

She gets the grades. *Woooo!!!*—Straight A's across the board. She studies the Russian romantic poets. She cruelly critiques the movement. It's all marginal and mystical malarkey. She links Polish piano pounder Paderewski to nattering Nazi composers of the oompah-band ilk. Her professors know that she's a gallivanting gadfly—but stress the solid soundness of her rigor. '39, '40, '41. Joan Marcelline Hubbard makes her mark and goes forth.

She graduates. She goes on to grad school. That crisp chronology cruised me through her academic life. Course names/dates/test scores/grades/the names of professors. The transcripts tripped by as La Joan's light fantastic. File pages blew by in a blur.

I hit late '41 and the cusp of '42. I hit my first chronological misfile. Spring '40: An Introduction to Polish Labor Movements/Professor Witold Kirpaski. I put the transcript aside and plowed through late '41. Then this, then this, then *THIS*:

Fall '39. The Political Content of the Post-Revolutionary Russian Novel/Guest Professor Constance Woodard.

The nite becomes me. I assume my Pervdog pose. My hophead side sidles forth and fuels me. I'm the Red Devil Bandit, one crazed chromosome removed. It's kid shit shorn of pretense. I've peeped since I was fourteen years old in bumfuck Massachusetts. Thus, I peeped *NOW*.

I parked outside Connie Woodard's pad. I popped three Dexedrine and adjusted my adrenaline load. Midnite marched to 1:00 a.m. All Connie's lights were off. I pondered a B and E—but abstained.

My wall graph walloped me. Lives and lines linked on paper. Fall '39. Connie Woodard links to Joan Hubbard. Connie's linked to Steve Cochran. Claire Klein links to Connie. She's marked a man for murder. She thinks Connie may know things. She knows I know things. She knows I've got L.A. hot-wired. I'm the Man to See. Claire talks to me through a mad medium. Listening posts broadcast *two* ways under her spell. She pounds me, paranoiac. Freddy, what thou hath wrought. She Bible-bashes me. The Book of Revelation 3:8. *I know all the things you do, and I have opened a door for you that no one can close.* She has made me the Man to Be Seen.

I eyeballed the Woodard house. I fought off B & E urges. I felt seen. I kept seeing things that might or might not be there. Cop cars clustered in close surveillance. Women wielding shivs. Claire stamped me stigmatized. We merged heartbeats. She marked me the Man to Be Seen.

I worked the phones all afternoon. I talked to Harry Fremont. He froze on the get-me-into-Connie's-house front. "I can't come up with a ruse or diversion, Freddy. Give me time to think this through." I talked to Stretch. She reported from the Sweetzer listening post and Lez Line #2. She said Claire and some unknown Russki talked mucho McCarthy. Jabbering Joe and his feckless Feds were working L.A., through and through. Joe was set to serve subpoenas and roust Red cliques clicking back twenty years. Joe needed *gooooooood* publicity *baaaaaad*. Newspapers gnashed him. Radio reporters rebuffed him. TV pundits punished him for his sins. Brother, I empathize. We're both Men to Be Seen.

I hid out at the Larchmont listening post and listened to listless dead air. I killed dusk and half the nite there. Connie called nobody, nobody called her. I dozed and dreamed of Stretch and Claire, nude like I'd never seen them. I woke up and drove two blocks to here.

Late nite becomes me. 1:00 became 2:00. I noticed empty milk bottles outside Connie's front door. I got This Nutty Notion That Just Might Work.

Time ticked. I chain-smoked and chewed Chiclets. The milkman arrived at 4:13 a.m. He grabbed the empty bottles and left a fresh four-pack. I grabbed my sodium secobarbital stash and removed eight capsules. Connie might mix milk with her morning coffee. If so, she's cooked.

I walked up to the door. I pulled off the bottle caps and whipped in my witches' brew. Four bottles/eight pills/Freddy O.'s merry milk shake. I shook the bottles and condensed the contents. I slid back to my sled to wait.

Dawn dimmed nightfall. Low clouds closed in and reigned rain. Connie opened her front door at 7:14. It was quick. She filched the four-pack and went back inside.

I waited. Waiting wilts me and wears me thin. I waited, regardless. 7:14 to 8:14. One hour, no more. She's had coffee or she hasn't. The kitchen's the likely location. It's peepable. Note those low windows facing the driveway.

I peeper-popped over. I peeped one window, two windows, three. There's Connie. She's passed out flat on the kitchen floor. There's spilled coffee au lait. She's inviting me in.

My #6 pick fit the keyhole. The back door wiggled wide open. I cut into the kitchen. Connie snored. She should inhabit Dreamsville for ten to twelve hours. I had time for a top-end toss.

The kitchen. Chromium and bleached-blond wood. Nothing succulent or suspicious. The living room. All mid-century modern miasma and murky abstract art. A blitzkrieg of black leather. Glare off glass walls. A Kandinskyesque carpet, cobalt-colored and loaded with goofball gewgaw shapes. Nothing succulent or suspicious. Just Connie's suspect taste.

I checked the downstairs bathroom. Nothing nudged me. I walked upstairs. No surprises sandbagged me, straight off. One bathroom/one bedroom/one office. I always work up to women's bedrooms. I checked the bathroom first.

No, *nein*, *nyet*. Cold-cobalt walls and threadbare throw rugs. No medicine-chest *mishpokeh*—no dizzy dope/no ribbed rubbers/no diaphragm dusted with cornstarch.

The office. Here it gets *gooooooood*.

Note the *red* walls. They're all poster-pinned. It's a treasonous triptych. Free the Scottsboro Boys!!!!! Communism is 20th Century Americanism!!!!! Ben Shahn's screechy screed: "You have not converted a man because you have silenced him."

I grabbed my crotch. Hey, Connie—convert *this*, you Red Reptile!!!!!

There's a desk/a swivel chair/a typewriter. There's three drawers packed with dumb desk supplies. Connie's column for today was tucked in the typewriter. The Marlborough School for Girls, the winter '54 ball, the Hancock Park elite attends.

I checked the top drawer. There's a red leather diary marked "1954." Yesterday was March 20. I dipped to the date and read *this*:

"I fear what I presume will be Senator McCarthy's last stand before a long-overdue U.S. Senate censure. I fear what will happen when less strident anti-Communists take up the cause that once he owned and has now all too overtly besmirched, and that those subtle fascists will assume an aura of respectability. I fear that my Party membership will be exposed, along with those in my cell—which seems likely, as Senator Joe has set up shop here in Los Angeles, rather covertly, and seems determined to do damage to those I love in the city that I love and call home. All of us have sworn allegiance to the Soviet Union. How could any sane person not? But I fear that we will never have the chance to put forth our public case, as we conduct our more pertinent tasks in secret. McCarthy has been our most consistent goad and the most persistent face of fascist vituperation since the early days in Korea. What will happen when he goes? We require intense persecution to prove the solvency of our war on capital. We must never be tolerated. Tolerance militates against revolution. We must be violently opposed, so that our reaction in kind will be considered the only true and sane reaction by the oppressed masses that we strive to liberate."

Woooo!!!!! That is some dippy dialectic and convoluted confusion!!!!! Connie's a stagnant Stalinist—with Uncle Joe now a year dead!!!!!

I dipped diary pages backward. It was more, more, more—maladroitly more of the same. I hit February 17. Simple sentiment stunned me and stopped me in my tracks.

"JMH is dead. *She* is dead, the only *she* I've ever known. It was in the papers and briefly on the radio. The police suspect a burglary gone awry."

I flipped back to New Year's. It was all agitprop and agitation. I got no more Joan jolts, no incriminating initials, no named names.

I bopped to the bedroom. I saw more red walls. They were garlanded with Goyaesque portraits of women. *Ooooh*—they were nuke-bomb nude and clad in the wicked wardrobe of revolution. They wore black boots and fur-trimmed hats emblazoned with hammer and scythe. They wielded whips and laid the lash on men marked "Fascist Oppressor."

I *got* it. It's Goya as comic-book artiste. It's savage satire. It's the annihilating antithesis of Connie Woodard's *tooooooooo*-tame life as a Hearst hack. It's communism as contraband pornography. It's a staggering strain of the jejune jive *WE ALL* jerk off to. It's the jack-off juvenilia that has enslaved half the world.

I opened a closet door. Connie's spinster threads channeled Chanel No. 5. A top shelf featured comely camisoles and slithery slips. I ran a hand under them. Scented envelopes slid out. I knew they were lesbian love letters.

I let the butch billet-doux lie. A file cabinet couched against the wall caught my eye. Three file drawers. All unlocked. I tornado-tore through them.

Red-leather diaries. Connie's Red message, beaming back to '38. The Moscow show trials. Connie justifies Stalin's purges. She confoundingly cosigns death, death, and more death. There's photographs tucked between pages. Connie cultivates young women and preens proud with them. Perdition, catch my soul—there She is.

Connie and Joan Hubbard. A UCLA backdrop. The foto is dated 8/12/41. There's Joan. She's twenty-two. It's faded Kodachrome color. Connie's russet-haired and knock-kneed at forty. Joan wears a red beret.

I tore through Connie's August '41 diary. I went to 8/12/41 and found *this*:

"I spent time with Joan H. today. I think she's ready to join the Party. I told her my cell was small and all were utterly loyal to one another. She'd be safe there."

It wasn't enough. I wanted more of what all of this was. I found diaries dated up to 1946. Connie's prose went crypto-clipped. Initials replaced names. "All of this" had to be Commie cell minutes.

I hit my first "JH" in May '42. I followed "JH" at weekly intervals, up through V-J Day. "*JH,*" "*JH,*" "*JH.*" My Joan's a certified subversive.

I know who "CW" is. Who's "SA"? Who's "RJC"? Who's "EPD"? I didn't know and didn't care. I only wanted Joan's name and Connie's scent on the pages.

JH, JH, JH. She's mine throughout the war years. She's left UCLA. I'm in the Marine Corps and dodging combat duty. She translates for the California State Senate. I join LAPD. JH, JH, JH. We're into '46 now. I'll murder Joan's husband in three years' time—

Googie's. My unfailing fallback and righteous retreat. The Tattle Tyrant held sway here. *Confidential* was king. Bondage Bob Harrison's handouts bought me all the love I could take.

Late-a.m. tipsters almost toppled my table. Orson Welles snuffed the Black Dahlia. The rumor raged now. I told the tipsters to fuck off and bought them off with chump change. Joe McCarthy's in town. No shit, Sherlock. Yeah—but he's shacked at the Chateau Marmont with Danny Kaye. Okay—here's ten scoots, don't bug me, my heart's heavy, and I'm all alone with some shattering shit.

Boo-hoo, boo-hoo. I'm in existential exile. I've got boocoo opportunity, but the love eludes me.

I wolfed pancakes and pondered my doofus dilemma. I told my wetback waiter to bring me a phone. I called Harry Fremont at the City Hall DB. Harry boo-hoo'd me. He hadn't rigged a ruse or devised a diversion to get me inside Casa Connie. I told him I got inside. I trashed my tracks and blew a blistering shot at reentry. In the meantime, I'll pay you to do *this*:

There's Feds in town. They may be running rogue. They're jungled up in jumpy juju with Joe McCarthy. They must have a field office somewhere. Find them and suborn them with Bondage Bob's payola. I need three hours with their files.

Harry said, "And this pertains to Joanie?"

I said, "Yeah—it sure as shit does."

Harry coughed up compliance. I hung up. Claire Klein and Rock Hudson sat down with me. They held hands. I held up my hand and showed them my stigmata. Claire laffed. Rock went *Huh?*

They looked good together. They glowed. They were actors

to their core. They were Strasbergites maimed by the Method. The homo heartthrob marries the sicko psychopath. This mock marriage sends them, Daddy-O.

Rock said, "You're green at the gills, Freddy. You should take a Bromo and hit the sack."

Claire said, "Freddy has things on his mind."

I laffed. "Have you set a date yet?"

Rock lit a cigarette. "Jimmy's working on it. He's with Liz and me on *Giant*, you know. He thinks two ceremonies is the way to go. Claire's Jewish, and I'm a Presbyterian. Jimmy wants to emphasize the interfaith angle. You know, one synagogue gig, and one church gig."

Claire lit a cigarette. "There's no need for Rock to convert. I know a rabbi who performs a good ceremony and works cheap. We met in the Sinai, back in '48."

Rock said, "Claire's got a history."

I said, "Don't I know it."

Autograph hounds hit the table. Rock threw up his hands and winked at Claire. *I'm in demand, babe.*

Claire winked at me. Rock signed autographs. Claire slipped me a note under the table. I peeped the piece of paper.

Tipster Claire. The insidious insider. She's got news on the celeb smut film.

The start date had been moved up. They shoot tonight. Here's the address. It's an abandoned motel in Cathedral City.

The Jolly Jinx Motel. A desert dump. Off a deep-rut road between Indio and Palm Springs. It's sandwiched by sand dunes and next door to nowhere. It's a baleful bank foreclosure, circa '31.

It's a film set tonite. *Thirteen Women and Only One Man in Town.* Steve "L'Auteur" Cochran mans the megaphone. The Jinx is a horseshoe-shaped hellhole. There's twelve beat-to-shit bungalows, sans doors. Note the parked cars. Note the arc lights outside bungalows 8,9, and 10. Note the camera up on casters and the boom mike. There's a cameraman and a soundman. I've seen them at

Googie's. They're headed-for-hell hopheads and rancid racetrack touts.

Dig: it's *finito*. The A-bomb wipes out the world. It's Steve the Stud's delicious duty to repopulate it. He's got titillating talent to siphon his seed and assist. Joi Lansing, Anita O'Day, and Babs Payton. Plus ten call girls headed for Holly*weird* stardom and felony smut raps.

I hid hip-deep in a high sand dune. I brought binoculars and Bernie Spindel's sound-receiver. It was battery-juiced and sent sound to headphones-cum-earmuffs. The set was forty yards down. I had open-door and smashed-window sight lines. The arc lights and malignant moonglow made me Johnny-on-the-spot.

The courtyard was Cochran's command post. Steve mingled with the thirteen lucky ladies. They wore crocheted bikinis cut hairpie *looooooow*. The girls scrolled script copies and learned their lines. They moved their lips and traded quips.

"How can we live with such devastation?" and "I don't want our kids growing up with Strontium-90 in their bones." Joi said, "First, we've got to have the kids. Do you think Big Steve's up to the task? The motel is the Garden of Eden. Big Steve is our Adam, and all thirteen of us are his Eves." Babs said, "I heard he's hung like a barracuda." Anita said, "People blame the Communists and the Soviet Union for everything bad in the world. But I say, 'Let he who is without sin cast the first stone.'" And, dig: "It's the good old USA who A-bombed the Japs."

Ooohhh—Studly Steve's script toes the repugnant Red line. Shuddering shades of Red Connie Woodard!!!

Steve walked actress to actress. He pulled down their bikini tops and *looooooow*-leveled the bottoms. The arc lights lit hairpie glow. Steve lined up the cast. They stood thirteen strong. The nite was cold. Goose bumps popped pandemic. Steve microphone-mauled his talent pool.

"*Achtung, meine Kinder*. Comrade Steve speaks, and your job as my Fertility Guard is to listen. We're shooting scene one now. Bungalow nine has been decorated with some Nazi gear I've collected.

Babs portrays Hilda, She-Wolf of the SS. My job is to impregnate and reindoctrinate her. Chop, chop, comrades. Babs and crew to bungalow nine. The rest of you huddle up in your cars and stay warm."

Twelve girls beat feet out of the courtyard. Steve and Babs as Hilda hit Bungalow 9. The camera guy and sound guy followed them. The setup took six seconds. I had live sound and a smashed-window view. Roll it, Big Steve.

Lights, camera, action. Big Steve rolls it. The camera caught the swastika wall banners and the rising-sun bedspread. Steve as Adam and Babs as Hilda squared off.

Steve/Adam: "Look, you fascist bitch, you've got to atone for your sins and submit to reeducation, like Comrade Stalin did with the Moscow trials in the '30s."

Babs/Hilda: "Don't sound me, *muchacho.* The Moscow trials were a shuck—and I know it because I subscribe to *Klansman* magazine. I'm hip to geeks like you. If you think you're going to repopulate the world with me, you'd better stow the lecture and show me what I'm getting into."

Steve/Adam whips it out. Man, what a *schvantz*!!!

Babs/Hilda says, "I'm impressed, but *der Führer* was bigger. Eva Braun told me he packed a hard yard. But I guess twelve inches is better than nothing, especially if the fate of the world is at stake."

Steve/Adam says, "I'm radioactive, baby!!! You know what I want!!!"

Babs goes *woo-woo* and shucks her bikini. Big Steve dumps his duds. They forgo foreplay. They hop on the Jap bedspread and instigate insertion. Steve's a two-minute man. It's over that quixotically quick. Steve climbs to a climax and wails in rapturous Russian. *Say what?* Babs/Hilda chortles and lights a cigarette.

The whole night went listlessly likewise. Up to the pustulating point that it changed.

Babs/Hilda does it with Steve. Ditto Anita as Nuke-Bomb Nellie. Joi plays Evil Eve. She does it with Steve—and fails to jolt me jealous. The collective call girls strip and dog-pile Big Steve. Half the sizzle sex fizzles. Steve can't get it up. He's a wilted wonder boy. His beast is bushed. He's auf Wiedersehen, adios, sadly sayonara. His priapus is *proschai*.

I watched for hours. My vulturous voyeurism nudged toward its nadir. It bid me to boredom. Man, what a drip-dry drag.

The camera guy and sound guy packed up their shit. Steve moped around the courtyard and mumbled to his muse. I bent my binoculars to Bungalow #7. I saw Anita O'Day and Babs Payton prep jolts of Big "H."

They cooked it. They fed a spike. They tied off tourniquets. They geezed and went smack-back. They hit Cloud 9 as Steve entered the room.

He backhanded Babs. She hit the floor. Anita backed up to the bed. Steve stood over her. Anita brandished the spike. Steve grabbed it and stabbed her in the leg.

Anita screamed and sobbed. I heard it high up on my dune. Steve stormed out of the bungalow. He glowed radioactive red. The red was Strontium-90. It's got a half-life of ten thousand years. I glowed rage-red myself.

Stretch was asleep. Lance the Leopard cleaved close to her and snarled at me. They ordered room service. Lance left paw prints on the white tablecloth.

I changed clothes. I put on black gloves, black slacks, and a black turtleneck. I stopped at an all-nite novelty store on my way over. I bought a rubber red devil mask.

I tried it on. I posed in front of the bathroom mirror. I'm George Collier Akin, reborn. I capered and preened.

Havenhurst was a short shot up Sunset. I got my sled and slid there in the slow lane. I cut south and parked. It was 3:00 a.m. His lair lights still glowed.

I put the mask back on. The Red Devil Bandit resurrects. I bee-lined to his door and rang the bell.

He opened up. He screeched and backed away. Size isn't everything. I pulled my beavertail sap and bitch-backhanded him.

It tore him a high harelip and took out some teeth. The reverse shot ripped him a new widow's peak. He hit the floor like Babs Payton did.

I picked up a Russian-helmet ashtray and dumped butts on his head. I hurtled high and drop-kicked him. I heard ribs crack. Rib bones sheared out of his shirt.

He screeched. His eyes rolled back. I forced open the lids and put my red devil face upside his. He sputtered and coughed up Camels and Kool Kings. I wiped ash off my red devil face.

ROGUE FBI FIELD FACILITY

Office Building at Wilshire and Mariposa

3/22/54

Harry said, "This is pricey. I've got palms to grease. Bondage Bob'll have to dig deep on this one."

Some office. One confined cubicle. Thoroughly threadbare. Bare-bones and strictly cut-rate. It's twenty feet by twenty feet. There's three desks/three chairs. There's one file cabinet, no fone, no Teletype.

"These guys are black bag, all the way. McCarthy's kaput. He can't call old man Hoover and say, 'Hey, Johnny—I need some men to hunt Reds.'"

Harry shrugged. "They've got some Federal motor pool vehicles. At least three, by the looks of this place. Remember that plate number I ran for you? That car was checked out to these guys."

I said, "See if you can put a name to it, okay? The car might have been specifically assigned."

"Sure, kid. You and Bondage Bob say, 'Jump,' and I say, 'How high?'"

I thought it through. The word *Hollywood* hit me. I prowl Casa Connie. Her current diary drivel drills me. She fears jumped-up Joe McCarthy's last gasp and fears for her cell. Joe's working a Hollywood angle. It's in tight and spicy specific. He thinks he'll bag big names somewhere down the line. It's his loopy last hurrah. It's a

Hollywood headline hunt. Here's a hunch. He doesn't quite know where it all is or what he's got.

Harry harumphed. "Freddy, get *to* it. We've got three *hours*, not three weeks."

I popped the top file drawer. It was Bug City. Bug mounts, bug mikes, bug transceivers and cords. Plus *loooooong*-range broadcast shit. I popped the middle file drawer. It was Hurt City. Brass knucks, rubber truncheons, ball-bearing saps.

I popped the bottom file drawer. It was Rat City. A file sticker spelled it out: "Security 1-A: Coded Informant Index."

Four thin files. Thin gruel. Thin carbon sheets couched within.

File #1. Code name: "Big Duke." These notes: "No remuneration. Subject has said his motive is 'love of country.' Has numerous contacts within the entertainment industry."

I'll say. It has to be John Wayne. He's ratted Reds since the ice age. It doesn't say he's a cross-dresser. He's strictly straight—but *still*. My Marines foto-fucked him at the Big Girls Boutique in Balboa. He bought his way out of a *biiiiiiig* exposé.

File #2. Code name: "Mama Zee." These notes: "Noted writer (Negro) turned anti-Communist zealot. Has numerous contacts within the Negro community in Los Angeles."

I'll say. It has to be Zora Neale Hurston. She rats Reds to Bondage Bob. She's fetchingly featured in *Confidential*'s "Darktown Strutters' Ball" clips.

File #3. Code name: "Mr. Webfoot." These notes: "Subject hosts local L.A. kiddie show. In hock to bookmakers. Always needs $ & knows people within the CP."

I'll say. It has to be Jimmy Weldon. He's a venal ventriloquist. Webster Webfoot's a downscale Donald Duck. Jimmy's a Googie's geek. He peddles piles of the Carole Landis nude morgue pix.

File #4. Code name: "Redbird." No summary notes. One bank-deposit summary.

The deposits ran from March '47 up to last month. $150 per week. '47 to '54. Almost seven full years. Account #8309. The bank branch: the B of A at Melrose and Cahuenga.

I'LL SAY. Melrose and Cahuenga. It's four blocks from the Horvath House of Death. Red Stromwall found a B of A passbook in Joan's undie drawer. The balance: fourteen g's. The weekly snitch pay stopped last month. Joan Horvath *esta muerto.*

I'll say. What would you say? How does this sound to you?

My Joan. Communist Party infiltrator/FBI snitch.

I'm a Pervdog. We're nativistically nocturnal. Our genus genuflects at moon fall and comes alive at nite. We seek succor in the scent of secret lives, half hidden. We peep, prowl, break, enter, *SEEK.*

Day dimmed to dusk. I parked across the street from Connie Woodard's house. I was half gone on high-test lemonade. The Pervdog percolates.

I holed up at the Larchmont listening post, all afternoon. I called the B of A branch at Melrose and Cahuenga. I impersonated Joe Fed. I demanded the name attached to account #8309. The timid teller gave it up: Joan Hubbard Horvath.

It felt right. It felt wrong. I reacted, reflexive. I sought Connie Woodard's scent.

I hooked on headphones. I caught calls. Connie called her cleaner's and a Chevy dealership. I heard backup bips on my line. My hackles heaved.

The *looooong*-range transceiver. It's packed at the pathetic pocket office. It's expensive equipment. It hints of a centralized eavesdrop apparatus. Jolting Joe McCarthy. Not as pointedly pathetic as one might think? Communist Connie—quite possibly bugged and tapped?

Rain clouds eclipsed the moon I came to howl at. The sky unzipped and ripped rain. I ran my heater and warmed my canine coat. Connie Woodard walked out her front door.

She wore a formal kilt ensemble. A tartan sash was cinched across her embroidered black crepe blouse. Tartan pleats ran down to her knock-knees. White kneesocks and black brogues filled the ensemble out.

She shagged her '52 Chevy and cut southbound. It felt right. It felt wrong. I felt summoned suddenly. *Take note of what you are seeking, for it is seeking you.* Some sweaty swami said that. I get it now, Daddy-O.

I walked across the street and picked the back-door lock. Connie left the kitchen lights on. She left lurid leads out in plain sight.

The broken milk-bottle glass and milk mulch in the sink.

The Milk of Magnesia bottle on the counter. Milk of Magnesia absorbs ingested barbiturates.

Connie's coldly outraged. She's been vilely violated. She's left those leads out to address me. You contemptible coward—will you fling your hands high and flee?

I wimp-wavered. I almost flipped out and fled. Her summons seduced me. I ran upstairs instead.

Connie left the bedroom lights on. I went straight to her clothes closet and her scent. I opened her file drawers. She left her 1949 diary out and bookmarked for me. 9/10/49. Connie carves her pen across the initials JH and scrawls *"Traitor"* boldface.

I sat in a red leather chair. The red walls closed in on me. I pulled my roscoe and jammed it under the seat cushion. I looked over at the bed. She'd left those lezbo love letters out for me to read.

Take note of what you are seek—

I read at them and through them. I looked for the name Joan and/or the initials JH. They weren't there. There were no torrid texts. It was all *kiss* and *swerve* and *breath* and *scent*. I failed to determine gender or genus—male/female/moon-mad beast.

I shut my eyes. I summoned seconds of safety and solace and slid into sleep. It was *kiss* and *swerve* and *breath* and *scent* and scent on wool and black crepe. *Take note of—*

I stirred and stretched and saw her. She stood by the bed. She held a Makarov automatic. The kilt ensemble caught me and held me. She was fifty-two. We're May and September. She dressed this way to meet me. It's some furtive first or one-and-only blind date.

I said, "Redbird. You must know that this is about her."

She said, "There's some high points here. She betrayed the Party, and you killed her husband. I saw your photograph in the paper. I thought, He is certainly a young man who intends to go places, and you certainly have. 'Tattle Tyrant' suits you, but 'Peeping Tom' and 'Slander Merchant' might be more apt."

I sprawled. She stood. Her bed stood between us. I felt underdressed and outmaneuvered and called out in calm contempt. She's verging on rude rebuke, and I still want to touch her.

"You're wearing battle kit. I saw you at Jack Kennedy's bomb party, and you didn't evince this sort of flair. I've found some things out about you, and you know me by reputation. That stands as the basis of some sort of discussion. I'm a peeper, and you want me to see you. You left your diary and your letters out for me to read. You're begging a stranger who's assaulted your home and your person for intimate comprehension, and I want to know why."

She messed with her Makarov. She had fast hands. She racked out the round in the chamber and popped out the clip. She tossed it on the red leather chair. My piece was stuffed under the cushion.

" 'Intimate comprehension.' It works both ways, you know. Perhaps I should tell you what I know about you, so that we might turn this into an opportunity."

I said, "Tell me."

She said, "I was in love with Joan Horvath. You weren't the only one inclined to park outside her house and moon. I've counted the money you left in her mailbox on more than one occasion, and I'm convinced that you intend to kill the person who killed her, since the man that you've already killed certainly didn't do it. You have my consent for this, and my word that I won't report the act, or any act that might have transpired between us up to this point."

I said, "I've read your diaries. Comrade, your whole life's a deception. Your word's about as good as mine is, and that's hardly an indictment."

She put one knee on the bed. Tartan battle kit. The pleats/the wool/the scent. One long leg exposed.

"It's all about Joan, you see. It's your willingness to act, and my willingness to suborn your intention. I would never betray anyone who possessed the grit to do what you intend to do, despite my shoddy track record with veracity for its own sake."

I stood up. Connie stood still. I reached under the seat cushion and grabbed my piece. I have fast hands. I racked out the chamber round, popped the clip, and tossed it all on the bed.

Connie said, "Say her name."

I said, "Joan."

She said, "Well, then."

I said, "I intend to see you again."

She said, "Yes, of course."

I made for the door and brushed by her. I touched her back and nuzzled her hair. She leaned into me one mad moment.

INFERNAL INTERMEZZO:

My Furtively Fucked-up Life

3/23–4/4/54

It started like that. We were joined in Joan and forged in forgiveness. Sex saturated us. I've decided to dim the details by dint of decorum. "Freddy & Connie." Initials cutely carved on a tree. I'm thirty-two, she's fifty-two. You know what *I* am. Connie Woodard defies cloying classification. Commie, lezbo, sweltering switch-hitter. Take your punk pick. She's all of it, some of it, none of it.

I'm being dizzy disingenuous. Connie's a righteous Red. She's a treasonous true believer with her hooks hitched into me. I'm foiled and fucked five thousand ways. Perdition, catch my soul. And she won't let me all-the-way *SEE* her.

I needed names to know her and to know who killed Joan. Known associates, rancid Reds, fractured front-group front men. Fellow travelers, pusillanimous pinks, lily-livered leftists. Give me names/no, I won't/Connie takes the *farshtinkener* Fifth Amendment. Tell me the names of your Commie cell mates. I've already memorized their initials. Who's SA? Who's RJC? Who's EPD? I've scurvily skimmed your diaries—and I'm tweaked. I told you I killed the Red Devil Bandit in cold blood. You must reciprocate in kind.

No, Freddy. I'm your recidivistic refusenik. Besides, there's one name that you've withheld from me.

Yes, that's true. I refused to name Claire Klein. I equivocated here. I told Connie that a dangerous woman was orbiting her orbit. She wants to kill a man—but she won't tell me why. She won't *name* the man. She's my other ripe refusenik. I'm not naming her. She's one of the other two women that I love.

"Freddy & Claire." "Freddy & Stretch." More names cutely carved on a tree. Unconsummated communions. That's fine for now. I'm beat-to-shit busy. I've got to find a man and kill him, myself.

Connie won't name names. I vow to kill Joan's killer. Connie won't name names. I vow to jerk Joe McCarthy's chain so that he won't expose her. Connie *still* won't name names. Why's Jack Kennedy's name in your address book? Oh, *pshaw*—Jack's just an old pal. Why's Steve Cochran's name in your address book? Here, Connie withers and wilts me: he was my last tortured and torturing male lover—before you.

I'm thirteen days in with Constance Linscott Woodard. It's tender and tortured. I'm beat-to-shit busy. I'm rolling lucky and unlucky thirteens.

Lucky 13: Harry Fremont frosted out my assault on Big Steve. He greased the Sheriff's bulls investigating the caper. They put it off to a B and E man out to clout Big Steve's Nazi gear. *Unlucky* 13: *Thirteen Women and Only One Man in Town* debuted a week later.

In Harry Cohn's rec room. Popcorn and cut-rate booze. I'm there. Big Steve's there. He's beat-to-shit bandaged and mummified like Pharaoh's granddaddy. Jack the K.'s there. Bill Knowland's there. They yuk-yuk and wolf-whistle. Joe McCarthy's there, his own self.

The flick made me squirrelshit squeamish. I've got no beef with the A-bomb. We should have mushroomed Moscow after we juked the Japs. Joi Lansing was my ex, and I had a wolfish wingding with Babs Payton. It was the *sex*ploitation aspect. That's what gored my goat.

Bondage Bob bagged me outside the rec room. He said he was killing the Cochran exposé. Big Steve was tight with some powerful pols. He pimped for Jack K. He juiced Jack's pill habit. Freddy, let this one go.

I did. It rudely rankled me. I compensated, commensurate. I bore down big on the who-killed-Joan and the spare-Connie-from-Joe McCarthy fronts.

I gave Harry Fremont a *gooooood* gig. The rogue Feds *had* to have a long-range listening post. Find it for me, Dads. Lucky 13: Harry hit it, hard. *Un*lucky 13: I found bugs and taps in Connie's living room and bedroom. Lucky 13: they were mismounted and mismatched and malfunctioned. The broadcast beams barely made it next door.

Lucky 13: Stretch worked my Sweetzer listening post. *Un*lucky 13: she picked up Lez Line #2 chat. Claire Klein tricked with V. J. Jerome. She pressed him on "Robin Redbreast"—but venal V.J. purported to know zilch. Claire pressured him on Connie Woodard. V.J. said, "Don't sound me—she's just a dilettante." Stretch told me his tone was deadly demeaning. V.J., you speak with forked tongue.

Thirteen days. I want names. Claire wants names. V.J. won't name names. Connie won't name names, most of all.

I vow to find Joan's killer. Connie won't name names. I vow to save her from Joe McCarthy. Connie won't name names. We make love. We pillow-talk around the whirlwind woman who brought us together. Connie won't name names. She won't say whether she and Joan did or didn't do the deed and were or were not rapture-rapt lovers.

I read Connie's diaries. The sex sent me. It remained *kiss* and *swerve*, *breath* and *scent*. I read through years of Commie collusion. Delusion deluged me. Pathos pounded me. Connie and her cell siblings suck up Soviet yak-yak and proudly proclaim it as truth. They dialecticize purulent purges, cold conquest, mass murder. Connie says she's Sovietizing me. I roll my eyes. It makes her laugh. She covers her mouth then. Some Central Committee of Kremlin kreeps might be listening.

Connie won't name names. She won't reveal Robin Redbreast's real moniker. She won't name names. I'm on her side as much as she'll let me be—and more. She won't name names in Joan's memory. She memorializes Joan and tells me how much she loved her. She loves me with her body and won't say the worshipful words. I explore the world's secret shit. I excoriate it and explode it in *Confidential*. I live to do this. I've peeped windows since 1936. Connie joined the Party that same year. She joined the Party to run rogue in the squarejohn world and live *baaaad* bourgeois while she did it. We bit the same cancerous coin and spit it back at the world. Shared blood blooms in our veins. We both know this. She still won't name names.

THE SWEETZER LISTENING POST

4/5/54

The noxious nite shift. Torrid two-line tilts. Pizza pie and beer and Pink's hot dogs. Stretch worked Lez Line #1. I worked Lez Line #2. We held hands and swapped nifty nuggets.

Gamal Abdel Nasser's in town. He's scrounging funds to overthrow Egypt. He's a fellow camel jockey. He's banging butch girls, three at a throw. Go, Gamal, go!!!

Biff Stanwyck's ensconced at a hot-sheet hut on Highland. She likes it fresh and heavenly wholesome. There's a dyke slave den near Hollywood High. The den doyenne's an old studio scrape nurse. She "reeducates" nymphets and feeds them dope and the lewd lore of Lesbos. Currently embroiled: ex–kiddie star Natalie Wood. Jimmy Dean told me she's hot to trot, across the sex spectrum. Biff's got first dibs.

Art Pepper's at it again. He's gone foto fiend. He's now the King of the Sapphic Snapshot. He's snapping pix at a fuck pad on Fountain. Go, Art, go!!!

I was big-time bored. My headphones itched. Lance went home to Liberace. Stretch and I boo-hoo'd his departure. The lez line pickings were thin—but tasty. Then Harry Fremont called, two hours back. Go, Harry, go!!! Once again, Harry delivers.

That Fed car. The rear plate I saw. Outside the Horvath crime scene. It's on loan to a Fed fuck named Charles Fullerton. He's in

Joe McCarthy's posse. He's a rogue Red basher from Jump Street. And, Freddy, dig: I've located the longrange listening post. It's a shit shack in Silver Lake. They're running bug-taps up the yammering ying-yang. I hit my PC Bell contact. Dig: the phone bills run three grand a month.

Woooo!!!—that's one nifty nugget!!!

I yawned. I scratched my balls. I ogled Stretch in basketball silks. I got insistently itchy. I wanted to *slooooooooow*-cruise the Fed pad and lay some late-nite love on Connie.

I yawned. I scratched my balls. I ogled Stretch in basketball silks. She went *Wowie-zowie* and scribbled up her scratch pad. She hurled off her headset and went *You, too.*

I hurled my headset. Stretch *glooooowed* and dished *this*:

"Claire and Babs just tricked with V. J. Jerome. I got forty minutes of grunts and groans, and then Claire starts pumping V.J. on Robin Redbreast again. V.J.'s vexed and bored, but he *finally* cops that Robin Redbreast was a crackpot scientist and a CP flunky named 'Sammy.' But that's as far as it went, because they all started up with the woof-woof again."

We lounged in the red bedroom. Connie wore a half-slip and her tartan skirt. I was stripped down to my skivvies. We ran the radio. Some Russki piano putz rippled Rachmaninoff.

I was *toooooo* tense and caught-up constricted. I went by the Fed pad and reconnoitered. I got a Big Dumb Idea. It was cold-calculated and meant to make Connie name names.

Connie lay languorous. We stretched and struck poses and draped off the bed. I kissed Connie's knock knees. She ran her hands through my hair.

"Don't start hounding me again, dear. My lips are sealed, and I won't let you ruin this lovely moment."

I parted her legs and tossed her skirt and kissed my way up a bit. Connie made this soft sound that she makes.

"*I'll* name some names that you might recognize. You don't have to respond, but I'd be happy if you would."

Connie laffed. "It's our ongoing game, isn't it? Freddy interrogates Connie. Connie takes the Fifth. Freddy and Connie. Has it ever occurred to you that our names lack dignity?"

I smiled. Connie said, "I'll indulge you, if you promise that you won't press me too hard. I'm out to sustain this mood that I'm in."

I pulled her skirt down and patted it back into place. I looked up at her and fixed on her eyes. I'd know if she dissembled or flat-lied to me. I'd know if she knew the names and went refusenik.

"Robin Redbreast. He's allegedly a 'crackpot scientist' and a Party flunky named Sammy. There's also an FBI man named Charles Fullerton. He was at Joan's house with all the other cops, and I saw him there myself. You should know that he's in Joe McCarthy's posse—which is, quite frankly, out to get you, given the bugs and taps that I've pulled here."

Bingo/Eureka/Three-Cherry Jackpot. The refusenik reacts. Tears fill her eyes. Her hands fly to her face.

I know you, Constance. You'll wipe your face on a pillowcase. You'll light a cigarette and blow smoke at the ceiling. You'll say, "No comment" or "I'm not telling you."

I nailed the first part. I blew the second part. Connie said, "You're never going to quit, are you? You will always insist on this, and in the end, I'll either lose you or never have a moment's peace."

I pulled myself up close to her. I got our eyes close.

"Sammy. Charles Fullerton. The 'SA,' 'RJC,' and 'EPD' in your cell. I want full names and confirmations. It's all for Joan. You know that's true, and since you're a dialectical materialist who's always looking for a payoff, I'll offer you a doozy if you'll do this for me."

Connie kissed me. I wiped some tears off with my thumbs. She kissed me again. I pulled her slip up and kissed her bare back.

"'A doozy,' you said?"

"Yes. If you tell me what I need to know, I'll burn down the McCarthy gig. You'll never set foot on a witness stand. It'll spare some other people a good deal of grief, whether they're for-real traitors, or just bleeding-heart fools like you."

Connie said, "It's not nice to betray your friends, you know. People you've lived History with."

I said, "Joan."

Connie said, "We'll always come back to her. She's our deus ex machina."

I said, "Joan." Connie stubbed out her cigarette and turned back to me.

"Yes, we were briefly lovers, and that's as far as I'll go to sate your curiosity there. Charles Fullerton turned Joan out as an FBI informant, and served as her handler for years. He also introduced Joan to Ralph Horvath. Sammy is a physicist named Samuel Ahlendorf—and, yes, he was Robin Redbreast in our cell. 'RJC' was a Negro man named Robert Jones Crawshaw. He wrote for the *Daily Worker*, and now he writes cheap paperbacks about Negro pimps. I know that he's friends with your friend Billy Eckstine, for what that's worth. 'EDP' is Eleanor Price Donnell. She was one of Joan's professors at UCLA."

She snitched. It hit me six ways from Sunday. I rolled away from her. I stared at the red walls and faux-Goya garlands of women. Connie clung claustrophobe close.

" 'The citadel of my integrity has been irrevocably lost.' That's from T. E. Lawrence, in case you were wondering."

I wasn't. "Don't shit a shitter, and don't playact with me. It was the right thing to do."

Connie stage-sighed. "I'm twenty years, one month, and nine days older than you. I was born in 1902, and you're in love with two other women. Why did I do what I just did? Am I really that desperate to keep you?"

I stage-sighed. "You're just self-absorbed. Are all Communists as self-involved as you?"

Connie laffed. "Frankly, yes."

"Including Joan?"

"Yes, and Joan more than most."

I said, "She made the rounds, didn't she? Men, women—she had the appetite."

Connie said, "She was faithless, yes."

I said, "I'm sorry about that."

"Don't be, dear. You're like that yourself."

I pulled down her skirt. I caught her scent and kissed her breasts.

"I've fulfilled my part of the bargain, dear. How will you derail the evil senator and save me?"

"I'll do something brave and stupid, and it will damn well cost me a great deal."

Research. Reading-room rigor. Know your foe. They might have YOU made, going in. You're the Tattle Tyrant Who Holds Hollywood Hostage. You're the Freewheeling Freddy O.

I felt *goooooood*. Connie fed me a big breakfast. I chased it with three dexies and four jolts of Old Crow. I hit the library early. I collated a cavalcade of *goooooood* dish. I tapped solid sources.

The *L.A. Herald* and the *L.A. Sentinel*—L.A.'s colored rag. *Who's Who In America/1953*. *Who's Who In American Academia/1953*. Plus *Downbeat* magazine, the *Daily Worker*, and a call to LAPD R & I.

Dig:

Comrade Sammy Ahlendorf. Age sixty-three. That's "Robin Redbreast" to you. He's a physicist. He got doctorates in his native Russia and the U. of Chicago here. He's also a kultural kommissar. He partied with bibulous bohemians in wicked Weimar Berlin and malignant Moscow. He knew Eisenstein/Nijinsky/Stanislavsky/Meyerhold/Okhlopkov. Sicko cinema, dipshit dance, stilted stage productions for the maimed millions enslaved by the Red Beast. Sambo emigrates to the U.S., circa '36. He's dumped off the Manhattan Project, circa '44. He was pro-A-bomb then. He's anti-A-bomb now. This guy gored my goat. I was hopped-up and out for Commo blood—*baaaaaad*. I might phone-book Sambo in the studly style of the Hat Squad.

Comrade Robert Jones Crawshaw/aka *"KKKomrade X."* Age forty-one. Labor agitator and scurvy scribe for the *Daily Worker*. Would-be "Racial Reconciler." Dig this: He tried to integrate the L.A. Klan, circa '40. Close pal of my pal Billy Eckstine. The august author of *Black Pimp, Black Bossman, Black Savior, Black Dictator, Black Kingpin, Black Bwana,* and the KKKontroversial *Black Führer*. Comrade Bob renounces Communism, circa '51. Comrade Bob heads hard right. He's pals with nativist *nudnik* Gerald L. K. Smith. He's got a righteous rap sheet. There's three pops for receiving stolen goods. There's the cancerous capper, circa '48. Ralph Mitchell Horvath bails him out on a burglary beef.

Comrade Eleanor Price Donnell. Age thirty-eight. Tenured history professor at UCLA. She's a shrill shrike and shrieky Soviet suck-up. She's the author of *Moscow Miasma*—an apoplectic apologia for the show-trial sins of Uncle Joe Stalin. You think you've got this bilious babe pegged, don't you? Well, fuckers, here's the *real* reconstructionist riff:

She's an ex–call girl. She pandered poon to the Party, circa '44–'45. She sold sex to CPers with gelt. She was part of a poor-working-girls/Stalinist stable. She gets popped V-E Day. A cadre of Commie construction magnates celebrates Hitler's surrender. It's caviar and call girls for these cats. La Donnell and her sick sisters turn tricks for striking dock workers. LAPD Vice intervenes. They raid a fuck pad-cum-millionaire's mansion. La Donnell and eighteen other confessed Commie girls get busted. La Donnell writes a memoir about her salacious sojourn. It's called *Party Girl*. She wrote it under the pseudonym "Miss X." Robert Jones Crawshaw's publisher published it.

My Connie's Commie cell. Add on the late Joan Hubbard Horvath: Commo, turncoat, licentious lover. Here's the tattle-tabloid tilt of a lifetime:

I'm marching into the maximum maw of madness.

—m—

They all lived in L.A. I installed an itinerary—north/south/north-west. Comrade Sam lived in the Valley. Comrade Bob lived in Watts. Billy Eckstine set the meet at Club Zombie. Comrade Ellie lived on the Wilshire corridor. It was *très* close to UCLA.

Sambo and Party Girl were door knocks. Knock, Knock—trouble treads your way. I'd browbeat them. I'd bring them to tears. I'd dig for the dish on Comrade Joan Hubbard. I'd yank them through the war years. I'd push the Claire Klein angle. This dangerous dame is out to kill a man. She thinks Connie Woodard might know him. So, how about *you*?

I bopped out to bumfuck Van Nuys. The Valley Vista Villas—hotbox huts off Hastings and Harlequin Heights. I parked and popped up to the pad. *Knock, knock*—trouble treads your—

Sambo opened up. *Ooohhh*—he's threadbare thin and cancer cough–consumptive. I flashed my State Police badge. All the HUAC humps had them. *Cringe, you Red rat fink.*

"Yes. I've seen that badge before. It's not like you people haven't sought me out in the past."

I said, "This is a new wrinkle, boss. It pertains to the murder of a woman named Joan Horvath. You knew her as Joan Hubbard."

Sambo let me in. He rolled an oxygen tank to his chair. He sucked air. He cancer-coughed and said, "Yes?"

I perched on a footstool. "I'm not here to nail you for your CP membership, pops. You should know that going in."

Sambo said, "That's white of you—and uninformed. I left the CP in '44, before I got cleared for the Manhattan Project. I was the first one to abandon the cell I was in, although all of the others, except for our den mother, ultimately saw the light."

The statement stunned me. Connie's diaries ditzed me. I saw Sambo's initials on cell minutes for the postwar period.

"I have documents, sir. These documents plainly state that you attended cell wingdings up to the late '40s."

Sambo sighed and sucked air. "Then they're fabrications. Especially if the den mother proffered them to you. I'm an apostate, Mr. Detective. I renounced the Party, and I've been vetted by a great number of committees, both State and Federal. And if Mr. McCarthy should subpoena me for this latest pogrom of his, I'll testify to that at the outset. You look like McCarthy, I might add. You share his black-haired, beetle-browed look."

Fuck you, pops—I got your beetle brows swinging!!!

"Joan Horvath, sir. She was Hubbard when you knew her."

"Yes, and I had an affair with that very lively and brilliant young woman, and I think you're bright enough to have deduced that I'm in no condition to drive to Hollywood, break into a house, and commit murder."

Esta la verdad, Daddy-O—I sound you loud and clear.

"What did you think of Joan?"

"I thought she was the single most self-absorbed human being I've ever met, and that she was a hot piece of skirt. I also thought that she was no sort of Communist, back when the rest of us were convinced that the Party was the light of the world."

I snorted. "That's it for Joan, huh?"

Sambo sucked air. "Yes, it is. Ask me about nuclear physics. I can talk physics all day long, but it might prove to be over your head."

I snorted snide. "Okay. Why'd you get dumped off the Manhattan Project? That must have been an ace gig for a guy in your trade."

Sambo sucked air. He rattled and racked. His lifespan loomed as next week.

"I'd made friends in the film colony, here in L.A. Young people— one in particular. I was antibomb then, even though I helped build the bombs the fascist U.S. dropped on Japan. It's believed that I was fired for scientific ineptitude. That's hardly the case. I was a political casualty, pure and simple. I may be a physicist, but I'm an idealist and a patron of the arts, most of all."

Sambo, the idealist. Sambo, the ardent artist. I ran with that ball.

"I know you swung with all those swinging artists in Russia. Eisenstein, Stanislavsky, Meyerhold—those were some hotshot cats."

Sambo laffed and coughed viscous vapors. *Pops, you contaminate me.*

"I knew them, yes. Their visions formed me in ways that you will never know."

Sambo sickened me. The interview inflamed me. I bounced a new ball. Let's get this over with.

"There's a dangerous woman, circling your cell. I know she's aware of your 'den mother,' who I assume to be Constance Woodard. Her name is Claire Klein, and she's not to be trifled with."

Ooohhh—did Sambo just glitch, twitch, shudder, cower, and cringe?

"No. The name Claire Klein means nothing to me."

That's okay, Sambo—I've registered your response.

"Constance Woodard. Your 'den mother.' Why would she fabricate cell minutes, after all the members of the cell had renounced the Party?"

Sambo sighed. "Because she was the only one of us who truly believed, and her belief transcended quite an onslaught of reality. And she was the loneliest woman I've ever known, and her fabrications must have convinced her that she still had comrades and friends."

The Club Zombie. A double dose of darktown. A danger dive. Discordant bebop and the Baron Samedi Cocktail—"One Sip Leaves You Zombified."

I knew the Zombie. I busted beboppers, mud sharks, and junkies here back in the '40s. The big buck bartender made me. Fractious Freddy's back. He still be *baaaaaaaaaad* muthafuckin' juju. I'll make him a Baron Samedi Cocktail. He *gots* to be Zombified.

He cooked up the cocktail. It glowed radioactive. I slipped him a Bondage Bob C-note. He went *You the man*. I guzzled the cocktail. It bebopified the dexies dosing my bloodstream. I went ZOMBIFIED.

Robert Jones Crawshaw walked in. He's aka Comrade Bob and *KKK*omrade X. He bypassed the bandstand and bopped to a booth by the bar. I made him off old mug shots. He looked bad to the bone. I dug his purple porkpie hat.

I joined him. He snapped his fingers. Two Baron Samedi Cocktails appeared. He bolted his. I sipped mine.

He belched, he burped, he bypassed all amenities. He gave me the Big This Is It.

"The Party is a crock of motherfucking shit. Ask Richard Wright or Zora Neale Hurston. Money and fame is the name of the game. I'm raking it in off *Black Bossman, Black Dictator,* and *Black Führer.* Billy told me you're investigating the murder of Comrade Joanie, and let me state at the outset that I liked her okay, but I never poured her the pork—not no way. Ralphie and me were tight—and I know you killed him, and it was a humbug deal, and now you got the guilts. I didn't kill Joanie, because the fuzz know it was a white man, because Joanie scratched his face good. I also know you know that Ralphie bailed me out on a 459 charge, back in '48. Are we all caught up, now? You think Bob Harrison would shoot me a gig, writing for *Confidential*? I'm hot shit in intellectual circles. *Black Führer* just went into its twelfth printing. Alfred Kazin and all them motherfucking intellectuals go for my shit."

I was zombified. I was beatified and transmogrified. The booze. The bebop. The dope. Comrade Sammy's sad take on my Connie. The mad musings of *KKK*omrade X.

"Known associates. Joan, Ralphie, or both of them. Can you come up with some names?"

*KKK*omrade X went *haw-haw.* "Some Fed mofo named 'Charlie.' He shot Ralphie the word on burglary scores. He knew Joanie, too, and he might have been her handler when she got hip and turned rat. Plus, I think Charlie might have introduced Joanie to Ralphie. That's the only name that I can think of, off the top of my head."

Charlie. Agent Charles Fullerton. It had to be.

"There's a woman named Claire Klein. She's got a very bad beef against a man in your cell, or in your general circle of the Party. Does *her* name ring any bells?"

*KKK*omrade X said, "*Nein*, Daddy. But there was only two men in the cell—me and old Sammy Ahlendorf. That said, there was this cast of thousands that the den mother knew, because she was always taking in strays. That also said, there was no man who jumped out of the crowd and said, 'Hey, remember me?'"

I stood up. I was Zombified, Commified, RATified.

"Go home and sleep it off, baby. And remember to chat me up to Bob H."

KKKomrade X called it. I took his advice and car-napped in my Packard pimpmobile. I woke up, unzombified. I remained Commified and RATified. My first thought was:

Lonesome Connie.

I pulled those taps and bugs at her pad. The McCarthy/rogue-Fed listening post was northeast in Silver Lake. Connie's place stood within long-range broadcast beams. Comrade Sam lived in Van Nuys. His place was *out* of range. KKKomrade X lived in Watts. His place was *out* of range. Comrade Ellie lived in Westwood. Party Girl's pad was *out* of range.

And:

Die Kameraden had ditched the Party and renounced Communism. Only my Connie carried the torch.

Ergo:

The Feds had targeted my Connie, *solamente*. Plus other Commos in cells unknown.

I whipped west to the Wilshire corridor. Party Girl had demon digs in a high-ticket high-rise. A valet parked my pimpmobile. I big-tipped him. He said Miss Donnell was in and walked me to the penthouse lift.

A glass rocket rocked me up twenty-four stories. It vibrated me, vertiginous. The door opened into Party Girl's parlor. Party Girl welcomed me.

She was tall. She was blond and waif willowy. She looked like Lizabeth Scott in *Pitfall*. Dick Powell leaves his wife for her. Now I know why.

I flashed my Statie badge. Party Girl said, "I already testified, and I thought I blew all the State HUAC guys, back when I was in the game."

She gored my gonads. She had Liz Scott's lisp and low purr down pat. She wore tennis whites to stay home and talk blow jobs to strange men. She defined noblesse oblige.

"Ten minutes, Miss Donnell. That's all I need."

"Who do you want me to fink on? I thought I was done there."

"I'm investigating Joan Horvath's murder. We're looking at the CP cell she was in. I've talked to Samuel Ahlendorf and Bob Crawshaw already. Quite obviously, you were on my list."

Party Girl went *After you*. I entered her demented demimonde. Glass walls winged wide on Wilshire. Dig the deep-pile rugs and lounge-lizard furnishings—all violet velour.

She walked me to a wet bar. She poured two Tom Collins, light on the lime. We sat on black leather stools and nudged knees.

"I didn't know Joanie that well. I wouldn't sleep with her, and I outgrew the Party before she did. I tried to recruit her for my stable, but she wouldn't hear of it. We ratted each other out to you State HUAC guys, but I forget who finked first. The den mother knew her better than any of us, that's for sure."

The Liz Scott lisp and low growl. The lioness-level gaze. She's leading you. *KKK*omrade X called and warned her. Freddy O.'s en route. He ain't no HUAC cop. Milk him, baby. He's money, once removed. He's susceptible. Spin him into your spell.

She wants to slander-slam den mother Connie. That's her intention. Field this changeup, bitch:

"Let me issue a warning about a woman that I consider to be quite dangerous—one that I've passed on to Mr. Ahlendorf and Mr. Crawshaw already. She has plainly stated that she intends to kill a man in your cell, or the general orbit of Party members you might have knowledge of. Her name is Claire Klein. She's quite persistent, and she has a way of getting up in your face that I would describe as unforgettable."

Party Girl lit a cigarette. "Well, there's one woman and one instance that I can think of, but the name Claire Klein sounds no gongs for me. It was back during the war. '43, I think."

I said, "Please continue."

"Well, it was some sort of Scottsboro Boys revival, and it was supposed to be all-Party—I thought one hundred percent. Then in walks a Wave officer, in her full-dress blues. She sizes me up as a girl who likes to gab, and then she applies the full press."

The war/the Waves/Lieutenant j.g. Claire Klein. *Perdition, catch my soul—*

"The funny thing was, it all pertained to Commie arcana in Russia, during the show-trial era. She was hipped on Vsevolod Meyerhold, his importance in radical-theater circles, and how Stalin liquidated his theater, made him attend a self-criticism session, denounced him for abandoning socialist realism, and had him tortured and killed. This is in '39 and '40, I think. Here's the worst part. The NKVD stabbed his wife's eyes out and stabbed her to death a few months earlier."

Meyerhold. Sambo Ahlendorf knew that cat.

"That's the extent of it? This Wave woman pressed you and moved on?"

"Right with Eversharp."

"Samuel Ahlendorf mentioned Meyerhold to me, earlier today."

"Sammy's old, and he's Russian. He's dined out on radical-socialist theater, all the time I've known him. I dare you to sit through one of Meyerhold's plays. Crassly put, they ain't *Guys and Dolls*."

I gulped. "Let's discuss the den mother. I assume you're referring to Constance Woodard?"

Party Girl crushed her cigarette. "That's right. Connie was our resident drag and expert on Joanie Hubbard. She was also Joanie's lover for an indeterminate period of time, during the war and after it, which means that she was awarded the Jealous Lover of All-Time Award for who knows how many years running, because you have *never* seen jealousy like that, and you have *never* seen anyone chafe under the yoke of it like Joanie did."

I said, "Keep going. There's something you've been dying to tell me."

Party Girl laffed. "I never liked Connie, but I grokked her existential anguish. Because Joanie was a Venus fly trap, and she had men, women, and who knows *what* else standing in line to get in her bed. Connie pulled a gun on *two* of Joanie's would-be suitors, and one man—a lefty lawyer in Marin County—vanished from sight altogether."

Now, I'm Commified, reconstructivized, social-dialecticized—

"Get it—Mr. State Cop who's not a state cop? The den mother killed that man, and *that's* what tore our dumb Communist cell asunder."

That man." Claire's Meyerhold fix. Dead men and dead Joanie. I was dungeon-deep with dead men and castrated by Communist women. Here I am in the den mother's bedroom. I'm crapped out on the bed. The red walls *clooooose* in on me.

I thumbed a library book. I'd bipped by the West L.A. Library, post–Party Girl. I did microfilm research. The *San Francisco Chronicle*, '48–'49. An emphasis on local murders.

The book. It's a big and boring Baedeker on Russian radical theater. There's big ink on Vsevolod Meyerhold and his actress wife, Zinaida Raikh. Party Girl told it true. Stalin's goons tortured and shot Meyerhold dead. They stabbed Zinaida's eyes out and stabbed her dead. They were one comely couple. The pix told it true. He's hero handsome as he waves a Red flag. She's beautiful in her babushka. The Red Wheel crushes them flat.

Meyerhold was a Stalin-era stud and swinging swordsman. He brought the brisket to women in Russia and abroad and left bawling babies behind. Those facts fanned me. Ditto this fact. *Somebody ratted Meyerhold to the NKVD.*

Murder in Moscow. Murder in Marin County. It's September '49. "Lefty lawyer" Will Hartshorn vanishes. Will's a wicked womanizer. Scads of scurrilous Commo women are questioned, to no avail. Wicked Will dips off and disappears. There's no corpus delecti—case closed.

The den mother's downstairs. She's cooking our dinner. She'll call up to me.

I left the library and sidled up to Silver Lake. There's the rogue-

Fed listening post. It's a shit shack on Ewing off of Duane Street. Harry told me they run three monitor shifts and lock up at midnite. I drove to Higgins' Hardware and bought what I'd need. Charles Fullerton lived in the Miracle Mile. The mid-Wilshire fone book said so.

The den mother dipped upstairs. I heard her heels hit. She stood in the doorway. She smiled at me and read me. She went *What's wrong, love?*

I said, "I talked to some people who knew you pretty well. You know who I mean, because you gave me their names."

She said, "Yes?"

I said, "They hold you in the highest contempt, because you stayed the course after they walked, and that made you a dupe and marked you as naïve. You wrote hundreds of pages of cell minutes and spun fantasies. You loved them. They didn't love you. You carried the torch. You created a pretend world in this very room. That fact alone has convinced me to protect you."

Connie said, "I 'stayed the course.' It's quite the male concept, but it's not something I can accept in you, if it means that you consider me pathetic."

I laffed. "How could I? You killed a man with no compunction, in the Freddy Otash mode. 'Pathetic' hardly describes it."

"He brutalized Joan. He hit her and demeaned her, and I couldn't stand it. I shot him and dumped his body in a lime pit in Point Reyes. The police questioned me once and believed my denials. They never troubled me again, and my ex-comrades never informed on me."

"How did you feel, after you killed him?"

"I felt aghast and relieved."

Perdition, catch my soul—for I do KNOW her.

Charlie Fullerton, FBI. Harry Fremont tagged him a booze-hound bachelor and a cloistered closet queen. He juiced at the Raincheck Room, Rick's Riptide, and Roscoe's Reef. He had an above-garage crib off 6th and Dunsmuir. Harry advised a midnite snatch-and-grab. Dump him in his doorway and go in strong.

Sound advice. The lock snapped easy. The crib was cloistered-closet claustrophobic. Small kitchen/small bathroom/small front room. *Whew*—it's Suffocation City. It's suffused with stale cigarette smoke and spilled booze.

I kept the lights off. I lurked and listened, doorway-close. 12:19 a.m. Fumbling footsteps. Charlie's key in the lock.

The door opened. I sandbagged Charlie, coming in. I kicked his legs out from under him. He moaned and mewed. I banged his head on the floor and hankie-gagged him. I dragged him into the kitchen and hit the lights. *Heh, heh*—there's this hot plate.

I handcuffed Charlie. I plugged the plate in. The coils glowed hot, *hot*. I hauled Charlie to his feet and shoved him up to the counter. Charlie bug-eye beseeched me—don't scorch me, boss.

I curled his right-hand fingers into the coils. I scorched and scalded him. My hankie-gag muffled his screams. I caught the french-fried fragrance of burned skin.

Charlie bawled and buckled and tore free of me. I kicked him in the balls and jackknifed him. A frigid Frigidaire was right there. I opened the door. I pulled Charlie upright and jammed his scorched hand in the freezer compartment. *Yeah!!!*—it's a skin-fry *frappé!!!*

Charlie tried to scream. The gag mumble-muted him. The cold ice cauterized his scalded skin and made streams of steam rise. I pulled his hand free and shoved him into a chair. I stood over him and laid out my Bill of No Redress.

"Joan Hubbard and Ralphie Horvath. Connie Woodard and her CP cell. This latest jive crusade of Joe McCarthy's, and how Connie fits in. Who you've got wired out of that long-range post in Silver Lake. Nod once if you want to live, and twice if you want to die."

Charlie nodded once. I yanked his gag. His muffled scream screeched out, sissy soprano. I pulled my pocket flask and fed him bonded bourbon. He gargle-gurgled it down and glowed booze-hound red.

I waited. Charlie went *Gimme*. I ran a refill down his throat. I tapped my wristwatch. Charlie went *More.* I ran Refill #2 down his gullet. *That* got him. His booze glow glissandoed into plain old pink-red.

I said, "Give."

Charlie coughed and cleared his throat. Phlegm flew into his hankie. He went from refusenik to running dog in one second flat.

"Joanie was never a Commie or a Comsymp. She was an FBI plant at the gate. We financed her radio show and gave her a stipend she could live on. She was always *ours,* and we planted her in Connie Woodard's UCLA class, because Connie was lez and loved young-idealist cooze, and because Connie was the den mother of the L.A. Left. Joanie was bait from 1939 on. She was nothing but a promiscuous gang girl with hotshot college degrees, and she was on the Federal payroll up to the time of her death. *I* set Joanie up with Ralphie Horvath, and they got a 459 thing going. So fucking what? Burglary isn't treason, the last time I checked."

I sucked bonded bourbon. I passed the flask. Charlie sucked bonded bourbon. He was booze-bombed and hurtin' for certain. He took on this weird white witch doctor look.

"So, the cell. There's a joke for you. Sammy A., that hump Crawshaw, and Ellie Donnell. They were smart, though. They recanted before they got named, which left the den mother all by her lonesome. And *she* was a joke, but she *knew* everybody, and *everybody* confided in her. She's the linchpin of this new thing Joe M.'s running, and we wired her place, but the bugs and taps went on the fritz. Joanie was set to testify, as a friendly witness. She was going to lay out the *criminal* misdeeds of Ahlendorf, Crawshaw, and Donnell, as sidebars to their recantings, to tell the whole world that onetime Commies never change. *But,* Joanie gets snuffed. *So,* there's a hot-prowl hump on the loose. *So,* the LAPD keys on him as a suspect, and blows him up. You were there, you should know."

I ran through the rat-out. One riff rang false.

"I can see Crawshaw and Donnell as criminals—sure. But Ahlendorf didn't hit me as the criminal type."

"Yeah, but Sammy's bent. We knew that, at the start. He emigrated in '36, but he kept going back to Russia, under false pass-ports that the Party fixed him up with. He was embroiled in some shifty stuff over there, but we never figured out what."

I said, "That long-range post you're running. You didn't set that whole deal up just to nail the den mother."

Charlie said, "That's correct. We've got nine other cells wired up, lockstep. The members are all Hollywood types, including some very large names, and most of them are linked to the den mother. Joe M. wants to squeeze her and get her to roll on them. She's never rolled before, but we've got her for Murder One, up in Marin County. A lawyer went missing, and we know why. You know how we know? Because Joanie told us. This guy was putting the boots to her, and the den mother got jealous and snuffed him. We can get her full immunity, if she rolls. If she doesn't roll, she's got a hot date with the green room."

I sighed. "Constance Linscott Woodard will never roll."

Charlie said, "Freddy, you're blushing."

The post was spiffed, spangled, and space age. Joe McCarthy scrounged the latest and greatest new stuff.

Long-range broadband transceivers. All-weather bug mounts, suited for outdoor use. Camouflaged microphones. Long-play tape recorders. Automatic voice activators. Static-eliminating headsets.

Plus work desks. Plus twelve file cabinets. All of them unlocked. All stuffed with bug-and-tap transcripts. Nine Commie cells headed for Hell.

I stuffed 12-gauge shotgun shells in the file drawers and spread gunpowder on top. I placed paper bags full of fertilizer and ammo-nium nitrate under the desks. I splashed two-gallon gas cans full of Mobile Supreme on the floor. I left the front door open and blasted seven ACP rounds inside.

The post blew up mauve and pink. It harked me back to Hiro-shima and that blistering blast at Jack K.'s bomb bash. There's this magnificent mushroom cloud, all aglow.

THE GOOGIE'S PARKING LOT

4/7/54

Googie's. Early-bird peeps from my Packard pimpmobile. A peremptory peep for Claire Klein, specific.

I popped dexies and chain-smoked. The a.m. *Herald* was due. Fullerton wouldn't rat me. He was in deep with a putrid pol soon to implode. I had him for all his Joanie-Ralphie 459 shit. The listening-post blast would blare headlines. The Feds would stagnantly stonewall it. The words *McCarthy/black-bag job/rogue action* would not pry their way into print.

I peeped the back window. Four shadows whipped by my windshield. Sergeant Max Herman. Sergeant Red Stromwall. Sergeant Harry Crowder. Officer Eddie Benson.

The Hats. Pearl gray suits and white Panamas. Trouble treads my way.

I waved faux wolfsbane. They deadpanned it. Max and Red yanked me out of the car. Harry and Eddie cuffed me. They tossed me in the backseat of their K-car and sandwiched me in tight.

Max drove. Red whistled "Funeral March of a Marionette." We ran Code 3 downtown. We hit City Hall and took the freight lift up to the DB. They dumped me in sweatbox #3 and cuffed me to a chair. Note the fat fone book on the table.

Max said, "You're fucked, Freddy. Metro's been spot-tailing you since February."

Red said, "We know everyone that you've seen and everything that you've done."

Harry said, "The moment of truth approaches, Freddy."

Eddie said, "Your camel-fucking ass is grass."

I said, "Maybe we can pin my grief on some random lowlifes. The *Herald*'s always willing to go that route for you guys."

Max phone-booked me. He threw a top-of-the-head/leave-no-marks shot. He cracked my cranium *gooood*.

"We know every sleazy thing that you and your goons have pulled for *Confidential*. We saw you and Bernie Spindel hot-wire Steve Cochran's place, and we saw you pull that red devil stunt with him the night of the film shoot. We know all about your wing-ding with the den mother, who seems a little long in the tooth for a young stud like you. We tailed you to your interviews with Samuel Ahlendorf, that geek Crawshaw, and Ellie Donnell. We boom-miked your assault on Agent Fullerton, and we saw you blow up the Fed post."

Red phone-booked me. He threw a cause-great-pain/leave-no-marks shot.

"You're fucked, Freddy. We know all of your shit, inside out."

Harry phone-booked me. "You're not our pal anymore, Freddy. You're just some jamoke that's outlived his usefulness."

Eddie phone-booked me. "We've got you for Treason, Sedition, and boocoo Smith Act violations. You'll burn, just like the Rosenbergs."

Max phone-booked me. He employed his love-tap/this-ain't-so-bad swing. "We'd appreciate it if you'd recount your interviews with Ahlendorf, Crawshaw, and Donnell. That would go a long way toward earning our favor."

Red phone-booked me. He tossed a love-tap uppercut.

"We'll let you think about it. We'll put you up in a tidy cell, away from the riffraff. I know the Chief is looking forward to speaking with you."

Harry phone-booked me. "Freddy O.'s wild ride has just ended."

Eddie phone-booked me. "R.I.P., Freddy."

They tossed me in a holding cell. My bunk was bare-bones. My hurt head hit a hard pillow. It caromed me into a coma.

I wasted Ralph Mitchell Horvath. Joi gobbled Steve the Stud's *schvantz*. I beat up Johnnie Ray. I peeped ten thousand houses. I popped penance payments in Joanie Horvath's mailbox.

I must have cried. I soaked my pillow down to the mattress. My head felt homogenized. My cerebellum sang sad songs. My cranium creaked.

William H. Parker racked the door and sat on my bunk. He wore his full four-star blues.

"The Los Angeles Police Department now owns you. As of this moment, *Confidential* has ceded its claim. We will let you skate for everything that you have done. You will skate for your assault on Agent Fullerton, and for blowing up the listening post. You will skate for your rogue actions on the Joan Horvath snuff. You will skate for any and all of your illegal actions while in the employ of *Confidential*. We will allow you to avenge Joan Horvath, however you deem fit. In recompense for the above stated mercies, you will enter my direct employ."

Parker paused. His Bible gaze burned my soul. The Book of Revelation 3:17–18: *And you don't realize that you are wretched and miserable and poor and blind and naked. So, I advise you to buy gold from me—gold that has been purified by fire.*

I said, "Yes."

Parker said, "You will sign a detailed confession regarding your work for *Confidential*. You will serve as my personal informant and agent provocateur, and assist me in my efforts to destroy the magazine. We are going to bankrupt it, expose the breadth of its evil, and slay it dead in Federal court. As of now, you are my personal snitch, rat, stool pigeon, and squealer. Say 'Yes' or 'No' immediately. Your answer will dictate the course of the rest of your life."

I said, "Yes."

—◊—

Tough tasks. Deep duties. My vows to first fulfill. WOMEN said it all.

Joan, Claire, Connie. Linked in cause and effect. Calamitous causation. Let's extract the truth thereof.

I bopped to Beverly Hills and beat feet to my bungalow. I stood by my wall graph and linked lines in black ink. I linked Joan to Connie, straight up.

Connie knew every Commie in captivity. Joan's killer lurked there. The '30s and '40s CP in L.A. Comintern cads coursing through. Fractious front groups established and unions usurped. How many dark-haired/heavy-bristled white men lurked and looted within?

On to Claire. Let's craft a chronology. Let's link lines. Let's answer this quivering question: who's the man that Claire wants to kill?

A nihilist notion nudged me. It was all circumstantial and based on thirdhand dish. Claire's out to get Sammy Ahlendorf. Here's my line links:

Lez Line #2. Stretch monitors it. Babs Payton dishes per her three-ways with Claire. Claire tricks with Russian consulate humps. She speaks Russian. Ahlendorf *is* Russian—but emigrated here in '36. Claire pumps out the code name "Robin Redbreast." V. J. Jerome says it's a former Red named "Sammy." Samuel Ahlendorf belonged to Connie Woodard's cell. Claire carries a Makarov pistol. Claire hates Reds and has finked them to HUAC. Babs dishes *this*: Robin Redbreast was a crazy Commo in the '30s and '40s. He's stale stuff in the '50s. His expulsion from the Manhattan Project underlines this.

Then, there's *this*:

Sammy digs Russian revolutionary art. He rankly revealed it to me. Ellie Donnell told me the tale of Meyerhold's maiming and murder. Meyerhold was a fitful formalist. He renounced socialist realism and pissed off the punk Politburo. Meyerhold is snuffed, circa '39–'40. His wife Zinaida Raikh is torture-stabbed and slain. A Wave officer braces Party Girl at an all-Party bash in L.A. It *has* to be Claire. She presses Party Girl per the whole Meyerhold deal. Claire's armed with supple suppositions now. She's got Sammy gun-sighted. That's a probable certainty.

Harry Fremont was tight with a U.S. Customs cop. I called and asked him to run passport checks on Claire and Sammy A. Check for Russian excursions. Post-'36 for Sammy. He might be using forged Party passports. Look for variants on the Robin Redbreast code name. Do this per Claire: check birth certificates per her surname and DOB. Check her parents' surnames. Check Claire's passport travel: '39 and '40. She was of legal age then. Did she connect to Robin Redbreast in Russia? Meyerhold was a sweltering swordsman. Did he siphon his seed in '20 and '21 in New York? Did he somehow spawn spectacular Claire? I pledged Harry a grand and told him to get back to me *faaaaast*. He told me it was all far-fetched. Yeah, but you never know.

I ink-linked lives. Claire, Joan, Connie—shakedown shills, rabid Reds, knock-kneed succubi. I ran them all through the Book of Revelation and found that they fit right there.

The fone rang. I picked up. Harry said, "I'll never doubt you again."

"Tell me why."

"Claire and Robin Redfield—that's the name on Ahlendorf's passport—crossed paths in Moscow in late '39 and '40, but they traveled separately."

I said, "Don't stop now."

Harry said, "Who's stopping? Customs ran the Klein skirt's DOB in New York. The guy was smart, because he cross-checked 'Claire Klein' with birth-parent names, and got Meyerhold and Zinaida Raikh. The Meyerholds granted custody to Mendel Klein and his wife, Clara, who were both big Party and radical-theater people. They gave the baby *their* name, and it all fits, just like you said it would."

The Book of Revelation 2:9–10: *I know about your suffering and your poverty. . . . I know the blasphemy of those opposing you.*

I owed Sambo a warning. I sensed his malevolent move, back in Russia. He finked Meyerhold and his missus to the Politburo and the NKVD. He cited reconstructionism, recidivism, formalism. He kissed Commie ass as only Commies can. His motive was most likely envy. He didn't want to be a bomb big shot. He wanted to be a radical-theater rajah. He wanted to mesmerize the masses, à la Meyerhold in his hoodwinked heyday.

Dusk hit. I looped Coldwater Canyon northbound and hit the Valley. The Valley Vista Villas loomed. I surveillance-circled the block and came back behind the buildings. I noticed a series of second-floor terraces with connecting walkways.

Let's surprise Comrade Sambo. Pick the sliding-glass-door lock and enter his crib. Hey, Sambo—it's dues time. Run while you can. Claire Klein is radical theater beyond your corrupt ken.

I parked and schlepped it up to the terrace walkway. Sambo's pad was three glass doors down. I heard shuddering Shostakovich bursting from within. The muted message was Fuck the Soviet Beast. The doors were heavy glass and locked from inside. I thought I heard one single screech.

I was too late. Sambo ran toward the terrace—and me. He was naked. His pubic hair had been shaved. His eyes had been stabbed out. His chest and legs had been stabbed. Claire chased after him. She wore a wooden Kabuki mask. Kabuki masks were a Meyerhold trademark. Claire's mask bore the face of Zinaida Raikh.

Comrade Sam couldn't see me. Zinaida-Claire didn't see me. Comrade Sam tripped and fell. Claire ran her shiv between his legs and eviscerated him.

Rush-hour traffic. It slowed my trek back. I stopped at a pay phone to kill time. I called Bill Parker and gave him a loose lowdown. He said, "Thanks, Freddy." He said, "Better dead than Red," and hung up.

I hung up and snail-trailed back to 6th and Dunsmuir. Charlie Fullerton lived above his garage. His garage enticed me.

Old police detectives and Feds. They saved their most fecund files and stored them in marked boxes. They piled said boxes in their garages—more often than not.

Charlie would be off at the Raincheck Room or Rick's Riptide. It was 7:45. I had lock picks and a penlight. I had Whiskey Bill Parker's home number if I fell in the shit.

It went as predicted. I picked the lock and picked through stuffed boxes. They were code-named and listed code-numbered rat-outs. I found the "Redbird" boxes and counted numbered snitches. Who killed you, baby? There's just numbers—no names.

Fullerton inked occasional comments. Rat-out #114 stood out. This guy was Hard Red and Deep Red. Sammy Ahlendorf mentored him. He talked up the need to snuff Federal snitches. He did this incessantly. Joan ratted him in May '49. He never joined the cell. Fullerton called him a fellow traveler. He was a closeted Party member. He drifted off for parts unknown, fall '49.

I wrote "114" and Fullerton's comments on my scratch pad. I wrote down numbers and comments for a dozen other snitches. I planned to pop the den mother with Pentothal. I believe in coerced confessions. How could I not? Bill Parker just made me his snitch.

I beat retreat feet to Googie's. The Tattle Tyrant turns tail. He slinks in defeat.

Rock Hudson sat in my booth. He was anchored in anguish and locked in loss. He's all worrisome and woe is me.

I sat down. Rock said, "Ask me why I look like warmed-over shit. I'm a movie star. I can't afford days like this."

"Tell me—but it's not like I can't guess."

Rock said, "Claire robbed me. She cracked the safe in my den, and stole twelve grand in cash and forty grand in gold Krugerrands. She'll be long gone by now, and I know I'll never see her again. I called Lew Wasserman, and, man, is he pissed."

"You got off easy, brother. Some day I'll tell you why."

Rock slid me a slip of paper. "She left this in the safe. It's for you. You get a good-bye, but I don't."

I read the note. It was bravura brief:

> *Freddy, love:*
>
> *Rain check, okay? I'll be thinking of you.*
>
> *All best,*
> *C.K.*

THE DEN MOTHER'S RED BEDROOM

4/8/54

I said, "It's for Joan."

She said, "You know exactly what to say to get exactly what you want from me. Truth serum, *really*."

Connie sat in the red chair. I sat on the red footstool. She held out her left arm. I swipe-swabbed it with alcohol and measured a mainline. I spike-speared her and jammed her the juice.

She sighed and went loosey-goosey. I said, "Count backward from one hundred and feel free to shut your eyes."

She moved her lips. I barely heard it: 100, 99, 98, gonesville. I took a brief breather and consulted my control notes.

Joan rat-out #84. Code name: Lazy Maizie. She's a San Marino socialite. She makes big donations to the Strikebusters' International. It's a known Commo front. Joan rat-out #204. Code name: John Henry. He's a male Negro. He's right tackle for the Detroit Lions. Charlie Fullerton's comment: "All the mud-shark girls go nuts for him."

I said, "How do you feel, Connie?"

Connie said, "Loose. But what if I don't feel inclined to . . ."

"Name names? That's okay. I'd be satisfied with simple, candid responses."

Connie, *très* loose: "Love, I'm sure that's all you'll ever get from . . ."

I said, "Lazy Maizie."

Connie, *très, très* loose. "She smoked hashish. She . . . put . . . her . . . hand on Joan's leg . . . and Joan slapped her."

That was *gooooood*. It was Joan-centric and Joan-phobic. I laid John Henry on her.

Connie, yet *more* loose: "He was . . . a steel-driving man in a Negro spiritual. We . . . sang that song at all the Scottsboro Boys rallies . . . we knew that something like half of them were guilty, though."

It was half good. Connie voiced un-Commie-esque candor. I gave her a brief breather.

Rat-out #114 was un-code-named. I'd have to mention Sammy Ahlendorf to rouse recollection. The papers toed Bill Parker's line, per dead Sammy. It's suicide, case closed. Connie believed that horseshit.

I said, "Joan informed on this man. She must have felt very strongly about him. He said he wanted to murder all FBI snitches, but I don't know his name. He never joined your cell, although he was very much in the thrall of Sammy Ahlendorf, and I think it's safe to say that he shared Sammy's anti-A-bomb mentality, which is to say he was pissed off when we A-bombed the Japs, even though they were fascists, and even though they dropped those eggs on Pearl Harbor."

Connie sighed. Her hands twitched. Her eyelids fluttered. She's digging deep here.

"I . . . remember him. . . . He said, 'We've got to expose the bomb before it wipes out the human race, and I'm going to build my career on it.'"

She snapped awake then. She didn't name names or say *his* name. She didn't need to. She'd already said this to me:

"*He was my last tortured and torturing male lover—before you.*"

Fullerton's file facts fit. They surged circumstantial. Joan's rat-out rang true. It did not mean that Steve Cochran killed her.

Connie snapped *très* awake. She blinked, blank-faced. She didn't recall what she'd said.

"Did you learn anything provocative? I'd hate to think that I let Joan down."

I said, "You did swell."

—m—

A-Bomb party. The U.S. Army's set to launch at 9:00 p.m. It's a tête-à-tête this time. It's *my* bungalow roof. Stretch, me, frozen daiquiris and corn chips. My transistor radio for the countdown. Two cozy deck chairs.

We held hands. Stretch lounged low and leveled out our height disparity. The radio murmured musings on mach 10 and beyond. Supersonic rockets are now passé.

I said, "You're not a Communist or a psycho killer, are you? My friendship's not sending you over the bend?"

Stretch said, "Uncle Freddy's having conscience pangs. He's sleeping with this nutty old lady in Hancock Park, when he could be here with me."

I laffed and lapped my daiquiri. The nite was cool. Stretch wore her USC letter coat. I wore a Beethoven sweatshirt that Claire left at Googie's for me.

"She'll break it off soon. It was a situational sort of deal. You and I are eternal."

Stretch laffed. "Older man, younger woman. *That's* a news flash. It's on a par with 'dog bites man.'"

I laffed. We swung our hands. The radio reporter cut to a commercial. Bucky Beaver hawked Ipana toothpaste.

"I saw that note you tacked to the board. *Really*, how blithe. 'Rain check, okay?' And don't tell me C.K. isn't the dread Claire Klein."

I said, "She's ephemeral. Forget all the bad things I told you about her. Don't listen for her on the tap lines. She got out, right on cue."

Stretch squeezed my hand. "You're being disingenuous, but I'll let it slide, because we're about to witness history."

The radioman rang out the countdown. *"Ten, nine, eight, seven, six, five, four, three, two, one—blastoff."*

I missed the mushroom cloud and the mauve-and-pink sky. Stretch strong-armed me into a kiss.

Ashes to ashes, baby. Ask the rental rabbi. Sammy Ahlendorf eats the dust.

LAPD quick-processed the stiff and released it. The graveside service was bilingo and brief. The rabbi ululated in Hebrew and extolled Sambo in English. He was a bomb builder, a *macher*, a *mensch*.

I stood graveside. The den mother stood with me. Grave diggers grappled the casket into the ground. The rabbi lit a cigarette and split the gig. It was a rush job. Who's this Ahlendorf *schmendrick*?

Connie and I came in two cars. She insisted on it. We walked toward the street and the Big Splitsville. Connie lifted her veil and dropped my hand.

"You brought a whirlwind into my life. We were united in common cause for a moment—and one that I'll never forget. But the walls between us stand too high to breach, darling. It's best that we end this thing now."

I said, "Stay strong, Red. It was a gas knowing you. You're History's child. Someone has to carry the torch, and I'm glad that it's you."

Connie touched my cheek. "Oh, Freddy—I knew you'd understand."

I winked. "Rain check, okay?"

Connie winked back. Her eyelash stuck. She pulled out a hankie and wiped it free.

"Always, love. For you, the world."

I walked away. She walked away. I felt ghastly and relieved.

The Ranch Market. My eye in the sky. It felt feckless and familiar and *gooooood*.

It's where I plot and plan and scrounge and scheme. It's a shake-down shack. It's a divorce-work dive. It's a scandal screen that sifts gold. The hard heart and sick soul of *Confidential* thrive here. I'm a police informant now. It's where I'll plot and plan and scrounge and scheme to take *Confidential* down.

It's ghastly. I'm relieved. It's an opportunity.

I popped three dexies and gargled Old Crow. I put my feet up on my desk and scratched my balls. Bernie Spindel walked in. He carried earmuffs and a tape spool.

I said, "*Qué pasa*, baby? It's a good day to be alive, *n'est-ce pas*?"

Bernie went *Oy*. He spooled the tape through my desk rig and earmuffed my head. He said, "It's our standing mount at the Miramar Hotel. I'll destroy the tape after you hear it."

I molded the muffs down and got comfy. Bernie flipped switches. I heard mattress moans and fucky-fucky exertions. I matched moans to my megamillions of women. Oh *yeah*—it's Joi Lansing in the sack. Oh *shit*—that's Steve Cochran with her.

Steve Cochran. Joan Hubbard rats his ass. He's Commie #114.

Steve and Joi light cigarettes. I hear match flare and exhale. There's fucky-fucky/goo-goo sounds. Oh shit—there's two full minutes' worth.

Joi says, "Your scars are healing, baby. That plastics guy knows his stuff."

Steve says, "I hate to say it, but so does your ex. I never bought that bill of goods the Sheriff's fed me. Some World War Two buff in a red devil mask? That dog don't hunt. It had to be Freddy."

Joi said, "Let it go, baby. He's just a stooge and a gofer. What's that you always call him? The 'running dog of capitalism.'"

Steve dog-bayed. Steve said, "Guys like Freddy are the fuckboys of the American Oligarchy. They've spawned this whole atomic nightmare we're enduring. Freddy's the ne plus ultra of the fascist gestalt. He's Camus' *l'étranger*. He's the guy who goes to his death knowing exactly jack shit."

Joi laffed. Joi giggled. Steve tickled her—I knew those squeals.

Steve said, "Credit where credit is due. It's Freddy who got me started on this big roll of mine. He blew up Joanie Horvath's husband, and got me thinking that maybe Joanie herself should go. For one, she was an FBI snitch, which mandates death in my book. That's why I bugged her pad. Two, she'd snitched me once already, and with Joe McCarthy in town, I figured she'd mount the revival."

Joi said, "You 'revivaled' her, baby."

Steve said, "You mean I *de*rivaled her."

They laffed. Steve was swarthy and dark-haired. I recalled that bandage he wore two months back. Joan scratched him. In that exact spot. I read the autopsy protocol.

Joi: "Don't tell me too much, baby."

Steve: "You're right. Mum's the word."

Joi: "And you be careful. Freddy's pussy-whipped, and he's got this thing for dead chicks. He might come after you."

Steve hooted. He coursed contempt. He pilloried my pathos. He decreed my damned destiny.

"I've got Freddy fail-safed. Charlie Fullerton told me that he torched that Fed post. I lifted some of his prints off his office at the Ranch Market, and placed them on a booze-bottle accelerant at the crime scene. If Freddy acts up, I can hang Treason on him. And that bottle is now in a Fed evidence vault."

Joi laffed. Steve said, "Ralphie to Joanie to now. The big karmic circle. When the revolution comes, your ex will be the first one to go."

I hit the off-switch. Bernie went *Oy* and walked out.

I felt reckless and feckless. I felt striated and stretched bare. Phantasmagoric '54 had me morally massacred and fearfully fucked-up.

Rain check, okay?

I made the rounds that night. Rock Hudson was having people over. Jimmy and Liz were there. Johnnie Ray saw me—and scrammed out the back door. Claire left some undies behind. Jimmy told me and showed me. I took a few farewell sniffs.

Jimmy dished Rock's new wife candidate. She was one Phyllis Gates. She worked for Rock's agent and came recommended. Jimmy said Phyllis was squaresville. She wanted to wait for her wedding nite. Phyllis was clueless. She swooned for Rock and did not know that Rock swooned for boys.

I got half gassed and bopped back to Beverly Hills and my bungalow. I went inside and watched Stretch sleep. I tucked her too-long legs back under the sheets.

Rain check, okay?

Pervdogs are scent dogs. We often loop by locations that recently roused us to lust. I drove east to Hancock Park and pulled up to the den mother's digs. I cut my lights and peeped her windows in the dark.

I whistled "Willow Weep for Me" and "My Funny Valentine." I saw Connie walk across the red bedroom and turn off the lights. I drove by Camerford and Vine then. A family had moved into the Horvath house. Their kids romped out on the porch.

I drove southeast for no good reason. I stopped at Ollie Hammond's Steakhouse and juiced in the bar. I peeped a tall redhead and watched her walk out of my life.

Opportunity is love. Hey, there—you with the stars in your eyes.

GONESVILLE

Freddy Otash Confesses, Part III

CELL 2607

Penance Penitentiary
Reckless-Wrecker-of-Lives Block
Pervert Purgatory
9/4/2020

I'm beastfully *back*. This concluding confession covers spring '55 to spring '60. The freewheeling Freddy O. is now a sniveling snitch. I'm Chief Bill Parker's back-room bitch and punk pawn in his crusade to take down *Confidential*. It's a fucked-up fin de siècle. The madcap magazine is doomed, Daddy-O. And I'm the ardent architect of its dipshit demise.

I've lost that lush life. I'm bopping the byways of big boo-hoo. Joi Lansing's gone. Connie Woodard's gone. Claire Klein's gone. Stretch Perkins went licentiously lez and snagged herself a barmaid at Linda's Little Log Cabin. Jimmy Dean's pulling away. He's a movie star now. He toplines *Giant* and *East of Eden*. He's been shooting a teen turkey called *Rebel Without a Cause*. It's filming on some loopy L.A. locations. I'm his main mentor no more. Director Nicholas Ray has replaced me. Nick Ray's a sweaty switch-hitter and a carcinogenic Commie. *I'm* Jimmy's real faux dad.

Boo-hoo, boo-hoo. I'm surfing a sicko surge of self-pity. *But*— this thunderous thought keeps me poised to pounce.

I know people. I'm now the pills-and-cocaine conduit for Senator Jack Kennedy. I broker scrapes for the contract cooze at Columbia and Metro. I've got L.A. bugged, tapped, and hot-wired here to Hell. I'm all repugnant resource and the withering will to survive.

Opportunity is love. Confluence is opportunity. I move in a mélange of *machers*, grifters, and graft-grabbers, and the sex-soiled sycophants so indigenous to L.A. Something has to pop my way. Something's coming. Something's telling me that *IT* is a *SHE*.

The wheelman lot. It's the *baaaaaad* bane of wicked wives and horn-dog hubbies, hot to trot. Divorce begins here. Lowlife lawyers call the pay phone by the lube rack. Punk PIs hustle off to hot-sheet huts and kick doors down. There's flashbulb flare and *eeeek* and *shreeek* and fuckee-suckee singed on celluloid.

The wheelman lot. It's my lurid launching pad today. *Confidential*'s cornholing Art Pepper. Artful Art's an alto sax hopping high on the *Downbeat* poll. He's a junkie with a jacked-up jones for high school honeys. He's nailed Miss Belmont High and Miss Lincoln High already. He's meeting Miss Franklin High at the Leechee Nut Lodge in Chinatown, one hour hence. I'll be there to instigate fuckus interruptus.

I'm serving two masters here. *Confidential*'s calling the piece "Sax Potentate Pepper: Junk and Jailbait Call the Tune Now!!!!!" LAPD Vice laid on the lead to the meet and laid down the law: *We'll* be there to slam this slime for Stat Rape/1st Degree.

Bill Parker hates hopheads and jailbait jumpers. Bill Parker's out to keester *Confidential*. He wants to catalogue *Confidential*'s coercive methods and march the mag to Indictment City. He's implementing a *loooooooooooong*-range strategy.

I lounged in my Packard pimpmobile. Ward Wardell and Race Rockwell reclined in their surveillance van. Donkey Don Eversall worked the outside spot. Miss Franklin High had her own sled. She handed out hand jobs, at five bucks per, and glommed a beat-to-shit '48 Merc. Donkey Don would call the pay phone. He'd say *It's on* and tail the twist to the Leechee Nut Lodge. The desk clerk was an LAPD lapdog. He told Don that putzo Pepper was smack-back in Room #9. Two Vice Squad goons were mainlining mai tais in the Lily Pad Lounge. They were set to grind Pepper while my camera crew rolled film.

I'm a snitch. I'm a rat fink. I'm a doofus double agent. *I'm* LAPD Lapdog #1.

I eyeballed the lot. Six wheelmen reposed in their rides. They drove hellacious hot rods and blew their gelt on booze, kustom kar kits, and cooze. They *lived* at the lot. They slept in their sleds. They poked B-girls from the Kibitz Room at Canter's Delicatessen and bounced their backseats, six at a pop.

Ward Wardell walked to the phone. Race Rockwell *schmoozed* a wigged-out wheelman with pizza-pus zits. The cat was a cop buff. He said the Hat Squad was chasing two 211/rape-o's. They stormed steak houses at closing time. They tapped the tills and took wallets. They purloined purses and made the women strip and dispense snout jobs. The Hats were out to take scalps on this one.

I tuned it out. The Hats and I had shared some shimmering shit. Fuck them—more current shit shivered through me.

Bondage Bob called me this morning. He beefed a southside radio station and a late-nite show called *Nasty Nat's Soul Patrol*. It was all pimp patois, cool-cat consciousness, and jive jazz. A woman called in three nights running. She came off winsome and *waaaay* white. She called herself "Miss Blind Item." She jawed with Nasty Nat and aped *Confidential's* alliterative prose style. Bob had no gripe there. *But*—she crossed some *craaaaazy* line and madly mauled the magazine. She *baaaaad*-beefed the August '52 piece on "Red Light Bandit" Caryl Chessman.

The piece bawled boo-hoo per Chessman's tripartite conviction. It's *baaaad*: Kidnap/Armed Robbery/Forced Oral Cop. Dig: the tone was apoplectic apostasy. The tone disregarded the magazine's perpetual fry-the-fucker stance. Chessman was convicted in spring

'48. The Little Lindbergh Law applied. Hanging judge Charles Fricke righteously mandated *DEATH*. Chessman professed his innocence. Chessman excoriated capital punishment. Lunar-looped liberals took up his hue and cry. '48 to '55. He'd held off his trek to the green room for seven full years. He filed appeals. He wrote screechy screeds and peddled them to pinko publishers. Now, this wiggy witch was mocking *my* magazine, and lambasting its *one* lamentable lapse in moral tone.

Bondage Bob told me to tune in Nasty Nat tonite. He said the witch called in at 1:00 a.m. and motormouthed till 3:00. I said I'd jump on it and take boocoo notes.

The pay phone rang. Ward grabbed it and grinned. He said, "*Arriba*, boss."

I banged Beverly, straight downtown. My Packard pimpmobile *performed*. A supercharged V-12 va-va-voomed me due east. My sled featured lake pipes, cheater slicks, and a Nazi death's-head shift knob. It was two-way-radio-rigged and synced to the surveillance van and Donkey Don's '53 Chevy. Our frequency number? *What else?* It's 69.

I ran the lead slot. The surveillance van dogged me. Donkey Don tailed Miss Franklin High southbound on the Arroyo Seco. She's crazoid Chrissy Molette. She's a hot-hormoned hellion out to bang all the bopsters on the '54 *Downbeat* and *Metronome* polls. She plays mean skin flute and hides hatpins in her big beehive. Her high school homeroom teacher was hotsville with Donkey Don. *She* tattled Chrissy's crazed yen for men.

Confluence. It's who you know and who you blow. Thus, this shimmering shakedown—

My radio cricked, crackled, and spit sputters. Donkey Don said, "69-Baker to 69-Alpha. Come in, Freddy."

"Alpha to Baker. I hear you, Don."

Don gargled garble talk. Sputters, stutters, static—his real voice shimmied and shot through.

"Chrissy picked up a tail at the York Avenue on-ramp. It's a '49

Ford ragtop, tan over blue. I got the plate number and buzzed the DMV. It's her brother Robbie's ride. Robbie's got a green sheet. One fall for pandering, one for 459."

I said, "Shit, this is grief." I brain-broiled a cool countermeasure.

"The Vice guys at the Lodge have a walkie. They're tapped in at 69, D-for-Dog. Buzz them and tell them to grab Robbie, plant some dope on him, and hold him. He's out to mess the gig up, and we need Chrissy and Pepper in the sack and *at it* for this deal to work for the magazine *and* Bill Parker."

Don tittered and tee-heed. He giggled, guffawed, and laffed lewd.

"Yeah, plus full bush, insertion, Pepper's sax and groovy dope paraphernalia in view."

Wire warp froze the frequency and cut the call off. I knew Don would field a follow-thru and buzz 69-Charlie. He'd rig the rendezvous. We'd converge and collide at the Lodge. Chrissy knocks on Door #9. Pepper opens up. He might be noxiously nude. We'll airbrush in a two-foot schlong and redact it, down to his knees. Our randy readers will get the gestalt. Ward and Race will roll film from high cover. I get the kick-the-door-in shot. The Vice cops pile in behind me.

Oooooooh—it's Stat Rape/1st Degree for Bill Parker. *Oooooooh*—it stacks my status as LAPD Rat #1 and brings me brownie points with the pervy puritan I hocked my soul to!!!!

I hit the hill by Belmont High. Beverly bywayed to 1st Street. I goosed the gas eastbound. I cut north on Broadway and east on Alpine. There's the Leechee Nut Lodge, up ah—

There's a car cavalcade, curbside. Chrissy's '48 Merc. Robbie's '49 Ford ragger. Donkey Don's '53 Chev. The Lodge is horseshoe-shaped, one floor only. Chrissy's cutting through the courtyard. She's anxiously angling toward Door #9. Robbie's skulking by the door of the Lily Pad Lounge. He's peeping the courtyard. He's insidiously intent. There's Donkey Don and the Vice cops. They're crapped out in deck chairs outside the office. They're sharing a short dog of Old Crow.

I parked behind Don's Chevy. The surveillance van parked behind me. I grabbed my righteous Rolleiflex. Ward and Race wrangled out their movie-camera shit. The *whoooole* scene sizzled in *SIN*-emascope and slid into a slithery *slooooooow* motion.

I signaled Don and the Vice cops and pointed to Robbie. They booze-barged over and braced him. He went *Who, me?* Don went *Yeah, you—cocksucker.* Robbie resisted and refuseniked. He put up his paws in a punk fighter's pose and bop-de-bop danced on his toes. Vice Cop #1 nabbed his neck and whacked his head against the wall. Vice Cop #2 kicked him in the balls and cuffed his hands behind his back.

Robbie baby-bawled and bitch-squealed. Don grabbed his greasy hair and pulled him inside the Lily Pad Lounge. I scoped Door #9. I saw *craaaazy* Chrissy crash in and crotch-dive Art Pepper. Man—it's a deep-focus door shot, *delicioso!!!!!*

The door slammed shut. I signaled Ward and Race and pointed to my wristwatch. The second hand tick-tocked toward fuckus interruptus. *Tick, tick, tick*—it tapped the two-minute mark. Donkey Don said, "Banzai."

We ran to Door #9. Ward and Race rolled film. Donkey Don worked the sound gizmo. The Vice cops ran up and stood behind us. They put on palm-weighted sap gloves and got het up to hurl some hurt.

Ward counted down. "Ten, nine, eight, seven, six, five, four, three, two, one—*zero.*"

I flat-foot kicked the door-doorjamb juncture. It juked the door hard off its hinges. The door flew back and in. It dumped a nightstand and pulped Pepper's sax.

Man—it's *suckus* interruptus.

Chrissy gobbled Ardent Art. Ardent Art geezed Big "H" in caustic concurrence. I got my shot. My boys rolled fuckee film. Chrissy went *eeeek.* Art Pepper said, "Oh shit." The Vice cops charged the bed.

The Hats hard-nosed Robbie Molette. I observed. The City Hall DB/sweatbox row/two-way-mirrored walls and outside-corridor speakers.

I perv-peeped the action. Sweatbox #3 snap, crackled, popped. I goosed the wall volume dial and caught every nasty nuance.

Robbie sat in a bolted-down chair. Note the bolted-down table and fat phone book. The Hats hovered. Max Herman waved Robbie's green sheet. Red Stromwall riffled Robbie's wallet. Harry Crowder crowded Robbie and caused a case of the sweltering sweats. Eddie Benson tapped the table and looked *meeeaaan*.

Max said, "Pandering. Pleaded down at arraignment, March '52. You're the most raggedy-ass-looking pimp I've ever seen, Robbie. *Successful* pimps take considerable care with their appearance."

Es la verdad. Robbie dressed pure pachuco. He wore a see-thru Sir Guy shirt and slit-bottom khakis. Pointy-toe fruit boots cinched the enchanting ensemble. Robbie evinced bad hygiene. Dandruff debris dusted the table. Robbie picked his nose and noshed the nuggets.

Red said, "459 PC. Three counts. Tossed at prelim, January '53."

Robbie said, "I quit pimping, and I quit burglarizizing. Actually, I don't know what the beef here is. You boys and those magazine shitheels kicked my ass, when all I was doing was lounging in the vicinity of a room where my underage sister was about to get devirginized by a notorious junkie and degenerate."

Harry laffed. "Your sister's three weeks and one day under the age of consent. The DA will never file Stat Rape on Pepper."

Eddie laffed. "He'll file for possession of narcotics, and leave it at that. And your sister lost her virginity back in the Coolidge administration."

Robbie laffed. "Yeah—just like your mama."

Eddie phone-booked him. *Whap*—a real noggin-knocker. It scoured his scalp and raised blood blisters. His dentures dipped to the floor.

Robbie reached down and replaced them. Bill Parker walked up to me. He weaved a tad. I knew the signs. *El Jefe* was half in the bag.

I said, "*Hola*, Chief."

Parker passed me his flask. I gargled Old Overholt and popped two Dexedrine on the sly.

"The kid's dirty. I've got a theory. I think he wanted to catch Pepper in the kip with his sister, and extort him with it."

Parker yukked. "Never let it be said that Freddy Otash doesn't know from shakedowns."

I passed the flask back. Parker yodeled Old Overholt. I rescoped the sweatbox hullabaloo.

Max said, "There's a few items we'd like to discuss with you, Robbie."

Robbie shrugged. Robbie said, "Okay."

Red said, "Here's the first item. There's a note from the Boys Vice Principal at Hollywood High attached to your green sheet. He states that you were seen at last year's Hollywood-Fairfax football game, attempting to pass yourself off as a 'talent scout' and recruit high school girls for your stable of underage prosties."

Robbie stut-stuttered. He blanched and blew spit bubbles. They pop-pop-popped.

"That's a humbug accusation. I've gone straight. I'm gigging as a busboy at the Beverly Hills Hotel. Talk to the desk manager. He'll tell you I'm revered by both my fellow employees and all the guests."

Max said, "Here's the second item. An hour ago, we sent two plainclothesmen from the Highland Park Station to the house where you live with your mom and dad, and your sister. They tossed your room and found a stack of forty-two beaver photos of Chrissy, all of which were marked '$1.00' on the back. Robbie, you would spare yourself a lot of grief, in this room and beyond, if you admitted that you were peddling those photographs, and that you and Chrissy were engaged in an attempt to extort Art Pepper, based on his somewhat specious relationship with Chrissy herself."

Robbie sputtered and stuttered. His dentures popped out. He crammed them back in.

"That is a no-good, goddamn lie. The cops planted those pix, and—"

Harry phone-booked him. *Whap*—a real cranium-crunch. Robbie's head bounced on the table. Ashtrays hopped, cigarette butts flew.

Parker said, "You called it on the extortion."

I said, "The Hat Squad. Accept no substitutes."

Robbie quivered and quaked. He shook, shimmied, and mewed for his mama. Max pulled his pocket flask and whipped it on him. Robbie suckled and siphoned it. His Adam's apple bob-bobbed.

He drained the flask dry. Max tossed him a pack of cigarettes and a matchbook. Robbie lit up and surged with a sudden savoir faire.

"I'll concede that I'm quite the racketeer, and that you'd do well to utilize me as your personal secret informant. I've been known to provide young stuff to the guests at the hotel, so they might utilize this young gash for what you might call 'casting-couch sessions,' which ain't illegal the last time my high-priced Jew lawyer checked. Also, 'Rapid Robbie,' as I'm known in the trade, has been known to supply maryjane to the geeks working at film locations, throughout the southland. I'll be candid here. I utilize the inside scoop on the locations off of tips the guests feed me."

Max said, "You're a criminal mastermind."

Red said, "I've never doubted it."

Harry said, "People dismiss you as a dipshit kid, in over his head. They fail to see the real, dynamic you that lurks beneath the façade."

Eddie said, "Keep going, hotshot. You've got us utilized."

Robbie blew smoke rings. "Right now, I'm moving maryjane to the gang on *Rebel Without a Cause*. That's this juvenile delinquency lox being shot all over L.A. This jamoke Nick Ray's directing it. He's got the hots for all these rough-trade boys he's hired to stand around and look tough in crowd scenes. I'm doing high-volume biz here. Nick the Dick's signed up an all-hophead cast, and—"

Parker hit the speaker switch. Rapid Robbie ran his mouth and made mute-mime gestures. Nick the Dick. That shitbird. He holds swishy sway over Jimmy. I should look into—

"I'm working up a brainstorm, Freddy."

"I'm listening, boss."

"I want you to build a derogatory profile on the filming of *Rebel*

Without a Cause. Deploy your pal James Dean and your usual gang of thugs, and sell Bob Harrison on the notion of a big spread in the magazine. You see where this is going? The piece is written. You improperly vet it. That leaves your shit rag that much more open to slander and libel charges, and in the meantime, you'll be passing whatever hard criminal dirt accrues on to me through the Hats."

I orbed the two-way mirror. Rapid Robbie mute-motormouthed. The Hats har-har'd and haw-hawed. Max Herman mugged at the mirror. He rolled his eyes and made the jack-off sign.

Parker passed the flask. I doused my dexie dose. *Yeah!*—a blistering blast of straight rye.

I said, "This gig packs potential. Cut dipshit loose, and I'll see what I can do."

Max made the meet. 6:00 p.m. at Ollie Hammond's. He'll be there, Freddy. It's an ass kicking, otherwise.

I arrived early. I worked the pay phones for two hours flat. I called Bondage Bob Harrison first.

Bondage Bob bemoaned the Art Pepper fiasco. All that shakedown shit for *one dope bounce?* Bob bitched: The demonizing—dope fiends craze has crapped out. It's *muerto,* you dig? I said, *Au contraire,* Daddy. It's seditiously segued into the jejune juvenile delinquency craze. To withering wit: the filming of teen turkey *Rebel Without a Cause.*

I laid it *aaalll* out. Jimmy Dean's my "in" on the shoot. Nick Ray's a carcinogenic Comsymp. There's sure to be horny hijinx with all the hot hunks and honeys on the set. Dig, Daddy: I'll dive for the dirt, you'll deliver the dish. Ten thousand words in the nuke-bomb November '55 issue.

Bob bought it, *big.* We seamlessly segued to the Rock Hudson–Phyllis Gates mock-marriage *mishegas.* Universal instigated it. Rock was one gallivanting gay caballero, and Lew Wasserman wanted all ripe rumors quashed. He hired me to find Rock a wife. My first candidate ran rogue and ransacked Rock's pad for cash and Krugerrands. Phyllis Gates seemed like a safe and sedate second bet. She was Rock's agent's secretary. She *seemed* to catch a secret scent of Rock's man-lust modus operandi—but would most likely keep her mouth shut. *Confidential* planned to publish a dizzy-disingenuous piece. How's *this* fly? "Rock's Trippy Triangle—*With Two Women!!!!!*" How's *that* for yuks and fucks/lies and sighs?

Bob said, You've got to *find* the other woman first. I said, Yeah—and I'm meeting Phyllis and Jimmy Dean at Googie's tonite to discuss it. Bob signed off, per usual: *L'chaim, boychik.*

I called Jimmy's pad and got no answer. I called his answering service and left a message: Nine tonite/Googie's. I called Phyllis and told her to make the meet. She gassed on the tricky triad scenario. She said it should culminate in a catfight at the Mocambo.

I hung up and scoped the barside crowd. *Shit*—there's Robbie Molette. He's hard-hustling a high-toned blonde and causing an undulating upscut.

Shit—

I fast-walked over and grabbed him. Rodent Robbie squirmed and squeaked. I frog-marched him to a back booth and shoved him in. I said, "Behave." Robbie sulked submissive. The barside babe blew me a kiss.

A waiter waltzed up. I ordered two double Old Crows, quicksville. Robbie smirked smug. The waiter dropped our drinks off and vamoosed.

Robbie said, "I know about you. My dad's a grip at Metro. He called you 'Mr. Fear.' He said you're the king of the shakedown."

I lit a cigarette. "What are you trying to tell me?"

"That we're two peas in a pod. That you should consider taking me on as a protégé. You could teach me the tricks of the trade and make me the new you. You could retire and ride off into the sunset then, knowing that you've got a vital young stud to fulfill your legacy."

I cringed. "Let's change the subject."

"How about boxing? Ray Robinson versus Bobo Olson. I think Ray's stale bread. Bobo's a vital young stud, and it won't go four rounds."

"How about *Rebel Without a Cause*? Lay the full dish on me. If I like what I hear, I'll let you run loose for a while. If I don't, I'll send you back to the Hats. You can play the role of the vital young stud in the queens' tank at Mira Loma."

Robbie cringed. "What's to tell? Nick Ray's a switcheroo man. He likes it young and hung, and ripe and saucy. The word is he stakes out one quiff of each gender on all his flicks. On *Rebel*, he's got Jimmy Dean for the brown eye, and Natalie Wood on the distaff side. Natalie's sixteen, in case you were curious. She's also a nympho with lezbo tendencies, for what that's worth."

Rodent Robbie. Reptile Robbie. He delivers the dish. He's cruel-credible so far.

"Keep going."

Robbie chugalugged his drink. "So, I drop off the maryjane and toke with the actors. I observe the gestalt, and to my way of thinking, this actor Nick Adams is Nick Ray's head honcho on the set. He's the court jester and the instigator, the boss pimp and the guy who drops the hammer and fulfills Nick Ray's skeevy hopes and dreams."

I killed my drink. "What hopes and dreams?"

Robbie went *tee-hee*. "Getting all these punk, fruitcake, hophead actor kids to 'fly without a parachute,' 'work without a net,' and all that other movie horseshit, when all he really wants is limitless young woof-woof, and to manipulate people in the guise of his jive, so-called art."

I clapped. I went *Ole!!!* I wolf-whistled and went *Woo-woo!!!*

"You're not stupid, Robbie. That's the only attaboy you're ever likely to get from me, so enjoy it while you can."

Robbie beamed *biiiiiiiiiig*. "Nick Ray's got all these hood-type extras under his thumb. He says he's testing their 'motivation.' He's sending them out on 'chickie runs,' like in the flick. Nick Adams is straw-bossing these deals, and Jimmy Dean's along for the ride. I don't know what's actually happening, but Jimmy calls them 'panty raids.'"

I chained cigarettes. "Where do you drop the dope off?"

"The set, the location, or Nick Ray's bungalow at the Chateau Marmont."

I peeled off five C-notes and slid them across the table. Reptile Robbie rolled his eyes and went *Oooh-la-la.*

"I'm in the White Pages. Call me at home or page me at Googie's the next time you've got a delivery."

Robbie scooped up the cash. "Two for the road? A couple of aperitifs to keep your whistle wet?"

I sighed. "All right."

"Hey, he's acting bored and vexed already."

"Robbie . . ."

"Okay, okay. Here's aperitif number one, straight from Nick Ray's mouth. Jimmy goes to leather bars and has guys put out their cigarettes on him. He is therefore known as the 'Human Ashtray.' Aperitif number two's more predictable. Jimmy's putting the moves on this kid actor, Sal Mineo. Pretty good, huh? Especially from a guy you only met a few hours ago."

I flashed back. Jimmy at Googie's. Little Band-Aids on his arms and neck. A solvent scent wafting my way.

Robbie stood up. I grabbed his waistband and slammed him back down to the table. He yelped and flailed. I held the table candle up to his face. Flame flutters scorched his pachuco pompadour and fried it to frazzled split ends.

"Jimmy and I go back. I'll concede my soft spot. Watch what you say about him."

GOOGIE'S ALL-NITE COFFEE SHOP

West Hollyweird

5/11/55

The 8:00 p.m. rush. Prosaic-predictable. Folks tumbled tables, noshed and shot the shit. Niteclub action accelerated around 9:30. Ditto, late-show movies. The Strip/the Boulevard. Ciro's, the Mocambo, the Crescendo. Grauman's Chink and the Egyptian. Googie's bopped close to all.

I took my table. Tipsters tagged the Tattle Tyrant as fair game. They salaamed and sucked up. They delivered the dubious dish.

Orson Welles sliced the Black Dahlia. *That* choice chestnut. Here's five scoots—please go away.

Here's a ripe wrinkle. Orson Welles sliced the Black Dahlia. *Yeah*—I know, it's day-old bagels at half price. Yeah, but dig *this*: Rita Hayworth held the Dahlia's legs while Orson sawed her in half.

Okay, here's ten scoots—*now* go away.

Van Johnson's at it again. The old semen demon's always up for a taste. He siphoned Tab Hunter's python in a back row at the Admiral Theatre.

No, I can't prove it. *Yeah*, I need gelt. There's a sneak peek at the Iris, and I'm short on the freight.

Here's twenty scoots. Uncle Freddy's a soft touch. The popcorn's on me.

A guy peddled Carole Landis morgue shots. *Yawn*. A guy peddled pix of Marlon Brando with a dick in his mouth. *Shit*—I thought

I cornered *that* market, back in '53. A call girl tossed me a tip on the steakhouse rape-o/robbers. They were holed up in a hot-sheet flop on 54th and Vermont. They were geezing Nazi-made morphine and meth speedballs. I slid her forty scoots. She slipped me her phone number. I told her to tattle the tip to the Hat Squad. She told me she banged Red Stromwall at an Elks Club smoker, back in '46.

Juan the fry cook passed me a message. Jimmy was 86'ing the Phyllis Gates meet. Nick Ray culled the cast and called for a script read. Nick Ray ran regular "Motivational Missions," as in tonite. Sorry, babe—give Phyl my love.

Neuter Nick Ray. "Motivational Missions." Robbie Molette's mad monologue. My pal Jimmy. The "Human Ashtray." I felt god-awful gut-punched.

It was 8:55. A late nite loomed. I had a batch of bilious back issues to study for Big Bill Parker. *Nasty Nat's Soul Patrol* popped the airwaves at 1:00. Miss Blind Item might call in. She'd castigate and condemn *Confidential*. She'd evince righteous rage per Red Light Bandit Caryl Chessman. The deal instantly intrigued me. Chessman was sure as shit guilty. I wanted him to burn, baby, burn.

My dexie dose fizzled, drizzled, and withered to wisps and gnashed nerves. I popped two more and awaited the *aaaaahhhh*. Phyllis walked in. I stood up and bowed. She walked up and curt-sied cute. She wore twill slacks and a cashmere cardigan. She radi-ated rectitude and a reserved ring-a-ding.

A waitress brought menus. Phyllis sat across from me. She went *Where's Jimmy?*

I said, "He couldn't make it. Something about a script rehearsal."

The waitress whipped back. Phyllis ordered a dry martini. I held up two fingers. The waitress scrammed. Phyllis said, "Drat."

I laffed. *"Drat?"*

"Well, yes."

"Should I decode that?"

"Well . . . Jimmy and Rock were pals on *Giant*. I was hoping that he might provide . . ."

"A perspective on Rock's bent, and your conundrum? Maybe buffer you and me getting down to brass tacks?"

The martinis materialized. Phyllis mainlined half of hers. She said, "Drat. What have I gotten myself into?"

I lit a cigarette. "You love him, right?"

"What's not to love? He's every Minnesota farm girl's dream. But *this* girl has lived in Hollywood for a while, and I've heard the rumors, and I know how to read signs."

"How discouraged are you?"

Phyllis laffed. "Not that much. Part of me knows that it's more than a little bit of a lark."

I mainlined my martini. It payload-packed the dexies. I rippled resurgent and revitalized.

"I'm on your side, and Rock's side. 'Love conquers all,' and all that happy horseshit. The magazine's on your side, and Rock's side, but the magazine is *Confidential*, with all the skank that implies. We've got to dispel one set of rumors, and create a contradictory, second set to eclipse it. Bob Harrison's committed to an eternal triangle scenario. That means we need to find a bait girl, and L.A.'s the bait girl capital of the world. And, for what it's worth, I like your idea of a catfight at the Mocambo."

Phyllis popped the olive out of her drink and snarfed it. I tossed my olive on her place mat. She snarfed it, quick-quick.

"Rock's a sweetie pie. Who am I to demand perfection in a man?"

"You've got every right to demand more than you damn well might have to settle for."

Phyllis said, "Ouch."

I said, "I'm sorry. That was harsh."

Phyllis went *Pshaw*. "It's not like I'm a hundred percent discouraged."

"Give me the good news, then."

"Rock took an inkblot test once, in the Navy. He saw butterflies and snakes, which symbolize a feminine nature and the penis. He took a second test, after the war—and this time he scored much more butch."

I sighed, sad-ass. "Shit, don't break my heart."

Phyllis snatched my martini and drained it dry. Her eyeballs boinged. Now, she's all rectitude—ripped to the gills.

"It's a lark, right?"

"Right."

"And there's no guarantee it'll *remain* a lark, right?"

"Right."

"So I should be prepared for any and all outcomes, right?"

"Right."

"Didn't you say something about us getting down to brass tacks?"

I leaned close. Phyllis leaned close. We deep-dialed our eyes and *cleaved* close. She wore Chanel No. 5. I wore Lucky Tiger. Our separate scents sizzled and merged, *molto bene.*

"You'll want out sooner or later. You won't want him hurt in the press, but you'll want your fair share of the pie. I'll handle the entrapment and all the other shitwork for ten percent of the initial property and revenue split, and ten percent of your alimony, in perpetuity."

Phyllis kissed me. She found the fit and held my head and leg-clamped me under the table. The kiss lingered *loooooong.* We wrapped ourselves into it. Our scents merged that much more. Some geeks at adjoining tables whistled and clapped.

11:00 p.m. Googie's is late-nite lulled. The dinner crowd's thinned threadbare. Phyllis split. I brooded and brain-broiled my *Rebel Without a Cause* caper.

My dexie decibel helped. Vodka shots sheared the rough edges. I worked the pay phone. I called Harry Fremont and my contact at Sheriff's R & I. Dig: Get me homo-hive roust sheets on Jimmy Dean, Sal Mineo, Nick Ray. Check for juvie sheets on Natalie Wood. Solicit hometown paper per Nick Adams.

The counter man divvied dish. Nick Ray placed take-out orders nitely. Juan the fry cook schlepped the shit up to Nick's boss bungalow at the Marmont. The orders came in late. There was bupkes tonite. I told Juan to burn a batch of burgers and send them up *now.*

The Marmont was four blocks west on Sunset. I shagged my Packard pimpmobile and crawl-cruised on over. I saw three hunky hot rods stashed just off the Strip. *Craaaaazy* chrome creations. Kool kandy-koat kolors.

One '40 Ford coupé. One '46 Merc. One *cholo*-chopped Chevy van, replete with flame paint job. All three flew flags for the "Nick's Knights Kar Klub, Limited."

The flags wiggled on whip antennas and flat-out flew in the wind. I fantasized shivering shit.

Nick Ray in tight toga and a simpering Caesar haircut. He's holding a movie megaphone and sporting a spiked collar. He's Mr. Fasco Fantastico at the all-boy bacchanal. As *real-life* proof—there's Nick's Knights, poised and posed by their sleds.

Three hunky monkeys. Ruff trade tricksters and buff B-boys. Black leather jackets, pomade pompadours, and pegged pants. Rodent Robbie ratted these punks. They were Nabob Nick's crowd-scene extras. They went out on "chickie runs" and "panty raids." Nudnik Nick held swishy sway over them.

I pulled up and parked on the bungalow access road. Juan the fry cook's junk jalopy was parked just ahead. I walked up to bungalow row. I peeped whipped-wide windows. I saw sapphic *soixante-neuf* and Marilyn Monroe blowing Joe DiMaggio. I saw a dusky dominatrix whip producer Sam Spiegel. I saw Funky *Führer* Nick Ray blaspheme, bloviate, and bluster to his actor acolytes.

He's the Father *Führer*, the Daddy Despot, the Doofus *Duce* who's exhumed mad Mussolini. He's brewing up bracing bromides. It's populist pap across all specious spectra. He's stamping it Stalinist. He's looping in Lenin and marginal Marx. It's the actors' art to subsume the rule of law and the ordered society. It's ART to sack sacred synagogues, chain church doors, and retorch Joan of Arc at the stake. It's sicknik sexual liberation, by way of the maladroit Marquis de Sade. He's pitching *Sex/Sex/Sex/* and *Love Me/Love Me/ Love Me*—and I will beatifically bestow upon you the gilded gift of MOTIVATION—which will unlock all the doors of your life.

His kiddie korps is digging it. They're bopped back in beanbag chairs. They're biting the burgers I bought them. They're big-eyed behind Big Nick's bullshit. There's Jimmy Dean and Natalie Wood. There's sloe-eyed Sal Mineo. That blond cat's Nick Adams. I've seen that Dennis Hopper hump on TV. They're Nihilist Nick's hip Hitler *Jugend*, ten years post–V-E Day.

I unpeeped the window and broomed back down to my sled. Memo to Chief Bill Parker: I got your derogatory profile, hanging a hard fucking yard.

Something was brew-brew-brewing. It had to break up and boil over, *soon*. I hunched low and peeped the hot rod punks. They popped hoods and adjusted fan belts. They poured quik-start in quad carburetors and goosed the gas *loud*. They made big noise. They torqued and toxified the air outside the Chateau Marmont. Then the moment of *Achtung!!!!!* arrived.

The punks froze. Eyes right, all *Kameraden*. There's Nick Ray in a cool khaki jumpsuit. He's Rommel, reborn. He's got an Iron Cross pinned to one pocket. He's wearing a Desert Korps hat. He's got a movie camera strapped to one shoulder. Jimmy Dean and Nick Adams stand behind him. They're his suck-up subalterns.

The punks salaamed and saluted. Nick Ray ran to the Chevy van. *Raus mit uns!!!!! Mach schnell!!!!!* All subalterns and B-boys to the Chevy van now!!!!!

The crew cringed and complied, toot-fucking-sweet. The van U-turned and booked west on Sunset. I U-turned and tailed it.

We struck off down the Strip and bombed through Beverly Hills. My Packard pimpmobile hovered three car lengths back. Beverly Hills to Holmby Hills to the East Bel-Air gate. Up to Westwood and the UCLA campus.

The van cut south on Hilgard. It decelerated down to a crawl. I crawled and kept perfect pace. We were on Sorority Row now. Note the big Tudor and sparkle-Spanish houses. Note the Greek symbols embossed by the doors.

It was midnite. It was quiet and moon-muzzled dark. The driver rolled down his window and pointed across the street. Somebody said, "Establishing shot." A back window slid down. Nick Ray held his camera out and rolled film. I decelerated and pulled to the curb. The *Führer* van U-turned and parked in front of a faux-château sorority house.

The Desert Korps decamped. That's the B-Boys, Nick Ray,

Jimmy, and Nick Adams. A B-boy held Ray's camera cord and a spotlight gizmo. Ray gave the high sign. They walked six abreast. They crossed the sidewalk and trampled the front lawn. They hit the porch. Nick Adams pulled a set of picks and unlocked the door. It's *soooooo* sinister—the six sickos slide and slither inside.

I heard nothing. I saw nothing. No light went on. I got out and jogged up to the door. It stood ajar. I heard wicked whispers and *sssshhh, sssshhh* upstairs.

The camera light snapped on. A beam bounced across upstairs walls and closed doors. I heard a door open. A girl said, "What's that?" A girl said, "Who's there?"

Then door kicks/shrill shrieks/light beams on dorm doors and double sets of bunk beds—

Then college girls in nightgowns and pajamas. They're kicking off their covers and tumbling out of bed. They're running straight into bright light and the Desert Korps with their hands out to GRAB.

Nick Ray yelled, "*Chickie run!!!*"

Jimmy yelled, "*Panty raid!!!!!*"

Spotlight beams bounced. I saw short shots of grabs at pajama tops and nightgowns. I saw panties pulled down to the knees. I heard screams overlap.

I ran upstairs. Half-nude girls dodged grabbing hands and bouncing light and ran from *der* Desert Korps demons. I pile-pounded into them. I dumped the fucko *Führer's* camera and smashed the bouncing-light machine. I got a fade-out shot. It's Jimmy Dean with pink panties pulled over his face.

I saw a fire-alarm switch wired to a wall mount. I swatted the switch and instigated deep darkness. A siren shrieked shrill. The girls screamed into it. They ran left and hit the back stairs. The Desert Korps ran to the main stairway. They couldn't see me. I couldn't see them. I pulled my belt sap and sapped black leather and coarse khaki. They made with the motivation and bitch-bleated. I might have sapped my pal Jimmy. So what if I did?

MY BOSS BACHELOR PAD

West Holly*weird*

5/12/55

I ran the radio. KKXZ—le jazz hot levied with listless bop ballads that blew blue and nodded off to nothingness. A low-watt/store-front station. Above Sultan Sam's Sandbox and Rae's Rugburn Room.

I was laid low, bent bare, and stripped to striation on the Isle of Deep Despair. The Westwood caper cornholed me. I humped Hilgard to Sunset. I ripped rubber just as the fuzz and fire engines arrived. The Afrika Korps beat it southbound. Their goofy getaway masked their insidious intent. A moment to maul my memory: Jimmy Dean, with pink panties stretched eyeballs to neck.

Nasty Nat's Soul Patrol popped the airwaves. Nat read local news spots before he samba'd back to his soporific sounds of the nite. He kicked off with his "Cutie."

UCLA. Sorority row. Panty raid at Chi Beta Gamma. The fuzz arrive. There's a garland of girls, wrapped in robes and issuing indignation. Four girls put it off on the SAE boys or USC football studs. One girl called it "more evil than that. These guys were older. One guy carried a camera. They ripped our robes, and tried to shoot a nudie film right there."

Nasty Nat put down some pooh-pooh patter. "UCLA ain't the ghetto, sisters. And I'm sure those young buck cops will be back to ask you to stage in-the-buff reenactments."

Ouch.

Nasty Nat said, "It's crime on the dime, tonite. The some might say infamous LAPD Hat Squad shot it out with those two steakhouse rapist-robbers. It went down at Tommy Tucker's Playroom on Washington and La Brea. One man escaped in the mad melee. *Muerto* at the scene: Richie 'The Dutchman' Van Duesen/white male American/age thirty-eight. Still at large: George 'Fat Boy' Mazmanian/white male American/age forty-two. The Fat Boy is purportedly armed and dangerous, so watch out."

Nasty Nat mimicked the *Confidential* style. It gored my goat. He cut from crime on the dime to bleak blues from the Synagogue Sid Trio. Dig: Sid on bass sax, Bobby Horvitz on flügelhorn, Aaron Adelman on drums. The piece: "Premature Funeral March for Gamal Abdel Nasser and King Farouk." Nat laid down the intro. He closed with "These cats run long." One, two, three—*shalom*, cats.

Synagogue Sid blatted his sax. Bobby Horvitz flaunted his flügelhorn. Aaron Adelman drilled his drums. I doused the volume. I got imperiously impatient. Where's Miss Blind Item? Where's her cruel critique of *Confidential*'s Caryl Chessman piece??? Where's her fry-the-cocksucker rebuttal???

I was itchy/antsy/fraught/fragged and dexie-ditzed out of my gourd. I got out my notepad and skimmed '52 to '55 *Confidentials*. I'm a snitch, a rat fink, a stool pigeon, a squealer, a quisling, a rogue dog who bites the hand that feeds him. Let's do legal prep work for Chief William H. Parker.

Bill Parker and me. We're like *that* now. Let's take down *Confidential*.

Back issues. Clipped-on legal files. Lawyers' notes and field reports. Look for loopholes. Dippy depositions to dice and deep-six. The mag hired ace legal beagles. The mag had Freddy O. for strong-arm vetting and verification. All our slurs and slander slams are true. We stand by our shit. Yeah, but if anybody's prone to fuck it all up, it's yammeringly yours truly.

I skimmed back issues. I read legal briefs and my own notes. I muddled through mellifluous memories.

December '52: "Showgirl Sells Shares in Self!!!"

Bland, by and large. A stock-market spoof. Vetted by a kid clerk. No slander slams or libel loops here.

December '52: "Exposed: Love in the UN!!!!"

Tattle text. The Multinational March of Miscegenation. Minor minions *j'accused*. I'm bored already. No vetting notes. Doofus diplomats never sue.

November '53: "Marked for Death: Walter Winchell, Bishop Fulton Sheen!!!"

Anti-Commie pap. Lawyers cite unnamed sources. Snoresville, U.S.A.

March '54: "Why Orson Welles Bit the Lip of Eartha Kitt."

Miscegenation—*Confidential*'s merry mainstay. Orson was boning irksome Eartha. A Vegas stringer fed us the bit. Eartha said goons broke down her door. She was right. I hired the goons. Eartha demanded cold compensation. I slid her ten thou. Orson said, "You're a shit, Freddy." I bitch-slapped him.

This piece was bad juju and a potential Parker payoff. It exposed the mag's strong-arm methods and exposed ME. I put it in my secret Parker dirt file.

November '54: "Christine Jorgensen's Romance with a Vanderbilt Stepson."

He-she hijinx. Ex-man Christine set Vanderbilt up and had me shoot sneak pix. She wanted the publicity—to goose her dead-stalled film career. I shook down Vanderbilt for twenty thou. Christine and I split the gelt. *Confidential* published a pablum-packed piece that went *pffft*. Christine was pissed. She wanted to see some wild and wet woof-woof. This piece could mulch the magazine, *baaaaaad*. Ditto, Fred Otash. It was *goooood* Parker file fodder.

January '55: "Eartha Kitt and her 'Santa Baby' Arthur Loew, Jr."

Miscegenation marches on. The old colored canary/white sugar daddy bit. It's Irksome Eartha *again*. Eartha threatens to sue. I'm the bagman. *Confidential* coughs up cold cash.

Synagogue Sid blatted on. I yawned. Where's Miss Blind Item? It's almost 2:00 a.m.

March '55: "The Wife Clark Gable Forgot." Yawn. "The Girl in Gregory Peck's Bathtub." Man, it's sacked-out soporific.

Synagogue Sid bleated bleak and deep diminuendoed. I heard the mike-magnified cough of coins dropped in a pay phone. I kicked the volume. Nasty Nat said, "Miss Blind Item's back—so I know we're going to be talking *Confidential* magazine and the infamous Caryl Chessman case."

Miss Blind Item said, "Hey, Nat. What's shaking?"

I dug her voice. It was cool contralto and *mucho* Midwest.

"Nothing but the leaves on the tree, baby."

"Locate me, Nat. Where did we leave off last time?"

"Well, we did the long-range overview of *Confidential*, and we both commented on how atypically liberal their coverage of the Chessman case was, given that *Confidential*'s been a Red-baiting and race-baiting rag from jump street."

Nasty Nat told it true. August '52. The cheesy Chessman piece. The mag was naïvely new then. I didn't sign on till fall '53.

Miss Blind Item laffed. "*Confidential*'s got style, baby. You're starting to alliterate already."

Nasty Nat wolf-whistled. "And you've got *cojones,* as our Mex cousins say, calling a Negro man 'baby.'"

Miss Blind Item relaffed. Phone-booth sounds went mike-magnified. There's a match strike and exhale. She's smoking a cigarette.

"I'm an actress, Nat. You can always count on me to go for a provocative effect."

"Disc jockeys go the same route. Our sponsors here encourage it. Come on, Sultan Sam's Sandbox and Rae's Rugburn Room? They ain't paying me for bland."

"Talk about alliteration, *baby.*"

Nasty Nat said, "You ain't Miss Blind Item, you the sexy succubus. Now, moving along, before you get me in trouble with the Klan, the Catholic Legion of Decency, and Chief Parker his own self, why don't you drop the basic lowdown on the Chessman case on all the folks out in Radioland."

Miss Blind Item refed the pay phone. Dimes dipped, nickels notched down the slot.

"It's early '48. Chessman's fresh out of Folsom. He's stealing cars and committing armed robberies. He's utilizing a hot '46 Ford as his rape vehicle, and he's affixed a phony red light to it, so he can pass himself off as a policeman. Now, he's prowling lovers' lanes in Pasadena and up above Hollywood. He's robbing young couples making out. On two legally affirmed occasions, he forcibly removes young women from *their* cars, and places them in *his* car. That legally constitutes kidnapping. Once they're in *his* car, he sexually assaults them, which constitutes a second, specific set of felony charges. His two *certified* victims conclusively identified him. He was convicted at trial and sentenced to death. Much has been made of the fact that Chessman did not kill anyone. *C'est la guerre*, sweetie. The Little Lindbergh Law applies. Now, that evil no-goodnik has become an ace jailhouse lawyer, and he's beaten back a slew of attempts to send him to the green room, where he most devoutly belongs. He wrote a book, which was published last year, called *Cell 2455, San Quentin*. In it, he fatuously asserts his innocence of the Red Light Bandit crimes and demands a redress of the entire American legal system."

Nasty Nat went *whew!* "I'm renaming you, and it ain't 'baby' or 'sweetie.' And you ain't really Miss Blind Item, you more the 'Vindictive Vixen,' which prompts me to ask you why you so het up on this case, when just about everybody *I* know thinks Chessman got railroaded, and these justice-minded folks *I* know are all doing their darnedest to make sure he *don't* go to that green room."

Go, Nasty Nat. You snagged it on the snout. Baby, sweetie, Miss Item—why you calling in to my radio show?

"It's dawning on me, sugar. *You* got a personal stake in this whole Chessman hullabaloo. That means there's something you haven't told us."

Miss Blind Item lit a cigarette. I heard the match flare and exhale.

"There was a third victim. She came forth and identified Chessman, but the DA chose not to have her testify at trial. The sexual assault that Chessman perpetrated against her was especially vile and vicious. Bluntly put, she went insane, and has spent the past seven years in Camarillo. The young woman was a friend of mine. We studied at a prestigious acting school in New York together, back in late '47. That's the long and short of it, Nat. I'm on leave from a gig in New York now, so I thought I'd make a little ruckus in my friend's hometown, and maybe take a little drive up to Camarillo."

Es la verdad. I was at Hollywood Station that night. I saw Miss Third Victim walk in and collapse on the squadroom floor.

GRIFFITH PARK

Above the *Rebel Without a Cause* Shoot

5/13/55

*O*uch!!!!!

Outdoor surveillance. The withering worst. Dirt on my duds and briar bristles brushing my ass. I'm up some hellhole hiking trail. There's a noxious noonday sun singeing me. I've got binoculars trenchantly trained on the Observatory lot.

It's lunchtime. The lot's cordoned off for cast and crew, exclusive. It's loaded with hot rod heaps and kool kat kids couched within. Robbie Molette's hopping, heap to heap. He's pushing pills and reefers. I'm peeping the transactions. It's a rippling replay of last nite's panty raid/chickie run.

There's Nick Ray, Nick Adams, my putz pal Jimmy Dean. The gang's got up in street threads. There's no Afrika Korps kouture and *Sieg Heil* today. There's the three B-boys. They're still dressed in blasphemous black. I memorized the Chevy van plate stats last nite. They came back to one Chester Alan Voldrich/white male American/age twenty-six. Dig: he bossed the nabobically noted Hollywood High Rat Pack, circa '49. They rolled elderly fruits and Mickey Finn'd Marymount girls and got in their pants.

That was *gooooooood* derogatory dish. Bill Parker would crap-his-pants *cream*. *And*—per Nick Adams/real name Adamshock/DOB 7-10-31/Nanticote, Pennsylvania:

No arrests/eight rousts on suspicion: GTA, flimflam, malicious mischief, Stat Rape, Peeping Tom, pushing pornographic snapshots. *Plus:* gay-bar roust sheets on Jimmy Dean and Nick Ray. Confirmed per Jimmy: Robbie Molette's "Human Ashtray" shtick. Confirmed per Nick Ray: rousted at the Saints and Sinners Drag Ball. Whoa, Nellie—Nick was a knockout in his Red Guard empire gown. *Plus:* Natalie Wood and Sal Mineo, popped at the "Jailbait Jamboree" at Linda's Little Log Cabin.

It's all Kids Run Wild/Kids Led Astray. It summoned me to serve Bill Parker *and* my *meshugenah* magazine. It summoned me to save Jimmy D. from himself.

I binocularized the big parking lot. Robbie pushed pills. Jimmy and Nick Adams shot craps on a Nazi-flag blanket. Jimmy called my service and left a message: "See you at Googie's tonite." *That* meant *this:* he didn't make me at the panty raid/chickie run.

I binocularized. Chester Voldrich and his B-boy buddies sniffed a glue-soaked rag. Natalie Wood basked in a bikini. She reclined on the roof of a '52 Eldo. Nick Ray walked by and kissed her thighs on the sly.

I walked into Hollywood Station. The desk sergeant moaned. *Oh shit—it's Freddy O.*

I walked up to the squadroom. A meter maid tagging tickets sighed. *Oh shit—it's Freddy O.* The squad lieutenant saw me. He rolled his eyes and slammed his door. *Oh shit—it's Freddy O.*

I looked for Colin Forbes and Al Goossen. They bossed the Chessman case, back in '48. There they are. They're Hollywood Squad lifers—they've still got the same two desks. They're workhorses worn weary. They're working. The squadroom was otherwise dead.

They saw me. They shared a look. *Oh shit—it's Freddy—*

I pulled a chair over. Forbes said, "Hi, Freddy." Goossen said, "Freddy's slumming. That means he wants something."

I said, "Chessman. The magazine wants to atone for that boo-hoo piece they published three years ago. There's some rumors percolating on the third victim. I was here when she came in, if you recall."

Forbes lit a cigarette. "That's right. You called Queen of Angels when she fainted."

Goossen lit a cigarette. "Chessman bit her forty-three times. *You'd* faint, too. She went straight from Queen of Angels to Camarillo, and the last I heard, she was still in shock. Don't put her in the magazine, Freddy. Show some class for once in your life."

I let it go. "Do you recall her name?"

Forbes shook his head *nein*. Goossen shook his head *nyet*. They revealed zilch. My reptile rep rubbed them raw.

"What's the story on her? Can you give me that, without naming names?"

Goossen kicked his chair back. "She was an L.A. girl, home for a visit. She was studying at the Actors Studio in New York, which is some sort of hotshot deal. So, she's home, and she's staying with her folks. She's also a lezzie, which her folks know nothing about. On the night in question, she picks up a girl at Rhonda's Rendezvous, and they parked on the shoulder at Mulholland and Beverly Glen. Chessman pulls his red light number, sees the girls making out and flips his lid. He throws the pickup girl out of the car, escorts the victim girl to his car, does what he does to her, and she makes her way here, under her own power. She never testified in court, and she didn't need to. Judge Fricke heard the story, and *that's* what convinced him that Chessman should burn. And he *will* burn, sooner or later, despite all his books and legal appeals, and Marlon Brando and all the other Hollywood geeks waving placards."

Forbes said, "Shove your 'rumors percolating' up your ass, Freddy. You've got your own perv-o agenda going on this deal, so take it with you when you walk out the door, sometime in the next five seconds."

—⁂—

Perv-o agenda." *Oh shit—it's Freddy O.* My old cop colleagues lay on the love. Freddy O's the Shakedown King. He's the Shaman of Shame. He's the Pervdog of the Nite. Where's the payoff here, Freddy? There's got to be a payoff with you.

Why mince words? *Cherchez la femme.* It's Miss Blind Item. She's scorched herself under my skin.

I drove by the Ranch Market. I checked my phone slips. Jack the K. called. "I'm at the hotel. Come by at six. I'm having people up for drinks."

I'll be there, Jack. Fetch, Pervdog, fetch. I'll go by your favorite pharmacy first. I know what you like. Why mince words? I like it, too.

Miss Blind Item. She studied with Miss Third Victim. They were New York friends. A "prestigious acting school." Late '47.

Al Goossen. *The* Actors Studio. "Some sort of hotshot deal."

So—

Quo vadis, Freddy? Where to now?

I know. Let's slam Mr. Blacklist. He always gives up the goods.

Jack Lawson. John Howard Lawson. Anglicized from Levy or some such. One studly Stalinist. He tramples Trotskyites and hexes HUAC to hell. Folks hate Jack. It's that perennial politics and personality parlay. Jack's determinedly dyspeptic. He's a *schmuck, a schlemiel, a schmendrick,* and a *schlimazel.* The PD and DA Ernie Roll own him covertly. Let's bop back to '40. Jack's the Party's Kultural Kommissar and hard-hearted hatchet man.

Enter Budd Schulberg. He's a ripsnorting writer and a marvelous *mensch.* He's writing *What Makes Sammy Run?* The Party demands rafts of revisions. Budd's a Party man maimed by *mucho* misgivings. Like Studly Stalin's purges that mowed millions dead. Jack mediates a meet and sets the spot. It's some comrade's casa off Hollywood and Fairfax. Budd is suddenly summoned. Jumpy Jack's there. Likewise the viperish V. J. Jerome. V.J.'s Jack's Ko-Kultural Kommissar. V.J. and Jack pack the Party's one-two punch.

V.J. and Jack. They berate Budd for two days, stridently straight. You *will* rewrite your bourgeois book. It must be proudly proletarian. You're a revisionist, a refusenik, a deviationist delinquent. You're a passive pawn of the fascist elite.

Here's the punch line. The comrade's casa is bugged, rugs to rafters. The comrade called in the cops. The Hitler-Stalin pact did it. The comrade ain't no Commie no more.

Jack berates Budd. Jack reads him the ripe riot act. Jack motormouths on many topics. Jack pounds popular front groups and takes them to task. Jack jacks off à la idiot ideologues worldwide. The PD shoots the bug tapes to State HUAC. Fourteen Smith Act indictments result.

The bug's still in place. Jack's sublet the comrade's casa since '48. Ex-Commies visit Jack. They juke him with jungle juice and get him to jaw. Jack jaws on overdrive. He's every Red Squad cop and dirt digger's dream. '48 to '55. That's seven years. The bugs remain in place. Jack don't know shit.

I drove over and parked outside Casa Comrade. I brought Jack a jug of Jim Beam. Jack sat on his front steps. I saw him. He saw me. It was *Oh shit—Freddy Otash*, redux.

I got out and walked up. Jack went *Sieg Heil* and hummed "Das Horst Wessel Lied." I yukked and tossed Jack his jug. He yanked the cap and yodeled a big blast.

"Freddy the O. *Gauleiter* for the occupation forces of Chief William H. Parker."

"You know who I work for, Jack. I'm a free-speech man, just like you."

Jack grabbed his crotch. "Free speech is a shuck. It's a smoke screen to cosmeticize the fascist agenda. *Confidential* riles up the *schvarzers* and *faygeles*. In that sense, it's an organ of revolutionary intent."

I laffed. "I'll tell Bob Harrison that."

"Tell Bob I saw his first wife at a Scottsboro Boys rally, back in '30-something. She was holding hands with a *shvoogie* and Pete Seeger's Filipina girlfriend. They were singing 'Swing Low, Sweet Chariot'—off-key, no less."

I stuffed a fifty in Jack's shirt pocket. Jack reyodeled Jim Beam. He hummed "Lili Marlene" and the love-death bit from *Tristan und Isolde*.

"Freddy the O. wants something. He never comes just to *schmooze*."

I said, "The Actors Studio. The late '40s. I know you go back to the Group Theatre, so I thought you might be able to help me."

"The Actors Studio. *Oy*. Not a revolutionary organ, susceptible to takeover by Comrade John Howard Lawson and the hundreds of young Red Guard majorettes eager to suck his big dialectical cock."

I said, "Come on, Jack. I was thinking you could give me some names."

Jack went *mucho* outraged. "*Me*? Name *names*? You think the *apparatchik* to end all *apparatchiks* would name names and betray the Fourth Apparatus of the Central Soviet?"

I said, "Jack, you're a pisser."

Jack stumbled into Casa Comrade. He left the door open. I saw him banging bookshelves and tossing tomes on the floor.

I lit a cigarette. Jack barged back outside. He passed me a school-type yearbook. It was buckram-bound and gilt-embossed. The cover read: *The Actors Studio/1946–47*.

"Thanks, Jack."

Jack hummed "The Internationale." "I know about the bug, Freddy. My *schvartze* cleaning lady discovered it when I first moved in."

I was floored and flat-flabbergasted. I grabbed Jack's jug and jammed down the juice. The world rippled and revised itself right before my eyes.

"You could have pulled it. You'd have saved some comrades of yours a whole lot of grief."

"Maybe I didn't want to. Maybe they deserved what they got. Maybe I thought I'd fuck with History and roll the dice for a while."

I traveled Trans-Jack Airways. The Lawson-Kennedy loop. It flew Casa Comrade to Beverly Hills. I buzzed by the Beverly Wilshire

Pharmacy and filled Jack the K.'s order. Spaceman Jack would orbit tonite.

I hit the Beverly Hills Hotel. It was a back-bungalow bash. I lit through the lobby and landed right on cue. Women outnumbered men six to one. It was all stacked starlets and porko politicians. DA Ernie Roll and AG Pat Brown. Both quash-*Confidential* conspirators. Governor Goodie Knight. Colored congressman Adam Clayton Powell. Note his "Kiss Me, I'm Irish" campaign button.

I crashed the crowd. I popped out to a poolside porch and straddled a deck chair. A brisk breeze induced *aaahhhs*. I studied the Actors Studio book.

I poured through picture-packed pages. No-name kids built sets. Lee Strasberg made like Moses and laid down the law. I noted name actors and nudniks I'd seen on TV. I hit a section marked "1946–47 class." Kids congregated on bleachers and smiled, heartbreak hopeful. Page twenty-two popped out at me. I *thought* I saw—

Some names and no-names mingled. Kim Hunter, Ralph Meeker. Two no-name males. I recognized Reed Hadley of *Racket Squad*. There's Julie Harris and boss Barbara Bel Geddes. There's the wounded waif I saw at Hollywood Station during the Red Light Bandit's rampage.

She's hopeful here. She's heartfelt. She's wearing a paint-smeared smock and saddle shoes. She's standing beside a lissome light-haired woman I'd never seen before.

A name list laid out the players. Miss Third Victim was Shirley Tutler. The light-haired woman was Lois Nettleton.

Jack the K. walked up. I tossed him the pharmacy bag. Pill vials vibrated and did the shimmy-shimmy shake.

"Dare I ask what it cost?"

I said, "Zilch. The pharmacist's a defrocked physician. He owes me numerous favors."

Jack relit his cigar. "I'll be a defrocked U.S. senator, if I can't raise a whole lot of money tonight."

"There's not a lot of money in the next room. The girls don't have it, and the political guys never give it away."

Jack chortled. "Give me a good one, Freddy. My sisters like dish on handsome young actors and their secret lives. And don't give me Rock Hudson, because that's yesterday's news."

I said, "James Dean is known as the 'Human Ashtray.'"

"That's fairly unsavory."

"Barbara Payton's on the skids. She's car-hopping at Stan's Drive-In, across from Hollywood High."

Jack said, "Old news. You set me up with Babs when you were a cop and I was a congressman."

I said, "Katharine Hepburn is really a man. *Whisper*'s running the story next month. She underwent hormone therapy in the Soviet Union."

"I'll live with it. As long as she's not a Commie or a Republican."

My time was up. Jack's eyes wiggled and wandered. He's Two-Minute Jack with his minions. He's Ten-Minute Jack in the sack.

"It was good seeing you, Freddy."

"Always a pleasure, Jack."

The sun salved me. The breeze went warm and bid me to bask. I dipped and dozed. The bungalow behind me went muffled and mute. I saw Shirley Tutler's picture and heard Miss Blind Item's voice. Soft sounds soothed me. Reverie. I'm rapt and reverential. I'm a kid back in church.

Wheels popped over pavement. Dishes rattled. Somebody said, "I didn't know you knew Jack."

I opened my eyes. Oh shit—it's Rodent Robbie Molette. A hairnet hid his fried hair. He's Busboy Robbie today. He's rolling a room-service cart.

"Everybody knows Jack. He exemplifies our new egalitarian society. It's why he talks to guys like you and me."

Robbie scratched his balls. "Be that as it may, I should take advantage of running into you, and tell you the latest scuttlebutt from the shoot."

I said, "I'm listening."

"You *should* listen, given the gist of what I'm about to tell you."

"Robbie, don't draw this—"

"Okay, here's the latest and greatest, which ain't so great in my view. A, Nick Ray's talking 'escalation.' He wants 'the kids' to 'plumb their motivation' and 'escalate their mischief.' B, he's talking hot-prowl 459's, liquor-store robberies, and making some sort of 'radical alternative movie,' that will 'complement and enlarge the meaning of,' this lox *Rebel Without a Cause*, which in my view is headed for the drive-in circuit in Dogdick, Arkansas."

I pondered the poop. Robbie futzed with his hairnet.

"You burned me, fucker. You messed with my good looks, because you're jealous of me."

Stood up, stiffed, dropped dry, and jilted. Dumped for some psycho Film *Führer*. Bereft like some left-behind belle at the ball.

Jimmy no-showed. I waited at Googie's. No Jimmy. I called my answering service. No messages. I called Jimmy's pad. No answer. I went by Jimmy's pad. No lights lit, no Jimmy. I cruised by the Chateau Marmont and bopped back to bungalow row. I peeped Nick Ray's bungalow. I saw Nazi Nick pour the pork to Natalie Wood while Sal Mineo snapped snapshots.

I bolted back to my sled and slipped southbound. I was whip-wigged and wound up *waaaaaaay* tight. A new notion nudged me. It pertained to Miss Blind Item. I stopped at a pay phone and called crime lab rajah Ray Pinker.

I outlined my plan. I pledged five yards. Rajah Ray said, "Sure—I'll do it." I ran back to my Packard pimpmobile and pointed it southbound. I *dove* into darktown. Vermont to Slauson, eastbound and *doooooooown*.

I passed Mumar's Mosque, Mama Mattie's Massage Paradise, and the Mad Monk Klub. I hustled by Happytime Liquor, Happy Hal's Liquor, Hillhaven Liquor, and liquor lockers lit by signs that said LIQUOR and no more. I saw the signs for Sultan Sam's Sandbox and Rae's Rugburn Room. There's my dizzy destination: KKXZ Radio.

A wino weaved by. I curb-parked my pimpmobile right by the Rugburn Room door. The wino whistled and gassed on the tritone paint job. I tossed him a ten-spot and told him to watchdog my baby.

Back stairs ran me past the Rugburn Room and up to Radioland. It was beat-to-shit bohemian and cultivatedly cut-rate.

A wastified waiting room. Album covers stud-stapled to bare walls. They were all Bird. Bird bought the farm and bid us bye-bye in March. Bird beamed beatific now—I'm *muerto, muchachos.* A myriad of mourners scrawled up the white walls. It was all adios, Big Daddy and Hail to the King.

"Write something, Mr. Otash. He won't mind."

I swift-swiveled. Nasty Nat stood there. I recognized his radio voice. He was tall and a fit forty. He dressed cool-cat insurrectionist. I dug his fez/combat fatigues/fruit-boot ensemble.

I pulled my pen and scrawled on the wall. Nasty Nat said, "You're pissed, right? I mean, the magazine's pissed."

"I'm not pissed. I'm intrigued more than anything else. I was thinking you could record a message for me, and make sure that Miss Blind Item hears it the next time she calls in."

"How about a message for Bird? 'Sorry I popped your ass for junk outside the Club Alabam in March of '49.'"

I said, "How do you know I didn't write that on the wall just now?"

Nasty Nat pointed to the sound booth. I followed him over and in. We took the two chairs. The booth boxed us up. We were nudged knee-to-knee.

The Synagogue Sid Trio trickled and trilled. Nasty Nat killed the sound and moved his microphone my way. I excavated my bold bass-baritone.

"Miss Item, my name is Fred Otash. I work for *Confidential,* and I'm a former Los Angeles policeman. I was there at Hollywood Station the night your friend Shirley came in. I agree with your assessment of Caryl Chessman's guilt, and I'd like to discuss with you a second Chessman piece that might serve to set the record straight."

Voilà. That was *gooooooood.* I was cool-cat commanding and concise. Nasty Nat smiled and hit the kill switch.

"I'm pretty sure she'll call in tonight, and I'll make sure she hears your message. And, before you ask, I don't know her righteous name, or anything more about her than you do."

I scoped the bare-bones booth. It's got that rat resort/proud poor folks gestalt.

"You get by on donations, right? Making the rent's a stretch, and you're always running on fumes."

Nasty Nat said, "That's right."

I said, "*Confidential*'s a sucker for good jazz, and we're in business to make friends, regardless of what you might have heard about me, or the magazine itself. I need a favor that only you can perform, and if you *do* perform it, the magazine will drop five hundred clams a month on KKXZ, indefinitely."

Nasty Nat lit a cigarette. "She's calling from a pay phone. I can hear her feed the coins in. Does this favor pertain to that?"

I smiled. "That's right. I need a trace. I need you to call a cop pal of mine within two minutes from the time she gets on the horn with you. It might not work the first time, but it should work sooner or later."

"She might leave town. This whole deal could go *poof.*"

"You still get the bread."

"Well then, okay."

I winked. "I'm going home, to sit by my radio."

"Tell me something before you go?"

"Sure."

"What did you write on the wall?"

"I wrote 'Dear Bird: Thanx for the sounds. Best wishes, Fred Otash.'"

Nasty Nat said, "You're caustic, but you'll never be hip."

Synagogue Sid serenaded me. I ran my radio low and laid low on my couch. Nasty Nat cut to commercials for Sultan Sam's Sandbox, Kool Kings, and the Cannonball Adderley Quintet. Then dimes dipped and nickels nudged and slid down a slot. I knew that noise now. I knew it was microphone-magnified.

Silence socked me. I knew why. Nasty Nat put Miss Blind Item on hold and buzzed Ray Pinker.

It's Tap Try #1. It's logged in at 1:16 a.m.

I heard fuzz, buzz, radio rasp, and dissonant dial tones. I knew why. Nasty Nat's playing my plea. I held my breath. Now, she's back in ripping rejoinder.

"I don't know, Nat. Is our Mr. Otash looking for a date, or justice for my friend Shirley?"

"It could be both, you know. One don't exclude the other."

I heard tap-taps. *Tension* taps. Miss Blind Item's crammed in a phone booth. She's drumming the wall. It's stagecraft. She's buying time to rig a response. That means she's tweaked, that means she cares.

"Mr. Otash has a reputation, Nat. It precedes him, you might say. I read a piece in the *L.A. Mirror*—last year, I think it was. It described his illegal surveillance methods and alleged that he resorted to physical force in order to quash lawsuits levied against *Confidential*."

"Well, you know that old saw, right? 'If you want to make an omelet, you've got to break a few eggs.'"

Miss Blind Item laffed. "Not that *Confidential* magazine is much of an omelet, right?"

"You sure got me there, baby."

Silence settled in. Silken, sullen, sickened—who knows? Ardent or artificial—who knows *that*? She's amply ambiguous. It's cold-calculated. She's *leading* me, she's *playing* me, there's something she *wants*.

"A casting director I know told me he beat up Johnnie Ray. *Really*, Nat—*Johnnie Ray*? I met him once, after his gig at the Copa in New York. He was certainly one of the nicest, and certainly *the* least offensive young man that I've ever met. Nothing that I can think of could ever justify that sort of behavior."

Baby, I know just how you feel.

Nasty Nat said, "Yeah, I dig on Johnnie Ray. I spin his discs on the show, every so often."

"Handsome is as handsome does, Nat. I saw Mr. Otash on Paul Coates' show, the last time I passed through L.A. I remember thinking, My, that surely is a most presentable man, which made me doubly sad to have heard the Johnnie Ray story."

Miss Blind Item. *I've got you under my skin.*

A.M. shitwork. Phone work and field reports. Two per *Rebel Without a Cause*. Mendacious memos to Bondage Bob Harrison and Bill Parker.

I called Nasty Nat at KKXZ. Pathos pounded me. He *lived* at the station. His noxious news: last nite's trace went blooey. Nat said he'd try again tonite. I bid the big bopster bon voyage.

Miss Blind Item. You've got me torched and scorched.

I wrote my report to Bondage Bob. I delivered the dish on Nick Ray's Afrika Korps and described the pustulant panty raid in delirious detail. I omitted Jimmy Dean's presence. I owed Jimmy that. I exorbitantly expanded my memo to Bill Parker. I reported Robbie Molette's dish per *Führer* Nick's "escalation" escapades. Dig, Chief: He's planning hot-prowl 459's and liquor-store 211's. He's the maladroit mastermind of the "motivation" crime. Addled actors bow to his bidding. Nazi Nick's applied the Stanislavskiesque stamp.

I called *Confidential*'s messenger service. A car schlepped down from Sunset and Vine and picked up the pouches. Chop, chop, fucker—deliver them *now*.

My desk phone rang. I picked up. Bondage Bob bored straight in.

"Lew Wasserman just called me. Rock's at the West Hollywood

Sheriff's Station. He was booked under his kosher name of Roy Fitzgerald, and it looks like he was drunk or maybe Mickey Finn'd, he might have been blowing some guy in a parked car, and what's for sure is he swung on a deputy, so now he's in custody. All this means I need you and your boys to get him out and clean him up before the press gets wind of it."

I said, "*Jawohl*, boss. I'll jump on it."

Bob bored back in. "We've got to safeguard our exclusive on the 'Rock marries a woman' front. Lew's a hundred percent behind us on this. He wants to call the piece 'Rock's Rocky Road to Marital Bliss,' and he's a hog for the eternal-triangle bit that you and Phyllis have cooked up. That means you've *got* to find us a bait girl to play the other woman. You dig, *bubi*? I want a fresh face, which means nobody we've used before. If Rock falls in the shit on this Sheriff's deal, we can lay the bait girl off as the 'sexy succubus who led the righteously religious Rockster to tasty temptation,' or some such happy horseshit."

I said, "I'll have Rock out inside of an hour."

Bob said, "Lay off the kraut jive. I'm one twenty-fourth Jewish, and I'm touchy about it."

Ward Wardell and Race Rockwell rendezvoused with me. We surged up surreptitious. We slid in slick and parked by the jail-exit door. Bondage Bob called ahead and bought the bail bond. Rock stood ready to roll.

Race remained with my sled and sluiced the engine. I'd called ahead and pledged the jail deputies a yard per. Ward and I juked through the jail door. We caught a corridor and sidled up to cellblock row. There's Rock. He's signing autographs for a filthy phalanx of his fellow jailbirds. *Wheww!!!*—they're malodorous *Menschen*—winos, weedheads, K-Y cowboys caught in the act.

Race wrangled Rock. I ran interference. Rock hurled hand kisses back to the boys and ran with us. He was sweaty and swack-back on some kind of hop. His feet flip-flopped on the floor.

We made the door. I barged us out. We ran right into a riotous raft of reporters.

Banzai!!!! Sneak attack!!!! It's Pearl Harbor perpetrated by the putz-oid Fourth Estate!!!!

Flashbulb flare. Hurled questions. I heard *Rock, Rock, Rock* and ARE THOSE RUMORS TR—

A cordon constricted around us. I pulled my belt sap. Ward pulled his belt sap. We sap-slapped cameras. Flashbulbs shattered and sheared into shards. We sap-bashed heads and scoured scalps and hurled Rock ahead of us. We slid into my sled three across. Race Rockwell goosed the gas. We surfed out to San Vicente and nailed it north to the Strip.

Dig it. *Escape from Stalag 69.* Rock could top-line the flick. He yukked, I yukked. Ward and Race yukked. There's blood in my soul and torn-out teeth stuck to my sap.

Race wound west on Sunset and dipsy-doodled south and north on Crescent Heights. Rock and I hopped out at Googie's. The coffee cave was midmorning lulled. We took my table. Debrief me, Daddy. *Escape from Stalag 69.* What's the priapic prelude here?

I fed Rock my flask and two dexies. I fed myself, likewise. Rock said, "Don't tell me. You want me to lay out the whole sordid tale."

I said, "That's right."

Rock lit a cigarette. "Here's what I recall. I was visiting this kid actor, Nick Adams. *Why?* Because I sensed susceptibility. He's got a little rental house, up north of the Marmont. Okay, I'm there. Nothing much is happening, except I go to the bathroom, and I notice this spare bedroom piled up with hi-fis, TV sets, movie cameras, and all kinds of radio consoles and electrical gear. It's like Nick's running a Sears, Roebuck out of this one room. Then Nick makes me a drink, and there *had* to be something in it, because I go gaga. And . . . well . . . there might have been another guy there, but I'm not sure . . . and . . . well . . . the next thing I remember is waking up in jail."

Nick Adams. "Motivation, escalation." Robbie Molette's 459 dish. Rock's Sears, Roebuck shit. It radiated *Burglary Swag.*

"I'll take you home. We've got that fake-wife caper coming up, you'll have two good-looking women fighting over you, and you should get some rest."

Rock went *Why me, Lord?*

I pulled into Stan's Drive-In. Babs Payton knew from bait girls. She had a history with Nick Ray. She cadged courses at the Actors Studio West. She knew all within her limited *perv*view. She tattled all for cash and cocaine.

I'd dropped off Rock and rolled by the Ranch Market. I read my two message slips. Bondage Bob and Bill Parker called. I returned the calls. I bagged big bravos for my *Rebel Without a Cause* report. Bob said the *Escape from Stalag 69* cost him six g's. It covered cameras smashed and busted bones set at Central Receiving. He laffed it off.

The *Rebel* report and Rock's tricky triangle made the money minuscule. Parker parsed attaboys. He told me Ernie Roll rhapsodized per the *Rebel* revelations. Meet us at Ernie's office, 4:00 tomorrow.

Babs skated up. She did her signature sideways dip and passed me a pineapple malt. The malt metastasized. A mushroom cloud toxified me. Babs laced *my* malts. Bonded bourbon and Benzedrine bits brought the brew to a head.

I slid our seats back. We got cozy. Babs tucked her legs up and skimmed her skate wheels on the dashboard.

"I need a hundred, Freddy. Regardless of how many topics we cover."

"Okay. Let's start with the Actors Studio. I'm looking for something very specific here. Do they keep a radio and TV tape library on the premises? I'm looking to identify a specific actress by her voice."

Babs lit a cigarette. "Yeah, they do. Their members put on these earmuff thingamajigs and watch the TV and movie stuff on some monitor-type gizmos."

I sipped my malt. The depth charge detonated. *Oooooohhh, Daddy—*

"Second topic. I'm looking for a bait girl. It's a long-range deal, and I'm looking for a new-kid-in-town, who-are-*you*? type."

Babs blew smoke rings. "Let's come back to that one. I've got to put my thinking cap on."

"Okay, here's topic three. Nick Ray. I know you worked as an extra on *They Live by Night*, so that's got to ring some bells."

Babs whooped. "That's the three-cherry jackpot and *two* chapters in my book, *Hollywood Creeps I Have Known*. To begin with, he's a perv of the fake-daddy ilk. He likes it young, and he likes sending young actors out on 'motivational missions,' which he films, and I assume that that would be for kicks in the moment and blackmail purposes somewhere down the line. Do you like it so far?"

I said, "Tell me something I don't know. This juvenile delinquency turkey interests me."

Babs tossed her cigarette. "Nick's got his head goon on all his pictures. On this one, it's this mean little shit, Nick Adams. He's also got his 'Love Boy' and 'Love Girl' on all his pictures, and this time it's your chum Jimmy Dean and Natalie Wood. He's always trying to push these kids into all kinds of scary stuff, and he's got it all justified and sugarcoated to the nth degree. There's an actor on the shoot named Dennis Hopper. He's a customer here, and he's got common sense enough to give Nick a wide berth. Now, Dennis told me that Nick's got Jimmy all hopped-up to play Caryl Chessman, and Jimmy's drooling for the part."

Click, click, click. *That's* a three-cherry jackpot. Yeah, but it's turgidly topical, it's *new* news, Chessman's a headline humper, but *still*—

"Freddy, are you even *listening* to me?"

I said, "Keep going. What else have you got on Chessman?"

"Nothing. Except who wants to see a vital young stud like Jimmy Dean play Caryl—"

"Whoa, Babs. Hold on. Where'd you get that 'vital young stud' line? It's something I've heard before."

Babs scoffed. "I got it from a would-be criminal mastermind named Robbie Molette. He's a regular here, and he's always referring to himself as a 'vital young stud.' I used to shtup his daddy when I was a contract kid at Metro. He also works as a busboy, at the Beverly Hills Hotel, and—"

I cut in. "Babs, *what*? What's with that lightning-bolt look?"

"Nothing. Except you're looking for a bait girl, and Robbie was in last night, and damned if he hasn't put together a stable, and damned if he didn't show me a merchandise book with some very fresh faces."

OUTSIDE NICK ADAMS' RUSTIC RENTAL PAD

West Holly*weird*

5/15/55

Stakeout. *Eine kleine Nachtwerk*. The mad march to 1:00 a.m. and Miss Blind Item. I'd run my radio loooooooooooow. I'd hear coins slip-slide down that slot. Nasty Nat would try for a trace. I'd hear *Her* voice.

Nutty Nick Adams. There's his chump-change chalet. I'm parked across the street and two doors down. It's a murky moon-mist nite. I'm cunningly camouflaged. Shade-tree shadows shield the shape of my sled.

It's peeper peekaboo. I see Nick's pad. Nick can't see shit. There's window lights. Big beams bounce my way. I possess Peepervision. No one else does.

There's a scurrilous script read. Nick Ray pontificates. Nick A. and Jimmy Dean declaim dialogue.

I hexed the house. I made mental mincemeat of the punks and mocked their motivation. Leave now, feckless fools. I've got work to do inside.

I brought my evidence kit. It contained print gear and Ray Pinker's stop-frame camera. I dunned the DMV. They fed me photo-stats of three drivers-license applications. I had right thumbprints for Jimmy Dean, Nick Ray, Nick Adams. Pinker's camera light lit latent prints and magnified tents, whorls, and arches. My game was confirmation and/or elimination. If they touched the B and E swag that Rock described, I'd know.

I turned on the radio. Synagogue Sid serenaded me. Sid's bass sax sallied forth. The flügelhorn flew with it. The drums drilled a cool counterpoint. Then that cacophonous coin cough cut in.

Adios, Sid. Nasty Nat's nudged you aside for Miss Blind Item. I ran the radio *looooooooow*. I listened for tone above text. Talk to me, love. Say something, say anything. *Give me your voice.*

Miss Blind Item riffed and rang rapport with Nasty Nat. I listened for tone above text. I nite-dreamed as she talked.

Caryl Chessman would be in L.A. As in soonsville. He had a court appeal downtown. Nick Ray wants Jimmy Dean to play the Red Light Bandit. It surged as subtext and nudged me nonplussed. It couldn't compete with Her Voice. Her vowels suggest the urban Midwest. It's a seen-it-all city voice.

A door slammed. I orbed the chalet. Mark it: 1:23 a.m. The punks pop from the pad. They bag Nick Adams' rental ragtop and roll northbound.

I rolled. It's late, time is tight, you need an hour inside. I *ran* to the door and laid into the lock.

Lock picks and penlight. It's up-close, in-tight work. I jammed a #4 pick in the keyhole and massaged the main spring. Two tumblers tipped. I pulled out the #4 and jammed in a #2. The door jerked from the jamb. I shoulder-shoved it and inched inside.

I locked myself in. I penlight-flashed the main room and dug on the details. Bullfight posters, bongo drums, a TV tuned to a test pattern. Natalie Wood nudie pix tacked to one wall.

It's cheesecake chiaroscuro. Natalie's backlit by flickering flames and feral faces peering out. It's the Afrika Korps, the B-boys, the Nick's Knights Kar Klub. The *Führer's* face peers out above them. Nick Ray's wearing devil horns and torquing a ten-inch forked tongue.

I cut down the hall. I flashed a bare-mattressed bedroom and a bathroom in bad disarray. My light speared the spare bedroom. My beam swung over the swag.

The hip hi-fis. The cumbersome consoles. The fetchingly fence-able TV sets and camera cascade. They were hurled haphazard and carelessly covered the floor.

I left the room lights off. I got out my gear. I made for the mountain of merchandise and went to work.

My penlight put me in close. I went contraband item to item. I marked manufacturers' ID numbers on my scratch pad. It was all B and E stash. I knew that. It might be traceable to specific burglary lots.

Prints next. That's the tuff part. Dust touch-and-grab surfaces. Daub contrasting-color powder. Put the stop-frame camera up to liftable latents. Expand the images and look for thumbprint configurations. Count tents, whorls, and arches. Compare them to the DMV photostats.

I went at it. I *had* at it, wholesale. I kept the lights off. I penlight-parsed and brushed purple powder over every touch-and-grab surface in sure sight. Finger oil brought up smudges, smears, paltry partial and full fingerprints. I went item to item. I dusted hi-fis/consoles/cameras/TV sets. Smudges, smears, and partials popped up. No glaring glove prints stood out. That was *gooooood.*

I caught two full finger spreads. They popped off a pinewood console. That meant bupkes/zero/zilch. I needed right thumbprints X-clusive.

I worked myself weary. I wound my way down to two portable TV sets.

They had hard-to-hold planes and no handles. They were cumbersome and unwieldy. They were hoist every which way items.

I dusted Set #1. I hit hard surfaces, crevices, cracks. I brought up a right thumbprint. I raised my camera. I zoomed close. I let fly.

The camera magnified. The camera impaled images and brought them up, white-on-black. I counted comparison points. I'd memorized the photostat points. I'd broiled them into my brain. I knew every tent, whorl, and arch.

I counted One, two, three, four, five, six, seven, eight, nine, ten—Nick Adams, it's you. You're fucked for 459 PC.

I dusted Set #2. It's hard to hold and pry off the premises. There's that hard-to-hold tube housing.

I dusted it. I pulled Right Thumbprint #2.

I put the camera up to the print. I magnified it. I counted common points. Six points saddened and sickened me. Nine points nullified me. Ten points pounded James Dean, courtroom conclusive.

Bait girls. Babs Payton shtups Robbie Molette's dad, circa '47. Rodent Robbie. He's running call girls now. No shit, Sherlock. Robbie's got a merchandise book. Babs reveals fresh faces. It's a nutty non sequitur. It indicates the brute breadth of my *craaaaaaazy* crowded life.

I broomed to the Beverly Hills Hotel. Robbie worked the noon-to-nine swing shift. I parked in the employees' lot and lingered by the locker room door. Robbie rolled up at 11:40. His '49 Ford fed fucked-up fumes to Beverly Hills and beyond. It laid out L.A. as a lung ward.

I coughed up to the car. Robbie popped the door. I scooched in. Robbie called in some cool.

"Hey, Freddy. What's shakin' today?"

I lit a cigarette. Robbie said, "Hey, watch it. Asthma runs in my family."

"Let's talk about your family. Like in your dad, who's a grip at Metro. I see nepotism at work here. Babs Payton and your dad were some kind of an item. And Babs is impressed with your new stable. 'Fresh faces' was how she put it."

Robbie reached under his seat. He pulled out a pink padded notebook. It was embarrassingly embossed "The Young Stud's Stable."

I riffled and ran through the pages. "Fresh faces"—yeah. Nepotism—yeah plus. They were Metro contract cooze. The innocent ingénue type. The Hollywood Heartache Class of '55.

Dad strung strings around Robbie. He passed on his pimp patrimony. I knew the Metro method. The casting cads culled and curried a type. Bryn Mawr, Vassar, Mount Holyoke. This was Ivy League woof-woof deluxe.

"Your dad wants you to keep it localized. The hotel, and nowhere beyond. You suck up to the guests and take it from there. Your dad palms the desk guys and gets the rooms. You do a little matchmaking, and take home your cut."

Robbie huff-huffed. His dentures dipped out. He's twenty-two. He's got dentures. He *needs* a dad.

I reriffled the girl book. A look lassoed me. She's tall and lioness lithe. She's chestnut-haired. She's heaven-sent in heathered tweeds. She's Bryn Mawr brought to life.

Robbie said, "That's Janey Blaine. She went to Smith. She's gigging with Jack tonight."

'*Jack*'? You mean Senator John F. Kennedy?"

"Well, *I* call him *Jack*, and I'm the one who set him up with Janey. He's meeting her at a Democratic fund-raiser here tonight. It's my patented 'Some Enchanted Evening' scenario, you dig? Janey's an out-of-town Party functionary, you dig? She sees Jack at the wingding, their eyes meet across a crowded room, and she goes back to his bungalow with him, and stays all night. There'll be movie big shots at the wingding, and they'll scope Janey and check out her pedigree at Metro. She'll get legitimate work out of this gig, you dig?"

I chained cigarettes. "I dig. And I'll be crashing the gig, by the way. And if I like the way Janey carries herself, I'll have a long-term gig she won't be able to resist."

Robbie sniff-sniffled. His eyes went wet. He trembled. His dentures clack-clacked.

"She resisted me, that's for damn sure."

I resisted the riposte. You'll always have your sister, kid. Chrissy's a hot sketch. She's yours as you live and breathe.

Ernie Roll sipped scotch. "Your *Rebel Without a Cause* summary is boffo. Don't you think so, Bill?"

Parker sipped scotch. The DA's sanctum sanctorum featured fishing trophies tricked up on wood-paneled walls. Monster marlin and ossified octopi.

Ernie crapped out at his desk. Parker and I sat in soft leather chairs. The seasick green leather went with the walls.

"It is. We'll get some indictments out of it, and we'll get Freddy to improperly vet the magazine's story, which will give us the double whammy when we put *Confidential* in the shit."

"Get us some good dirt on this James Dean kid, Freddy. He's a big movie star now."

"Freddy's tight with the kid, Ernie. We have to assume he's a source for a lot of this information."

I sipped scotch. "The Chief's right about that, Ernie. That said, I should add that I tossed Nick Adams' pad and took his prints off some hot TV sets. Harry Fremont's got the ID numbers off the merchandise. If the burglaries were reported, he'll nail that punk for a whole flotilla of 459's."

One more misdirection. One more mercy missive for Jimmy the D.

Parker said, "Freddy Otash. Accept no substitutes."

Ernie said, "Lay out some story vettings you were remiss or criminally culpable on, Freddy. And, remember, I'm voluntarily offering up that no-file sheet on you when all this goes to court, so you'll be in the clear on any and all criminal charges."

I cracked my knuckles. "The two Eartha Kitt jobs were dirty. I slapped Orson Welles around. We paid off Eartha on both of them, all off-the-books cash. The pieces were all lies. Race mixing was a hot topic, so we went nuts with it."

Ernie went *Hubba-hubba*. Parker said, "Freddy's prebriefed me. It gets better than that."

I scoured my scotch rocks. "Christine Jorgensen and I shook down the Vanderbilt kid for twenty grand. The piece we published was expurgated during the editorial process. I kicked the door down and took pictures. They'll make good courtroom exhibits or place mats at your next Elks Club smoker."

Ernie slapped his knees. "Like your stellar photos of Marlon Brando with a dick in his mouth."

Parker rolled his eyes. "A legendary item."

Ernie said, "Your legendary tiff with Johnnie Ray. That's a good courtroom vignette."

I cringed. "As tiffs go, it wasn't much. And it's not like I'm proud of it."

Parker held one finger up. Ernie ticked *that* topic off.

"We're working a two-way street here, Freddy. That means you've got a fat credit slip in Banker Roll's vault."

I said, "Caryl Chessman's got an appeal in superior court. He'll be here soon. I'd like a jail visit with him."

Parker said, "That evil cocksucker."

Ernie crossed himself. "Those poor girls. That girl in Camarillo."

Parker crossed himself. "Consider the request, Ernie."

I crossed myself. "I promise I'll behave, and I promise that anything *Confidential* puts up will atone for that boo-hoo piece we published in '52."

Parker beady-eyed me. "Here's a reminder to go with that request. The next time you witness Nick's Knights, or the Afrika Korps, or whatever you're calling them, committing first-degree felonies, you are to intercede with all due and vigilant force."

Match the voice. Make a voice print. KKXZ to the 1946–47 yearbook. She's not the noted Kim Hunter or Barbara Bel Geddes. She's not Shirley Tutler/aka Miss Third Victim. She's *probably* Unknown Actress #1 or #2. She *might* be the lissome Lois Nettleton. Her picture *might* not have popped on that page.

Babs bought me in. She called ahead and relayed my request. She artfully audited Actors Studio West classes and muff-munched member Mercedes McCambridge on occasion. She explained my kooky conundrum. A clearheaded clerk caught it quick. She snagged her yearbook copy. She found the faces. She rigged a TV clip/film clip/scroll-the-screen machine.

Unknown Actress #1 was Marjorie McConville. Unknown Actress #2 was Lana Linscott. Shirley was Shirley. Lois was Lois. The machine socked sound out of side vents.

The clerk cozied me up in a cubicle and cut the lights. I scrolled the screen. Miss McConville mangled *Major Barbara*. She stormed a stage in Belfast or Ballymora. She shoved Shaw at me in a brutal brogue. I rescrolled the screen.

Lana Linscott laid it on light. She played some doofus Doris in a dithering *Dinner at Eight*. Her voice wasn't *The Voice*. She was a salt-lick soprano. She came off as a comedienne.

I knew what was next. I scrolled the screen and got to it. There's Shirley Tutler, pre-Chessman.

She looked L.A. She *talked* L.A. She had the flat vowels and the vibrato drawl. She essayed Stella in *Streetcar*. She simpered and saw how it played. She started over and notched up her native dignity.

I replayed the nite we met. Her blood-soaked blouse *dripped*. I brought her a blanket. She said, "You're very kind." I brought her a cup of water. Colin Forbes and Al Goossen took over from there.

I touched the screen. I scrolled the screen. Lois Nettleton main-lined Maggie in *Cat on a Hot Tin Roof*.

It was Her Voice. She had *The Voice*. She jumped geography and subsumed a southern belle's timbre here. She withered her weak willy/bottle baby/homo-haunted hubby and begged him to sire her child. She pinnacled the pathos and wrapped back to the rage. Her Deep South diction dipped north to Chitown shaded with Sheboygan. I was glad. It was *Her Voice, The Voice*.

Lois, it's you.

Janey, *it's you.*

For Jack, it is. Tonite, at least. You look *goooooood*. You move magnetic. You roil the room and mug the men moving at you. You've got droves of dreary Democrats drip-dried. You might bag the bait-girl gig. I'll call you Rambunctious Rock's Squeeze, then.

I circulated. It was a big-room bash. It was committedly corny and panderingly partisan. Note the crepe-paper bunting. Note the coarse cardboard cutouts—Democrat donkeys at graze.

I'm crawl-crammed in with two hundred people. The women wear god-awful gowns and show too much shoulder. The men sport spring-weight suits and sweat them straight through. *I'm* sweating. I'm a Lebanese camel fucker and prone to the sweats.

Jack's immune to sweat. Janey's immune. Jack's got cucumber-cool chromosomes. Janey's loose-limbed in lavender linen. I'm tall, Jack's tall, Janey's tall. I'm a periscope. I'm peering over the heads of the heaving hoi polloi. Come on, kids. It's Some Enchanted Evening. This bum bash is one hour in. Orb those eyes. Orbit the room. Let's see you cull contact.

Some *nudnik* nudged me. Oh shit—it's Robbie Molette. He's passing out puffed cheese and seared tuna on toast. He slipped me a note. I brusque-brushed him off. The rodent rambled away.

Ooooga-booooga. There it is. Jack's moving *her* way. Janey's moving *his* way. It's a slow slog and a deep detour through dowdy folks. He's laughing. She's laughing. They move their hands in sexy sync. It's fate—*what can you do?*

There, they've met. They shake hands. They're speaking. Here's my speech balloons. She's calling him "Senator Kennedy." He's calling up his killer comeback: "Come on, call me Jack."

I watched them. The Pervdog of the Nite's a peeper from *waaaaaaaay* back. What's going on here? What's with this jungled-up juju? What *is* it that you two have got?

It's this:

You're decorous. It's a deft deception. You project a state of groovy grace as you sally forth in sin. There's a halo around you now. It hides your cold hearts and your constant calls to conquest.

Janey, it's you.

You were born to play bait gigs. I'm enchanted and appalled.

I barged out of the bash. I bopped over to the porte cochere and read Robbie's note.

"Nick's Knights are mobilizing. Tomorrow night, 9:00 p.m. at the Marmont."

—⟷—

I remade myself as Stage Door Freddy. I'm a sweaty swain swooning for my phone to ring. I know her name, she knows my name. Nasty Nat's our conduit and cupid. The Actors Studio clerk laid out the lowdown on Lois.

Born Oak Park, Illinois/'27. Miss Chicago, '48. The Art Institute of Chicago. East to the Apple. The Actors Studio. Lois meets Shirley Tutler. Her connection to the Caryl Chessman case is calamitously forged.

TV work. Film work. Stage work. Her zenith's *right now*. She's understudying Barbara Bel Geddes in *Cat on a Hot Tin Roof*. Here's a punchy parenthetical:

The play's all Broadway bravos *right now*. If Barbara bails behind a bad bug or lays up with laryngitis, Lois plays Maggie the Cat.

But she's in L.A. She knew her cruel critique of *Confidential* would somehow summon me. She knows things about me. She wants something from me. My pay-phone trace will work at some point. Yeah, but I'm *right here, right now*.

I caved on my couch. I'm Stage Door Freddy. I'm a cuckold, a *cornuto*, a juvie jerkoff, a chump. I hexed the phone. I brain-brewed an APB on Lois June Nettleton/white female American/DOB 8-16-27, Oak Park, Ill—

The phone rang. I picked up and risked ridicule. I said, "Hello, Lois."

She said, "Hi, Freddy. I figured you'd find me before too long. So I jumped the gun a bit."

"I'm glad you did. And I'm not going to ask you what you want, because I know you'll tell me pretty damn quick."

Lois said, "That's true, but what I want is evolving, and I'm not quite sure what it is."

I said, "I saw a clip of you today. It was in black and white. I couldn't tell what color your hair is."

"It's strawberry blond. And I saw *you* on Paul Coates' show, and you tried to tell the truth, but you faltered at it."

I said, "Meet me. Right now. It's not that late."

Lois said, "Not tonight. Before too long, though."

I said, "You've got this haunted tomboy thing going. Like Julie Harris, but earthier and more pronounced."

"I like men who notice things like that, and make accurate comparisons like the one you just did."

"How long have you been pulling this anonymous telephone stuff?"

"Since the war, when I was in high school. The telephone has always been my métier."

"I wish we could talk in person."

"We will, in time."

"Shall we talk about Chessman?"

"Not yet."

"You're right. It's more of an in-person conversation."

Lois said, "Shirley speaks of you, when she's capable of speaking. She's never forgotten those few moments you spent together."

OUTSIDE THE CHATEAU MARMONT

West Holly*weird*

5/16/55

Rolling stakeout.

It's 8:55 p.m. I'm parked perpendicular, down from bungalow row. I borrowed Donkey Don's '53 Chevy. It's innocuous compared to my Packard pimpmobile. I'm snout-out in a flat flower bed. I'm ready to roll.

I'm still stage door–stuck and looped on Lois standard time. We talked until 2:00 last nite. We tippled at topics and nodded off into non sequiturs. We laffed, we flirted, we surged toward and circumnavigated a path past Shirley Tutler and Caryl Chessman. Lois refused to divulge her L.A. hideaway. I called Nasty Nat and Ray Pinker two hours back. They'd trace-tracked three Lois calls. They got cloyingly close. Ray tracked transformer stations and logiced out a loose location. He made it mid-Wilshire east.

It's a booth call. Here's his best shot at a border-to-border bid. It's Western to the west/Vermont to the east/Beverly to the north/ Olympic to the south.

I *got* it. I *saw* it. My mind churned and channeled straight to Chapman Park.

The Ambassador Hotel's there. Ditto, the Chapman Park Hotel and the Gaylord Apartments. The Brown Derby's there. Dale's Secret Harbor's there. It's a lively locale. Lois would light there—I *knew* it.

The fone fungooed my whole day. Rodent Robbie called and ran me raw. He said, Jack loved Janey. I said, No shit, Shadrack—what's not to love? Robbie goosed me: You giving her the bait gig? I said, Yeah—tell her to meet me tomorrow nite/Frascati/ten p.m. It's a pithy party of four. She'll meet the players then. Robbie hung up. Harry Fremont called. *Caramba!!!*—Sheriff's Burglary called *him*.

It's a make. The Nick Adams swag matched the manifests for six 459's. Six B and E's—all within one mile of Nabob Nick's rent-a-pad. That's *goooooooood*. If Nick keeps the cache, he's cooked. Here's what's *baaaaad*. The Sheriff's lab dutifully dusted the B and E locations. They turned up no viable latents.

I called Bill Parker and tattled the tidings. He said, Sit on it for now. I called Bondage Bob and told him. He said, This *Rebel Without a Cause* caper is a cause célèbre.

I'm a snitch. I'm a rat fink. I'm an infernal informer. I beat both ends against some malignant middle. And the wide world *knows*.

I checked my mailbox, midafternoon. I found one piece of paper. Dig this vivid valentine:

> *Freddy,*
>
> Quit bugging me, okay? It's annoying. I've moved on to greener pastures. I'm a movie star now. I'm not the scuffling kid who used to jack around with you and your stupid band of thugs. Over's over. Quit persisting. It's undignified. Con-fidential's a shitrag, and you're a shitheel for working for it. Over's over. You're passé, bubi. You're not a name I want on my résumé.
>
> *Best wishes,*
> *Jimmy*

Jimmy, you shitbird cocksucker. I knew you when.

I bug-eyed bungalow row. I watched my watch. 9:00 p.m. nudged by. Bungalow row remained snoresville. The action accelerated at 9:14.

There's the filthy phalanx. *Farshtinkener Führer* Nick Ray stridently strides ahead. His *Untermenschen* unfurl behind him. Jimmy Dean, Nick Adams, Chester Alan Voldrich. The two black-jacket *Kameraden* from the sorority *soiree*.

Die Fahne hoch. Die Reihen fest geschlossen—

They're *all* Afrika Korps tonite. The jumpsuits, the big-billed caps, the Rommelesque regalia. Nick R.'s got his movie camera. We're back at El Alamein, '42. Rommel's resolute. He's readying his raid on the brave British forces.

It's a quivering quick-march. The Kiddie Korps follows their festering father—they goof some goose steps and hop in the Chevy van. Voldrich whips behind the wheel and peels out.

They looped left on Sunset. I looped left and lagged back. I caught cover behind a big bus booming eastbound. I rode the back bumper and kept their back bumper surveilled.

We headed into Hollywood. The bus barged due east. The van vizzed south on Wilton Place. A taco wagon wiggled between us. It was chopped and channeled. It surged, submarineesque. The sassy side panels read LOS INTRUSOS.

The van vipped ahead. I surfed behind the submarine. We're headed southbound and down. Wilton arced into Arlington. We passed Mount Vernon Junior High/aka Mount *Vermin*. The van angled east at the Jefferson juncture. The tacomobile tooled on south.

I lost my car cover. I dawdled three car lengths back and dug darktown by nite. Something Rodent Robbie Molette said sacked me.

Escalation. Liquor-store 211's. We're at Jefferson and Normandie. It's liquorland lit large—right *here*, right *now*.

Telepathy ticked—me to them. Don't read my mind, *Menschen*—don't cross this line.

The van wriggled to the right lane and crept curbside. I saw the lit-up liquor store window, jarringly just ahead. I whipped wide and nudged up to the north-side curb. The van stopped in front of the store.

Achtung!!!! Raus!!!! Mach schnell!!!!

The six sickos pile out. Nazi Nick's got the camera. Nabob Nick's got a pump shotgun. Jimmy Dean's got a bottle of T-Bird topped with a cotton-wick fuse. It's a sure-as-shit Molotov cocktail.

I froze, I watched, I *peeped*. I'm a peeper first and forever. Bill Parker told me to intercede and fuck up all felony actions. I didn't. I disobeyed. I sought succor in savagery. I was coldly complicit. I'm all vile volition, and—

They walked into the store. The counter clerk saw them and *guuuuulped*. Nick Ray rolled film. Chester Voldrich reached behind the counter and tapped the till. The clerk yelped. His mouth moved. I imagined a plaintive *please*. The two no-name *Kameraden* hopped the counter and taped his mouth shut.

Voldrich shagged a shelf bottle. He uncorked it and passed it to his putrid pals. Some reflex ripped me. I kept going for a gun I didn't have.

Nick Ray rolled film. No-name Nazi #2 pulled out a Minox minicamera and snapped stills. Jimmy flicked his lighter and lit the Molotov. Nabob Nick pumped his shotgun and blasted the booze shelves.

Glass shattered and sheared. Wino wine and rotgut rye and skunk scotch blew wide. Jimmy tossed the Molotov. It caught the cold cuts case and exploded. Fumes flared and flattened out at the ceiling. Electrical cords caught fire and sparked blue and white.

Smoke smothered my Peepvision view. The clerk ran outside and ran straight out of my frame. Nick's Knights walked out, en masse. They stood studly, six across. They rebel-yelled. They whipped out their whangs and pissed in the street.

MY BOSS BACHELOR PAD

West Holly*weird*

5/17/55

I confessed. I crawled my crib, cruciform. I drank myself draconian and drip-dried my dearly soul. *What* soul? They could have clipped the clerk and popped some pedestrians. I had to peep it and imprint the images. I'm the Pervdog of the Nite—past all rancid rationale and jacked-up justification.

I confessed to God and Chief William H. Parker. I wrote him a self-defaming memo and had it messengered, posthaste. I read my Bible and ripped right to Revelation:

Anyone with ears to hear should listen and understand. . . . Anyone destined to live by the sword will die by the sword.

That's Nick's Knights, that's me. That's God's conflagration called down on *Confidential.*

I sat by the phone. I willed Lois to call. She didn't call. I laid the phone in my lap. It rang. I picked up. It wasn't Lois. It was Reptile Robbie Molette.

He blathered. I listened, listless. I was shot to shit and half in the bag.

". . . and, Freddy, I figured I should tell you. Nick Ray's over at Googie's right now. He's got a group of his kids in tow, and they're all ragging on you pretty bad."

I hung up. I willed Lois to call. I voodooized the airwaves and tried to make the phone ring. It rang. It wasn't Lois. It was Chief William H. Parker.

He said, "You're absolved, Freddy. We've got those humps on Arson, Assault 1, 211, and six related firearms charges. They're sunk if Ernie Roll and I decide to sink them, and you've proved to me you won't sell me out to *Confidential*. Get it? You're not a coward or a quisling. You're a shitbird who played it smart for the first time in his life."

I blathered. Parker said, "Shut up, and enjoy your absolution and the rather astonishing fact that I'm starting to like you. And, while I have you, here's a suggestion. It might be nice if you let Nick Ray and his gang know that they should mind their p's and q's."

Absolution. Parker's sassy sanction. Dexedrine and strong coffee. I hurtled out of my haze and fumbled out of my funk.

Googie's was jam-packed. I tamped on my tunnel vision and bebopped in the back door. I saw them, they saw me.

Them:

That giant-ant flick, last year. Giant ants attack L.A. They raise a ruckus and eat good-looking women. I giggled and goofed on it. Freddy O.'s a giant ant.

Them:

Nick Ray, Jimmy Dean, Chester Voldrich. Natalie Wood and Sal Mineo. They're ensconced in a big booth. They're slurping massive martinis. Natalie and Sal are underage. It's a Beverage Control bust.

I adjusted my antennae and ant-ambled over. Don't fuck with Freddy O., the Giant Ant. The gang ignored me. I popped the olive out of Nick's drink and noshed it. I went *Yum-yum*.

Jimmy said, "Get lost. Can't you read? My days as your sidekick are *finito*."

Nick started to stand up. I nabbed his necktie and yanked. It put him face-first in his antipasto. He glug-glugged and heaved.

I twisted his tie and held his head there. He flap-flapped his arms.

Natalie giggled. Sal swooned, swishlike. Jimmy played it kool-kat quiescent. The Giant Ant *bored* him. The shimmy-shimmy shakes gave him away.

I dropped Nick's necktie. He glug-glugged and blew his bloody nose on his napkin. Chester Voldrich pulled a push-button shiv and popped the blade my way.

He was close. I ratched his wrist and sheared the shiv free. Voldrich yelped. I pinned his hand to the table and stabbed straight through it. Bones broke, blood blew, the blade cracked wood and tore through the tabletop. I put my weight behind it. Voldrich screamed. I pinioned and pyloned him. I crafted a cruciform seal.

Voldrich screamed. I said, "Natalie, pour your drink on his hand."

Natalie said, "What's my motivation?"

I said, "You're a juvenile delinquent."

Natalie said, "Okay." Natalie poured her drink on his hand.

Chester screamed. His purloined paw got freon-fried and scorchified. He screamed anew. He buckled the table and banged his back against the booth.

Sal said, "I'm a juvenile delinquent." Sal tossed his drink. It re-scorchified Chester's hand.

Chester screamed. I shoved a napkin in his mouth and muzzled him. Jimmy's still kool-kat quiescent. Now Nick's putting on *his* pose.

I'm Freddy O., the Giant Ant. Don't fuck with me.

Maiming mission to mortification. Giant Ant to peeper pariah.

I walked into Frascati. The maître d' moaned. He took me to my table. Dippy diners at adjoining tables moaned and moved away. Waiters whipped up. They plied plates and place settings and rescued the geeks. It's Exodus—let my people go!!!

There's Rock and the girls. *Hellllloooo*, Janey Blaine.

She's bravura. She's *mucho magnifica* in a madras shirtdress.

She held out her hand. I bowed and took it. Rock winked. Phyllis rolled her eyes and registered resentment. Come *on*—it's just a showbiz shuck and another mock marriage. It's Hollywood. Rock's Trippy Triangle!!! Let's lay in for some laffs.

I sat down. Rock motioned for more martinis. I smelled tossed gin on my coat cuffs. It made *me* moan.

Janey kicked it off. She went for the whammo, straight in.

"Forgive me for being precipitous, but exactly what do I *do*?"

I lit a cigarette. "You *act*. You're a Smith girl on the loose in L.A. You meet Rock at a dinner party. It's the Some Enchanted Evening scenario that I know you're acquainted with. Phyllis is with Rock. She's his fiancée, and she doesn't like what she's seeing with you two. I'll script a dinner-table dialogue for you and Phyllis. You'll debate politics and some other things, but it's all a smoke screen to cover the simmering feeling building between you and Rock. That's how it starts. We'll see how the kickoff goes, and we'll take it from there."

Phyllis said, "It's demeaning. It can only go downhill from there, at least in my case."

Rock said, "No heavy petting, Janey. I don't roll in that direction."

Janey laffed. Phyllis said, "Not *yet* you don't—but we're working on it."

The martinis materialized. We took a brief breather and boozed. I scoped Janey, sidelong. I came to cold conclusions.

She's peremptory. She's petulant and short-tempered. She gored Phyllis's goat at the get-go. Let's define the Tricky Triad. Rock's the passive putz—but now he's strictly *straight*. Phyllis brings the brains and the royal rectitude. Janey is what she is—*bait*. She's the torrid temptress who diverts Rock's idling walk down the aisle.

Janey sipped her martini. "What are you prepared to pay me, and how long will the gig last?"

I said, "Ten thousand. Be prepared for a series of staged encounters, to transpire over a series of months. There'll be a series of interviews with the celebrity press. Lew Wasserman has pledged a second-tier speaking part in Rock's next picture. You'll play the female lead's bitchy kid sister."

Janey lit a cigarette. "I'll upstage her, too. Won't I, Rock? Or should I start calling you 'sweetie'?"

Rock said, "Janey's a pisser. Isn't she, Freddy?"

I said, "She sure is."

Phyllis glowered and glared. *Hell hath no fury like*—

"Just remember who gets him in the long run, dear. Only one of us has the ability to facilitate his conversion, and that's me. So, in *that* sense, this tawdry charade of ours *does* reflect reality."

Rock said, "Keep referring to me in the third person. It sends me."

Janey crushed her cigarette. "I can tell you're quite accomplished when it comes to losing men, Phyllis."

"Let's just say I'm more practiced than you in general, dear. For instance, Freddy and I made out in a crowded coffee shop, not that long ago—and I would have slept with him, if he'd asked."

Janey said, "Freddy, you're a dog."

I said, "Woof, woof."

Rock high-signed me. I moved Janey's purse out of the way and pulled my chair close. Rock chaired in close.

"I'm coming out of that haze I was in when you got me out of jail. I'm remembering some things that happened at Nick Adams' place."

"Such as?"

"Such as arc lights. And, you remember that guy who I said was there with Nick?"

"Yeah, I do."

"Well, now I remember him touching me—if you catch my drift. And he was babbling something about Jimmy Dean playing Caryl Chessman."

It vibed blackmail/smut smear/cold-cocked Rock and some Nick's Knights perv. Some filthy-film fandango. *That* equals Extortion 1. Bill Parker would dig it. *Rebel Without a Cause*. The derogatory profile expands. Plus—Caryl Chessman, *again*.

A waiter passed me a message slip. I unfolded it.

Freddy,

> *We traced the calls. She's calling from a booth at Wilshire and Mariposa. It's behind Dale's Secret Harbor.*

All best,
Nasty Nat

I stood up. I grabbed the flowers out of the centerpiece and wrapped my napkin around the stems.

Rock said, "Freddy's leaving. I'll bet he's got a hot date."

The girls ignored us. They chitchatted and heaped on the hate.

Lois Nettleton at twenty-seven. Here she is, the first time I saw her.

I parked in the lot behind Dale's Secret Harbor. The booth stood by the back door. She talked to the phone. A booth bulb shined down and shimmered her. She's boldly backlit by nite.

She's lithe. Lissome, yeah—I figured that from her foto and film clip. She runs rangy but not tall. Her hair's red running to blond. She's unadorned. She goes to gaunt. It's that timeless tomboy gestalt. She's got bleached-blue eyes. They connote kulture-kooky and crazy. They confirm our fone-call contact. She works for effect, she shears short of contrived.

I walked up to the booth. Lois saw me. She cracked the door and smiled. She saw the flowers and stage-swooned. She said, "Nat, I have to go," and hung up.

I handed her the flowers. She said, "Freddy, you shouldn't have." Her bleached-blue eyes bounced. They were set too close together. They marred her good looks and served up her soul.

She'd leased a cool casita at the Chapman Park Hotel. It was a white stucco job with a tiled terrace. A green-brown walkway wound down to Wilshire. Stray headlights strafed skyscrapers and smart storefronts.

We sat on a serape-print swing. Room service sent lobster salads and white wine by. Lois wore a shift dress and a sheer cardigan. We laid our feet on a long ottoman. Lois had knobby knees. I dug that.

I said, "What if Miss Bel Geddes gets pneumonia? You'll be out here with me, brooding on you know who, and you'll blow your big break."

Lois twirled her ashtray. "Barbara will never let herself get sick. It's one reason why I scheduled the trip when I did. And you shouldn't be shy about saying his name. It's Caryl Whittier Chessman."

I twirled my ashtray. "What's another reason?"

"He has a court appearance coming up. I thought I might stand outside the Hall of Justice and hex the son of a bitch."

I stretched and plopped my feet close to Lois. She scooched close and bumped her feet up against mine. She wore ungainly lace oxfords. I dug that.

"There's a weird confluence going on, with that hump Chessman in the middle. First, you show up and start tweaking the magazine, and yours truly. Second, I get embroiled with some cop pals of mine *and* the magazine, as they pertain to this movie that my ex–boon companion, James Dean, is filming right now. I've been informed that Nick Ray has been urging Jimmy to play Chessman in some sort of biopic that he's got his hat set on making."

Lois lit a cigarette. "Jimmy's a shit. I knew him in New York, and I didn't like him. If he plays Chessman and portrays him as anything other than the evil bastard he is, I'll hex him with Aunt Lois' you-will-die-young hex, and he'll go tits up in some sort of embarrassing leather-bar altercation."

I laffed loud and lewd. Lois laffed loud and lewd and laced up our fingers.

"I might have a shot at interviewing Chessman, while he's in L.A. My pals the DA and police chief have okayed it, provisionally. Would you like to be there?"

Lois crossed herself. "As God is my witness."

I crossed myself. "Then you shall be."

Music meandered and wafted over Wilshire. The Ambassador

Hotel and the Coconut Grove were close by. I heard "How High the Moon" and looked up. Moonbeams stirred stars, all across the sky.

"Freddy, the mystic. Penny for your thoughts."

"I'm wondering how you'd summarize this whole Chessman deal of yours."

"I'd call it the central moment of my life, even though I wasn't there for the outrage."

I looked at Lois. "I'll buy that. I'm also wondering if you'll let me kiss you good night."

Lois said, "I haven't decided yet."

MY BOSS BACHELOR PAD

West Holly*weird*

5/18/55

Fone rings raked me and drilled through a dream. I was the Giant Ant, once again. I wrangled the receiver and scoped the nitestand clock. It read 8:12 a.m.

I said, "This is Otash."

A man said, "It's Jack, Freddy. Don't ask questions, just get out here, immediately."

It *was* Jack. He came off panic-pounced and scream-screechy. I said, "I'll roll now."

I rolled, *rapidamente*. I hit the Beverly Hills Hotel in one hard heart-beat. I ran through the lobby and out to Jack's bungalow. I banged the door. Jack opened up.

And stood stunned-o. In his tattered tartan skivvies. Note his dumb-dunce demeanor. Dig his dilated eyes. He's on some pillhead pilgrimage. He's Mongo Lloyd, late of the loony bin. He's broiled off brain cells by the billions. He's holding a wet washcloth.

"What are you doing, Jack?"

"I'm wiping fingerprints off the walls. That way, they'll think she hasn't been here. I sprinkled cornflakes all over the bedroom floor, so if they come in the back way, I'll hear them."

I stepped inside and shut the door. I double-bolted it. A table radio rumbled. I switched it off.

"Who's 'she' and who's 'they,' Jack? Lay it out slow."

Jack said, "I stripped the bed and sent the sheets to the laundry. I pulled two of her hairs off my hairbrush and flushed the butts she smoked down the toilet. Nobody saw her enter or leave. She hid in the bedroom when room service came. I'm a pro at this kind of thing, so—"

I slapped him, hard. Once, twice, three times. I raised red welts and blood dots. I grabbed his pencil neck and pinned him to the wall.

"Tell me what this is. Tell me who 'she' and 'they' are."

Jack trembled and trickled tears. I hankie-wiped his face and put my hand over his heart. His pulse popped to two hundred plus. His skivvies drooped, sweat-wet.

"This call girl. Janey something. She spent the night before last here. They found her body this morning. It was on the early news. She was dumped, off of Mulholland and Beverly Glen."

Shattering shit fuck. Jack the K., off to Shaft City. Robbie Molette's cold-complicit. He pimped Janey to Jack. Adieu, Janey. No bait-girl gig for you.

I pulled pills from my pockets. Jack gob-gobbled them. He'd pass out, pacified. He'd wake up goosed out of his gourd.

"Clean up the cornflakes, and stop wiping the walls. Call Jerry Geisler and tell him the truth. Tell Jerry to call Ernie Roll, and I'll call Bill Parker. We'll hang a shroud on this deal and make sure you don't get hurt."

Jack said, "You're a pal, Freddy. I knew you'd come through."

Nothing's free, rich boy. The ticket's fifty g's at the get. The PD's payoff goes up from there. Parker's got his eye on the FBI. It's common drift. Gay Edgar Hoover hates you. This could be *goooooooood*.

Jack weaved to the bedroom. Cornflakes crunched underfoot. He collapsed on the bed and burrowed under the covers. Muffled snores drifted up.

—〰—

Fifty g's. Lois and me. A madcap month in Montego Bay, Jamaica. Last nite's kiss multiplied *mucho* million times. I'll slip some bad bacillus in Barb Bel Geddes' coffee. Lois will revise and reprise her role and bring Broadway to its knees. We'll jump to Jamaica on *Cat's* closing nite. And, in the meantime, we've got Manhattan.

I popped to the porte cochere. I'd conked Jack comatose. I should call Parker and Ernie Roll and jump-start this. The valet saw me. I saw my Packard pimpmobile. Four big men lounged upside it.

Ever yours—the Hat Squad.

I walked up, *slooooooow*. The Giant Ant ankles, acquiescent.

Max Herman said, "Hi, Freddy."

Red Stromwall said, "How's Senator Jack, Freddy?"

Harry Crowder said, "Too bad about Miss Blaine, Freddy."

Eddie Benson said, "We found your prints on Miss Blaine's purse, Freddy. The Chief would like to discuss that with you."

City Hall. The Demon DB. Sweatbox #3. The Hats held me hostage in the hot seat. We've been here before.

The bolted-down table. The bolted-down chair. The ashtray. The fat phone book. It's *the* you-will-confess confessional.

The Hats straddled chairs. I kicked my chair back. Max passed out cigarettes. Red revealed his flask. It made the rounds. We took two pops each.

Red went *aaahhh*. "Breakfast of champions."

Max said, "Explain your prints on Miss Blaine's purse."

"I had drinks with her last night, but I left early. I moved her purse out of the way."

Harry said, "Where, when, and who else was there?"

I said, "Frascati, in Beverly Hills. It was a ten p.m. wingding. The other guests were Rock Hudson and his fiancée, Phyllis Gates."

Eddie said, "Rock's a fag. Don't tell me—you were cooking up some ruse for the magazine."

"That's right. I brought the Blaine girl in as the bait."

Max said, "Why'd you leave early?"

"I had a date."

Harry said, "Where, when, and who with?"

"About eleven-thirty. The Chapman Park Hotel. A woman named Lois Nettleton."

"How long were you with Miss Nettleton?"

"Until two a.m."

Harry sighed. "If the alibi is kosher, it clears you."

Max sighed. "We should bring Freddy up to date."

Red sighed. "Freddy deserves to be updated."

Harry lit a cigarette. "We've had you spot-tailed from the moment the Chief signed you up for his *Confidential* caper."

Eddie twirled the flask. "For example, I saw your outburst at Googie's last night. Voldrich lost two pints of blood and went into shock. I stiffed the call to Queen of Angels. Voldrich is a noted sack of shit, so I told the dispatcher to dawdle."

I laffed. "Give me the particulars on Janey."

Red checked his notebook. "It's rape and manual strangulation. The TOD is one a.m. She was dumped on Lindell Street, at the foot of the Mulholland embankment, right off Beverly Glen. It looks like she was killed in the bushes and dumped from there. A dog walker found her at four-fifteen. It made the a.m. *Herald* by a rat's snatch-hair margin. Doc Curphey's doing the autopsy now."

I point-by-point parsed it. She might have stayed late with Rock and Phyllis. She cabbed to Frascati or took her own car. She knew the guy. She tricked with the guy. It all went bitching *baaaad*.

"Vehicle at the scene? Did she *have* a car? Tracks in the dirt up on Mulholland or down at the dump site?"

Harry checked his notebook. "No vehicle at the scene, that we know of. We'll be running the canvass in an hour or so. She owned a '50 Buick Super, which is parked in the driveway of this little house she rented in Culver City. We've run the cab logs already. There were no drop-offs or pickups at Frascati from eight p.m. on."

I pondered it. Harry said, "You were spot-tailed the night of the fund-raiser. In case you didn't know, the public places at the hotel are riddled with surveillance ports, so I was able to observe you,

Senator Kennedy, and Miss Blaine—which, in retrospect, looks like a staged-date sort of deal. BHPD, by the way, has a roust sheet on Miss Blaine. She was soliciting at the bar at the Beverly Wilshire."

Max sighed. "You see what we've got, Freddy. The big question is, who hipped you to the Blaine girl and got this whole thing going?"

Eddie slid the flask over. I glug-glugged, deep-deep.

"You won't believe it, but I'll tell you anyway. It was that little dipshit, Robbie Molette, that you rousted on my Art Pepper gig. He's a busboy at the hotel, and his old man's a wage slave at Metro. He's recruited some contract girls at the studio, and Robbie's peddling them to the guests at the hotel, along with his other jive criminal enterprises."

Max said, "Holy shit. *That* jerkoff."

Red said, "Nice family. Daddy and junior peddle poon, and Robbie sells nudie pix of his own sister."

Harry said, "And, he sells maryjane to all the hophead kids working on film shoots. Remember? He revealed that when we were squeezing him, last week."

Eddie said, "Including *Rebel Without a Cause*, which Freddy knows all about, because the Chief's got him working up a derogatory profile on that lox, and I myself saw him bird-dogging the parking lot by the observatory, while they were shooting there."

Spot tails. Enterprising entrapment. I'm keestered every which way. Chief William H. Parker. Accept no substitutes.

I said, "Here's a word to the wise. Anything pertaining to that movie should go from the Chief, to me, and me to you. Robbie's dirty, sure—and dirty as far as that flick goes. I'm just making sure that this work I'm doing for the Chief doesn't get trampled on."

Max sneered. "And I'm sure the same goes for Senator Kennedy, when and if we clear him on the Blaine job."

Harry scoffed. "The Molette kid is pushing ass to a U.S. senator. I still find it hard to believe."

Red moaned. "We're buried on Fat Boy Mazmanian, and now we get reburied on this Blaine deal. Give us a ray of hope, Freddy. Tell us she confided in you, and you know all about her private life."

I sucked the flask. "Nix. Robbie set the senator up with her, and I just met her last night. It's a big canvass and known-associates job, when you'd rather be putting that Mazmanian shit in the ground."

Red laffed. "*Es la verdad*, junior."

I buzzed Harry. "Okay, you spot-tailed me at the fund-raiser. You were on the premises at the hotel. You observed the senator and Janey, so you kept your eyes open. I'm wondering if you noted anything inconsistent while you were there."

Harry shrugged. "Some unruly news photographers, outside the main lobby. At least one guy got loose and started shooting pictures through that big window that looks out on the porte cochere. A BHPD guy told me there were a couple of dozen dumped flashbulbs on the ground where he was standing."

Somebody knock-knocked the door. The Hats stood up, *rapidamente*. Bill Parker walked in. The Hats walked out. It took point-one-two fucking seconds.

Parker straddled a chair. "The senator brought in Jerry Geisler. Jerry called Ernie Roll. Ernie sent Miller Leavy over to take the senator's deposition. It appears as if the senator was indisposed with a second call girl while the first call girl was being raped and murdered, which clears him for Doc Curphey's presumed time of death. The second call girl has confirmed the senator's assertion that they were together at the senator's bungalow from eleven p.m. to four a.m., which handily covers all possible estimated times of death. Inexplicably, the senator wants you on this job. I don't know why, and I don't care. I am acceding to the senator's request, and I forbid you to utilize your dubious influence with the senator to in any way derail my incursion against *Confidential*. You will also deploy your goon squad and have them make every effort to dissuade newspaper, TV, and radio reporters from publicizing the murder of Miss Janey Blaine. Per that purported homicide, Doc Curphey has revised his first estimate of Miss Blaine's cause of death. He has officially announced that Miss Blaine died of injuries sustained by a fall from the Mulholland Drive embankment. Are you following me so far?"

I cracked my knuckles. "I am, sir."

Parker lit a cigarette. "Ernie Roll wants you to work with the Hats. He's issuing you DA's Bureau credentials and swearing you in as a special deputy. This will pave the way for you to *legally* contact municipal, state, and Federal agencies and request records checks on each and every member of the cast and crew of *Rebel Without a Cause*. I am, of course, aware that the disreputable Robbie Molette sells drugs to them, and I am *painfully* aware that young Robbie pimped Miss Blaine to Senator Kennedy. I want you to compile dossiers on any and all members of the *Rebel* gang. This will assist you in preparing *Confidential*'s smear job on the movie, and assist me in assessing the derogatory profile that you are preparing for my eyes only. It will also, dare I say, assist you and the Hats in your sub rosa efforts to seek justice in the matter of your dear lost bait girl, Miss Blaine. Are you following me so far?"

I follow, boss. Find the guy. Kill him. Buttress Doc Curphey's bullshit. Janey fell off a high hill.

"I follow, sir."

Parker dry-popped digitalis. He chained Chesterfields and chased it. He smoke-smacked Sweatbox #3, wall to wall.

"Concludingly, I want you to compile a derogatory profile on Senator Kennedy himself. I may direct you to publish your findings in *Confidential*. There's been talk that the senator may be tapped as Governor Stevenson's running mate next year. It might be just the right time for an in-depth smear."

William H. Parker. Accept no substitutes.

I parked my Packard pimpmobile in the City Hall basement. Back stairs bopped me down there. I saw Jack the K.'s Lincoln limo by the cop-car slots. The back doors were whipped wide. Roof lights lit the ripe rendezvous.

Jack, Ernie Roll, Bill Parker. There's a backseat bar and Baccarat decanters. Jack served drinks.

Fluorescent tubes ghoul-glared and lit the whole basement. I slid behind my sled and peeped the confab.

Jack sucked up to Bill and Ernie. Bill and Ernie sucked up to

Jack. They all sucked scotch and nailed that noon glow. Jack said he'd cadge a case of Cointreau and send it to Coroner Curphey. His postmortem postulations pulled them out of the shit.

Parker said, "Especially you, Senator."

Jack said, "Call me Jack."

Ernie said, "We're white men, Jack. Don't expect us to start calling chits in the second you land in Washington."

Jack said, "Ouch."

Parker said, "You feel bad about the girl, don't you?"

Jack lit a cigar. "I do. And, frankly, I'd like to see each and every conceivable loose end tied up, as well as see her avenged in some sort of clandestine and never-to-be-revealed manner."

Ernie said, "You won't be disappointed, Jack."

Parker said, "The Hats are good at that sort of thing. Freddy Otash isn't bad, either."

Jack said, "I rue the day I met Freddy. I don't think a case of booze will express the proper thank-yous for the Dutch uncle talk he had with me, as well as kick that cocksucker out of my life forever."

Parker lit a cigar. He blew smoke rings. The aroma dispersed and sweet-swacked me. *Aaahhh*, Cuba. It's a puppet regime. We've got our mob mascots making mad money. They grease Democrats and Republicans, fifty-fifty. Jack and half the House heels take tastes.

Jack said, "Batista's got a pet shark named Himmler. He lives in a big swimming pool, behind the presidential palace. Himmler eats Commie dissidents. Batista's goons toss them in the pool, and Himmler goes to town. Lyndon Johnson told me it's a show you don't want to miss."

Ernie said, "Forget about this whole damn boondoggle, Jack. We'll take care of it."

Parker said, "We've got resources, and we're not afraid to break a few rules."

Jack said, "Bury it. I don't want to know the whos, whats, and whys. She was just another girl, right? Maybe I'll run into her again someday."

Dusk. A meandering moon cleared away clouds and starlit chez Lois. We swung on the swing and held hands. Lois wore a cord skirt and a blouse like Shirley wore that night.

"I know what you're thinking. You're thinking how deep it goes with me, and that I'm a nutty actress who works out her motivation by assuming persona, because *her* persona is a drag, and that's what convinced her to become an actress in the first place."

I went *nix*. Lois laid a hand on my leg.

"You were kid roommates. You shared a cheap pad down in the West Twenties. It was just after the war, and things were exciting. Kid friendships are powerful. You can't let go of Shirley, and there's no reason why you should."

Lois burrowed into me. "You're right about that. And you know just what to say to defuse me. I hardly know you, but I know you've been looking wan, because Chessman's appeal has been postponed, and you know I'll be going back to New York soon, so what happens next?"

I tilted her chin up. I kissed her hair and caught almond shampoo.

"I'm not letting this go."

"Yes, but what will you *do* about it?"

I prickled. "Is this the part where you reveal that you contrived to meet me, because you knew Chessman would be out here, and I spent five minutes with Shirley, and you like to create drama, and you sure like to chase men while you're at it."

Lois slapped me. I let her. She slapped me again. I caught her hand and kissed her fingers as the slap hit. She cried a little. I kissed her neck and brushed tears back.

She said, "I need you to do things that I can't do. I don't know exactly what they are, but I need you to do something."

I said, "I'm putting together a smear piece on Nick Ray, Jimmy Dean, and *Rebel*. I've got special deputy status on a cop job that ties in, and I stiffed a call to the mail-room boss up at Quentin. Nicholas Ray and James Dean are approved correspondents of Chessman's, so I think the rumor that Jimmy and Nick want to make the movie about him are probably true."

Lois tugged my hair. We bumped foreheads. Our eyes locked too close in. We pulled back and found the fit.

"Let me explain something to you. I suck up to certain men and lean on certain men, and it's how I cull favors. I'll put the two of us in a room with Chessman, *if* I can keep culling favors with the guys who can make it happen, which will sure as shit serve to *make* it happen."

Lois said, "If James Dean plays Caryl Chessman, it will result in a publicity blitz that will serve to guarantee his exoneration. I don't want that to happen, and I want you to do something bold and brave and more than a little bit stupid, because that's the type of man I throw myself at."

A light rain kicked on. Lois pulled the serape spread around us. I ran my hand under her blouse and touched her bare back.

"Don't leave me, because you can't see beyond this Chessman deal. It's a drama, so it's half-assed unreal at the gate. Don't leave me, period, because I don't want to lose you."

Lois threw herself at me. I convinced her I was bold, brave, and stupid. We stretched out and gassed on the storm.

Rain.

Torrents tidal-waved the terrace. Puddles popped and soaked the serape. We swung off the swing and collided inside to bed.

We shivered and shucked our duds. We didn't do it. We got nuke-bomb nude and dove under the duvet. Wide windows gave us Wilshire by nite. Buses stirred and streaked water high-high. Rain racked the roof. We posed on pillows and whispered under the racket. We kissed and touched each other top to bottom and went back to words.

I spilled. I savagely self-defamed. I *confessed*. I laid out Bill Parker's crusade to crush *Confidential*. Lois called me a crazed crusader. It impelled me to impolitic discourse. I laid myself out as one servile serf. I dodged overseas duty. Men I pounded to perfection at Parris Island got Jap-juked on Saipan. I described the Johnnie Ray debacle as the nightmare nadir of my life. I ran through my *Rebel* wrangles and deliriously delivered everything that they did and I did. I ran down the Janey Blaine/Robbie Molette/Jack the K. conundrum and the official hoax to obfuscate Janey's cause of death. We played to Jack's vile vanity. He wanted the killer killed. Who killed Janey Blaine? Five of us were determined to traffic the truth, even as we assailed it as the penance pose of a hotshot politician too hot to touch. Say we catch the killer? It's devil take the hindmost, then.

And, per Caryl Chessman? What will I *do* about it? I'll think of something. What will it cost me? I don't know—but the price will be high.

Lois told me stories. Bond drives and beauty pageants in Chicago. New York and acting gigs. This scurvy schizophrenia, the Too Many Bedrooms Blues. Too many weak men with shaky psyches. All of them actors. All too-too temperamental and so-so sadistic, all of it aimed straight at *You*.

Freddy, I could tell you stories. Darling, you already have. I knew you'd have stories like the ones you told me. I think it's why I set out to find you. You're a dear heart, Lois. No, I'm just your midnight caller. Lucky for me you picked up the phone.

We fell asleep about then. The last thing I recall is the rain.

SUB ROSA INVESTIGATION (187 PC)

Jane Margaret Blaine (White Female American)
DOB: 4-19-29/Visalia, California
Personnel assigned: Sgt. M. Herman, Sgt. R. Stromwall,
Sgt. H. Crowder, Det. E. Benson, Spec. Dep. F. Otash
5/18–5/21/55

The Hats and me. Full-fledged partners. One rich run at the roses. We reckoned we could race three full days. Max had a cousin in Bremerhaven, Germany. He worked at a pharmaceutical facility. They manufactured Pervitrol. It was a loopy lozenge that *maxi*mized merriment and once drove the Wehrmacht Tank Korps to pound Poland to pulp in record time. *Anschluss!!! Blitzkreig!!!* We rendezvoused at Stan's Drive-In. Comely carhops hopped us pineapple malts laced with 151 rum. We popped Pervitrol and particularized our *werk*load.

We ran through our records checks to date. Dig: Janey Blaine dropped out of Visalia J.C. Her Smith–Bryn Mawr credentials were shucksville. She looked it, she didn't *earn* it. Dig: her phone records came through threadbare. She buzzed mom and dad in Visalia and Robbie Molette. That's *it*—sadly *solamente*.

We ran Robbie's records. He had his own line listed at mom and dad's Highland Park hutch. Dig: Robbie called Janey and the fourteen other call girls listed in his merchandise book. Harry braced the security boss at Metro. The boss vouched the names. He roundly ratted out Rodent Robert J. Molette, Sr. He'd been instigating ingénues into the call girl arts since '49. He told Harry he'd have a damning dossier for them soon. We returned to Robbie's records. *Re*-dig: Robbie called Nick Ray, Nick Adams, Jimmy Dean, Chester

Voldrich, and Nick Knight Arvo Jandine. Arvo was the so-called unit fotog at the liquor-store job.

We discussed the Robbie senior and junior jihad. We agreed: senior would seize a lizardesque lawyer, *faaaast*. We agreed: we'll hardnose Robbie and get him to give daddy up. I reported on *my* records checks. I lamentedly left Lois for a 3:00 a.m. to 8:00 a.m. fone stint. I ran the *Rebel* rascals and supply supplanted my existing records checks. Now, hear *this:*

Nick Ray's under subpoena from State and Fed HUAC. He ran Comintern-financed front groups, '42–'43. Among them: the Hollywood Committee for Artistic Freedom, the People's Party to Resist Censorship, and the Hands-Off Comrade Stalin Committee. Max interjected: he talked to a Sheriff's Burglary bull this a.m. Bingo, baby: the noxious numbers on Nick Adams' swag matched two recent 459 lots. We agreed: we'll haul him in and bat him around till he bitch-squeals.

I returned to my *Rebel* checks. It was all junk juvie shit—Arvo Jandine's excepted.

He was a whipout man. He tossed his tool during daring girls' locker room gambols. He hit Pasteur Jr. High, Nightingale Jr. High, Le Conte Jr. High, Foshay Jr. High, and Audubon Jr. High. We all agreed: this cocksucker mandates consideration.

Eddie reported per the crime-lab crucible. Dig: the rape-o/presumed killer was a savage secretor. Ray Pinker typed his blood, off his putrid payload. It's AB negative. Jammed upside Janey's body: plasticene and foam fabrics. Car seat-cover shit. Bad news here: said shit was indigenous to Mercs, Buicks, and Pontiacs, produced between '51 and '54. We all *groooaned*. That meant *mucho* millions of cars. It came down to *this:* we had to check all indigenous makes and models per our suspect pool.

Cars. This banged our bells per a big issue. How did Janey get up to Mulholland and Beverly Glen? She had no car. She called no cab. Rock and Phyllis didn't drop her. She didn't wait outside Frascati. Ergo: somebody picked her up near the restaurant.

It's in Beverly Hills. It's a short hill hop up Beverly Glen to Mulholland. It all came down to Janey's tricks, past and present. It all came down to Robbie Molette and whether or not Janey worked freelance.

Eddie riffed on the crime-scene canvass. It boded bupkes—nobody saw shit. Ray Pinker noted drag marks at the foot of Beverly Glen and the embankment. This indicated *one suspect*, pulling upward. A West L.A. squadroom dick disagreed. He studied a bunch of crushed leaves. They indicated *two suspects*, dragging Janey *down* that embankment. Per toxicology: Janey had a big booze load in her system. No shit: she sheared down martinis and most likely wine at Frascati. Yeah, and she gobbled or was force-fed four Seconol. Ray called her comatose at her TOD.

Max said, "I'm bored. Let's go get Robbie. Freddy and Eddie, you come with me."

Harry said, "We've got leads on Fat Boy I'd like to check out."

Red said, "Nix. You and I will go pick up Adams. The Sheriff's bull said we could have first dibs."

I *guuuullped*. Jimmy was Nick A.'s 459 accomplice. I failed to mention that—

We strode in strong. Max, Eddie, and me. We're overzealous. It's overkill. We're raiding the Beverly Hills Hotel kitchen.

We went in the employees' entrance. We staged a stir. We eyeball-orbed for Reptile Robbie. It's no sale, *papacito*.

Max braced the crew chief. *El Jefe* said Robbie was up by the bungalows. He had four breakfasts to clear.

We bopped back there. We saw Robbie's pushcart. Max and Eddie snarfed left-behind bacon and home fries. Robbie bopped out of a bungalow. He lugged leftovers off lox plates and dirty dishes. He saw us and went *Oh shit*.

He dumped his dish debris and went all punk passive. He shuddered and moved meek and mild. We tossed him in our K-car and drove him straight downtown.

Max and Eddie sat up front. Robbie and I hogged the backseat.

Robbie said, "It's about Janey, right?"

Max said, "Robbie's wising up."

Robbie said, "I'm just letting you know in advance that I plan to cooperate. I'm looking to avoid a thumping like the one you put on me last time."

Eddie said, "Tell him, Freddy."

I said, "You've got two choices here, junior. You give up your dad's girl biz, or I put the hurt on you myself."

Robbie's dentures dipped out. I dipped them back in. Max said, "He gets the picture. His family life as he knows it has just gone *pffft*."

We drove downtown. We hauled him up to the DB and sweatbox row. Red radioed in. He said he and Harry just nabbed Nick Adams. Nick got bad-boy belligerent. They kicked his ass and sapped some sense into him.

We ensconced Robbie in Sweatbox #2. Max bought him a candy bar and a Coke. Box 3 was reserved for Nick Adams.

Eddie said, "I turned the hall speakers on. The Chief wants to observe."

Robbie noshed his Nougat Deelite and chugged his Coke. Max, Eddie, and I straddled chairs. Robbie sat sidesaddle. He's a passive putz. He's here to help. He's a fellow rat. Who do I have to betray to leave here unthumped?

Max said, "You've got your girl biz and your dope biz. Your dad runs the girl biz. He recruits, and you peddle the tail, exclusively at the hotel. You run the dope biz on your own, and you sell mary-jane and pills to dickheads on film shoots. You suck up to film-biz guests at the hotel, and develop leads on the shoots in that manner."

Robbie said, "Right with Eversharp."

Eddie said, "For the record, did you kill Janey Blaine, or know who did?"

Robbie said, "No."

I said, "What's your best guess?"

Robbie glugged Coca-Cola. "I read the *Herald*. They said Janey left the restaurant alone. That means she's on the hoof, alone, in deserted Beverly Hills at midnight. She left her car at home. Maybe she was meeting someone, maybe she got picked up. Here's an insight. Janey was avaricious. Maybe a guy picked her up, and she sensed his interest. She offered him some snout for fifty clams, and it got all tangled up, and poor Janey got 86'd."

Eddie said, "Give up your dad. For the record. Let's get it out of the way."

Robbie scratched his balls. "For the record, my dad has been exploiting his job as a grip at Metro for the purpose of recruiting wholesome, Ivy League–looking ingénue snatch, for the purpose of turning them as call girls, for a fifty-fifty split. He's been pulling this shit since '49. Before you ask, I'll tell you he doesn't keep a trick book or a girl book. He keeps it all in his head."

Eddie said, "Describe his relationship with Janey Blaine."

Robbie picked his nose. "He recruited her. That means he made her strip, and he poked her, one time only. He didn't *kill* her. That's ridiculous. He never leaves the house at night. He's got home cooking, anytime he wants it—and he *always* wants it. My mom and my sister keep him well supplied."

Max said, "Tricks harassing Janey. What have you heard about that?"

Robbie said, "Zilch. And that goes for all my girls. They work a high-class clientele, strictly at the hotel."

I said, "Your dad doesn't keep a trick book or a girl book. But you keep a picture book—because I've seen it. Here's the question. Did Janey keep a trick book?"

Robbie licked his fingers. Yum, yum—Nougat Deelite.

"I don't know, but here's something you should know. I keep a trick list in my room at the house. Specifically, all the big-name guys who put the boots to my girls, and here's the rub. My room got burgled a few days ago. Shit was subtly out of place when I got home, and the trick list was gone. Lucky for you, I had the list memorized."

Max yukked. Robbie Molette. Accept no substitutes.

"Give us a preview. You can reconstruct the list on paper, later on."

Robbie rescratched his balls. "Besides our pal Senator Kennedy, we've got Senators Johnson, Knowland, Smathers, Humphrey, and Governor Stevenson, who likes boys, but my biz don't fly that route. We've also got Ike's chief of staff, Sherman Adams, DA Ernie Roll, Louis B. Mayer, Lew Wasserman, Jack L. Warner, and Darryl F. Zanuck. Not to mention Clark Gable, Gary Cooper, Van Heflin, and that froggy guy, Yves Montand."

Eddie went *Oooh-la-la*. Max whistled. My first thought: *BLACKMAIL*. Big-name men/call girls/some clumsy first approach. A list on *paper*? Prememorized names? It read AMATEUR NITE.

I tossed a tight changeup. "The *Rebel* shoot. Has anyone on it expressed interest in Janey or your other girls? The cast and crew are nothing but pervs and shitbirds. It's a suspect pool we should explore."

Robbie made the jack-off sign. "Nobody on the shoot *knows* about Janey or my other girls. I keep my two business worlds separate and compartmentalized. And, as far as *Rebel Without a Cause* goes, the shoot's wrapping on the twenty-fourth or twenty-fifth. I'll keep my ear down for you, but I've got to make one final haul off those weirdos, because once they go into postproduction, I'll never see any of them again."

Max said, "The Democratic fund-raiser. You were bussing tables there, so you saw your 'Some Enchanted Evening' scene play out. Here's what interests me. Were there any unusual occurrences *outside* of that that you can think of?"

Robbie dry-drained his Coke. "Not really. Some stray paparazzi guy got loose and started shooting pix through an uncurtained window, and me and Manuel, this other busboy, got tapped to pick up all these used flashbulbs where he was shooting."

I said, "We know that Nick Ray and Jimmy Dean have been talking up a Caryl Chessman flick. What else have you heard about that? The whole deal sounds unsavory to me."

Robbie shrugged. "Nick Ray and Jimmy Dean are unsavory. The whole biz is unsavory. Chessman's headed for the green room. If movie folks are gabbing up Chessman, it's just that he's a hot topic these days."

The wall speaker sparked. Bill Parker said, "Otash, get out here."

I walked out. Parker passed me his flask. I gargled Old Overholt and lit a cigarette.

Parker said, "The shoot's closing down. I'm thinking we should recruit Robbie and do a big dope raid. It would do the magazine good in the short term, and we should net a variety of leads on a variety of criminal matters out of it."

I said, "I agree."

Parker went *scoot*. We popped down to Sweatbox #3 and peeped the wall window. There's Nick Adams. He looks phone-booked and fit to be tied. Note the blossoming bloody nose and torn earlobe.

Parker said, "He confessed to the burglaries, and he gave up your friend Jimmy Dean as his accomplice. Red and Harry are out shagging him now. It may take a while. They're chasing a hot lead on Fat Boy Mazmanian, too."

I made the gimme sign. Parker passed his flask. I glug-glugged and got that glow.

"We've got the confession on Adams, Chief. That will stand up in court, and who knows what you'll get from Jimmy. But we need to cut them loose, so they'll be there if we run that dope raid."

Parker popped digitalis. Straight, no chaser. Gas on *his* glow.

"You've been saying 'we,' Freddy. I find that encouraging."

"I'm starting to think like a cop again, sir."

"Anything else before you go?"

"Yes, sir. Tell Red and Harry to give Jimmy a good thumping."

I soloed out to Culver City. My peeper penchant popped me out there. Pervdog, peeper, priapic pad prowler. You're a clue clown on a *biiiiiiig* case. Let's toss Janey Blaine's pad. Let's lay it low and look for leads. Let's sniff her panties while we're at it.

It was 1:00 p.m. I stopped at a pay phone and called my service. I had one message: "Call Mr. Kennedy at his hotel."

I did it. A stooge picked up. He asked me to drop by at 3:00 today. I said I'd be there.

To extort your boss, fucker. Ring-a-ding-ding!!!!

I found chez Janey. It was a peach stucco cube job off of Motor Avenue. Her '50 Buick was gone. The West L.A. dicks impounded it, posthomicide. A first-rate forensic revealed zero and zilch. West

L.A. left the case then. The Otash-Hats combine caught the duty. The pad was pristine to prowl.

I pinned my badge to my suit coat. It added official ooomph. I walked up and keestered the keyhole. Pick #6 worked. The door popped. I locked myself in.

The living room was squaresville meets hipsville. Persnickety Persian carpets and nifty Naugahyde chairs. The kitchen featured a gas range/Frigidaire combo. The fridge featured TV dinners and Tovarich vodka. Tovarich was high-test and cut-rate. Janey was jacked on the juice. She was a secret sauce hound. That's Clue #1.

I hit the bathroom. It was tidy, turquoise-tiled, and crawl-in cramped. I checked the medicine cabinet. *Aaahhh*—here's some good shit.

A diaphragm. A big box of cornstarch. Vivid vials of biphetamine and Nembutal. I popped two of Janey's biphetamine. Let's bond, baby doll.

I hit the bedroom. It was squaresville squared. The de rigueur ratty carpets. The small slipcovered bed. A small four-drawer desk. A matching four-door dresser. Cheap Picasso prints on the walls.

The desk blotter. It's a clue clown/pad-toss classic. Check *it* out. Catch some light and look low.

Jawohl. It's crisscross indented. There's cursive marks all over it. Janey wrote loose-leaf letters and pressed her pen hard. *Shit*—no legible words leaped out.

I rifled the desk drawers. An inconsistency inflamed me. They were all bare-bones empty. No pens, no paper, no envelopes. The wood had been washcloth-wiped. That meant print eradication. The gradations of grain gave it away. The light grain was dry, the dark grain was damp.

The desk had been tossed. The contents were picked clean. The thief carried off correspondence and/or personal pen-to-paper musings. He stole some called-up calculus of Janey Blaine's life.

I checked the one window. I saw tool marks sawed into the sash. He leaped off the lawn and let himself in, presto chango.

That left the dresser. Women's dressers always draw me. I'm a peeper and a sniffer. I've been one since puberty pulsed. Women's dressers drew me in 1936. Women's dressers draw me NOW.

I opened the top drawer. I saw the panties I sought. I pulled away, cold concurrent.

They were white. They were decorous-demure. There was one row, fetchingly folded. It was everything I liked.

BUT—

They were jizz-juiced, semenized, spurt-spattered, and sicko soiled. The B and E bastard laid his load on lace and cool cotton. It enraged me.

And it was *evidence*. I ran out to the car and grabbed my evidence kit.

The Jack-Freddy Summit. It's been set for 3:00 p.m. It gave me time to run the panties downtown to the crime lab. Ray Pinker promised results by 6:00. I whipped back west and made the meet on time.

I buzzed the buzzer. Jack opened up. He wore seersucker shorts and a Harvard Crew T-shirt. He was drawn dry. He was too thin. He had stick legs. His raw rib bones showed. He was still strikingly Jack the K.

He pointed to a chair. He said, "Sit."

I sat. He sat facing me. He lit a cigar. It was Cuban. I recalled *Jefe* Batista. His pet shark noshed dissidents.

"I need a promise, Freddy."

"I'm listening."

"It's no publicity of any kind on the girl. No sandbag job in your magazine. No shakedown attempts by any bent cops who might know the story—which, of course, includes you."

I said, "I have some questions about 'the girl,' as you describe her. I'm wondering what she told you about herself, during that brief amount of time you spent talking."

Jack flushed. "No. We're not discussing it. I'm not telling you, and this is the last time this matter will ever come up between us."

I called up some cool. "I set you up with Ernie Roll and Bill

Parker. You own them now. I overheard you guardedly state that you would like to see the girl's killer put down. There are five of us who intend to find him and kill him, which will surely save you grave embarrassment somewhere down the line. I expect to be compensated for this, and the price is fifty thousand dollars."

Jack flinched. "The price is way high, and your manner is entirely too brusque. You're not saying, 'Jack, I'm stretched,' or 'Jack, I need a touch,' or 'Jack, we go back a long time.' You're too brusque, Freddy—and you're rather out of touch with reality, given who I already am and where I'm going. So let's end this conversation and remain friends while we still can."

I said, "No. I expect to be compensated for what I've done already and what I'm going to do, and the price is nonnegotiable, and a bargain."

Jack fondled his cigar. "It's a shakedown. You're shaking *me* down."

"No, it's not. I've levied no threat of exposure. I'm presenting you with a bill for services rendered and services to come. Read whatever you like into it. I'll expect a call from one of your inbred Irish flunkies, sometime within the near future. We'll discuss the mode of payment and the time and place, and this is the last time you and I will ever discuss it."

Jack said, "I'll pay, Freddy. And this is the last time we'll ever discuss anything. You've just made an impetuous and small-time move—but then, you've always been that kind of guy."

It was fifty paces to the Polo Lounge. My legs quake-quivered and held. I ducked by some dowagers and dumped one on her ass. I helped her up and sent drinks to her table. She waved and went *Yoo-hoo!*

I boozed. I watched a wall clock. Ray Pinker promised semen-stain results by 6:00 p.m. I conjured Montego Bay, Manhattan, the mountains on the moon. I spent the fifty grand fifty million ways. I saw Lois naked by a wild waterfall and Lois naked at the Chapman Park Hotel. Belfast-born hoods killed me all the standard ways. I died by garrote, gun, brass-knuckle blows to the brain. Flags flew. Jack took the oath of office. I saw Caryl Chessman in Hell. He said, "Hey, baby doll."

6:00 p.m. boded and bopped close. A radio riffed near my booth. The Hat Squad closed in on fiendish Fat Boy Mazmanian. The cocksucker was doomed. I knew it. Nobody said it.

I found a phone and stiffed the call. Ray Pinker got the goods. The jizz-juiced panties matched the Janey Blaine autopsy discharge. Ray said shit like "identical cellular componentry" and "exudate cell formation." Ray said the sample was six to eight days old. *That* meant *this*: the killer left his load *before* he killed Janey.

I bolted. I drove straight to the Chapman Park Hotel and Lois. We got naked and tumbled into bed. We didn't do it. We held each other tight-tight and talked.

We made sense and no sense. My monologue on money/Móntego Bay/Manhattan. My rude riffs on the Janey Blaine job as really MURDER. Lois on Nick Ray and Jimmy Dean and We Can't Let Them Make That Movie. I heard what I heard and knew she heard me back the same way. I said We've Got Some Money twelve million times. She said Chessman and What Will You Do About It? twelve million times back. We talked *at* each other. We wrapped ourselves up together and tried to find some fit we never found.

I went out or passed out and went someplace Lois wasn't. It was booze and dope and Jack and Janey and Jimmy leaving me. I tumbled. I saw things that weren't there and went somewhere Lois wasn't. I woke up for real at 4:00 a.m. Lois was gone, her suitcase was gone, she left no note on the pillow. All I had was her scent.

The Hats were off hunting Fat Boy Mazmanian. I drove home and changed clothes. I checked my answering service. Nobody called me. I heard Chessman and What Will You Do About It?—but she wasn't there.

I called Jimmy's pad and service and got no answers. What Will You Do?/What Will You Do? She ventriloquized me. I heard her say it—but she wasn't there.

Jimmy had a crawl-in crib off of Wilshire and La Brea. He slid in there to sleep and be alone. It was an above-garage abode and a cool caterpillar's cocoon. I drove over and brazenly broke in.

It was easy. One lock poke, one shoulder shove. It's a room-with-bath/eat-off-a-hot-plate deal. I scoped the one room. Here's what I saw:

A Chessman shrine. The Chessman Taj Mahal and Sistine Chapel. The Chessman Mount Rushmore and National Cathedral. Newspaper headlines taped wall-to-wall. Chessman foto glossies shellacked to the ceiling. Movie-type test fotos stacked on the bed. Jimmy Dean made up as Caryl Chessman.

He's got darker hair here. It's been cut and kinked à la Chessman. A makeup man puttied his nose. That prominent prow is Chessman's choice feature.

Jimmy always looks peeved and pissed off. It's always there and always offset by his native pride and prettification. He embodies hip hurt and magnified maladjustment. It's his studly stock in trade. Here, he moves into MEAN. He looks older. He's usurped and channeled Chessman. It's a trenchant transubstantiation. He's made himself vicious and vile. It's a metamorphosis, man to monster.

Harrowing headlines hemmed me in. They were existentially Chessman/No Exit. They jumped from January '48 and jammed up to now. RED LIGHT BANDIT SOUGHT. RED LIGHT BANDIT CAPTURED! CHESSMAN CONVICTED—GAS CHAMBER LOOMS. VICTIMS DESCRIBE DEGRADATION. THIRD VICTIM HINTED AT.

The walls whipped around me. They coldly constricted me and cut off my air. Pictures popped out. Regina Johnson and Mary Alice Meza. Victims 1 and 2, weeping. Apoplectic appeals. HIGH COURT RULES NO STAY OF EXECUTION. WORLDWIDE PROTESTS: FREE CARYL CHESSMAN!!!

I gasped for air. I stumbled and fell on the bed. I looked up at Jimmy's Michelangelo art. He'd pasted Chessman pix to the bodies of Greek cherubs. They flew, flitted, and flung the face of the Beast down at the whimpering world.

Maladjustment. He's memorializing it. It's his movie motivation. He's a tortured teenager tempting teens to toss themselves at the abyss. He's a mad marionette of modernist depravity. And Nihilist Nick Ray is pulling the strings.

I shut my eyes and conjured Lois. I counted to fifty thousand dollars, one dollar bill at a time. I magically misplaced myself: Montego Bay, Manhattan, the mountains on the moon. I opened my eyes and saw the file cabinet by the bed.

Flimsy green metal. One file drawer. File-tabbed *C.C./San Quentin Correspondence.*

I opened the drawer. I saw dozens of envelopes dumped in. They were addressed to Nicholas Ray and James Dean and postmarked San Rafael, California. I recognized Chessman's handwriting. The *Herald* had run two of his prison letters in full cursive. He moved *these* missives past censors and guards and got them into the mail.

I plucked the first envelope and pulled the first page. The sassy salutation said, "Hey there, Jimmy and Nick." It was dated 12/18/54. The first line read, "Before we start, let me state that I want Elizabeth Taylor to play the Meza bitch. She's got bigger jugs, that's the main thing."

Chessman scrawled a script title here. *If I Really Did It—(heh, heh).*

I read my way through the whole file. I popped sweat and sweltered out toxins from my delirious last days. Some tears must have merged there. My eyes burned bad and felt funny. I kept wiping them.

Chessman admitted all of it. He copped to the most minute evidentiary details. It was a savagely sustained depiction of sexual horror. It was demonically descriptive. Chessman recalled sights, scents, and sounds. He reveled in the mess he'd made of lives for years to come. He described the Shirley Tutler assault and designated Shirley by name. He spent forty-three pages extolling each and every time he bit her. He said he sucked the blood off her blouse front. He wrote, "Maybe we can get Natalie Wood to play Shirley."

I read all of it. I read Jimmy's margin notes. He wrote, "Wow!" "Dig it!" and "This Caryl cat is cold," repeatedly.

I got my evidence kit out of the car. I walked back inside and prepped my shooting stage. I turned on all the room lights and photographed all the pages. I ran through twelve rolls of film and dumped the envelopes back in the drawer in approximate order.

My legs quake-quivered and almost caved. I walked into the bathroom and doused my face. I looked different. *What Will You Do About It?* I looked older. I wondered if Lois would notice.

Evidence. "This Caryl cat" was cooked. His rights of redress had run out. I just punched his ticket to the green room.

Dizzy spells. Discontent and discombobulation. Don't go for exultant. There's No Exit, Baby. Don't pop to your pad or rack out at the Ranch Market. Roll somewhere nobody can find you.

I'd lost a full day and a half at Jimmy's crawl crib. It was the next nite of the next day at least. I drove downtown and parked in the cop lot at City Hall. My car cocooned me and sent me soporific. I tried to count from one to fifty thousand. I fell asleep at two thousand-something.

Bill Parker rapped on my windshield and woke me up. I popped the passenger door. He stepped in and dropped the early a.m. *Herald* on my lap.

I saw the CALL GIRL HOMICIDE headline. Plus CORONER CURPHEY'S ACCIDENT RULING "HOGWASH," ANONYMOUS SOURCE SEZ.

Janey Blaine, hot off the press. There's one fab foto. She's fetching fine in '49. She's Miss Visalia JC.

There's zero per Jack the K. Ouch—PROMINENT POLITICOS AMONG HER MANY PATRONS. LAPD WITH EGG ON FACE. CHIEF PARKER PLEDGES REVIVED INVESTIGATION.

I said, "Who's the source?"

Parker said, "As if you didn't know."

"Are you saying you won't buy the pillow-talk defense?"

"No, and I would think you'd have figured out that you're being spot-tailed a goodly portion of the time, and would have learned to conduct your liaisons accordingly."

I lit a cigarette. Parker passed me his flask. I dunked deep and passed it back. Parker dunked deep. A barter bid's boding. He'd have bitch-slapped me otherwise.

I said, "Let's trade favors. Binding, as of now."

He said, "You ask first."

I said, "No reprisals on Lois Nettleton."

He said, "Granted. On my end, I want you to assist in the dope raid on the *Rebel* gang. We're going in at eight p.m. tomorrow. We're hitting the Marmont, instead of the set. The head shitheels are camped out there, and they're the ones we want to shake."

I laffed. "Is that it? I'm getting the better end of the deal here."

"No, not quite. I've decided that that Fat Boy Mazmanian is good for the murder of Janey Blaine, and I would like you to assist the Hats in wiping the egg off my face that Miss Nettleton put there."

Why not? Montego Bay and Manhattan moved into sight. Lois rabbited, ratted me, and ran. To forgive is divine. I had that hot hole card. The Chessman/Dean letters would light Lois up. I'm *locking* them up as of now.

Stage Door Freddy. He's back. He's finessing fuckups and finalizing favors at full speed. Rat, fink, sovereign suck-up. The man who shook down John F. Kennedy. Call me bold, brave, and stupid. Lois Nettleton could do worse.

Parker said, "Fat Boy. Are you in?"

I said, "Yes, sir, I am."

OUTSIDE THE CHATEAU MARMONT

West Holly*weird*

5/22/55

Dope raid. Preselected bungalows. Nick Ray's hip hutch. The cast and crew crawl pad. The B-level bedrooms of the Nick's Knights Kar Klub.

It was 7:50 p.m. Rodent Robbie ran the dope by at 7:20. Nazi Nick had assembled the Juvie *Jugend* at his place. He'll pitch one more motivation message. The flick wraps three days hence.

We perched on the access road. Four Sheriff's plainclothes cars, eight Narco cops, plus me. The Hats were off elsewhere. They had Fat Boy Mazmanian 94.6 percent pinned. That quashed our Janey Blaine job. Fat Boy punched the ticket for Rape/Murder One. He'd go down soonsville.

We were looping up loose ends. The shoot would wrap. Ernie Roll would run the evidence and finalize filings. The panty raid. The liquor store 211/Arson. The four burglary counts to keester Nick Adams and Jimmy Dean. The Hats thumped Nick and Jimmy and cut them loose. We were playing and plying a *loooooooooong* game here. Call it collusive convergence—cops and Fourth Estate.

The *Confidential* smear job and the issued indictments must hit concurrent. The big bonanza lay there. I ran rapaciously rogue through all this *Rebel* rigamarole. I would confess all at the *Confidential v. State of California* trial.

"Two years, Freddy. We'll be in court then. What you and I hath wrought."

Parker said it. I believed it. It vouched my visions of Lois and fifty grand. It stamped Caryl Chessman's insisted innocence Null and Void. I believed it. I *had* to believe it. So why hasn't she called?

The radio rumbled. The squawk box squawked. That meant go, goon squad—

We got out and barged up to bungalow row. We're heat on the hoof—eight cops up against hip hopheads and dizzy dilettantes. We hit the *Führer* Bungalow at a sprint. We prepeeped the door kick. Here's the big window view:

Nick Ray in white robe and sandals. He's serving up the Sermon on the Mount. His addlepated acolytes are attired likewise. That's Nick Adams, Jimmy, Natalie Wood, and Sal Mineo.

Reefer smoke smogged the air. The acolytes noshed home fries and Googie's burger bits. It's the Last Supper. Jimmy beat his bongo drums. Natalie and Sal made like Muslims and ululated to Allah. Nihilist Nick held up a cheesy chalice of cheap wine. He said, "Art is self-sacrifice in the fight against Squaresville America. Come, drink from my blood."

He's serving Commie Communion. T-Bird wine and burger bits for wafers. Natalie whipped off her white muumuu and stood starkers. No shit—she's the *altar!!!*

We kicked the door in. I went straight for Nick Ray. I elbow-popped his face and gnashed his nose in. His cheesy chalice flew. I kicked him in the balls and jackknifed him to the floor. I double-cuffed his hands to his ankles. I bow-bent him back ninety degrees. The fucker scree-screeched.

The acolytes made like Mahatma Gandhi. They went supine and sang Sufi songs to unnerve the fuzz. The cops shackle-chained Jimmy, Nick A., and Sal. They fondle–felt up Natalie and let her linger nude. They grabbed pill vials and reefer wrappers off the floor.

I ran down the row. I hit the crawl crib and crashed in the door. Four grimy grips groused and ground themselves deep in their bedrolls. I noticed no dope evidence extant. I ran down the row to the B-level bedrooms. I beat down the door to room #29.

It's a two-bed flop. There's nobody home. My roust sheet listed the occupants: Chester Alan Voldrich and fotog Arvo Jandine.

I eyeballed the room. A glossy glint gleamed on the dresser. I checked it out.

It was a black-and-white snapshot. Dig the built babe in a bikini. I'd seen her before. I knew where. Robbie Molette's girl book. This studette starred in his stable.

OUTSIDE FAT BOY MAZMANIAN'S HIDEOUT

2892 South Budlong

5/23/55

He's back there. It's a back garage setup. He's paying furtive fugitive rates for three hots and a cot. The front house is a sweltering sweatshop. A kiddie korps sews Sir Guy shirts and sicknik silks for L.A. gang goofballs. Ten cents an hour, *muchachos*. You're overpaid at that.

He's George "Fat Boy" Mazmanian. He's survived his pustulant pal, Richie "the Dutchman" Van Deusen. We've got him for the steakhouse/211-sex assaults. That mandates death by cop, all in itself. We've got him for the Janey Blaine homicide. He didn't kill Janey Blaine. Nobody's perfect—least of all him, or *US*.

We evacuated the sweatshop. The Hats bought *los muchachos* Eskimo Pies off a Good Humor truck. The kids gassed on the LAPD's largesse. We weren't LAPD or the Hat Squad plus Fred Otash today. We were the Men from Mars.

Dig it. We're spiffily space age. We're wearing spangle-sparkly bulletproof vests. The PD purchased a big batch of Chicom surplus supplies. They're *hiiiiigh*-density and heat-resistant. They'll deflect H-bombs and silver bullets. They glow candy apple green in the dark.

We reconnoitered behind the sweatshop. We adjusted our vests. We loaded our Ithaca pump shotguns with rat poison–laced buckshot. We slipped on our headgear. Dig: L.A. Rams football helmets rigged with antiradiation rays and Plexiglas face shields. Wobbly whip antennae for that space-monster look.

We were ready. We were armed and attired. *Uno, dos, tres—vamanos, muchachos—*

We blasted the door off its hinges. Double-aught buck punctured pinewood to pulp. Fat Boy fired. I caught two shots. Max and Red caught two shots. They singed synthetic fabric and fell off our vests. Fat Boy popped four more shots. Harry and Eddie took them. Ricochets riddled my football helmet and zinged off of me.

We advanced. We were the Men from Mars. We feared no man or beast. We stood in point-blank range and let fly. I pumped my five rounds straight at his head. He was my voodoo-doll substitute. I saw Caryl Chessman's face as I killed him.

GOOGIE'S ALL-NITE COFFEE SHOP
West Hollyweird
5/24/55

I tallied table tips. I autographed a.m. *Heralds*. Here's the headline:
MEN FROM MARS BATTLE CALL GIRL KILLER!!!!!

Not quite—but I'll take it.

I logged lowdown. It was all bullshit. I didn't care. Let's celebrate and gloat.

The *Rebel* wrap party was here tonite. The dope-raid arrestees had bailed out. Parker wanted it that way. Let's postpone the parade of criminal indictments. We'll sync them to the film's release.

I tallied tips. I rippled with resurgence. The money. Fat Boy dead and scapegoated for Janey Blaine. It buttressed Jack the K.'s peace of mind. That was *gooooood*. That meant it buttressed *me*.

Yeah—but why hasn't Lois called? I called her New York service fourteen times and got zilch back. I'd null-and-voided Caryl Chessman. Nobody knew but me. I was resurgent. That meant WE should be.

A tipster bopped up. He tattled the Secret Snatch Hair Auction at the Charlie Chaplin estate. Certified Jean Harlow locks went for thirty grand each. Certified Carole Lombard locks went for twenty grand, plus. L.A. County Morgue doctors certified the snips and attested to their authenticity.

Here, kid. Here's forty clams. Uncle Freddy can afford to laff. He's got Lois Nettleton and fifty g's.

The *Rebelites* wandered in. Nick Ray, Nick Adams, Natalie Wood, and Jimmy the D. Jimmy had that bruised-and-contused, I've-been-phone-booked look. His hacked hairline gave it away.

He saw me. He kissed his middle finger and flipped me off. He wheeled and walked back out the door.

You get the picture. I never saw him again.

INFERNAL INTERMEZZO:

My Furtively Fucked-up Life
5/25/55–10/14/57

Confidential fell. The mistrial mandated a move to excessive expurgation and bum bowdlerization. Jimmy Dean went tits-up in a car wreck. Tuff shit. His mopey martyrdom moves millions and redefines *Confidential*'s concept of epic boo-hoo. I felt next to nothing. *Nada, nix, nein,* nullification. Jimmy betrayed me. Jimmy dumped me. Jimmy left me for Demon Daddy Nick Ray.

Bondage Bob killed the *Rebel Without a Cause* smear job. Bill Parker dumped his derogatory profile on the teen turkey turned big hit. Ernie Roll rolled over and declined to file criminal charges on Nick's Knights et al. Parker and Roll succumbed to sentiment and success. Canonized kid actor, boffo box-office take. They capitulated to cultural consensus. Movie money made them meek. That big boo-hoo made them back off, bitch-like. That's the bilious *bi*-fecta. They're satedly satisfied. I'm not.

'55 to '57. It was all one speciously spectacular sprint. I served my two mad masters. I vetted vile stories for Bondage Bob as I bamboozled him. I tanked the verification process and trafficked the truth to Bill Parker. We built a defamous dossier. It topped two thousand pages. It was mucho more than any prize-prick prosecutor could ask for. It comprised one wicked workload. It detailed my libelous life as a smear merchant and thug and made for a massive missive of my misconduct. Why mince words? I'm a rat, a fink, a snarky snitch, and an insidious informant. And I revere Bill Parker for giving me the chance to become one.

'55 faded out. Rock Hudson married Phyllis Gates in November. Best of luck, kids. I give it two years. I'll work Mrs. Hudson's divorce gig then. Phyllis is a fine filly. We collapse in the kip once in a while. Phyllis pretends that I'm Rock. I pretend that she's Lois.

Barbara Bel Geddes never caught cold or laid up with laryngitis. Lois never netted the ripe role of Maggie the Cat. The show shut down in November '56. I remain Stage Door Freddy. I tune in my TV and watch the only woman I've ever loved. There's Lois on *Decoy*. She's dizzy and dykey in two prison-drama shows. Lois stuns on *Studio One* and mangles the motions on *Captain Video and His Video Rangers*. She's bravura on *The Brighter Day*. She called out to me on *Camera Three*, and told me we're still on.

Lois played Emily Dickinson. She was all Art and Loneliness. Her poet's passion pounded me. I know why. Lois lives longing the same way I do. She said, "What will you do about it?" I haven't told her I've done one big thing already. I haven't said, "I'll tell you all in time." I want to rig our reunion in Shirley Tutler's name and the name of Vindictive Justice. We've got time here. Three jolting jurists have told me that.

J. Miller Leavy prosecuted Chessman. He told me the hump should burn some time in '59. Ernie Roll's best guess is early '60. Judge Charles Fricke calls it '60–'61.

We've got time. Hotshot men owe me favors. We'll get our jailhouse visit. I promise you *that*. In the meantime, I've done *this*:

I stored the pix from Jimmy D.'s crawl crib in a bank vault. I B and E'd the crib the day Jimmy died. I stole his Chessman letters and stored them in Vault #2. I ripped his Chessman wallpaper to shreds and burned it. I contacted two high-ups at Quentin and begged for *all* the names of Chessman's approved correspondents. They've refused me so far.

We'll reunite. I know it. We won't ride as rich as I'd hoped. Jack the K.'s fifty grand sallied south.

The cocksucker stiffed me. A minion called and made the meet. The parcel weighed in weighty. I took it home and counted the cash. The bills boded *wrong.* I showed some to a Treasury man. He said the cash was counterfeit. Freddy, you're fucked.

I hexed Jack the K. It worked at first. He lost the veep bid in '56. '56 is not presumptive '60. Jack was right. My shakedown was short-range thinking and a small-time move. That made me a small-time man.

Yeah—but I took down *Confidential.*

Es not *la verdad.* I just helped. The gig was Bill Parker's bristling brainstorm from the get. We compiled the damaging data. Parker fed it to AG Pat Brown. He launched the official investigation and empaneled the grand jury then. The grand jury issued indictments on 5/15/57. Conspiracy to Publish Criminal Libel. Conspiracy to Publish Obscene Material. Conspiracy to Disseminate Information in Violation of the California Business Code.

Call it a clamorous cluster fuck. Bondage Bob hired Arthur Crowley to defend the magazine. Art was a divorce lawyer. He was not a libel-defense lawyer. Assistant AG Clarence Linn repped California State. I owed Bob a big beau geste. I was not indicted. Parker and Roll kept their word. I made a ham-handed play to pollute the jury pool. It cost Bondage Bob forty g's. I flew the fuckers to Acapulco. They lived large for one week. So what? Nobody noticed or seemed to care.

A load of lawsuits surfaced, postindictments. Maureen O'Hara sued. *Confidential* cornholed her in the March '57 issue. It alleged that she made out with a Mexican at Grauman's Chinese. *Oops.* Somebody futzed the fact check. It had to be me.

Robert Mitchum sued. Errol Flynn sued. Dorothy Dandridge sued. We miscegenation-mauled her on no evidence. The trial opened on 8/7/57. Prosecutor Linn called Bondage Bob "Mr. Big." He said Mr. Big had prosties lure celebs into compromising contexts. *No shit.* He said we paid known homosexuals to rat out those of their ilk. *No shit.* He said we employed strongarm methods routinely. *No shit.* Art Crowley preached the letter of the libel laws and freewheeling freedom of speech. It bopped back and forth. The courtroom socked in summer heat. Maureen O'Hara testified. She said she never made out with that Mex. The trial traipsed and trucked along until late September. The jury was deep-six dead-locked. They stood at seven to five for conviction on two counts. The judge closed the cluster fuck off and declared a mistrial.

Doofus Double Agent Freddy. He's the dippy deus ex machina of the whole mess. His secret depositions shaped the prosecutor's trial brief. He gave up his guilt. It cost him big gelt. It freed him to dream and scheme anew.

Confidential survived. It cooled down its content. It now publishes pap for a reduced readership. Our circulation circled downward. Bondage Bob pledged to publish "only wholesome stories." He went on a cost-cutting binge. Listening posts were abandoned. I'm on my way out. My goon squad squared up tall and went back in the Marine Corps. I'm a full-time private eye now. I work divorce gigs out of the wheelman lot and snitch to Bill Parker. A snitch fund pays me five yards per month. I make out okay. Robbie Molette and Nasty Nat Denkins work the wheelman lot with me. I'm their faux daddy who used to be hot shit.

I'm alone most nights. I talk to women who aren't in the room with me. I think about Janey Blaine and Shirley Tutler. Rumination to revelation. A *click* clicked in my broiled-to-burnout brain, much belatedly.

January '48. Shirley Tutler is abducted and assaulted. *Near Mulholland and Beverly Glen.* May '55. Janey Blaine is raped and murdered. *Near Mulholland and Beverly Glen.*

Rumination to revelation. I now see *replication* at work here. Movie madness. The *Rebel* shoot. *Craaaazy* crisscrosses at play. Robbie Molette and Janey. Robbie and the *Rebel* crew.

The *Rebel* remnants remain in L.A. Nick Ray's prepping a preachy lox at Fox. Nick Adams shows up on TV. The Nick's Knights Kar Klub is surely making mischief. It poses a What-Will-You-Do-About-It? dilemma.

I'm bored. I'm underemployed. I may be ramping up to do something bold, brave, and stupid.

BONDAGE BOB HARRISON'S SUITE

The Downtown Statler

10/14/57

The useless eulogy. The dippy de-brief. The rip-snorting ride is over, Sahib.

We took chairs. Bondage Bob poured mid-morning martinis. He wore a pink-puce toga. Note the lash marks on his legs.

"It's the end of an era, Freddy. And you're savvy enough to know why I've called you in."

I lit a cigarette. "You're 'Mr. Wholesome' now. I'm redundant. You've got no need for a strongarm corps, so you're cutting me loose."

Bob sipped bum Beefeaters. The suite was bargain basement. The booze was bottom shelf. His toga resembled a reclaimed Klan sheet.

"That's the long and short of it, son. There's a few clean-up jobs you can take care of—but that's it, over and out."

I went *nix*. "You've got qualms about the trial. The prosecutors came in, armed to the teeth. Somebody fed them a shitload of inside dirt. It was either me, or one of my guys. You're getting up the juice to ask me. You're sitting there in your toga, and you look like Julius Caesar at a drag ball. You're getting ready to lay some sort of '*et tu*, Freddy' number on me."

Bob went *te salud*. I went *so ask*. Bob scratched the whip scars on his ankles.

"I see Bill Parker behind the whole magillah. He ran the show and fed the dope to the AG's boys. He recruited informants, took depositions, the whole *schmear*."

I said, "Ask me, Bob. Accuse me and ask me, and I'll say yes or no."

Bob shook his head. "This is not the Freddy Otash of yore I'm seeing here today. This is some new *kamikaze* version, that I find disconcerting."

I drained my drink. "You're asking me to feed you cues. Okay, here's the first one. The shit I pulled for you and the magazine was wrong. You take it from there."

Bob made the jackoff sign. "You're jerking my chain, son. You don't get to take my money for as long as you did, and make me the bad guy."

I said, "I'm the bad guy. I knew it when I put the hurt on Johnnie Ray."

Bob shrugged. "I'm not going to ask you, and you're not going to volunteer. I'll tell you what gets me, though."

I went *so?*

"Here's what gets me, son. Whoever it was was some sort of insider, and that fucker sided with that pious son-of-a-bitch Parker, against me."

I stood up. "Here's a cue, dad. I'd rather be him than be you."

The wheelman lot. Legions of the lost light and *live* here. We scrounge for scraps. We dive for divorce dough. I'm El Daddy-O by default and decree. I'm a licensed PI. I'm a DA's Bureau special deputy. My ex-*Confidential* status still stamps me a stud. Bondage Bob fired me. I've still got my Ranch Market gig. Bob's got me doing clean-up jobs on a per diem basis. I'm closing out listening posts, tomorrow. Taps, bugs—they've got to go. Bob's divesting and dumping his properties. His profits have dipped *loooooooow*.

He's Mr. Wholesome now. He told the judge and prosecutors that. Call him Messrs. Bland and Blasé.

I slid low in my sled. I yawned and yodeled Old Crow. I popped two biphetamine and lashed the late-morning blahs. I shared my shit with Robbie Molette. He's my new sidekick, thus my new Jimmy D. Nasty Nat Denkins dozed in the backseat. He crossed the wheelman color line. He's now Mr. Darktown Divorce. He's still got his gig at KKXZ. *Confidential* still subsidizes the station.

Robbie said, "What's the deal today?"

I lit a cigarette. "France's Parisian Room, over on Washington and La Brea. The mark's an ofay stiff. The girl's colored. She hops cars at the Parisian and peddles it part-time. The mark's terrified of exposure. He's a preacher at a drive-in church in Van Nuys. The wife wants a divorce. Nat's playing a kitchen cook and bringing lunch over. The pad's right behind the Parisian. We'll take down the door and take the pictures. The girl's in on it. There's three of us and one of him. We'll kick his ass and take him to Wilshire Station. The wife and her lawyer want criminal charges filed."

Robbie *yaaawned*. He cricked and uncricked his neck. He slept on the lot. He slept in his '49 Ford. He left his mom and dad's house. He's now Mr. Apostasy. He quit boning his kid sister and peddling her beaver pix. The Janey Blaine job tested and torqued him. He cleaned house and wound up *here*.

I said, "I've been teething on Janey. Who she knew, who she tricked with, who she might have met in Beverly Hills that nite."

Robbie picked his nose. "We've been through all that. I've been through it with you and the Hats, and Max and Red braced my dad at Metro and polygraphed him. He came up kosher, and you and the Hats made Fat Boy for the snuff. I don't want to keep on plowing up this old dirt."

Nasty Nat stirred. "Fat Boy was framed. He's Emmet Till and the Scottsboro Boys, reborn. I'm referencing him on my 'Cutie' tonight."

I said, "Tell me why."

"Those Chicom space suits the PD bought spontaneously combusted, in this Police Academy storeroom. *Whoosh*, they go up in flames. They were defective from the jump. No bad deed goes unpunished."

Robbie said, "I never thought Fat Boy did it. He always worked with a partner, and he robbed the women first."

I laffed. The pay phone rang. Nat reached out his window and wrapped the receiver.

He said, "Yeah, we're here." He listened. He hung up.

"It's on. The girl says she's afraid of the mark. He's gone kinky on her."

The Parisian Room. A mock-moderne job with Frenchy accoutrements. The standard counter hut and outside park-and-eat slots.

We pulled in and parked. The girl walked out. She wore a white blouse and pink pedal pushers. She was gawky good-looking, in her own wild way. She wore a black lace hairnet. Her name tag read *Babette*.

She pointed up to a back-rear apartment. It was second floor/ stairway access/ three pads in a row.

She said, "Don't be too long. He's on his lunch hour, and he always moves these things along. And he damn sure always jumps on me first thing."

Robbie winked at her. She rolled her eyes and skipped off. Nat doffed his street duds and slipped on his cook-waiter's whites. I checked the camera and fitted in a flashbulb strip. Robbie eyeballed the second-floor stairway. He said, "Okay, she's in."

A real cook-waiter waltzed up. He handed Nat a big bag of burgers and fries. Nat paid him off.

I watched my watch. I gave the loser lovebirds five full minutes to find that funky fit. The girl screamed, three minutes and eight seconds in.

It rang real. I gunned my sled and peeled through the rear-exit alley. I came up by the stairway and double-parked, snout-out. Robbie moved, Nat moved. I went *No* and waved them back. I went *Sit* and *This Is Mine*.

I got out and ran up the stairs. Scream #2 rang real. The pad was three doors down. I did a spring-and-pivot move and flat-kicked the jamb juncture.

The door caved. I saw them. He had her flat-pinned to the couch. He was naked. She was naked. A foot-long rubber dick extender condom-covered his schlong. He blew on a lit cigarette. He lowered it and burned her back.

She writhed and screamed. He lowered the cigarette and reburned her back. I jumped him and pulled him off. He flailed and sissy-swatted me. His fake dick poked me. I pulled my belt sap and backhanded him in the face. I got his nose and his teeth and broke bridgework. I ripped one nostril loose. His fake dick dipped and wilted. I kneed him in the balls. He puked on my Sy Devore coat.

Somebody Jap-jumped me. A dogpile ensued. It was Robbie and

Nat, neighbors and cops. A fat cop applied a headlock. I got loosey-goosey ecstatic. I saw Lois as I went out.

Blackout.

I've had them before. I know the messed-up MO. You booze and abuse for weeks running. An altercation ensues. Somebody cuts off your carotid artery. You see shit that is and shit that ain't there.

Like Lois. Like the backseat of a beat-to-hell prowl car. Like the Wilshire Station drunk tank. Like Jimmy Dean at Ten-Inch Tommy's—and these bad boys butting Kool Kings on his neck.

Like Max and Red. Holy shit, Freddy—don't you ever *quit*?

I came to at Ollie Hammond's. Max and Red sat facing me. My neck hurt. Somebody snatched my Sy Devore coat. Where's Robbie and Nat? What's the dispo on the sicknik sadist and that colored carhop?

Drinks appeared. We imbibed. Max said, "We squared you up. Your boys took your car back to the lot. We got the girl settled in at Queen of Angels, and we booked shithead for Rape 1 and Mayhem. He'll do a doomsday dime somewhere."

Curb-to-curb service. Freddy O.'s our boy. Bill Parker wants something. They're here to ask.

I said, "I appreciate all this. Thanks. Now, let's go out and kill some 211 guys and blow off some steam. Maybe clear some pending homicides on the books."

Max said, "Freddy's miffed."

Red said, "It's a delayed reaction to Fat Boy."

Max said, "We did a favor for Freddy's pal, Jack. It's called 'snipping loose ends while you punch a shithead's ticket that deserved to be punched in the first place.'"

Red said, "Freddy knows the rules. He's got scalps on his belt. He's just momentarily aflutter with Senator Jack and his vision of 'an America that provides for all her people.'"

I laffed. I raised my drink. I went *Touché*.

Max said, "What did Jack pay you, Freddy? Don't disappoint us and tell us you didn't shake him down."

I said, "The bite was fifty g's. I got the package. Too bad it was all counterfeit."

Max and Red roared. I *re*-roared. Montego Bay, Manhattan, the mountains on the moon. O bird thou never—

Red lit a cigarette. "The Chief has a job for you. It pays three grand, cash, no counterfeit. It piggybacks a job you're embarking on for Bob Harrison."

I drained my drink. I faked a cough and dipped two dexies.

"He's got me packing up listening posts, and disarming the bug-and-tap feeds. Let me hazard a guess. The Chief wants me to play the recordings extant and compile intel files."

Max said, "Freddy was never dumb. He's always known up from down."

Red said, "I like Freddy, but I wouldn't go that far."

I blew smoke their way. "Sure, I'll do it. I'm starting the gig for Bob tomorrow."

Max twirled his glass. "You know what the Chief likes. You can't go wrong with sex, politics, and California Penal Code violations."

I noshed a bread stick. It was stagecraft. It covered my mean megrims and trembling tremens.

"I need a favor. I don't think it's a big one to ask."

Max went *tsk-tsk*. "Snow job alert. I sense one coming."

Red went *tsk-tsk*. "The shaky hands are always the tell."

"I need a look at the Caryl Chessman master file, and the PD file on Janey Blaine."

Max said, "No. Whatever you're thinking of, whatever you may be planning, no good can come of it. The Chief looks askance at your fixation with dead and brutalized women."

Red said, "No more dead-woman crusades, Freddy. That's over and out. Chessman's a dead issue, and Janey Blaine's been avenged. You should know—we killed the man who killed her."

Shitwork. Divestment duty. I'm a wage slave. Lift that barge, tote that bale.

There's six posts. Pack the furniture/box the bug-and-tap mounts. Take last listens. List damning dish Bill Parker would drool for. Look through bug-and-tap logs. Bootjack hot bug-and-tap tapes for Big Bill.

I started *here*. The Argyle post ran a *loooooong*-range transceiver. We bugged and tapped mid-Hollywood and the hip Hollywood Hills. Our bug-and-tap targets totaled twenty-four houses and apartments.

Film folk. Sullen subversives. Furtive fuck pads and nifty nests of stewardess call girls. Fly *me*—I'm Pam, Lizzie, Sally, Nancy, Kathy et al.

I scanned the logs. The indices listed bug-and-tap targets and their addresses. Tap callers were listed. Their call dates and times were marked. Two names nabbed me, straight off.

Ingrid Ellmore. Pan Am stew and poon panderess supreme. Ingrid invented the all-nite pajama party. She owned a six-bedroom A-frame on Bronson Hill. You got six girls/180-proof absinthe/all the poppable pills in the *PDR*. Ingrid had a heated pool. Ingrid had sauna and steam rooms. Two yards bought you the Debauch of the Damned. Ingrid rocked round the clock.

Ingrid's call-in list. Note some names. AG Pat Brown, Mayor Norris Poulson. Baseball boss Leo Durocher. Sheriff Gene Biscailuz. TV titan Sid Caesar. Bumptious Buddy Hackett and lounge lizard Louis Prima.

I boosted three bug-and-tap boxes. I'd listen in and cherry-pick some choice shit for the Chief. This was a listen-at-your-leisure deal. The second name shrieked *Listen Now!!!*

Dalton Trumbo. Commie *Caporegime*. Bugged and tapped at his worker's wigwam off Whitley Drive. Hollywood Ten hard-on. Gallivanting gadfly. Dig *this* name on *his* call-in list:

The Caryl Chessman Defense Committee. Dig Bernie Spindel's margin notes:

"CP-financed. Popular front-group remnant. Evolved from the Free the Rosenbergs Committee. Frequent celebrity call-ups to target's home phone. Names noted on specific call sheets."

I culled the call sheets. They coughed up *baaaaaad* Burt Lancaster and cheesy Chuck Heston. There's Calypso King Preston Epps. He's hard on the heels of his hit "Bongo in the Congo." There's Liz Taylor. There's Hugh Hefner. There's Mr. Mumbles himself—Marlon Brando.

Marlon mauled my main *mujer*, Joi Lansing, at a party. It was fall '53. I've ground that grudge for four years now.

I went straight for the call-in tapes. I was hopped up on hate now. I'd rereprised my role of the cornholed *cornuto*. I got a hot hit off the call-tap list: Marlon Brando *at* the Caryl Chessman Defense Committee.

I found the tape and wrapped it into a tape rig. Dig the date: 10/9/57. That's just last week.

I got cozy. I lit a cigarette and sucked my flask. I punched PLAY. Red rake Trumbo schmoozed Mumbles Brando.

Static cut through the call. I amputated the amenities and sundered some chitchat. Voices vibrated two minutes in.

Brando: ". . . and they've got that burglar-killer guy, slated to burn on the eleventh. What's his name, again?"

Trumbo: "Donald Keith Bashor. The Party was thinking of sending some pickets up, but this guy was just too vicious. He killed two women, and messed around with the good-looking one, post-mortem. We want him to burn, because it explicates the callous nature of fascist injustice. In fact, we want everyone to burn, including Caryl. The more the merrier. They're martyrs to the cause. We can really play that angle up in the press."

Brando: "You're right about that. And, you know, there's these rumors floating around that Caryl will be coming down soon for a hearing. I'm laying some groundwork on that. Can the Party bounce for two hundred protestors, at ten clams a pop? That's two grand, all in all. I'm leading a protest outside the Hall of Justice, downtown. Me, Preston Epps, maybe Liz Taylor. That's on the seventeenth, and I'm not floating this gig out of my pocket."

Trumbo: "I'll get you the bread, don't worry. That's what front groups do—they front their comrades money."

Brando: "Rumors . . . yeah, I dig that concept. Hey, have you heard the one about the third victim? That Caryl bit her nipples off, and she's been in the funny farm ever since? That she couldn't testify at Caryl's trial, because she was far-gone catatonic?"

Trumbo: "The fascist lie machine dreamed that one up. Of course, they made her a real baby doll, with tits out to here. Too bad she didn't really exist."

The call staticked up and stuttered out. Mumbles mumbled. Dial tones ditzed and dimmed Trumbo out.

I went back to work. Caryl Chessman *click-clicked* in my head. It felt like a fever. It's mutating and metastasizing. It'll maim me unless I do something soon.

I boxed up the Ingrid and Trumbo tapes. I called *Confidential*'s messenger service and told them to roll up here *now*. I added notes to Bill Parker:

"The Ellmore woman's a mother lode for Headquarters Vice. Duplicate and forward the Trumbo tapes to your Intel Division, plus State and Fed HUAC. More to come/F.O."

That fever. Festering, mutating, metastasizing. I could feel it. I could feel *him*—this malignant microbe inside me.

I called my answering service. I had one message:

Mr. Nat Denkins called. He said Miss Blind Item called him and will call the show tonight.

Festering. Mutating. Metastasizing. *The malignant microbe inside both of us.*

I messengered the bug-and-tap boxes to Bill Parker. I blew off my other work gigs. I popped home and perched by the phone. I'm Stage Door Freddy, resurrected.

She didn't call. The wait wilted, withered, and wiped me out. I boozed, I chain-smoked, I popped pills to push the clock forward. A paradoxical effect popped me. They slowed the clock down.

I made midnight. The clock climbed to 1:00 a.m. I ran my radio. The Synagogue Sid Trio blatted and blasted their intro. They went topical tonite. The microbe moved within *them*. Dig their composition: "I Got Dem Caryl Chessman Blues Again, Mama."

Bass sax, flügelhorn, drums. A crash-out crescendo. Then the silken sound of coins slid down a slot. Then *her* voice: "Hey, Nat—what's shakin', baby?"

Nasty Nat said, "Miss Blind Item, her own self. Man, it has been way too long!"

My heart thudded and thumped and threatened to blow on the spot. Lois said, "Over two years, sweetie."

"*Sooooo*, are you back to finalize your beef against *Confidential*? Is that what brings you to town?"

"What's to finalize, Nat? That trial last summer pretty much emasculated it."

Nasty Nat said, "Yeah, *Confidential*'s been declawed and devenomed, that's for sure. *Hhhmmmmm.* Let's see now. Could the purpose of your visit be the fact that Caryl Chessman will be coming here for a court appearance later this month, and because there's a big protest rally scheduled at the Hall of Justice tomorrow, with Marlon Brando and numerous other celebs slated to appear?"

Lois laffed. "You've lost me there, Nat."

"Hey, baby. You're an actress, I hear tell, and I know you've done some things in New York. You ever cross paths with the Mumble Man?"

Lois said "*Weeelll*, I'd be remiss if I didn't say we shared a history."

My heart shook, sheared, and shuddered—and almost shut down on the spot.

Nasty Nat said, "Here's a question, Miss Item. Chessman's court appearance hasn't been announced in the press, but it certainly has been a persistent rumor. How did *you* hear about it?"

Lois laffed. I saw her bleached-blue eyes bounce and almost cross *craaaazy*.

"Well, Nat. I flew out for a fund-raiser for your attorney general, Pat Brown—who's running for governor next year. Mr. Brown mentioned the appeal, and also the fact that Vice President Nixon will be touring South America next spring, where Communist-backed protests against Chessman's death sentence and American foreign policy in general have already been announced, which poses the question, 'How can one evil man command such attention, and *what can we do about it?*'"

Well now, baby. Here's where it gets really *goooooooooood*.

Ooooga-booooga. There's the protest. That's two hundred college kids. Note the Party putzes passing out ten-spots. They're buying a Commie cacophony. The kids are chugging out chants: "Chess-Man is Inn-O-Cent!!! Stop the Death Machine!!!"

There's Brando. He's in with the kids. He's signing autographs and popping a placard high in the sky. He's the solo celebrity. He's top-lining this gig. He's wrapped in a fulsome phalanx of fans. He's a hog for their *looooooooove.*

The Spring Street sidewalk shook with their shouts. I curb-crawled and slid my sled inch-by-inch slow. I looked for Lois. I saw her not. I circled Spring to Temple and drove around the block. I saw counterpickets congregate. Their signs said BURN CHESSMAN NOW!!! They were weary working stiffs. The college kids packed more panache.

I full-circled the shit show and shot back to Spring. I saw a solo college boy by the bus stop. He looked bored.

Heh, heh. I had the antidote for *that.*

I pulled up. He saw me. I waved him up to the car. He ambled on over. Man—this kid's entrenched in *ennui.*

I said, "Hey, junior. How'd you like to make a C-note for a half hour's work?"

He said, "Doing what?"

I held up a stack of my Marlon Brando fotos. They're a cool cultural touchstone and define our time and place. It's Mr. Mumbles, gobbling *schvantz*.

Junior perused the pix. Junior's jaw jerked and dropped to his drawers. He filched the fotos. I laid out the loot.

He said, "Gee, thanks."

I said, "Distribute these to your pals. What's a protest without some smut? Maybe he'll autograph them."

I went back to work. I had four more listening posts to dismantle and disencumber. The microbe moved within me. Lois lived within me. Janey Blaine bloomed off by herself. Justice for Caryl Chessman? Fuck that shit. Justice for Janey and Shirley Tutler.

Left brain/right brain. My paid work boded boring. That protest prodded me proactive. I felt radicalized and detectivized. My brain quadrants melded and merged. I realized *this*:

The Sweetzer listening post. It's Bug-and-Tap Central. We kept the master bug-and-tap logs for *all* the posts there. That meant *all* the typed transcripts. Going *aaaaalll* the way back to *Confidential*'s first issue. It's got *aaaalll* the callers' and callees' names and fone numbers. It's nothing but names, names, and names. It's *the* ripe repository of L.A. vice.

It's still a long long shot. But confluence causes coincidence. It's who you know and who you blow. L.A. vice. That wicked world. Everybody *knows* everybody. Everybody *talks*. And *Confidential* had that wicked world *wired*.

I drove over and let myself in. It was midday musty. I kicked on the air-conditioning and cooled the place off. The master logs ran to eighty-eight volumes. Twelve for '52/seventeen for '53/eleven for '54/eighteen for '55/twenty-one for '56/nine for '57. My confluence was Chessman/Blaine/the *Rebel Without a Cause* connection.

The convergence culminated in '55. The *Rebel* shoot ran from March to May. Nick's Knights escalated in May. The loose Chessman chatter escalated in May. Janey was murdered in May. I knew of no bug-and-tap mounts at the Marmont. That might or might not mean they weren't there. Bernie Spindel installed independent of me. The Marmont was a mother lode of L.A. vice. Certain units had to have been bugged and tapped.

I didn't need to hear voices. I needed typed transcripts and named names. I pulled Log #9/May–June '55. I noted a Marmont bug-and-tap listed. I finger-walked to page 483.

I noticed the names first. "Voices ID'd as actors Nick Adams and Dennis Hopper." I noted the listed location: "Bungalow 21 D/Chateau Marmont." I knew who lived there in May '55. It was Nabob Nick Ray. I'm a bug-and-tap pro. I know the work. This talk reads like a living room conversation.

I *get* it. Nick and Dennis Hopper. They're alone in Big Nick's boss bungalow suite. It's 5/14/55. Something Robbie Molette said tweaked me.

Nick Ray's "alternative movie." It refracts *Rebel* and then some.

The bug's laid in a lamp or wired to a wall. The transcriber typed out bursts of static, dead air, and *this:*

Adams: "The boss has got some more escalation shit he's concocting. He's calling it the 'final filmic thrust.'"

Hopper: "I think he's a fucking psycho. That's why I've kept my distance with him."

Adams: "All geniuses are psycho. Look at Bird and Lucretia Borgia. You don't get one without the other."

Hopper: "Nick's out of his gourd. He keeps hopping around the set, asking everyone from the camera guys to the grips, 'Can you spell the word *rape?*'"

That was it. The conversation coughed to static and dead air. I found the work order and the transcriber's signature at the bottom. Bernie Spindel ran the gig.

We met at Googie's. I'd read the rest of the May transcripts. Nothing else slammed me. *"Final filmic thrust." "Can you spell the word* rape?*"* The conversation occurred 5/14/55. Janey Blaine was raped and killed 5/18. Confluence abets consequence. I grokked a cause and effect.

We sipped coffee. Bernie said, "I remember the job, but it wasn't for the magazine. Whatever you're looking at, this conversation plays sideways to."

I lit a cigarette. "Who put in the work order?"

"The security chief at Warner's. He didn't trust Nick Ray not to go over budget, and he didn't trust him with all that young pulchritude around. He was just keeping tabs for the studio execs. It was a nothing kind of Hollywood job. I did all the transcriptions, and nothing I ever heard was worth a shit."

I said, "Shit."

Bernie said, "Yeah, 'Shit.' Just what I said. One thing you should check, though. One of my guys misfiled a bunch of the May transcripts in the July log. Since the gig never came to anything, I just let it lie."

Lois Nettleton at thirty. The second time I saw her for the first time.

Gaunt subsumes *goooood*-looking. She's winsome and wary, all wound up. She's much more of whatever made her. She's a runner stirred in the starting blocks. She'll run from you but not herself.

Once again. Lois the Lithe. My midnight caller. We're outside Dale's Secret Harbor. She's boxed in a booth. She's haloed in a heathered crewneck sweater and cord slacks.

I walked up. She saw me. She closed her eyes and probably prayed. It was a *whew!!!* prayer. We worked through conduits and cupids. Her sudden summons worked.

She talked to the phone. I pulled out the Chessman/Jimmy D. letter and placed it flat on the booth glass. Chessman rags Shirley Tutler. He adamantly admits the assault.

I gripped the door hinge. Lois laid her hand there and laced up our fingers. I heard the phone drop.

We got naked and tumbled to bed. We didn't do it. We conjured a rainstorm, like last time. It time-machined two years away. It rained hard and hurled hailstones. We sealed our circuit of time lost. '55 to '57—our window view's a wonderland by nite.

It was *now*. We did what we did *then*. We kicked the sheets off and burrowed deep-*deep*. I told her how I found the letters. I forgave her Janey Blaine blurts to the press. She winced and wept at that. I put it off to pillow talk. I didn't tell her I killed a man to spare her exposure.

Lois talked. She said Chessman's L.A. court date had been moved up. We had forty-eight hours to make the meet and no more. I talked. I said Ernie Roll retired. Bill McKesson had his job now. He was a tough piece of goods. Bill Parker would have to persuade him. Lois said, The Chief should see the letters. I said, He should. She said, I want to read every one.

The bedroom spun. It arced on an axis in sync with the rain. It rendered me reluctant and muzzled me mute. I wanted to riff, ramble, and laff. I wanted to predict our prosaic future beyond this sacred cause. I stayed still. Our future ended at the green room. We both knew that.

Lois grabbed my briefcase and walked to the kitchen. She left the door open. She chain-smoked and drank coffee and read Chessman's letters. I watched her. She wept and kept her sobs as mute as me.

I hid in her heartbeats. Her silent sobs put me to sleep. Time hurtled haywire. She slid into bed and moved me to murmurs. I said, "Do you love me?"

She said, "I'll think about it."

*E*scalation."

"*Final filmic thrust.*"

"*Can you spell the word* rape?"

All synced to Janey Blaine's date of death.

I popped into the post. Bernie's boys misfiled some May '55 transcripts. They were master-filed *here*. I felt moon-mad in broad daylight. Lois was back. I was raking in righteous results.

I'd messengered a missive to Bill Parker. It included photostats of four Caryl Chessman to Jimmy Dean letters. Ernie's out, Chief. Bill McKesson's in. Remember that favor I asked? Twenty minutes with the Fiend?

Parker called McKesson and messengered me back. We got ten minutes with the Fiend.

I blew out of my pad then. I hopped to Hollywood and *blitzkrieged* Hollywood Station. I blew into the records room and cruised crime-scene pix. I found Shirley Tutler *and* Janey Blaine. '48 meets '55. Mulholland meets Beverly Glen. The abduction spot for Shirley. The probable dump spot for Janey. Five fotos total. They were point-by-point duplicates.

Here's what's hair-raising. The '55 foliage had been trimmed back to '48 dimensions. I did *not* imagine this. I saw tree and leaf clippings on the ground.

Escalation meets replication.

I locked myself up in the listening post. I pulled the July '55 book and skimmed for misfiles. I found the Nick Ray/Chateau Marmont work order. The room-bug transcripts preceded the fone taps. The room bugs revealed jack shit.

Neuter Nick blathers and bloviates. Jimmy D. and Nick A. blather back. Nick pokes Nifty Natalie and Sassy Sal on the couch. Bernie's notes note "low and high-pitched grunts and sounds of sexual frenzy." Fourteen pages of garbled-voice overlap follow that.

I hit the phone-tap transcripts. The section ran sixty-two pages. A separate column listed callers. It got boring, fast.

Nick Ray calls Googie's forty-three times. Cal the counter man picks up. Nick calls Jimmy/Nick A./Natalie and Sal. They discuss movie motivation. Nick promotes underage woof-woof.

Nick calls his agent. Nick calls twenty-nine unknown men and women. Forty-one unknown men and women call Nick. Bad-boring to languorous and long-winded. No ripe revelation. No talk worth jack shit.

I hit twenty-six pages of fone static. Bernie marked it as such. I hit a noodle-nudging non sequitur: Nick calls NO-65832 nineteen times.

It's a pay phone in Silver Lake. It's by the Black Cat Bar at Sunset and Vendome. Bernie lists it as a "known bookie drop."

Nick and Unknown Man #21 talk. It's 99.9 percent voice voids and static crunch. Yeah—but there's nuggets in with the dross.

Nick, 5/11/55. Bookie Call #8: *"Setups," "lights," "the girl."* Interlaced static throughout. Eleven minutes of line static follow.

Unknown Man #21, 5/13/55. Bookie Call #9: *"Props," "the '46 Ford," "some sort of real-life location."* Interlaced static throughout. Sixteen minutes of line static follow.

Nick, 5/14/55. Bookie Call #16: *"Of course, Jimmy wants to play the Bandit."* Interlaced static throughout. Four minutes of line static follow.

Three more pay-phone calls follow. There's no transcribed talk. So what? Calls 8, 9, and 16 dumped the dirt.

The calls precede the Janey Blaine snuff. It's movie talk. *"Props,"* "*lights*," "*setups*." Janey's "*the girl*." Caryl Chessman drove a "'*46 Ford*" on his rape jobs. Mulholland and Beverly Glen is the "*real-life location*." Jimmy wants to play the (Red Light) *Bandit*? If the shitbird weren't dead, he could do just that.

The booth calls belatedly bugged me. I considered them conclusive. They surged circumstantial. The "'*46 Ford*" cinched the whole deal. I wanted more. I wanted to place Janey Blaine's killer in that phone booth.

I called Al Wilhite at Headquarters Vice. He knew *that* booth and the bookie-drop gestalt. He said, "Freddy, it's just a run-of-the-mill pay phone. Yeah, it sees a lot of bookie traffic—because bookies book a lot of action at the Black Cat. But what's to stop some neighborhood denizen with no phone from making calls there? Or your two callers arranging calls there, because the callee lives in the neighborhood, and he doesn't want his number listed on any calls-received list?"

It made sense. I drove by Sunset and Vendome and eyeballed the booth. I saw bookie types exit the Black Cat and enter the booth. I saw them take and make calls and fill out bet slips. I got half gassed at the Cat. I called up concepts and threaded theories through my head. One stuck stern and *held*.

Phone calls. Letters. Codes of communiqué. Caryl Chessman writes to Jimmy Dean. Jimmy probably writes back. It's *Nick Ray's* repugnant replication film. Wouldn't Neuter Nick want to *talk* to Caryl Chessman—at least once?

I whipped west. The concept coursed through me. I ran by the Ranch Market. I kept my *Rebel* cast and crew records check paper there. I ran through the address index. *Nein* and *nyet*. Nobody lived near Sunset and Vendome/the Black Cat.

Nick Ray called Chessman. I sensed it. Death row cons caught calls at the attorney room. The Quentin switchboard put them through. Nick Ray called Chessman in May '55. His hotel bungalow was bugged and tapped. He might have sensed it. I was hurling heat at him then. What would he do? He'd place a switchboard call.

I moseyed over to the Marmont. I badged a dippy desk clerk and played special deputy. I laid it out. Nicholas Ray/the *Rebel* shoot/ May '55. Did Mr. Ray make any switchboard calls, here in the flesh?

The clerk said he seemed to recall it. He was on the desk that month. He checked his call records and went all aglow.

Here it is. *Now,* I remember. He called San Quentin Penitentiary. He spoke for fourteen minutes, and he used that phone right here at the desk.

I slid him a C-note. He palmed it, *perfecto.* I went all dippy disingenuous.

I would *never* accuse you of eavesdropping, but—

Well, I recall one thing that Mr. Ray said. He said, "Jimmy and I consider you our technical adviser."

I checked the call list. The call went through at 3:16 p.m., 5/17/55. Janey Blaine was murdered the next morning.

Picket punks. Slogan slammers. College kids and movie morons moved to outrage. Their main martyr's up in the DB. He's hard-wired to a hot seat. We're heading that way.

"Chessman Is Inn-O-Cent!!!" "Stop The Death Machine!!!"

I ran interference. Lois lugged a prop steno machine. Picket punks posed and paraded. They were packed tight and pissed off. They bristled with bromides and placard-plumed the air.

I stiff-armed us through them. We maneuvered by Marlon Brando. Lois said, "Hi, Marlon!" Brando said, "Lois, what are you doing with that putz?" I flipped his necktie in his face.

There's the steps. We tumbled over, up, and inside. Max Herman and Red Stromwall played escort. They doffed their Hat Squad fedoras. Max ogled Lois. Red went *Woo-woo!!!*

We made the freight lift and the DB. We walked to sweatbox row. The Fiend's in #2. I looked at Lois. She looked at me. I winked. We held the Holy Shit moment close and linked hands. I pushed the door in.

There he is.

Beelzebub. 666. The Biblical Beast. The red-horned/trident-tailed/cloven-hoofed apparition. He emits dust and sparks. Serpents coil through his hair. He's assumed human form today. He's thirty-six and pale. He's got that bumpy nose. He's skinny, he's prissy, he wears jail denims. He vibes World's Smartest Convict.

He sat cross-legged. I pulled a chair up. Lois perched her steno machine on the table. I brought my briefcase.

Chessman said, "You were at Hollywood Station. I recall you at the squadroom there."

The Beast speaks. He's a brazen braggart. I know that about him. He's brought his so-soft voice today. He's surgically circumspect and silky self-effacing. He's the watchful world's Victim of This Time and Place. He's Sacco and Vanzetti, and Timothy Evans, framed for Reg Christie's grief.

I said, "Yes, I was there. I saw Colin Forbes and Al Goossen interview you, and I was there when Shirley Tutler came in."

Chessman said, "Who's Shirley Tutler?"

"She's the woman you assaulted between your assaults on Regina Johnson and Mary Alice Meza. I state that knowing full well that you've denied those crimes, and will certainly deny assaulting Miss Tutler."

I let the moment meander and metamorphose. He'll deny it. He'll say there's no proof. Lois futzed with her machine. Dear Lord, her eyes. Such righteous hate.

"I don't have to talk to you. The court will invalidate the stenographer's transcription, and I surely will not confess to yet another crime I did not commit."

I popped my briefcase. I pulled out the forty-three-page depiction of Shirley Tutler's bite wounds. I put the pages before the Beast's eyes.

He looked down. He saw, he recognized, he willed himself nonreactive. His hands palsied, his neck veins pulsed.

"It's not my handwriting. And even if it was, I've attributed those crimes to someone else."

I lit a cigarette. "You only looked at the top page. You don't know it's crimes plural you've described here. I didn't mention the attribution, and the only way you could have known that was if you'd written this document yourself."

Chessman pushed the pages back to me. He's Camus' *l'étranger*. He's beset by bourgeois burghers who just don't understand. He's implacably withstood their stupidity and indifference. He's read Gandhi and Sartre. He knows how to trenchantly transcend.

He said, "No." That one word. Existentialism 101. To refuse is your right of redress.

I passed him a pen. "You will write the following on that top page. 'These are my crimes, as told to the late actor James Dean, and attributed to an unnamed rapist. Thus, they are *my* crimes, and these documents in the aggregate stand as *my* confession.'"

Chessman said, "No." The Beast's beset by Bourgeois Burgher Freddy. It's his lot in life. Who's that red-haired wraith? *She's* rape bait, for sure.

Chessman said, "No." I backhanded him and banged him to the floor. He went sullen silent and nonreactive. Bourgeois Burgher Freddy kicked him in the balls.

"You have two choices here, Caryl. Sign the confession or get kicked to death. The latter option leaves you no option. The former option permits you to survive, cultivate yet more public acclaim, and further dissemble in court."

Chessman shape-shifted. He went maladroit Mahatma, coming off the railroad tracks. He couldn't call up a costume change. He couldn't shave his head and don his granny specs.

He stood up. He winced from my nut shot. He wrote out my confession text and signed his name below.

Lois said, "Jimmy Dean wanted to play you. That must have appealed to your vanity."

Chessman said, "Hi, Red. I knew you'd have a kicky voice."

I locked his confession in my briefcase. Chessman kicked back in his chair.

"I'm beyond vanity, Red. I've seen too much and had too much done to me. You're a woman, so I'm sure you'll understand."

I said, "Too bad Jimmy crapped out. I would've dug on the movie."

Chessman said, "There's always Nick Ray's alternative movie, not that it will ever surface. I was the technical adviser on it, so I'm sure it's got some verisimilitude."

Lois said, "Things went awry there, didn't they? It seems that always happens with you."

Chessman shrugged and grinned. Ring-a-ding. The Mahatma meets the Rat Pack.

"The game's rigged, Red. That's why I always take what I want, and take it where I can find it. And I always find it, because I'm not choosy. Johnson, Meza, and Tutler surely attest to that."

That's it, then. It took eight minutes and sixteen seconds.

I hustled Lois out to the hallway. The wall speaker spritzed and sparked static. Bill Parker and the Hats hooted, howled, and clapped.

I had no name/no at-the-scene proof/no certified murder suspect. I had the infernal inspiration for the crime itself and the cancerous contexts that had caused it. Lois and I laid siege to the *Bacillus chessmanitis*. At some point of prickly protraction, the strain would strangle by gas. That was the unforeseen *then*. Janey Blaine revenged ran me resolute now.

I dropped Lois at the hotel and nudged north-northwest. I hit Mulholland and Beverly Glen. The two crime-scenes crisscrossed and merged as one hellish whole.

'48 to '55. The perfectly preserved historical location. Jimmy D. didn't kill Janey. Ditto, Nick Ray. It was some suck-ass subaltern. He'd prowled Janey's pad. He rifled her desk and jizzed up her undies. *Somebody* stole Robbie Molette's list of Janey's johns. That somebody was circling Janey in advance of the alternative film. Nick Ray called *that* man at the pay phone by the Black Cat. They discussed the details of the shoot. The Hats cleared Robbie Molette's dad. The killer was a *Rebel* set flunky. He possessed technical and/or logistical skills. He 459'd Robbie's pad. That meant he knew Robbie. That meant Robbie knew *something* about him.

I walked the merged crime scenes. I climbed hills and claimed clues. I found used flashbulbs off the Mulholland embankment. That meant *photography*. It linked the lead of the used flashbulbs at the Demo fund-raiser site. He was stalking Janey then. It was furtive foreplay. He knew Janey would be there to culminate with Jack K. Robbie set Janey up with Jack. That meant Mr. X knew Robbie.

I humped hillsides. I claimed clues. I found a roll of red cellophane by a tree trunk. *Red* cellophane. It covered the headlights on Chessman's '46 Ford. It covered the headlights of the '46 Ford prop car Nick Ray discussed with Mr. X. The Red Light Bandit posed as a cop. Jimmy revived the role. *This* red cellophane was weathered and worn. It looked to be two-plus years old.

Robbie didn't kill Janey Blaine. He showed me his foto ID once. He had O-positive blood. The killer had AB-negative blood. His jizz secreted his blood type. Robbie had a name for me. I sensed it, sure thing.

The wheelman lot. There's Robbie. He's listlessly lounged by the lube rack. The lot's listless, today. There's no *trabajo*, no divorce *dinero*.

I pulled in and hit my horn. Robbie rubbed his eyes and walked over.

I popped the passenger door. Robbie scooched in. I passed him my flask. We traded pops and glommed up a glow.

"I had a few questions about Janey."

Robbie said, "Boy, that's sure old news."

I smiled. "Well, something's come up."

Robbie heh-hehed. "You mean Fat Boy doesn't fit the bill anymore? Not that he ever did, to the cognoscenti."

I went *nix*. "I'm recalling something you said, and how you said it wistfully. You said, 'Well, she resisted me,' and I'd like you to elaborate on that."

Robbie choked up. "Aw, Freddy. Don't make me say it."

"Say what, Robbie? That you were in love with her?"

Robbie wiped his eyes on his sleeve. Robbie blew his nose on his shirttail.

"Okay, I'll say it. I was in love with her."

"And your dad set you up with her. And she joined your stable at the hotel."

Robbie said, "You're rubbing it in. I divested the stable, as you damn well know. I'm a wheelman now. I'm on the straight and narrow."

That made me laff. "Your dad introduced you to Janey, right?"

"No. Chrissy, my sister, did. She knew Janey, independent of my dad. Even before she got her contract at Metro."

"Are you saying they were pals? Running partners?"

Robbie snatched the flask and deep-dunked it. He got this kid wild-man glow.

"Chrissy and Janey were movie-mad. They costarred in these jive, skeevy-ass shorts. You know, so-called experimental films where nobody gets paid, you never see the flicks in theaters, but copies circulate. I'm not calling them smut, but I'd call them 'bodice rippers,' with a lot of skin and some pretty smutty scenes, if you get what I mean."

I said, "Keep going. Don't make me prompt you."

Robbie deep-dunked. "They were historical-type pastiches, and they were all based on famous crimes where women got raped and sliced. You know, *The Last Days of the Black Dahlia*, Fatty Arbuckle and Virginia Rappe, the girls that guy Otto Stephen Wilson shanked. Chrissy always played the sidekick, and Janey always played the victim. That's how they met, and how they got tight."

I said, "Who made the films? I mean photographed and directed them?"

Robbie said, "I don't know. Just some fucko movie guys who wanted to push women around and see some skin."

"Did any guys like that work on the *Rebel* shoot?"

"Not that I know of."

"Did you know that a film like the ones you described was being shot, and that it pertained to Caryl Chessman?"

"No, but it don't surprise me, because, like I told you back then, that sick twist Jimmy Dean was all hopped up to play Chessman, and that yet sicker twist Nick Ray was promoting the idea. I also passed you the tip on that so-called alternative film."

I lit a cigarette. "Do you know a bar in Silver Lake called the Black Cat?"

"Yeah. It's a bookie joint by day and a fag joint by night."

"All right. Did you know anyone from the *Rebel* shoot who lived near there? Right off of Sunset and Vendome?"

Robbie shook his head. "Not exactly. Not back in '55, I didn't."

"What do you mean?"

"Well, I knew a guy who lived *up the hill* from there, and who frequented the Cat, and who moved his studio to a couple of doors down from the Cat, maybe last year."

I tensed up. Say the name, Robbie. We just tipped telepathic. I should have tapped the guy already. I nabbed the name a split second back.

"*And?*"

"And, *what?* It's Arvo Jandine. He was the unit fotog on *Rebel*, and he's another sick twist of the Jimmy and Nick Ray ilk. He don't strike me as the killer type, so that's why I didn't mention him when you started in on the *Rebel* guys."

I shut my eyes. I *saw* it. Jandine. The *Rebel* records checks. He's a whipout man. He habituates junior high schools. He invades girls' locker rooms. He's a photographer. He snapped stills at the Liquor Store Inferno.

Plus, the dope raid. Jandine's flop. The bikini pic from Robbie's girl book.

Robbie said, "Freddy's in a trance. It's like he's on some new species of hop that's just been discovered."

I opened my eyes. "You said 'sick twist.'"

"Yeah. He's the guy who took those beaver pix of Chrissy. That, and he whipped it out on my mom."

I reshut my eyes. Robbie said, "Do you ever get ashamed of your life, Freddy?"

I said, "Only most of the time."

Escalation. Mine and his. I escalated my efforts to know him. I escalated my master plan and primed it for profit. I called LAPD

Vice and filched a *full* fotostat of Arvo Jandine's green sheet. It revealed his rude escalation.

Arvo Jandine, one *sizzling* sick twist. Born 6/8/19, bumfuck Nebraska. Arvo's a shifty shutterbug. He's sneaking snaps in girls' locker rooms, *eeeaaarly*.

His first bust is back in Omaha, '37. He's peddling candid nudes at CCC camps and WPA wingdings. He's sent to a compassionate youth camp. It's committedly coed. He wires the girls' locker room and rigs an automatic shutter flap. He compiles and catalogues candid nudes by the thousands. He escapes and peddles the pix at truck stops and gin mills throughout the Midwest. He's Mr. Smut now. He makes his move and hotfoots it here.

He becomes a unit fotog. He pops pix at Paramount and calls Columbia home. He rigs automatic shutter flaps in female stars' dressing rooms. They snap sneak pix on overdrive. He's Mr. Beaver Bounty and Mr. Stark Naked Star. Word of mouth mainlines him to the L.A. Perv Elite. He manufactures nude actress trading cards. Myrna Loy, Carole Lombard, Norma Shearer. Rita Hayworth, Ella Raines. One Ann·Sheridan trumps two Betty Grables. He spawns a *craaaaazy* craze. He makes a fat fortune. The fuzz fox him and entrap him. He sells shunt shots to an undercover cop and gets five to eight in quivering Quentin.

He's paroled in '49. He returns to L.A. He's Mr. Subtle till his fall '51 flameout. He gots to have it/see it/fotograph it *young* now. He's popped outside Le Conte Junior High, June '52. He does eighteen months at Chino and pops out on parole—January '54.

He's *escalated*. He's ready to *collaborate*. He seeks sick twists who twirl to his delirious delusions. He finds his way to Nick Ray and *Rebel Without a Cause*. He's cringingly crossed the path of Freon Freddy Otash. That's where Arvo erred.

Escalation. His and *MINE*.

I creeper-crawled Sunset and Vendome and stared at storefronts. Jandine Art Photography was two doors down from the Black Cat.

Noxious nitefall fell. I wound my way west to the Fox lot. Nick Ray was shooting his latest lox there.

Party Girl. Robert Taylor and Cyd Charisse. Costarring studly

John Ireland. Jungle John's Hollywood's reigning tape topper. He measures in at a mighty 17½.

I knew all the gate guards on the Fox lot. I knew I could bluff my way in.

I did. I cited a pokerfest at Pandro Berman's office. The guard bought it. I slid him a C-note. I parked my Packard pimpmobile and noodled over to Nick Ray's bungalow.

I burgled my way inside and paved paths by penlight. I planted a mini-mike and a battery pack under Neuter Nick's desk. It was a flip-switch gizmo. I'd flip said switch on Judgment Day.

It was 11:14 p.m. I barged back to Silver Lake and orbed Jandine's studio. It was deep dark and devoid of all movement. I circled the block and saw a back door off the alley. I stashed my sled and slid on rubber gloves.

I carried a camera case and a Leica loaded with infrared film. I loped up like I owned the place. Two pick pokes popped the door. I locked myself in. My penlight paved paths once more.

I got the gestalt. Arvo lived for his work. I flash-flared three storerooms laid with lights and camera gear. I slid by a sleeping cubicle. Arvo conked on a couch-bed combo and cooked on a hot plate. He hung his threadbare threads in a freestanding wardrobe. The sink, shower, and toilet stall stank of rat turds and sprayed piss.

Arvo the obsessive. Arvo the unkempt. He'll keep malignant mementos. These sickniks save souvenirs.

The cubicle catty-cornered a corridor. My penlight lit a shut door. I nudged the knob. I got no give. I put picks in and pushed counterclockwise. The door gave and bent in.

It's one room. Ten by ten, tops. It's windowless and suction-sealed, tight. I tapped the walls and tipped a switch. Gooseneck floor lamps lit four walls of *this*:

The combined shoots. *Rebel Without a Cause* and *Red Light Bandit.* Glam glossies by Arvo Jandine.

Jimmy Dean in his red *Rebel* jacket. Nifty Natalie and Sassy Sal, costumed per the flick. Shots from the shoot. Shots from the Sorority Panty Raid. Shots from the Liquor Store Inferno. Natalie, nude. Sal, nude and nervously embarrassed. A nude Jimmy Dean, banging his bongos. Jimmy Dean, costumed as Caryl Chessman. The '46 Ford rape car, replicated. Nite exteriors at Mulholland and Beverly Glen.

Janey Blaine done up as Shirley Tutler. Janey, with mock blood blotting her blouse. Janey and Jimmy, tussling in the Ford. Note Janey's bare breasts.

Then we escalate. Note this wraparound wreath of shots:

See Janey, nude. See Janey and Jimmy, nude. See Janey and Jimmy coiled in coitus in the backseat of the Ford. See Janey in the clothes she wore to Frascati. See Janey body-dumped at the crime scene. She's handspan-strangled and dead.

NABOB NICK RAY'S OFFICE
20th-Century Fox
10/20/57

I sat and tamped up some tension. I conjured Lois and moved money to new mountains on the moon. Nick notched his final take an hour back. His office slaves slid out early. I booby-trapped the doorway. I kept the lights off. I brought Exhibits A and B in my briefcase.

My pix of Jandine's pix. My pix of his diary pages per *Red Light Bandit*. He kept his diary cached under his couch-bed. He kept his Junior High Hall of Fame pix close by.

Jandine recounted his revelatory fix on Janey Blaine. He met her at Robbie Molette's place. Chrissy introduced them and called her a friend of her dad's. Janey got him unit fotog work on *The Last Days of the Black Dahlia* and the Fatty Arbuckle flick.

His obsession per-per-percolated. He 459'd Janey's pad and stole *her* diaries. He read them and got to the hard-hearted heart of her yen for men and money. He tried to seduce her with his own blackmail scheme. He enlisted Nick Adams. They Mickey Finn'd Rock Hudson and took nudie pix. He 459'd Robbie's room and stole his list of powerfully perved clients. Janey laffed his black-mail scheme off. He fotographed Janey and Jack K. at the Beverly Hills Hotel. He had the unit fotog gig on *Rebel*, already. He ran up a rapport with Nick Ray and Jimmy Dean. They concocted *Red Light Bandit*. The shoot went swell. Janey jumped Jimmy's bones for real, right out in the open. It made him mad. He said he'd drive her home after the wrap. It got out of hand. He didn't mean to rape her and kill her. Shit like that happens. Thank goodness nobody blabbed.

The door opened. Nabob Nick hummed "Lisbon Antigua" and walked this way. My trip wire tripped him and proned him out flat on his face. His head hit the floor. He snagged his snout. He's Nosebleed Nick now.

He groaned. I got up and stepped on his neck. It pinned him and muzzled his mouth. I penlight-flashed the pix and the diary pages. I ran them by his flattened face sidelong and *slooooow*. I gave him time to digest his dilemma and ponder Jandine's every word.

"You're going to pay me twenty-five percent of your net earnings, for the rest of your life. That means twenty-five percent of every dime you make. You're going to cut me in for twenty-five percent of all your current bank balances, and you're going to liquidate any stocks and bonds you might possess and pay me twenty-five percent of their value, now. You're going to pay me twenty-five percent of the assessed values of any properties you might own, now. You will pay me my salary cuts on the first of each month, beginning on November 1, 1957. I called your bank in Beverly Hills this afternoon. I impersonated a Federal bank examiner and learned that your current balance is forty-four grand. We're going to the bank together, tomorrow. I'll take the first eleven grand in cash."

Nick Ray squirmed and squinted back tears. Freon Freddy Otash. The Giant Ant ascends.

Low clouds unzipped and reigned rain. I broomed northeast to Sunset and Vendome. I parked on that same side street and sidled to the same back door.

The same two picks popped the lock. I stepped inside and *eeeaaased* the door shut. I heard his snores, straight off.

The sleep cubicle. Eight paces and flank sharp right.

I brought a .44 Magnum revolver. It blasted loud. The pro suppressor soaked up all attendant sound. I walked toward the snores and flashed my penlight. It haloed Arvo's face on the pillow. I aimed and fired six shots.

He vaporized. I smelled dissipation and desiccation in the bone-and-blood mist. I snatched his diary and his wall-to-wall fotos. I jacked the wall heat up to ninety. Let the demon decompose.

Jolting jam session. Walloping world premiere. Live in-studio: the Synagogue Sid Trio.

The piece:

"Trippy Triptych: Dirge for Shirley Tutler and Janey Blaine & Caryl Chessman's Gas Chamber Chaconne."

It's hastily composed. As in *right now*. Sid and his boys embody improvisation. There's four kool kats here for the bash. As in Lois, Robbie Molette, Nasty Nat, and yours truly.

We're celebrating. I bought KKXZ outright and dumped the deed on Nat. Nick Ray paid the freight. I pocketed two g's in chump change and paid Lois' air-fare back to the Apple. She's got an *Armstrong Circle Theatre* gig pending.

I'm bleak, blue, and shorn to shit. We defanged the Beast. We radically revised the sexy secret history of our nation. Lissome Lois leaves me for ten minutes on TV.

Sid and his boys cranked it. Bass sax/flügelhorn/drums. It only goes so far.

I got itchy and Giant Ant antsy. I kept thinking of fatal fuckups and the loony lore of decomposition. I walked to the waiting room and ran some deep breaths.

It helped. I de-antsified. I scoped the Charlie Parker tribute wall. I noticed a new screed scrawled below the *Live on 52nd Street* album.

"Pack up all your cares and woes / Here you go, swingin' low / Bye, bye, blackbird."

It was signed, "Much love, Lois N."

INFERNAL INTERMEZZO:

My Pensively Pent-up Life

10/22/57–5/1/60

It came and went. *Confidential*, the whole *Rebel* rigamarole. I waltzed on the Arvo Jandine snuff. Decomposition devastated all possible inquiries. Stagnant stomach gasses gasped out of the stiff and ignited. The studio blew up. Nobody made it a murder.

I burned all of the listening-post tapes and tape logs. *Confidential* and I went kaput. The mag moseys along without me. Bondage Bob's been raked by residual lawsuits. Savaged celebs now savage him. He's putting out ten and fifteen g's per pop. Nuisance suits are draining him dry. The mag's corrosive content has wizened to wispy white bread. There's no vindictive va-va-voom and scandal skank. There's no strongarm goons to dash dissent and fight that fierce First Amendment fight.

I'm shit out of luck there. I'm Ex-Officio Freddy. I'm a former PI and a dervish of divorce at the wheelman lot. I shook the shake-down tree and bled Nosebleed Nick Ray for a spell. Sustained extortion withered my wig. I blew my take on booze, dope, and women. I sold myself into sin and saw a certain sickness eat me alive. I divested to climb clear of the serpent sucking at my soul. I told Nosebleed Nick this. He genuflected and wept.

Opportunity is love. I've always known it. I doped a racehorse named Wonder Boy and tried to rig a run of races. I got popped for it. The L.A. DA issued indictments. Bill Parker interceded and rerouted my Quentin trek. I lost my PI's license. I'm still Big Bill's back-door bitch and informant. I'm still a rat, a fink, a snarky snitch. I've gone from tattle tyrant to tattletale. It's the work I'm best suited for.

I'm still the Pervdog of the Nite. I still trawl for trouble and peep potent windows in my path. I've cruised and crashed a load of lives on said path to date. I'm lonely in my loss of them. I peep them from afar and peruse the paths they've chosen.

Jack the K. was resoundingly reelected to the Senate. '58 boded big for him. Pat Brown was elected governor of California. The *Confidential* trial trounced the notion that Pat was a putz. Rock and Phyllis are Splitsville. I negotiated the divorce. Nick Ray remains the awful auteur. He makes miasmic movies that slide folks to sleep. The *Rebel* rigamarole marked his slide into evil. Confluence is destiny. He had help there.

Jimmy D.'s dead. I killed Arvo Jandine. Natalie Wood and Sal Mineo are movie stars. Nick Adams has his own TV show. Chester Voldrich lost the hand I mangled to gangrene. I slide him five yards a month, anonymous.

I see them all as the specious spawn of Caryl Whittier Chessman. The cancerous conjunction of vicious thug/victim/hard-hearted hipster left them too weak to resist. Escalation. The Sorority Panty Raid, the Liquor Store Inferno, the film *Red Light Bandit*. Spring '55 et al. Chessman hovers in ellipsis. I cannot and will not forfeit the thought of him. He's insistently intertwined with Lois Nettleton. *They* collectively colluded and marked my one shot to become someone else.

Chessman continues. He files appeals and writes books and claims the ownership of a fatuous phalanx of folks given to dime-store notions of redemption. He'll fry sooner or later. I trust that legal consensus. *Here's* what my most heated hatred and powerful perceptions tell me.

He's struck Lois with a strain of his virus. It lives within that part of her where the hard-hearted careerist and ardent artist coexist. Lois worships a tricky trinity. It's Art/Chessman/Shirley Tutler's Desecration. She found me because she needed me and sensed my susceptibility and rage for romance. She's discarded me twice now. She sees me as a Chessman casualty, as I see her. She knows that I'm love-struck in a way that careerist-artists are not. I torch for her as she does not torch for me. She's unfit to live a squarejohn life. So am I. I'd try it with her. She won't try it with me. I must change my life. She will not abet this design. She considers the design pathetic and inimical to her Drama of the Artist Alone. I've got one last shot at Lois Nettleton's love. I consider it a curtain call. We must stand together the day Chessman burns.

THE GREEN ROOM

San Quentin Penitentiary

5/2/60

There it is. This stark steel contraption. It's ghastly ghost green and riven with rivets and big bolts. It faces the spectator seats. It fits one condemned convict. The door's plied with a Plexiglas window staring straight at us. The hot seat features cinchable restraints. A vat socked with sulfuric acid sits beneath it. The cyanide pellets scoot through a chute and dissolve there. Thus begins the big adios.

I sat with Lois. Bill Parker booked our seats. Colin Forbes sat two seats down. Chessman drew a full house. Sixty seats. Sixty newsmen, politicos, and those with clear-cut clout.

We parked in a lower lot and pried through protesters to get here. A thousand people jostled, jeered, shoved, and shrieked. Marlon Brando mugged into a megaphone. He told the folks he was set to play Chessman in a forthcoming flick.

It's 10:01 a.m. There's the Beast. He's entered through a side hallway. Two guards hold his arms. A third guard pops the door. They strap Chessman hard in the hot seat. He's strapped legs, lap, and chest.

A doctor appears. He hangs a stethoscope around Chessman's neck. The death dudes pop back out. Chessman's alone in the green room. It's 10:02 a.m.

The Warden spoke. Wall speakers sent sound our way.

"Do you have any last words?"

Chessman said, "I am not the Red Light Bandit."

A green-room mike cranked out his credo. I winked at Colin Forbes. Colin went *Freddy, you dog.* Lois caught it and swatted my leg.

The pellets dropped. It was soundless. I saw Chessman feign nonchalance. Cyanide fumes filled the chamber. They were invisible. Chessman buckled and gasped and dripped drool.

His head lolled and sat sideways. His mouth stretched wide-wide. His lips curled over his teeth. His tongue torqued. His arms trembled and palsied palms-up. He looked sure-as-shit deadsville to me.

Time slipped slow and stood still. The fumes dissipated and died. The doctor reentered the green room. He held a handkerchief to his face. He donned his stethoscope and put it to Chessman's chest. He said, "I pronounce this man dead."

G uards got us through the throng. Protesters pressed against us. Lois looked at them and waved at kids in papoose-style pouches. We trudged and tripped down some stairs. The slogan chants and shouts sheared off to a low roar.

We made the lower lot and my Packard pimpmobile. We lounged upside it and lit cigarettes.

I said, "Let's head into the city. I'll get us a suite at the Fairmont, and we'll lay low for a while."

Lois blew smoke rings. "I'm getting married, Freddy. I thought you should know."

I slumped into my sled. "Well, shit. Who is he?"

"He's a playwright, and he has his own radio show. Before you ask, I'll admit it. I took to calling in, and one thing led to another."

I laffed. "Okay. L.A., then. We'll hit Trader Vic's or Ollie Hammond's. I'll drop you at the airport tomorrow."

Lois said, "Marlon's driving me back. Don't look so glum, and don't pretend you don't know. It was always about the three of us, and with What's His Name gone, we'd just be fishing for compliments, and making conversation."

—⚡—

An evil rape-o burns. I lose the girl. My confession ends right here, right now.

The bridge traffic was brutal. News trucks traipsed to and from Quentin. Outbound cars carted slogan slammers and protest pros out to hatch havoc. Placards plumed out their windows. STOP THE DEATH MACHINE and KENNEDY IN '60. Hey, kids—I used to pimp and cop dope for that guy!!!

I dipped downbeat and bopped with the blues. Dig my big boo-hoo. Lost Lois and a dizzy decade out to castigate and confound me. I'm shivering under my shroud. I'm a rogue cop and strongarm goon with too much past and no future to lose.

The traffic thinned. I hit the bridge and goosed the gas. It propelled me past a caravan of Kennedy kids. Sheer movement gored my gonads. L.A. was four hundred miles south. Opportunity is love. I'm gonesville, Daddy-O.

A NOTE ON THE TYPE

This book was set in Albertina, the best known of the typefaces designed by Chris Brand (b. 1921 in Utrecht, The Netherlands). Issued by The Monotype Corporation in 1965, Albertina was one of the first text fonts made solely for photocomposition. It was first used to catalog the work of Stanley Morison and was exhibited in Brussels at the Albertina Library in 1966.